On the Plus Side

Shadows in the Strobe Lights

BOOK 1

By Jhonny Steppes

Editor/Publisher: Alexander McCarty

Editor/Cover Designer: Gabriel McCarty

Front Cover Art: White Namikaze

ON THE PLUS SIDE: SHADOWS IN THE STROBE LIGHTS Copyright ©
2021 Sphere of Compassion

ISBN 978-1-943733-37-8

Published by Sphere of Compassion, Inc.

https://sphereofcompassion.com

authoralexandermccarty@gmail.com

https://facebook.com/authoralexandermccarty

http://www.instagram.com/sphere_of_compassion

https://twitter.com/KExps

https://www.tumblr.com/blog/sphereofcompassion

Front Cover design by

White Namikaze

https://m.facebook.com/WhiteNami

https://www.deviantart.com/whitenamikaze

Table of Contents

ACT 1: THE PARTY PARADISE

ACT 2: KNIGHTS IN TRAINING

ACT 3: LAIR OF THE PUPETEER

EXTRAS

Acknowledgments

(From the Original Author)

I want to thank Alex and Gabe for supporting Plus Side and reviving it from a five-year slumber. Without their positivity and interest, this book would not be published at all. It certainly wouldn't become an ongoing series, so I'd like to thank them most of all.

I'd also like to thank Francis for being the first person to ever read Plus Side and tell me that it had potential.

Special gratitude to my mother, who also read Plus Side and greatly enjoyed Stella and the big twist involving her.

This book is dedicated to those who are stuck in unhealthy habits. May we all muster up inner strength and listen to the wisdom of our loved ones so that we may become happy, free and shine that light upon the world.

Introduction

This book took me five years to bring into fruition. It was my first full length project I'd ever written, and I started back when I was in college. Unlike some of my later work, it is very routed in the feeling of the Twenty-Tens. It's a sort of a post-Steven Universe, pre-She-Ra (Netflix She-ra) kind of adventure. Back then, I truly believed that this first book was going to be a blockbuster hit, but I got some negative feedback and I canned it. Plus Side was on the shelf for several years before my good friend Alex offered to purchase it. He was smitten by the story, the characters and the world I had created. He loved the book as it was but also saw potential for it to grow. Now a part of their Sphere of Compassion company, Plus Side is a time capsule from a period long past, and thanks to the McCarty siblings it's now been unearthed for everyone to read. They've edited it, changed some of the dialogue and had me write some more chapters specifically for the occasion.

Revisiting Plus Side is like relearning some old steps, but now it's got some brand-new moves. Stay tuned for the sequel. For now, enjoy your journey into the City Electric!

Act 1: The Party Paradise

Prologue: The Dance of the Gods

Two opposing aspects: fire and ice, boy and girl, smooth and sporadic mixed the day the two dreamers found themselves face to face on the dance floor.

The female dancer's skin was a pinkish brown, and her hot pink hair was styled as twin drills. She was a Summerein.

The male dancer had skin that glistened like silver and dark hair that hung over the right side of his face in an arc that he gracefully swept from his eyes when he bobbed his head. He was a Winterson.

To prepare for the dance, the girl had kissed her lucky boots before coming onto the stage. The boy had held firmly onto a pendant dangling on his necklace. As they approached one another, she bounced intuitively in her go-go boots, and every step in his curved heels was taken with methodical precision.

The amphitheater was silent, except for the light whirls of the competitor's movements. The two dancers could also hear the light drum of their heartbeats.

The silver boy aimed for honor, and the brown girl aimed for the stars. They had both overcome all challengers of their own race to get to this point, the final round. Despite their different styles, both dancers were determined not to lose. They knew that they were dancing for a chance to take part in protecting their planet, Aleatore.

The youths met at the center. They looked into each other's eyes, refusing to be blinded by the spotlight or the other's gaze. The girl couldn't help but smile, proud of the distance she had come to get to this day, but the boy was still and unresponsive.

A slinky accordion stirred up on the surround system, and they seized each other by the hand, sizing up the unfamiliar touch. They had practiced with dancers of their race for years, but this was their first-time dancing with one of the opposite culture. Each had a personality the other had to adapt to the moment their hands met. After the slightest of pauses, the two began to tango.

She believed every extra step and every additional nuance was all a natural part of dancing; while he had honed every move down to a rigid, unfeeling science. They twirled, and when she kicked her legs in the air an extra time, he had already moved on to the next step. She was forced to stiffly land and catch up to him. She still smiled, but her eyes winced slightly as he continued to drag her along on his mechanical routine. In this way, the two gathered energy within one another. Any misstep could cause a dangerous discharge of energy.

The two moved together again, and then he set her up for a spin. With overzealousness, she launched into it too close; rotating fast and whipping him in the face with her pigtails. Disoriented, but refusing to lose focus, he stopped her and tipped her back, rebalancing the energy. Their eyes met. She knew that to balance their chemistry her chaos needed his order. It was the only way to bring harmony to this evolving dance.

The dance was a re-enactment of the mythic first union between the two cultures, and the two felt as if the goddess was watching them just as she had watched their ancestors in the past.

They split apart and ran to the edge. From the sidelines, she was tossed two red glow sticks, and he was tossed a blue one. The girl began to whip her body round and round, channeling her aura into the wand until two bright red whips of fire shot out of her neon sticks. The boy raised his hands, making zig zags in the air while spreading his feet together and apart in a bewitching tempo, willing his energy into the catalyst. His neon blue stick shined, and the boy and girl ran together, lighting up the stage.

The boy, with poise, shot an ice blue projectile from his glowing wand, and the girl struck it with her fire whip. The projectile shattered with a diamond like sparkle; lighting up the air and enticing the silent audience to 'ooh' and 'ahh'. He spun around her at an alarming rate, and she blasted beams with accompanying twirls, leaving clouds of permafrost floating like fireworks in the night sky.

Claps and swoons from the audience were audible as the diamond light brightened the darkened faces of the crowd. The enchanted watchers cried out for the show stopper, and the boy grabbed the girl before launching her into the air.

Her body flew higher and higher. She was defying gravity by channeling the energy she had accumulated into her special power. She had only used short bursts up to this point to assist her to remain light on her feet. She soon reached the ring of ice projectiles surrounding her. She spun as she rode her self-made gravity well, hitting every single target…or so she thought. One had slipped beyond her reach. Before landing, she blasted the final ice projectile. It burst the moment her feet greeted the ground.

The audience roared, and the girl's eyes were full of diamond sparkles as she slowly rose up. The ecstasy of the moment caused her to lose focus. Her gravity well was dispelled, sending her into free fall. The boy had dived beneath her as she came down. And now she was lifted atop his shoulders.

With that final feat, the semi-decannual Dance of the Gods ritual came to an end.

The girl took the boy's hand and bowed, gazing at the audience. They embraced, as the sacred ceremony decreed. He ignored the cheers from his father while she scanned the audience for her mother.

10

The boy seemed almost unphased of his triumph, as if it was pre-ordained by the goddess. Even so, there was certainly worry in his eyes about what came after the ceremony.

Despite her victory, a sense of dread came over the girl as she stared at the glowing crowd of smiling faces.

It was the last dance before the year 3000 would arrive and the war with the Winterson's and Summerein's mutual enemy would begin. The heroes of both races were decided that very night, and they bowed before the adoring crowd, unified in both body and spirit.

Step 1: Humble Beginnings

Waking up from her dream with a sudden jolt, Stella popped out of her bed. Stella whirled around her room like a sewer jeeg on ecstasy. It was a quarter to ten and she had to be at the station in two hours. She wasn't going to miss out on the chance of a lifetime. This dreamer wasn't the kind to sleep in, but she was the kind who'd stay up all night on a crazy midnight odyssey. She was never subjected to the harsh consequences for tardiness until today.

After she sprang from her dayglow sheets, she grasped a brush off her adjacent dresser and began shaping her bed hair using a towering mirror. Her hair was a dull dirty brown that was kinking left and right. The messy locks were begging for a good straightening session; maybe some bright neon dye too. Her rosy auburn face was small and thin, though the rest of her frame was athletic. Every limb had a definitive dancer's proportion, though they were completely unadorned at the moment.

"When I get settled in my new home, I'm def getting a makeover," she told herself. Regardless of her current drab appearance, her face still curved upwards with her teeth flashing.

As she finished shaping her hair the best she could, she began to gather things for her travel bag. The first thing her eyes targeted were dark go-go boots with small spikey moldings. Normally, people didn't leave shoes of any kind on tables or shelves because of the germ factor; but Stella felt these deserved their prestigious place upon her dresser. They had won her second place in the international dance competition known as the Dance of the Gods, and she displayed them like a golden trophy.

Despite being confined to her hometown of Bronsberg, she had a nearly encyclopedic knowledge of all dances from various cultures and had mastered most. The exception, that had brought her trouble many a time, was the tango. It demanded perfect match-making to truly shine. She had invested blood, blood and even more blood into perfecting her skill, but the tango was something she still hadn't yet mastered. When she arrived at her destination, she planned to flaunt those boots down every street and in every building.

Stella lifted the boots like they were sacred, and reverently placed them in her bag. "There's no way I'm going to the City Electric without my prized lucky shoes."

Her bright blue eyes darted to a poster beside her mirror. Pressed onto the poster was a triad of cel-shaded cartoon women. Each possessed a unique bright hue, body shape, and sense of triumph in their poses.

They were the Mighty Fruitsaders; the heroes of the same titled telescreen show who brought messages of love, empowerment, and feminism to its young viewers. These acrobatic paragons of virtue always saved the day with their morals and the power of teamwork. At the ripe age of 23 this dancer still ate the show up like a packet of fruit shaped gummies—which were conveniently marketed by the show itself.

Every Friday night she stayed home from her frequent rave parties and wrapped herself up in a snug cocoon of blankets just to catch her daily dose of Vitamin-She. With the likes of Orange Ornacia, Passionfruit Patel, and Tammy Mato, she was sure to get a cornucopia of fun. She rolled the poster up into a tube and quickly ran to her drawer to snatch a rubber band to secure it in a padded tube.

Returning to her dresser, she quickly scooped up a family portrait. Though the family all sported smiles, it betrayed how they were today. Her dad and her two brothers had moved on to bigger but not essentially better things, while her and her mother stayed behind for their own reasons. Before Stella's victory in the Dance of the Gods, they were both stuck in a rut.

It felt like her dad and her brothers had given up on them and tried to move as far away as possible. If it wasn't for her dad sending money to assist in paying rent, Stella would have loathed him. Even after winning the Dance of the Gods, they still stayed away while doing their own jobs. She brought the picture over to her neon green travel bag.

As she packed it, Stella found herself thinking that if the same picture was taken today, she would be the only one smiling."

She charged back and forth, tossing clothes and other debris into her bag and accidentally knocking a certificate off her dresser. It was sher ticket to a life outside Boring Town. No longer would she have to drive more than an hour to go to a party and perhaps she'd even make some Winterson friends too. Boring Town was a sunny villa with only Summereins in sight.

Stella deepened her voice as she read the certificate aloud. "Congratulations on ranking second in the Dance of the Gods. You've won an all-expense paid stay at the Raveopolis Suite and an opportunity to meet the groovy Daddy D, the King Mayor of the City Electric." Stella's eyes widened, "I certainly can't leave you behind. You are my passport to awesome!"

Stella was a dancer who aimed for the stars. The only place on planet Aleatore where a young, aspiring dancer could bask in the limelight was the City Electric. With the approval of the King of Dance himself: Daddy D, she would no doubt be the word on everyone's lips and comphones. She'd be re-blogged and printed everywhere: "The Best Dancer in the City…or at least, the second best." The city's perpetually flashing lights and dance clubs would allow Stella to indulge in her other hobby—raving. With her ticket to fame and success, she could rave and party until the jeegs came home.

After cramming everything into her bag, she swept it up and made for the door in the far corner of her room. Her foot stepped on something that

13

provided the traction of a banana peel. After nearly falling over, she looked down to see what was beneath her foot—it was one of her old school textbooks. "Geez, I totally forgot I had these," she said while gritting her teeth. "Can't wait to throw them away when I become a pro dancer."

Stella kicked the books aside—a page or two falling out and fluttering about as she did. She was the kind of girl who kept her dancing shoes on the dresser and school books on the floor where they belonged.

At long last, after years of having nothing but sheer athleticism to speak for her, she could finally move on to a career that wasn't stocking shelves or flipping patties. Her friends had long surpassed her with their studies and jobs, but this was finally her moment to take a ballerina's leap to the stars. With a big white grin, she rushed down the stairs and out of her house. "Bye mom, I love you!" she hollered as she rushed out.

Getting to the edge of the gravel pathway that stretched in front of her house, Stella halted to prevent herself from colliding with her mother.

She was a woman who also shared her auburn skin; but in addition, had enormous dark circles under eyes. Her hair was knotted into a loose bun with scraggly curls sprouting in every direction. Despite this worn look, her voice still possessed a certain warmth to it.

"Stella." She put her hands on her hips, and gave her daughter a very loving, but stern look. "You're going to leave without hugging me goodbye?"

Stella blushed and moved her legs up and down in an antsy fashion like she had to go to the bathroom. "I'm sorry mom. I just have to catch the train. You know I love you."

Her mother gave her a knowing smile. She had raised Stella since birth so she knew her daughter's flaws. "Well, my shooting star, I think you're forgetting something other than your hug."

"Oh no. What is it?" Stella looked left and right while hastily waiting for the answer.

"Your medicine. It's on the kitchen table dear."

Stella let out a big gasp of air. She stuck her arm out and smiled. "You're a real life-saver, momma bear." She quickly charged back into the house with her feet loudly pressing the gravel into the dirt.

Stella's mom hollered after her, "I know my daughter so well! She'd forget her head if it wasn't attached!"

Sprinting from the foyer to the kitchen, Stella shuffled inside and loudly started narrating to herself, "Where is it? I'm so late!" She started shifting everything around the piles of magazines on the kitchen table.

Some pertained to celebrities, others to real estate; they were all Stella's. She loved her tabloids in equal measure to her hatred of books; especially the ones that told tales of sorrow and success and the great details of fine living. She also adored the magazines that showed a diverse amount of living spaces, imagining them as new homes.

Without some assistance from her father, Stella and her mother could barely get by, and window shopping through a magazine made a world of difference to her. It's why the opportunity to live in the City Electric was so important, as were finding those darn pills.

Stella shoved a towering pile of magazines to the left of the table, successfully knocking them off it. Behind it, she found herself a thin clear orange tube with a shiny white safety cap fastened on top. There was a paper label hugging it that gave the pharmaceutical information:

"Doctor J. Proto. 271 Alphabet St, the City Electric" the prescription read "Yellow Plus. Adding more with subtraction."

Stella took away the cap just as she intended to take away her anxiety. The pills rattled around, and she deftly jostled one into her hand. It was a circular yellow pill with a plus sign at the center and a small semi-circle underneath. It looked just like a smiley face; an excessive amount of which she'd use at the end of a sentence in an online LYFI conversation. She flipped the pill into her mouth and closed her eyes as she swallowed. She could always count on it to dissolve away her depression the second it dissolved in her stomach. The anticipation of the ensuing relief gave her a placebo effect.

Before saying goodbye to her home, Stella skipped to the kitchen. The sink was cluttered with dishes, and some empty jugs that didn't belong there either. There was a dented two-slotted toaster with an extension cord that was a dangerous neighbor to the sink. There were tons of magazines and debris piled up all over the fridge, with newly added magazines on the floor around a field of dust balls. Every single area was filled with unnecessary baggage. The pill began to take effect, giving everything more shine, like hi-definition telescreen. Stella knew that aside from the magazines, most of this mess was her mother's. She had been too depressed to clean.

Stella didn't blame her mother. After all, her father wanted very little to do with them and wouldn't even tell her why. There were mood enhancers like Yellow Plus that could cure her mother of her depression, but the doctor advised against it. Yellow Plus was only intended for people below forty because it could cause dangerous heart palpitations to those longer in the tooth. Stella found this to be heartbreaking because the little yellow pill had helped her stay motivated during the grueling Dance of the Gods tournament, and she knew it could do wonders for her mom. Despite all her pressure, her mother refused to take any medication.

After quickly shoveling the magazines, she knocked over into a messy pile back on the table, she turned and charged out the door.

When the dreamer rushed outside, her face was as bright and wide as the smiling pill. The effects hadn't kicked in yet, but she could already feel the ensuing sunshine and the rainbows. She ran to her mother and embraced her in a running tackle. "I love you mom!"

The older woman was startled by her daughter's sudden need to behave like a linebacker, but quickly put her arms around her little star. To Stella, her mother felt as light and airy as an angel. She gave some saintly words to Stella too. "Stella dear, I know the meds are helping you, but I also know you can move past them. You're stronger than any chemical."

"I'll try, mom. Look how far I'm getting in life because of them. I almost won that dance competition because they gave me focus."

Stella's mom put her hand on her daughter's cheeks. "No honey, you did it yourself. I was watching from the crowd, and it was my little girl who did it with the power of her own positivity."

"I did do it, didn't I? Thanks, you're proof that old people are wise."

Stella's mom took one look at her daughter before putting one her hand on hip, raising her opposite eyebrow and giving a you-got-to-be-kidding-me smirk. Stella intimidated, started to back pedal. "Uh I mean beautiful, young, foxy people are wise?"

"You did NOT just call your mother foxy."

Stella took one look at her mother's arched brows of tough love and quickly took off down the street. Her tote bag swinging back and forth and she lifted her legs. "Sorry mom. I got to chase my dreams now! I love you, momma bear. Although maybe panda bear is more accurate."

"Haha, yes I know have bags under my eyes." Her mother sighs. "I love you too, but you're not my little cub anymore. When you get back here, you're cleaning the kitchen from then on. If I have seniority, I'm going to damn well use it."

And with the terrifying idea of having to scrub the filthy kitchen, Stella took off on her journey to the City Electric.

Step 2: The Bumpy Road to Stardom

Stella hustled past several blocks of suburban houses in her little town of Bronsberg. Her drive and athletic body allowed her to make short work of the distance to the Northern Gardens Station. It was a small station with a simple parking lot for sky cruisers, had a simple grey platform with a black railing, and only a single ticket machine. Talk about merciless.

Upon arriving at the station, her relief that she hadn't missed the train quickly turned to panic when she realized she still had to deal with the ticket machine and a daunting line of passengers in front of it.

Stella quickly shuffled herself to the back of the line. She looked ahead and observed those who stood in front of her. They all had heads of grey except in the case of a few men who were bald with just a few wispy hairs left.

"Geez, what's going on today?" Stella inquired to the elder in front of her.

The man gave a pause Stella felt lasted longer than his existence before recalling why he was there. "Why don't you know missy, it's Mortal Coil Day?"

"Mortal…what day?"

"The City Electric is having a day where all us seniors can boogie down one last time. They invented a brand-new dance called the mortal coil shuffle where we wiggle our replaced hips until we collapse and wait for the sweet release of death. Well, after taking a miracle drug of course."

"That's uh…nice." Stella grinned, trying to smile off what she just heard. "I just hope this line goes fast."

The old man slowly raised his thumb skyward. "Don't worry, missy. We're all super speedy."

"Yep. I'm sure you guys are the Greased Lightning Geriatric Dance Squad." Stella muttered, rolling her eyes aggressively.

"Pardon?"

Stella's face immediately shot back to a perky smile with wide innocent eyes. "Nothing. I hope you have a fun time."

Five seconds passed before the old man at the front of the line screamed, "Aw rave darn it, I dropped my wallet and all my K fell out."

"Don't worry, Fred, we'll help you," another oldie responded.

17

All the seniors bent over to reach for the small bills that fluttered all over the platform. The wind scattered some into the air and other fell on the ground, causing the seniors to bend over and fill the air with the cracking of ancient spines.

Stella continued to sport a grin, but her eye twitched. There was no way she was going to miss out on the chance of a lifetime. As all the seniors continued to clutch their backs and search for stray coins, Stella zigzagged around them; sneaking around on the tips of her toes like a black ops ballerina. She did not remove the med addled grin from her face the whole time. The swift girl made it to the front of the line and punched the machine's touch screen with the tips of her fingers.

"Welcome to North Gardens Station, please select your destination," the machine announced.

"Shhhh," Stella whispered to it, as if the machine would listen.

"What?" the old man said, whose place in the line was unknowingly usurped. "Darn hearing aid, it's acting up again."

Stella let out a sigh of relief, and with a swift press of the touch, screen selected "The City Electric, North Side Station." She slipped the bills in, the remnants of her unsuccessful stints as an odd-job worker. "Oh, yeah! I'm going to the City Electric!"

A homeless man eyed her from the back wall. "Better be careful. That city has been having some dark occurrences recently. If you're unlucky, then you'll end up in a real bad spot."

"Well, I am extremely lucky. So no worries, dude." She reaches into her bag and tosses the man a water bottle.

"May the angelic knights protect you, miss," he said with a warm smile.

"Thanks, homeless guy!"

The machine let out a high-pitched whine, and from a small slit came her tickets to success. Overcome by ecstatic feeling, Stella pranced off, leaving the old folks in a vain search for Fred's lost bills.

Stella felt a rush of wind, and a sleek black train swept in a few inches beside her face. She spit and coughed as a mat of her hair lashed in her mouth. She quickly yanked it from her mouth, and observed the train; it was illuminated with flashing rainbow strobe lights and a neon sign that advertised its destination. "Your one stop destination to the City Electric where life is always a party. Bask in our dayglow 4ever."

The strobe lights flickered in Stella's eyes, and she could feel her heart race. She was overcome with the need to rave, and as soon as the glossy sliding doors on the train opened, she charged in. Inside, she could instantly feel the train's air-conditioned interior, and saw seats of lime green and hot pink pleather. She was moving at full speed, giving the finger to the laws of momentum as she slammed into the conductor. She could feel her body spin in midair as she fell towards the ground. She let out a loud scream as she prepared to collide with the floor.

But she never met with the ground because when she opened her eyes, she realized she was in the arms of a familiar figure.

She looked at the face of the person who held her. He was a boy of twenty years whose skin was a shining shade of silver. His raven hair was shaved on half his head while the other half flipped in his eyes; he also tied parts of his hair into little knots for what Stella assumed was his culture's fashion. He had a look of disdain; and when he spoke, his tenor voice reflected the same. "It's beyond me how someone so gifted at dancing could be so uncoordinated and clumsy."

As grateful as she was for him not allowing her to get a fractured skull, Stella was still put off by the boy's sour attitude. "Gee, thanks for the anti-compliment, Dan."

Stella had just realized she had been caught by Dan Dorphin, her competition in The Dance of the Gods tournament, and the one boy who bested her at it. Stella wasn't sure how she actually felt about him due to his cold, detached demeanor, but she still had respect for his seamless abilities. She enjoyed their little rivalry too.

Dan calmly continued to lecture Stella. "I see what you were doing though."

He held his hands out between the area where Stella had crashed into the conductor. "If you had waited until the conductor had walked a few more inches past my seat, you could have dismounted off him at a better angle, causing your torpiroette to be manageable."

Stella sat up, and not only rolled her eyes, but moved her whole head gently along with them. A smile came over her. She knew he was only a merciless perfectionist who was enslaved by the need to master his own craft and help others do the same.

The conductor rose to his feet and proceeded to glare at the young dancers with his hands on his black khaki trousers. Dan looked at Stella, and patted her on the back. "Regardless if you hadn't botched it or you did, you'd probably still have a lawsuit for assaulting train employees."

Stella giggled, and tried to look as innocent as possible at the train conductor while holding out her tickets. He swiped them from her hands and muttered, "I'll let it go this time."

19

As soon as he was gone, Stella peered over the seat. With a self-satisfied smile and a wink said, "Pays to be cute."

"Or he had more important business to attend to." Dan said, paying less attention to her now.

Stella ignored him and continued, "Well how are you? I haven't seen you after you barely beat me."

She cringed, remembering how she lost: the accursed tango with Dan of all people. His lust for perfection and the demands he made of his partner and himself was all a carefully masked mind game to drive her insane. It was cute and amusing on its own, but it really shot her nerves when she had to work with him, and how he'd call out even an out of place breath. When it came to judging, her free-spirited movements were praised on their own, but they paled in comparison to his flawless mannered poise. Normally, something like this would embitter someone, but Stella wasn't that petty. She had a respect for his devotion to the arts and a handful of happy pills to sweeten her attitude regarding second place.

"Well, you only won because you stepped ever so in time with that beat. You're like a damned metronome in heels," Stella said, smiling but twitching all the same.

She wasn't as entirely over her defeat as she had convinced herself. Her sharp breathing through grinning gritted teeth could attest.

"I'm doing fine by the way, since you asked. How are you holding up?"

"Everything is super peachy!"

He stops and looks up at her with concern. "Good. My rival must be strong-willed. We are here to become knights, after all."

"I'm just here to vacay and impress!" Stella strikes a fashionable pose.

"This isn't a game."

"Hey, you said you were fine! Or were you just being polite?

Dan turns away from her bright gaze. "I'm still trying to move out from underneath my father's shadow."

Stella let out an exasperated sigh over his giant statement. "Your father, huh? That's gonna be hard."

"Don't remind me," The boy groaned.

Stella knew Dan's father quite well, and not because the two had shared more than a casual greeting, but because Dan's father was a retired megastar.

Dorian Dorphin was one of the most talented Dance of the Gods champions the esteemed competition ever had. Legends say that when he moved, time would stop and the world would center on his gravitational pull instead. With these mythical powers, he disseminated the worldly competition when it paid a visit to the City Electric. Like most cherished athletes, however, his story ended with a tragic retirement.

It was during the final faceoff on The Dance of the Gods, and fate had pitted him against his self-proclaimed arch nemesis, Madame Mimi. She was a performer so heinous that she earned her the misnomer: the Madame of the Damned. It was clear that this ultimate tango was going to be among the most legendary ever featured in the stadium, not only for the skill level, but the spiteful chemistry that broiled between the two. The dance had reached its height of tension, and it was clear the two were evenly matched. They stayed on each other so close that the Madame had never been caught. In the whirlwind of passion—so hot and fast that no one could notice her below-the-belt tactics—Mimi like a bullet bug from hell, quickly rammed her knee right between Dorian's thighs with enough momentum that it sent him reeling onto the floor in a spiral of agony. It caused him not only to forfeit the match, but to turn down the chance of an heir as well. With biology no longer on his side, Dan came into his life through an adoption agency, and took his rightful place as his child and successor to his prowess.

Through many widespread tabloids and gossip headlines, Stella knew the story of Dorian Dorphin better than that of her own father. She sympathized with the obstacles that Dan must have dealt with on his journey to become his own legend. His situation made her loss tolerable; she knew his victory would pave way for his own independence.

Stella and Dan sat in silence, taking in the ambience of the train for a lengthy minute. It rolled and bounced every five seconds, jostling their bodies. Blasts of air condition hit them, causing Stella to shiver, and make a mad grab for the hoodie inside her travel bag. Upon standing up and pulling her bag off the railing, the train came to a swift stop, and caused her to lose her balance and knock her back in her seat. "Um, I meant to sit down," she blurted.

She could have sworn she saw the normally solemn Dan smile from the corner of his mouth as he gazed out the window.

Her eyes lit up when she looked outside. The train had arrived at a platform quite like Northern Gardens; it was small with a single ticket machine, but the locale was entirely different. In its background, Stella could see the sparkling ocean, its neighboring beach, and a bunch of cottages; no doubt built for the bright shiny locale.

"Now arriving at Seaside Station. Next stop, the City Electric North Side," the intercom announced.

21

As soon as he heard these words, Dan reached underneath his shirt and removed a long necklace. There was a long rectangle shaped gem stone at the end of it. He gazed at it with widened eyes for the first time.

"Ooh, what's that?" Stella questioned.

Dan, startled by her words, scrambled to grasp the object. He made a fist around it, turning flushed all of a sudden.

"Sorry," Stella said grinning, a hand behind her head, "I was distracted by the shiny."

Dan glared at her. He did not judge annoying people silently. "What are you part feline?"

"Well, I do have a great cat crawl." Stella wiggles her eyebrows.

Dan raised his hands above his head, almost like he was trying to petition the great overseer to make this train ride end. But then he took a breath and said, "If you really want to know, it's my charm."

"Is it a lucky charm?" Stella said and pointed to her belongings. "My go-go boots have won me so many matches so I count them as my special relic."

"No, it's not a childish tool of convenience," Dan said, narrowing his eyes, "And I didn't figure you'd believe in something so absurd. Pitiful!"

"What? How can you say that?" Stella stuck up her lip in an offended pout.

Dan crossed his arms and spoke with a harsh tone to strictly discipline Stella. "When people say they're lucky it's because they're not confident to admit the merit of their own work."

"So you're saying…."

"There's no such thing as luck, only hard work. You belittle yourself…disgusting."

Dan paused for a second to size up Stella. He motioned to her. "Grace, I may have seen you fall on the floor more often than a child drinking his first vodka shot, but you came in second without any help. That is hard work personified."

Stella felt her face go warm. That was probably the nicest thing she ever heard him say, not just to her but in general.

"You're really good with those anti-compliments, you know," Stella spoke, ego having been struck, "Complinsults."

"I know." Dan responded, but paused before deciding he really had something he wanted to tell Stella. His stern face eased to show that there was a vulnerability behind such a strict mind. "But if you really want to know, this was something my birth mother gave me."

The dancer opened his hand to reveal what he had previously vice gripped: it was a large head carved in marble. Upon closer inspection, Stella could tell it was the head of the goddess, Ravenous. It was funny Dan claimed he didn't believe in superstitions, because the legend surrounding Ravenous was that whenever she came to a party, the party was the greatest in the land. Ravenous' influence was responsible for the construction of the City Electric. Her followers had all had elected it to be the world's first metropolis, whose primary export was partying to commemorate her. Ravenous had vanished. Books, myths, and legends were all that remained, yet people still carried around jade carvings of her head in order to bless their parties to be on the same level as the ones Ravenous hosted.

"I can tell what you're going to insinuate. But I don't believe in its powers. I believe in the love that was put into it when she gave it to me…her faith is more powerful than any goddess. It reminds me that I was loved…at a time."

Stella heard his voice crack a little when he muttered those last three words so quietly that she could barely hear them. She had heard rumors his tragic story. Dan lost his biological family, and the man he lived with now wasn't the one who raised him. Considering what a successful dancer the man was, he probably wasn't particularly easy to live with either. Since she wanted to add some positivity to their day, she decided to not dwell on that subject. Fortunately for her, the best subject was on the horizon.

She hops in excitement. "Oh wow…look out your window. You can see the city."

The City Electric stood in the middle of the ocean. The buildings were tall, cylindrical, and black and were covered in seams where liquid lights of electric blue, hot pink and otherworldly green that ran in between the windows. They flickered at such rapid pace, that if you weren't a raver, you could expect them to send you into an epileptic fit.

Fortunately, it was midday so the hot purple sun in the sky outshined them.

Stella remembered stories about how the sun went purple during a great war. That couldn't have been true, right? What kind of weapon can change something so massive?

She shook away her worries and took a deeper look at the city.

23

The giant pulsating billboards could compete in limiting your vision as well with advertisements for a smorgasbord of parties. They included the time, the place, and the style required to enter each respective club. Stella noted one for neon bikinis, and got more ecstatic than she normally was. Her body was cut, shaped, and waifish, so all she'd have to do was walk into a club and the eyes of both men and women would be all over her.

Electrical nodes rose from the tops of the buildings; they were shaped like glowing bright purple spheres. Stella learned from her fine-living magazines that these electrical nodes were used to absorb sunlight to keep all the incredibly bright flashing lights of the city powered all night long. They were modified specifically to absorb purple sunlight because a few years ago, the sun had turned from orange to purple, which caused normal solar power to die like dub step. The crisis was overcome by the City Electric's management. Like the drinks that were served all throughout this city, the people were smart and ecofriendly, and they had designed their town accordingly. Granted, they did not take into account the amount of light pollution their city caused. People complained from far off continents because they could see the city as bright as a nuclear explosion. Oh, but that wasn't even the whole story. Apparently, the city's internal bass was pumping on levels so high they caused tremors.

Speaking of, Stella could see the beat pulsate through the train's windows. She started to groove along to it, raising her hands above her head and wiggling her hips. They begged to be free of the confines of the seat and to dance the night away.

Dan looked at her like she was moving as the result of a concussion. "Why are you dancing?"

"Why don't you dance with me so I don't look like a dork?" Stella smiled, rocking back and forth to the rhythm.

Once again, Dan's inner politics came forth. He would share them at any given situation; no matter how jovial it was. "I don't dance unless there's an adoring audience and awards to win. Training is another exception, of course."

"Aww, party pooper." Stella stuck out her tongue and teased him. "You better get adjusted to it because where we're going; we're gonna party until the end of our lives."

As soon as Stella uttered those words, the whole train went dark.

Step 3: The Intruder

The train car holding both aspiring dance stars was blackened by the tunnel. The only lights came from the small flashing floodlights outside that imitated rave lights with a few neon swirls of green, red and blue. They illumined Stella's concerned face. "Whoa, this is kind of spooky. The lights don't normally go out when I ride down this way."

Dan sneered in response. "Must be a power failure. That's why you never ride in second class."

While Stella admired Dan's logicality, she was annoyed by his condescension. She quickly realized that rich boys like him weren't accustomed to the inconveniences of the lower-middle class, so she decided not to call him out. "Yeah," she said, trying to change the subject. "When we're both celebrities, we won't have to deal with this."

The lights quickly flickered on, and the door at the end of the car opened revealing a frazzled and angered conductor.

"If manic girls crashing into to me weren't enough," he said as Stella winked again, trying to avoid looking guilty. "I've got hooligans messing around with the breaker switch for this car. If I catch who did it, I'm tossing them out."

"See Grace, it's just pranksters," Dan said with a flamboyant lift of his hand. He always tried to bathe in the opportunity of being right.

The raver turned away from Dan to grit her teeth for a second before turning back. "Call me Stella, please."

"I thought a last name basis would be better since we're simply going to be colleagues from now on and that's it," he said, an inherent coldness in his voice.

Stella pursed her lips in disgust. She wanted to know him better since the competition, but maybe it wasn't worth it. This man was turning out to be a conversational cadaver.

They sat in silence again. Stella plugged her earbuds into her Interstellar Music Player, cranking up the latest top 40 electro-pop songs. She kicked back with her feet on the opposing seat, while Dan gazed at his reflection without much movement.

For 15 minutes, their only movements were the bumps caused by the train, but eventually, the bumps ceased. The air had become dry and stale, but Stella paid no mind to it, assuming it was merely from the awkwardness.

Dan jostled Stella who had her eyes closed as her head bopped to the beat.

Stella yanked the earbuds out and glared at him. "What?"

With a solemn look, Dan said, "We've stopped moving."

With no warning, the lights shot out again. This time they cut out with a loud buzz. The passengers surrounding the dancers chattered. "What's going on?"

"Why does this keep happening?"

"I heard from my friend there's a hijacker," a woman said, particularly loud.

"No, it's vampires! They are here for our blood!" yells a crazy old man, running to the front of the train.

The mumbling of the passengers increased, becoming more worrisome. Stella could feel her heart race. What if it was true? Would she die on her special day?

She looked towards Dan in the darkness; he had very little reaction to the news. She wished she could feel as numb in a situation like this.

"Will you just shut up," the conductor snapped. "If there was a hijacker, I would have been notified."

Through the dim lights, the conductor grabbed the sliding door leading to the outside of the train. "It's just some punk screwing around; and like hell, if I'm not going to do something about it." He slammed the door as he stormed out.

The whole car was silent for a moment until the sound of inordinate thumping was heard outside the car.

"What's going to happen to us?" One of the passengers asked.

Stella shivered. She looked at Dan with his solidified expression of not-caring. If one of her friends was sitting next to her, she would have nuzzled up against them for comfort. Unfortunately, she was with Dan, so the scared dancer just sank down in her seat.

Abruptly, someone's head came smashing through the glass panel on the door outside of the train. Shards of glass sparkled in the dimly lit car as it danced among the blood. Stella covered her eyes, but left a crack open to peek through. She squinted to see the face was the angry conductor all twisted and bleeding from impact. The door swung open and everyone watched stunned as the body of the conductor hovered in mid-air as if it was supported by an invisible person. The slumped body was flung across the car like it was spirited away by a specter. It slid past aisles of seats before stopping right before the dancers.

Stella gasped, and suddenly felt someone grasp her body. She looked and saw Dan holding on to her arm with an expression of terror on his face. Normally Stella would have been disgusted by this after what he said, but she comforted his head against the sleeve of her shirt. "It's going to be okay."

The intruder spoke. "I didn't come for you, low energy man who can't dance. I came for the prized morsel that lies within."

Stella and Dan both looked up after hearing a voice that would sound smooth and velvety if the circumstances were different. It was deep and reverberated around the whole carriage. It brought a chill that made Stella's hair on her neck dance with every enunciation.

A tall man in a nauseating bright green and purple pimp suit stomped through the car. Sharp spikes protruded out of his shoulder and his long silver hair curled just as sharply. His nose was his most prominent facial feature—hooked and long like a beak. It was so long it partially covered the smirk on his face. His skin, like his hair, was a shining silver. When he opened his mouth in a snarl, Stella could see not only did he have fangs, but they were the color of neon rainbows. The only time he was visible was when he walked into one of the flashing strobe lights from outside the car; every time he disappeared and reappeared, he switched his body into a different pose.

The man stopped right by the body of the conductor, and turned to Stella and Dan. His vision went right through the peppy girl and straight to the handsome young man. He licked his lips as his meal quivered behind its lady friend.

"Mmm, my senses don't lie. You, my friend, have the skin of an enlightened man of Gris." The man looked at the platinum skinned boy with a ravenous gaze.

Dan shuddered. "W-what do you want with me?"

The man's eyes grew wide and manic. "You have so much rave energy inside you. I need it."

"I'm not a raver, I'm a formal dancer," Dan said, with a nervous tic in his voice. Even in a dire situation, the perfectionist couldn't help his need to be right.

"What you don't know will hurt you, boy." The man extended his hand, giving a great big flash of his rainbow fangs as his deep voice echoed again. "My name is Vincent Crane. And to live, I will feed off the richest electromotion in the land—yours." The man's smooth voice transitioned into one that was comically deep and spooky, as if he watched too many horror movies.

Crane lunged with his hands outstretched, but Stella jumped out of her seat, plunging into him. They both fell to the floor where the conductor lay groaning.

Stella tried her best to intimidate a creature she was far more afraid of and released a grr befitting a great feline. "You're not touching him," she growled, lowering her light, airy voice. "I won't let you."

Crane gritted his teeth and quickly advanced on all fours to the feral obstacle. "I don't care about you, insignificant woman. You may have electromotion, but a pink girl is so much weaker and mealy to the tongue."

Stella kicked him in the nuts and tried to poke his eyes but missed.

After slamming his head into her, the slim looking man stood up as he lifted Stella over his head. With the strength of a wonder beast, he threw her half-way across the train.

Stella hit the glass panel door before falling flat on her face.

Having taken care of his annoying little problem, Crane continued to advance on his real meal.

Stella muttered to herself as she pushed herself off the floor. "Mom always said it doesn't matter how badly you fall down, just as long as you get up."

She quickly scrambled to her feet. While lacking book smarts, she knew how to move fast and think fast too.

She carefully opened the broken sliding glass door, and entered the small antechamber that connected both train cars. It was there she found a metal panel that had been left open by the ghoulish man. Inside was a switch operated by pulling, but it was broken. The creature must have snapped the handle off.

Stella stomped on the ground in frustration, and her foot slid on something. Crouching to regain her balance, she looked down. It was the flashlight the train conductor was using. She smiled to herself. "Falling down isn't always so bad."

Stella ran back into the train car just in time to see Dan yell at the monster, while waving a sword of ice. She had to squeeze through the crowd to get to him.

"Please, go away! I...don't want to hurt you."

The ice sword broke apart as Dan's confidence was shaken.

"Leave me alone!" Dan stuck out his hand in a very poor attempt to fend off Crane.

"Ah, you're offering me a well to drink from your veins. I thank you for that, child."

28

Crane grabbed Dan's arm and sank his multicolored fangs into the platinum skin. His face and arms glowed bright blue as he did.

Dan began to slowly wither out of consciousness.

Stella ran up to them, and shined her flashlight   in their faces.

Crane's face turned to one of extreme discomfort, and he quickly flickered from visibility.

Dan still shuddered in the corner. His eyes were so fearful.

"Dan. He's gone. Are you okay?" Stella rushed to his aid.

She heard an electric crackle and she turned around. There was a woman standing about two heads taller than her. She wore a black outfit highlighted by a glowing purple that looked like a cross between a rave suit and armor. It illuminated the whole room, and Stella could see the rest of her features: a blank expression, pale skin, black hair that was cut into an uneven bob and eyes that shined an intense orange. A thin unibrow hung over her eyes. She clutched a staff that emitted bright green, yellow, blue and red lights from both ends.

Stella was overloaded from the sight of Dan visibly suffering. "Can you...please help...my friend?" she said in tears as she held onto a passed-out Dan, his arm glowing where he was bitten.

The woman ignored her and continued to run through the train as Stella continued to plead. "Please, I don't want him to die."

One of the passengers, an older woman from the Greased Lightning Geriatrics Dance Squad, raised her phone. "Don't worry sweetie, we've already called the authorities. Just sit tight."

Stella looked at Dan's arm; there was now an enormous seam of rainbow shining through his otherwise silver skin. His arm looked like it had a rash of dayglow. She looked at his face. His eyes were closed, and his mouth hung wide open. Stella realized that this was the closest she had been to him since their tango all those months ago. She desperately wanted to bring back that snarky annoying perfectionist.

Step 4: A Doctor's Priority

Suddenly, the whole car was filled with masked soldiers sporting glow-in-the-dark camo. Stella observed that the masks looked more like the kind used to inhale things rather than to prevent inhalation. She quickly realized that these were the police of the City Electric, and they probably liked to party just as much as everyone did.

Everything that happened after that was a blur to her. The train had to be started up again. Stella was informed that the engineer was murdered; presumably by the same creature that attacked Dan. She informed the police that she and Dan were the two finalists in the Dance of the Gods tournament as well as what had happened on the train. They had gotten a stretcher for Dan and the sturdy conductor as well. For the rest of the train ride, Stella sat in silence until it reached its destination: the City Electric's North Side Station.

Stella was escorted by two police officers in thick-tubed masks that connected to a tank on their backs, while a masked paramedic pushed Dan on a stretcher. They stepped from the train onto the underground platform into a shadowy station.

The walls, when not covered from dirt and grime, were tinted by a glowing neon graffiti that did a better job of illuminating the cavernous station than the dim bulbs hanging overhead.

Stella had been here a few times; but on much more cheerful occasions, where she could step over the withered husks of burned-out users lying on the floor with no difficulty. After what happened on the train however, their gaunt appearances only whispered of death and depression. The shaken girl pulled out her pill bottle. She knew she wasn't supposed to take more than what her doctor prescribed her; but in a situation of high anxiety, she didn't know what else to do.

As the stretcher wheeled itself onto the elevator, a deathly thin young man who lay on the ground with a cardboard sign called out to Stella. "Please lady, I'm on my last plus, can you spare one. I don't want to withdrawal."

As if Stella wasn't already mentally on the edge, seeing the sad victim of drug abuse asking for some of her plus startled her even more. The elevator closed and she sat in the claustrophobic space with the three other police units and the stretcher. She carefully stored the pills in the top of her tote bag, and resolved not to take them out again until they had reached their destination. She leaned to one of the soldiers. "Where are we going?"

"The clinic," replied one of the soldiers. "There's one in this station. We can get your friend all patched up and ready to go."

The elevator opened up and they wheeled into a more crowded underground area. It was brighter, and there were a mess of people scrambling to get to their next destination.

"Paramedic Unit coming through," yelled one of the police officers. Fortunately for Stella, the stretcher served as a battering ram that managed to break itself through the overpopulation until they reach the destination.

It looked like a store in a rundown shopping mall on the bad side of town. Red neon letters that had faded read above the entrance: "Cherry Blossom Clinic."

Stella could not believe how her perfect day had fallen so far off course. As she walked inside, she opened her bag and clutched her pill bottle tightly.

Stella sat alone in the waiting room of the Cherry Blossom Clinic. The wood chairs had stiff cushions that provided little comfort when she tried to sink into one. The radio built into the wall had the cheerful lilt of Diva LaSweetfa's top 40 song, I Ain't Your Candy Girl playing an instrumental version with only the relaxing piano keys. Even so, it did little to shake Stella free of her mood.

After everything that had happened, her mind was in total chaos. She grabbed some magazines off the sitting room table and grimaced as she looked over them. It was great to read up on the latest celebrity news, but when the magazine of "latest celebrity news" dated back five months, the freak-outs and euphoric behavior of your favorites are literally old news. Stella plopped the magazine on the table loud enough for the receptionist behind the glass panel window to leer at her.

In Stella's eyes, the receptionist's short grey hair, plastic framed glasses with attached strings, and easily agitated demeanor made her look something between a librarian and an old lady who takes bingo night way too seriously.

Stella glanced down to avoid the laser like hostility of her glare. As soon as the gaze was diverted, Stella pulled out her pills from the tote bag that had been along the same hellish journey as her.

Stella held her prescription bottle in her hand. She thought back to the discussion she had with Dr. Proto, her psychiatrist, and a man so reclusive that she had only ever heard his voice. In his cold, grey office, his assistant gave her an elixir to end all of her misery. But even a magic elixir comes with side effects—this one caused manic excitement, disorientation and if she ever ran out, she could go through a dangerous withdrawal. Proto however, hadn't spoken to her about the side effects of taking more than the prescribed amount.

Stella really wanted to obey his orders, but she knew that she was in dire need for the kind of positivity the Yellow Plus offered. She wanted to forget all the horrifying things that happened.

31

"I don't want to spend my time in the City Electric clawing my eyes out, I just want to party and be happy," she said to herself as she swayed her feet around. She knew that one couldn't hurt her, and that one was all that it would be. She popped the little yellow pill into her mouth and swallowed. She closed her eyes and leaned back.

Fifteen minutes elapsed and then Stella opened her eyes. A smile crept on her face. Her mind did a superhero leap from the pit of despair onto a rainbow. Her mind then focused on what was playing on the radio: pulsating electronica.

Stella's foot moved in time to the synthesized rhythm and her mouth lip synched to the vocoded vocals. She moved her whole body out of her chair and began to wiggle. Just as soon as the bass dropped, she began cutting shapes on the waiting room floor. Her feet moved in rapid-fire steps that propelled themselves further with every time they synchronized. The waiting room was barely big enough for people to sit in, much less dance. When she spun, her foot locked with the magazine loaded table and flipped it over. Stella lost her balance and landed next to it.

The door to the waiting room opened and Dan stood right in front of Stella and the deluge of magazines that covered her. "Oh my stars, I'm sorry," Stella said, hiding her face in embarrassment.

"You're lucky I saw the receptionist making tea in the breakroom," Dan replied in a voice that was playful for him. "You always make a grand mess whenever you spin."

"Umm hehe," Stella said, her face behind the veil of her hands. Her eyes widened and she threw her hands down. "Dan, you're alive!"

Dan muttered, "Yeah…technically." He held out his arm. It came clad in a black bandage covering the seam on his arm.

"The doctor says it's called a rainbow burn." Dan gestured at his arm. "People have been getting them in incidents like this."

"Ooh, at least the name is fun," Stella said, again with a quick and flighty response. "It's like what you'd call a super gay comeback."

Dan groaned and slouched in a way that contrasted with his stiff upbringing. "It really hurts and it makes me feel tired. Really tired."

"Aww I'm sorry. I didn't know."

"Lucky for me, the doctor gave me this containment patch to keep it from spreading…and…I think it's working."

Dan took a breath in and choked in a moment of silence. He looked down and walked forward to Stella. "And, one of the officers told me that if you hadn't stepped in on the train…well…I would have been dancing in the afterlife."

"Huh?" Stella's eyes widened. "What did I do?"

Dan blushed; his pale complexion shaded brightly. "You saved me."

"I did?" Stella put a finger to her mouth and her eyes sparkled with curiosity.

Dan's forehead wrinkled. He was feeling that Stella was toying with him to get him to praise her further. "Do I need to spell it out for you? The officer told me that some woman told him that you shined a flashlight in that monsters face and drove him away."

"Oh yeah, I guess I did do that, didn't I?" Stella chuckled with an uncertain laugh.

Dan shook his head. "Stella, what are we going to do with you?"

Stella blushed and nibbled her lip. It was the first time she ever heard him ever call her by her first name. She hid her red face by gathering fallen magazines.

Dan crouched down and joined her; carefully picking up the magazines with his good arm.

"Well since I saved you, do you owe me one?" Stella smiled at him and extended her hand.

"Yes, I owe you a clumsiness debt. Every time you knock something over, I'll help you pick it up." Dan hesitated for a second before raising his hand to reach hers.

He paused for a second. "That doesn't include train conductors. Especially if they look as angry as that one on the train. Non-living things only. Is that clear?"

"That one looked like he could pick me up and throw me over his head." Stella giggled then paused.

What could have possibly gotten into Dan that made him so friendly all of a sudden? She hoped the rainbow burn hadn't sucked out his original dour personality and replaced it with something more colorful. Even if she much preferred him this way, she feared something wasn't right.

"Why are you being so nice all of a sudden?"

"Well…I—"

33

The door of the waiting room creaked, cutting him off. Out stepped a man whose curly dark beard covered the lower half of his face. The top half of his face was painted with stars—it clashed with his doctor's outfit—a black collared coat that pulled all the way down past his thighs.

"Wow this guy looks amazing!" Stella exclaimed. To her, most doctors were boring figures, and the fact that they prodded and poked you with needles was the only thing attention grabbing about them. This guy looked like a glam rock star.

"Thank you for the compliment, girly. I do try to look sharp." He licked his fingers and slicked back his hair while sporting a grin.

"Dr. Move?" Dan inquired.

"Yes, boy. I'm here to talk to you about my manner of payment."

Dr. Move pulled out a small notepad, flipped through a few pages. "It's come through to about fifty-three thousand K."

The currency K was as old as the city itself and was created to give it interdependency. Many of the nearby areas weren't too happy with such a loud and flashy neighbor. Outside the city, the currency is utterly worthless, but most people who visit end up staying until their final mortal coil dance.

Dan's eyes widened and he dropped the magazines he was holding. "That many Kinetics for this containment patch?"

Move was quick to respond, but his answer beat around the bush. "Partially, my boy."

"But we discussed the price earlier and it was to be two-thousand three-hundred K." Dan whined.

Dr. Move started feeling his beard. He lowered his equally bushy brows before he gave the prognosis of his cruelty. "Yes, but that was before I realized who you were: Son of Dorian Dorphin."

"What…so?"

"I'm sorry, but I am a simple physician, I may cure ills just like a magician, but this isn't celebrity rehab. That costs extra. Those with more to give should be forced to do so, it's only fair," the doctor said with a smirk.

Stella saw a rage billow up in Dan's face. He grimaced and she witnessed a long vein sprout from his neck. She put her arm on his shoulder.

The doctor extended his hands into the air. "And of course, you'll also have to allow me the following headline when I go to the papers: "Wonder Doctor Cures Dorphin Heir of his Ills.""

Stella stomped into the conversation. "This isn't fair. Mr. Doctor, you may look cool, but what you're doing is mega uncool."

A darkness grew in Move's face and his bushy eyebrows sunk low. "Nothing in life is fair, sweetie. Do you think I'm happy running a clinic in a train station? Of course not. I...."

This time it was Dr. Move who was interrupted.

The entrance door to the waiting room slammed so hard it crashed into the wall, leaving a dent. In stepped a woman who was just as eccentrically dressed as the doctor. If there was one motif of her outfit, it was thunderbolts. From her face which had small mini bolts painted underneath her eyes, to her shocking yellow hair that looked electrocuted from use of frizzy hair products, to her electric blue, white and yellow corset; she resembled a powerful streak of electricity in the sky. The woman in addition had high-heels where the part of the heel was molded just like a lightning bolt, and when she kicked the door open, Stella could hear them crash just like real thunder.

As this commanding woman smiled with dominance over the doctor who trembled before her. Stella puzzled her mind with who this woman was. She knew she'd seen her before, but where?

"May I interrupt?" She asked in a husky voice.

"Charlotte? Wh-what are you doing here?" The doctor stuttered.

"I was just informed by my close associate that the winners of the contest I sponsored were in this shamble of a hospital." She raised her eyebrow and whispered. "I would like them back, thank you."

The proud woman advanced, and the doctor withdrew in her presence like he was that freak Crane when he was confronted with a flashlight. Charlotte raised a neatly manicured hand, complete with sharpened bright yellow nails, and helped Stella and Dan Dorphin to their feet.

Stella was overwhelmed from the whole day, but when she finally managed to determine who this important woman was, she became star-struck. "Charlotte. Oh my stars. I remember seeing you at the judging table at Dance of The Gods."

"Yeah, and judging is not the only thing I'm good at, sweetie," the foxy woman replied, pulling her finger forward in a provocative manner.

Stella recounted all of the things Charlotte excelled in. She was the owner of CharLuv, the largest chain of dance clubs in the City Electric and those dance clubs were the sponsor of DOTG. In addition, she was voted last year as the City Electric's second most influential person, both financially and as a socialite. She may have been nearing the age of forty-five, but she was ageing with glamour and grace; and perhaps, as the tabloids suggested, a little help from renowned skin carvers. Stella made sure to leave that last part out.

Stella's gushing was interrupted when Charlotte's D-sized cup knocked into her as she stood up.

"O-M-G!" She yelled to the heavens. "Charlotte's boob just touched me! Pinch me, I must be dreaming."

This sentence caused the middle-aged receptionist who had returned with her freshly made cup of tea to spit it out all over her desk.

Dan rolled his eyes. "Uh…don't mind her, Charlotte. She's had a big day."

"No excuses needed, luv. She's a fangirl whose just met her idol. I would give her some time to cool her brain down." Charlotte gave a toothy smile that brightened the room like a flash of lightning. "I was the same in my youth. Though I never had an idol quite as electric as me!"

She took another imposing step forward, causing Dr. Move to back into the door. "Now for the matter of that payment you are demanding of Mr. Dorphin…"

"Y-y-y-e-s," The Doctor stammered.

Charlotte reached into her purse and whipped out a blank note and a pen. "Helena," She called, "Write this check for me."

A heavy-set girl stumbled into the room from the entrance. She had short brown hair, enormous brown eyes and a strawberry complexion, much like Stella's. A yellow pixelated flower in her hair tipped off Stella that this girl was the eighteen-year-old Helen Wheels, another competitor in The Dance of The Gods. This doughy dancer placed third and was known for her masterful jam skating and absolute distaste for Dan Dorphin and his father.

It was as if she was personally engineered to hate on the Dorphins by the Madame herself. She loved filling young Helen's impressionable head with rumors and old-wives' tales about the dour duo. Dan and his father would often fire back, and with their numerous ties, caused their in-crowd supporters to boo at Helen. Stella tried as hard as possible to stay out of the pageant-like nature of Dance of the Gods, but that didn't mean she wasn't paying attention. She just wanted to dance; toxic gossip would just dilute the experience.

Helen's round face flipped up into a shy smile upon seeing Stella. "Hi Stella. Back in the city again," she said as Stella waved hello back.

Her pudgy face wrinkled like she ate a mouthful of sour candy when her eyes turned to Dan. "Bleh, Dorkphin is here. Probably to get a prostate exam."

"Ahem," Charlotte said, coughing, "I do believe I have a check that needs writing, Helena."

"S-s-sorry, Ma'am."

Charlotte put one of her long finger nails to her lip and tapped it. "What was the price again, doctor?"

Move looked like he was having trouble forcing words out of his mouth. "Fifty-three thousand K. But don't think I won't tell the press I saved Dorphin's life."

"I don't think a broken nail is life-threatening," said Helen, sticking out her tongue.

Stella walks to her. "I had no idea you were working here. Congrats, pen pal."

"Ah," Charlotte said, her eyes and face unwavering as she glared at Move. "Helena, write me one for one-hundred thousand Kinetics. I'm going to pay you a teeny extra if you carry on your mediocre practice in silence."

Helena scrawled on the note and then handed the pen and paper to Charlotte who scribbled her name and planted a kiss next upon it. A tight smack of bright green lipstick marked the note; which was then planted on top of Move's head.

The greedy doctor scrambled to grab it as it fluttered above his hands.

Charlotte, without a trace of emotion turned around and walked away. A giant smile lit up on Move's face as he read the numbers on the check. "Hehehe, that Charlotte is quite the philanthropist."

"Mmm, a pleasure doing business with you," said the endowed woman in a velvety tone of voice. "Well, are my future stars coming?"

"I can't believe you just bought him," Stella said, taking a step back to marvel at the costly strings Charlotte had pulled.

Electra pushed up her ponytail. "Never underestimate a demure woman with big bucks."

Stella and Dan hustled, not wanting to be in the presence of Dr. Moolah any longer. They left the waiting room and went out into the lobby where Charlotte commanded Helen to "hold" the automatic sliding door for her and the two finalists. As soon as everyone walked out of the clinic and into the station, Charlotte put her arm around Dan, lifting him up. She had strutted swiftly so she could talk with him alone, leaving Stella and Helen behind. Charlotte was a speed demon despite her heels. Stella and Helen had to power walk together just to keep up with them.

"I'm so glad I get to meet the little baby Danny. Isn't he so cute?" Charlotte smiled and poked his cheek. She loved to flirt with boys who didn't know how to handle her large personality. It made her feel all the more powerful.

Dan turned away, but Charlotte continued to talk to him. "But seriously, I'm just happy you survived in one piece after the train fiasco. I'll have you know, if it was up to me, you would have been flown to me in first class."

"I wish that was the case." Dan finally spoke.

Charlotte side-eyed Dan and flicked her manicured hand at him. "And I would never let my kids get treated by that fourth-rate quack of a doctor. Let alone you, and you're much more important than my kids."

"You don't have kids," said Dan under his breathe.

"Oh, you spoiled the punchline." Charlotte started laughing and gripped Dan's shoulder tightly. "Don't do that again."

As Dan and Charlotte weaved through crowds of people in the subterranean station determined to find the exit, Stella and Helen walked at a brisk pace while chatting it up.

Unlike Dan, Stella was well acquainted with Helen, having shared the same dressing room in the tournament. The plussed out pep girl often found that Helen was one of the few people who she had real conversations with, though mostly online.

"That Charlotte sure is a lot more down to earth than I imagined," Stella said. "She also makes mom jokes, which I adore."

Helen pulled her face close to her and whispered, "She's nice as long as you don't work for her."

"Yeah? I haven't seen you since the Dance of the Gods. By the way, you kicked total ass in it," Stella said, pumping her guns.

Helen's large round eyes shimmered and her whole face lit up. "You really think so? I could never hope to be as good as you. You did beat me, after all. I got third place along with that Winterson boy that Dorkphin demolished. I honestly barely beat the Winterson in the deciding battle for third."

Stella stopped and held Helen's shoulders, "You're really masterful on wheels. I nearly crashed into the stands if you don't remember. If they didn't think it was all part of my chaotic performance, you would have won."

"Aww, thank you Stella. And you took that misstep and turned it into your shining moment, blasting me off my feet!" Helen's cheeks became rosy. "My only regrets are you didn't beat that no good dirty rotten Dorkphin and use his stupid hair as a toilet brush."

"He's really not that bad…at least, not lately," Stella said with a polite shrug.

Helen frowned and the acute anger she felt towards the Dorphins showed as her cheeks went red with rage. "Don't tell me that pale prissy princess is working his sleazy charm on you…"

"No, it's nothing like that."

Helen puffed out her cheeks in anger, "Good, because I've heard from so many dancers that he's a heartbreaker, and that's not all."

"Children," Charlotte hollered from far ahead, "I don't want to have to send out a scarlet alert because you get lost in North Side, hurry it up. Especially you, Helena."

Helen rolled her eyes, "See what I have to go through? Word of advice: if you don't win, never get bronze."

Stella laughed along with her chubby buddy. The two made a mad dash while dodging station goers left and right. So many had commuted from the suburbs in order to get away from the drudgery of their lives, throwing caution to the wind so they could have a chance to bask in the City Electric. The two girls caught up to Dan just as soon as they reached a staircase that presumably led them to the streets. The electric diva stomped up the stairs.

After at least thirteen flights, they reached the top and were greeted with blinding bright lights and a gust of night air that came from the heart of the city. The buildings were flashing, the bass shook the ground and thousands of people moved to the rhythm of the streets. "I'm finally here. This is where my dream finally begins." Stella exclaimed, taking in the sights and the very bright lights.

"Dream on, little starlet," said Charlotte with a smirk.

When thinking about the situation, Stella realized that this powerful woman who had all of their futures in the palm of her hands.

Step 5: Ultra Bright Lights, The City Electric

Charlotte, standing by her limousine, beckoned the three dancers who had stopped in their tracks from sensory overload. The awe in their eyes was a clear sign they were tourists. "Come on now kids, don't get epilepsy from staring at the lights too long! Why so starstruck? You've been here for the competition, no?"

"We arrived in the day time. The city at night…it's like a whole different animal!"

"It truly shines like the stars," said Dan with a dazzled look.

"I'm just trailing behind to make sure Dorkphin doesn't try anything," said Helen, pulling Stella by the arm.

Stella's attention was drawn primarily to a towering building that stood at what seemed like the center of everything. It divided the roads beneath it into two separate pathways. The building stretched in both directions and was constructed of what seemed to be highly reflective rainbow glass. A giant '42' in red and yellow shined above it. With its power and regality, it made the roads seem like two important but different decisions in life.

On this central street, perched at the center of the building was a giant screen. At first it only broadcasted adverts for clubs and flashy outfits, but as Stella had emerged from the underground it changed.

A man's visage stretched the pixels at least a yard long and beamed over the city. It was man of some seniority; he had closely cropped silver hair. It was completely unknown if he kept it that short on purpose or he used to disguise any hair loss he was suffering. His eyes, though divided into lines by neon green aviator shades were still visible, and they were bright blue and vibrant. His outfit resembled a white leisure suit but with more chest hair exposed than any modest disco dancer would bear to show, along with a giant rainbow popped collar and a large medallion hanging over his clothes. With a giant toothy grin on his face, the man had all the charisma of a dad free styling on open mike night.

"Wassup, its five to dime in this party city and Daddy D. is in the house; king mayor of the City Electric to all you newcomers. I'm broadcasting from Building 42 to give y'all the Shoot the Breeze before ya start partying hard. First for my royal degree: technically, this may be a monarchy, seeing as I am the king, but I hereby declare this city to be in a state of total anarchy. We're gonna party to infinity, and the only thing that's gonna stop us is that ball of purple light rising in the sky. He's a real sun of a bitch I tell you, ruining our party time on a fine night like this."

Charlotte cut into the man's speech, "Stella, honey, if you want to hear the Shoot the Breeze, you can watch it in the comfort of my limo...on mute."

She hollered at the chauffer who stood outside the car, ensuring everyone made it inside. "Driver, if you would be so kind, take us to the Raveopolis suites."

Stella looked around her and noticed that Dan and Helen had both boarded. She also judged from Charlotte's menacing glare that Helen's dislike of being in close proximity with Dan was outweighed by her fear of the mega-woman in thunder heels.

The slender dancer quickly followed suit to avoid being left behind. She still wanted to see Daddy D's famous speech, which were talked about all over Aleatore for his use of partying rhetoric.

She had read all kinds of pieces written about the influence that the man had despite his questionable get-up and mannerisms. She knew that he was an ambassador of peace back in the main land. Whenever the two warring nations of North and South Aleatore were on the brink of hostility, he would invite their leaders over to the City Electric. Once there, he'd seduce them with a long night of dancing, stimulants and questionable shedding of clothing. By the end, things would flow much smoother back on the larger continent. Weary people would often come to this land to seek the leisure the large nations didn't offer with their instability and Daddy D. welcomed all into his disco dreamland.

The big D would never turn away any soul who was ready to party it down. All you had to do was bring a libido, a working liver, some shiny neon outfit, and an urge to move your body. If you check those boxes, then you were welcomed into this sanctuary of celebration. That was his life's goal, which he broadcasted nightly with his announcement. As Stella climbed inside Charlotte's sleek ride, she heard it on the tiny screen that lowered down from the ceiling.

D put his hand to his chest in a patriot stance and spoke, "Citizens of Rave, I can guarantee that you will never have a night that isn't the time of your life. I will personally see to it that each and every one of you can kick back and enjoy yourselves. That's the will of our party goddess, Ravenous, and our demi-goddess, Kouyate, founded this nation on. As the Pharoah of funk, it is my mission to uphold their party decree. So, get up off the floor and make all your troubles disco dance into oblivion! Just free your mind and your ass will follow. That is the Breeze for tonight, peace out."

The screen returned to its casual programming, and now Stella could finally admire the interior of Charlotte's limo. The plush seats were yellow and bright green- the electric diva's favorite shades of hue. There were glass holders, a mini cabinet for electrolyte-filled beverages, and a glass window separating the chauffer and his passengers. The floor had illuminating titles that flashed like a dance floor. They were here in case anyone wanted to bust a move before they arrived at their destination.

A cool jet of air landed on Stella's face. She would have loved to lay on these plush seats, but she feared the eternal rest it could bring.

Stella caught a glance of Charlotte who had gritted her teeth, furrowed her brow, and was staring with her pupils dilated at the little screen that had played Shoot the Breeze. She clicked a remote and the television screen quickly hid itself, as if in fear of the fuming cougar.

Stella pondered about what could have upset the powerful woman so much. She then recalled her celebrity history.

Back in the day, Daddy D. and Charlotte were not just an item; they were the power couple! They were the two most powerful people in the city, and with Daddy D's overwhelming influence and Charlotte's ultra-successful dance clubs, they were said to throw parties on the level of Ravenous herself. The people of the City Electric cherished their union and believed that it together the lavish lovers would usher in a whole new era of greatness.

It was even said that Charlotte and Daddy D. gave each other their names. Before they met, they were Charlie and Darius. Darius was twelve years her senior and their romance led to fitting nicknames that eventually caught on when they reached the general public.

They were so in love that it was clear to the world that marriage and a joint-ruling was guaranteed, but one day, the two split. They never gave a reason, and nobody knew why their romance went dim, it just did. Stella was itching all over to know the deets, but she didn't feel right asking about something so sensitive.

Daddy D. decided to shed his bachelor status and take many wives afterwards, none who lasted more than a few years. Charlotte remained single, preferring to run her night club empire alone.

Stella realized even quicker that if she didn't want to have her face through the glass window it was best to change the subject. Her eyes darted around the car from the stoic Dan to Helen who was pouring a cup of mercy milk with caution. She smiled and asked, "So is Helen going to be working with us?"

Charlotte's face, changed from an expression of disdain to delight. "Why yes, Stella. You and Danny boy might have been the finalists, but sweet Helena is the true winner: She won herself an internship of a lifetime. Imagine being chosen to work under me as my own personal soy girl."

Stella tilts her head. "Soy...girl?"

"Yes, you see contrary to the rumors about my body, I believe in an all-natural lifestyle and that involves Helena bringing me all kinds of glutton free products whenever I call."

With cup in hand, Helen tapped on Charlotte's shoulder. Her milk mistress let out a yell and expressed as much shock as a botoxed face could possibly muster.

"Your...soy milk...Ms. Charlotte," the temp girl said with a nervous smile, hoping she hadn't given her employer an early heart attack.

As Charlotte was holding her heart and breathing heavily, Stella giggled, "Got to admit Charlotte, she's soy-lent but deadly."

Charlotte paused for a second before letting out a high-pitched belly laugh, "Haha, I thought I was gonna Soy-el myself. But I'm not *that* old yet."

While the two enjoyed a laugh, Dan looked like he could cringe so hard his face would move backward ten feet, while Helen looked at the floor nervously, wondering if her employer was mad at her or not.

Charlotte stopped laughing and let out a sigh. "I've always liked you Stella Grace, your effervescent personality really helps you stand out both on and off the dance floor."

"Wow, thank you Charlotte," Stella responded, clearly flattered. "You're a living legend! I'm so happy I'm going to be a mainstay at your club."

Charlotte gave a large grin, flashing all of her ambitions. "I have a feeling you and Dan are going to be a valuable addition to CharLuv."

Stella gazed out the window as Charlotte continued singing her praises. She marveled at all the people, many waiting outside in long lines waiting to gain entry to their personal parties.

She squinted her eyes at one person, she could barely make it out, but the darker face looked sort of like her mother. She shook her head in disbelief. Was it her mother? Stella looked again, but couldn't find the spot her eyes last focused on as the limo quickly zoomed out of view. The dancer was baffled. It either was someone who looked like her mother or her mother was finally celebrating that all her children left her house and was going clubbing. The latter idea put a big smile on the girl's face.

She put her hands behind her head in V formation and lounged. It had been a long day, but thanks to her persistence, and a little prescribed assistance, she felt great.

For the rest of the ride, she continued to joke with Charlotte and maybe brown nose a smidge. After all, Charlotte was the empress of influence, and if there was anyone who was going to move her from the floor of adequate to the lap of luxury, it was this woman.

The limo arrived at a building fit for a red-carpet event. There were people gathered everywhere outside of a hotel. The building was bright silver and as sleek and upright as a space shuttle ready to launch.

Stella narrowed her eyes at the building that towered so high they nearly reached the clouds. She could just barely make out the penthouse balcony that Dan had the fortune of staying at. She looked at the group that gathered before them; they were armed with towering cameras that shot white light at them.

"The paparazzi!" Stella put hands to her face, letting the cameras sparkle in her eyes.

She was so happy to have her time in the limelight she forgot entirely about their parasitic nature.

Dan, reacted the polar opposite way. He sunk down in his seat like jelly and whined, "Must I really swim through that filth?"

"Damn it, Howard! I thought that bumpy detour you took was to lead them astray. I guess you're not as good as I pay you to be," Charlotte snapped at her driver.

Turning to Dan, Charlotte spoke, "Danny, when you sacrifice obscurity to be a big shot like me, you have to deal with these clothed flashers. Just let them know you're a certified boss. Strut like a monarch, Danny sweetie."

Charlotte yelled at Helen who shielded her face. "Kitten, I want you to distract them while I make a break for it."

"Yes, Lady Charlotte."

Stella saw an opportunity to make the headlines and quickly cut in front. "No, I'll go." She opened the sliding limo door and dashed out to confront the swarm. Charlotte and the remaining two looked at her with shock on their faces before the influential woman smiled and nodded. "This will be good."

Stella stopped at the end of the red carpet that stretched all the way up to the rotating doors of the hotel. She looked to the left and right of her. Many of the reporters were shouting at her at once, making most of the questions they asked inaudible. The peppy girl grinned and struck a playful pose with a wink and a two fingered salute. "Hey guys, you ready to see a true star in action?"

She took off running across the carpet, which began to bunch up as she ran. Larger kinks appeared in the carpet until one caught Stella's boot. "Whoa!" she yelled when she found herself airborne.

Her whole body went somersaulting through the air, and as soon as her feet were parallel to the ground, Stella landed right on her crotch with her legs spilt on the floor. "Huff, huff…ta-dah!"

Some of the accosters were so shocked by her performance that they dropped their cameras and applauded, but the elite remained on their toes.

A female reporter, with a large floppy grey hat pulled over her eyes and nose leaving only a lip stick coated sneer, approached her to talk, "Bravo Ms. Grace. Can you tell us how it felt to be runner up, even with moves like that?"

Stella had barely noticed the barb from the reporter. She sported a confident grin when she spoke, "You know, it just inspires you to learn even more moves. I know my competition would be lying on the ground right now if he tried to pull off what I just did."

A sadistic smirk crept upon the female reporter's face from underneath her large hat, "Kind of like what happened to Dorphin's father, Ms. Grace?"

Stella was caught off guard by the female reporter's cutthroat low blow question aimed at Dorian Dorphin. "Uhh…you might want to take that up with him."

Dan had just emerged from the car and was walking with Charlotte and Helen when he heard what had happened and approached Stella and the female reporter. He looked nervous but agitated all the same. "What did you say about my dad?"

"Ah yes, young Mr. Dorphin," the reporter continued, "Has your father ever mentioned the nutcracker incident to you and how it's the reason you were adopted?"

Dan angrily responded. "My Dad adopted me because he wanted me." He did not like to wrinkle his features, but they creased in rage over the woman's words.

"Did you ever read any interviews how he said he would do anything to continue the Dorphin line even if he had to adopt a child to do so?"

Dan's face looked as if he'd been submerged 20 feet underwater, but just as fast it transformed into a look full of rage. Dan took his non-moving patched up arm and slammed the reporters recording device out of her hands, bits of tape and metal falling out as it impacted on the ground.

The reported gasped as Dan howled in pain.

Stella had never seen this fiery rage from her rival. She emerged from her split on the ground and stood up, holding Dan as he staggered away. A bunch of reporters took advantage of this and flashed their cameras at Dan.

Charlotte stomped quickly over and started talking, "Please excuse, Mr. Dorphin, he's been under the weather. But if you would like someone to talk to, please consult with our beloved bronze beaty place winner, Miss Helena Wheels."

45

The soy girl shuffled in front of the reporters like a hapless insect inside a tank full of lizards waiting to slurp her up. "Um...hi guys," she said as Stella, Dan and Charlotte walked off towards the entrance.

"Umm, I'm ready for my close-up." Helen put one hand on her hip and another on her head and gave a shy smile.

"So, what's it like working with Dan Dorphin and Stella Grace?" asked one of the reporters. Helen looked like she was about to cry, but composed herself.

"Working with Stella is a dream; Dan on the other hand, is more of a nightmare. The amount of lotion he spreads on himself, let's just say you need a tanker...and his father, I've seen better looking toupees made out of sewer animals."

Charlotte and Stella helped Dan get to the silver revolving doors. "Danny boy, you sure are costly. That reporter is the second person I'm gonna have to pay to silence; remind me not to be your date."

Dan looked like he was about to puke and not because of nausea related reasons. "I don't know what came over me."

"She asked you a loaded question," Stella responded. "I'm surprised they didn't bring up the rumors that my star-shaped birthmark is really a tramp stamp." She giggles in an attempt to make the silver statue smile.

"Honey, there are always gossip dealers waiting to score their next round of rumors to those who crave them," Charlotte added. "They don't care what they push as long as it's effective and gets people addicted."

Charlotte continued, her aged but botoxed face showing knowledge of the paparazzi. "In fact, I would love to get my hands on the people who started the rumor about me having implants. I am just naturally swollen, unlike what their head will be when I..."

"Charlotte," Stella interrupted her, "we should get Dan inside now."

"You're right, Stella baby." Charlotte motioned with a wave into the crowd. "Hey lumpy, you can come now. Don't keep Mistress waiting."

Helen's ears perked up and she came running across the extended carpet. "Sorry guys, I'd love to share some more of my mom's dirt on the Dorkphins, but I gotta go."

As she jogged, the female reporter with the big hat whispered to another cohort. "Wow, that skater girl, she's more bloodthirsty than all of you. I'd love to have her in charge of writing my headlines."

Everyone huddled inside the lobby, where everything from the chairs, tables, walls and ceilings were a sleek, reflective white. Stella felt that if she spilled anything it'd stand out gruesomely, but then she saw the obsessive-compulsive looking staff worker armed with a cleaning laser that would blot out anything dirty in mere seconds. With a shield-like visor with a white X over their face and a giant chemical pump on his back, he looked more like a hazmat worker. A gentle but uplifting rhumba played from over the PA causing the worker to shimmy as he was zapping things.

The rainbow mustached suit and tie wearing concierge at the central desk saw Charlotte in her pumps and his face grew unamused and pale as he asked in a posh and agitated accent, "Oh dear Goddess, are these the winners of this year's Dance of the Gods?"

"You don't need to look so depressed, sweet stache. They are those very stars," Charlotte said, putting her face close to his and making him take a step back.

"Charlotte, these kids get to stay at my fabulous hotel for free." The man frowned. "They have been known to trash the rooms with their rowdy antics. I have every reason to be depressed."

"Well, this year's batch isn't so sour, right children? You'll behave yourselves for Mr. Raveopolis, won't you?"

"You can count on me, Mr. R," Stella said, "I'd only be practicing my dancing in there."

Dan Dorphin despite his pain, managed to get a few words in as he leaned up against the far edge of the counter. "Stella, you're pretty much a one-woman demolition specialist when you dance."

Hellen crossed her arms. "At least she knows what fun is! You're as bland as a brick wall!"

Stella giggles. "Chill out, buddy. I like demolition."

Mr. Raveopolis held his heart. "Oh Goddess, give me strength. This is almost as bad as Mr. B. Bop when he first started rooming here five years ago."

"Stop being so dramatic, Raveopolis." Charlotte crossed her arms. "No one is as bad as B. Bop."

Stella giggled. "That's such a funny name. I remember he was that jazzy guy whose feet had a mind of their own."

"Yeah, and they had a one-track mind: Destruction." Mr. Raveopolis sighed and fanned himself with a paper.

Stella wanted to meet Barvarius Bop, the last winner of the Dance of the Gods. He was markedly old fashion, but he was just as wild as her. She knew he worked for Charlotte, so hopefully the chance for a frenetic encounter would arise. It was a goal of hers to see someone as chaotic as she was when dancing up a storm.

Charlotte continued to play with the owner much to his dismay. "Listen up, they will personally answer to me if anything happens, so don't worry your not-so-pretty little head."

The man glared at Charlotte, but reached into a slot from the wall behind him. "And which of these rooms belongs to which of these troublemakers?" He asked in his deep, unimpressed voice.

"My golden trophy boy is Dan Dorphin," Charlotte said, nudging at the depressed Winterson boy. "He won himself room and board in the penthouse."

Charlotte with theatrics laid her hands in front of both Stella and Helen. "The other two are the silver and bronze sisters: Stella and my soy girl. They get to share the runner-up suite."

Mr. Raveopolis pulled out two card keys and handed them to Charlotte who gave them to both Dan and Stella.

"Oh wow," Stella exclaimed, clutching her card tightly. "I've never shared a room with anyone before."

Helen looked up at Stella; her face had a reserved smile. "Neither have I, but I'm glad it's with you. Will we…" She looks down and taps her fingers together "pillow fight."

"Hah, yeah. We'll have the awesomest sleepovers! Staying up all night eating fried toaster tarts in our jammies, watching the Mighty Fruitsaders."

"What's that?" Helen asked, wide eyed. "A telescreen show? Cartoon or live action?"

Stella's eyes glistened with excitement. "Oh girl, you are in for the ride of your life. It's not only a cartoon; the lady who makes it, Brenda Splenda, is a revolutionary."

"Splenda," Charlotte said, beaming proudly with her hands upon her hips. "I know that little firecracker."

"Wow, do you?" Stella asked.

"I quite enjoy that show too and since I'm rather wealthy, I decided I would have dinner with her. Nice woman, even though she doesn't really understand the danger of sugar supplements."

"Whoa Charlotte, you are like the coolest mom lady ever."

"Hey watch your language," Charlotte snapped. "The only people who can call me momma are wealthy young men and only when I'm in the mood."

"Yeah, everyone else has to call her Mistress," said Helen with a scowl.

"Sorry," Stella said, still smiling.

The way Charlotte was so concerned about her age reminded Stella of her mother. Stella, without thinking, put her arms around Charlotte.

The electric woman was shocked at first and lifted her arms above Stella like she didn't want to touch her; but slowly, she put her arms back around the touchy-feely girl.

"Thank you for the opportunity of a lifetime, foxy momma," Stella said, hugging Charlotte like a long-lost maternal figure.

"Um…you're welcome. And I noticed some of your parents are MIA so I guess you can call me mom." Charlotte grabbed Stella's shoulders and dug her nails into them. "But I'm one of those young hip moms, got it?"

"Sweet I got two moms! I'll call you other mom, 'kay?"

"Oh, I can't say no to that face," said Charlotte, pinching Stella's cheeks with a teasing tone.

Dan, having stood there watching all this, became quite irksome. "Can we go? My arm's killing me?"

Stella nodded her head a dozen times in agreement. "Yes, lets. I can't wait to see my new digs."

"Try not to make too much noise." Mr. Raveopolis lowered his hands to represent his ideal volume.

Stella jutted out her lip with a sassy retort. "I can't believe that someone with the word rave in their name is so stuffy."

"It was my father's name he was just like you all, an uncouth chatterbox."

"Why not just leave the city?" asked Helen.

"Oh, that's easier said than done. There's no way to transfer currency so once you're in, you're stuck here." He sighs. "Stuck here with air-headed gossipers."

"Aww, thanks." Stella giggles and tucks the key in her pocket. She was ready to reside among the stars.

Step 6: My New Digs

Though she was five years older than eighteen-year-old Helen, Stella burst through the door of her brand-new room like a child while Helen walked in with reservation.

Stella observed the whole place with a hanging mouth.

It was double—or maybe even triple—the size of her room back home. There was a kitchen area complete with a microwave built into the wall. It was Chef Stella's number one choice of cooking devices and the only one she knew how to use. She loved how it made the icing on her toaster tarts melt. There was also an oven and an electric stove, but those were just over-complicated knock offs. A mini fridge lay next to the cooking devices and so did a sink; ideal for tossing all those kernel-filled bowls of blamcorn and sticky soft drinks in with a loud clunk.

The bedroom area was separated from the kitchen by a room divider, and there were not only two large beds fit for a queen, but a telescreen that took up half the size of the two beds. Everything was so sleek to Stella; there was a bubble-like chair that hovered as well. It was perfect for lounging in the shining white interior. The beds also levitated and looked fluffy enough to send you to cloud nine.

"Ooh I call the window bed!" She dashed in and threw her travel bag.

It landed onto a bed lying parallel to a wide reflective window that showed off a city skyline in bright neon colors. She then threw herself onto it; flying midair in a relaxed position as she hit the bed, but the impact caused her to rebound and sent her flying onto the floor. "Ow my butt," she said as Helen giggled at her. "That wasn't my clumsiness; that was just bad luck."

Helen eyed the window bed, but lowered her head in compromise. She laid her bag out on the other bed with a hum. "So, Stella, what will our new room be called?"

"Hmm, the Room of Doom?"

"Nah, that's too evil."

"Paradise Found?"

"Too pretentious."

Stella's eyes lit up. "I know, we shall fuse our names together and call it Stellen!"

Helen peered at Stella with warm eyes and even warmer rosy cheeks. "I like that one Stella. Especially because it's our room to share together."

Stella ignored Helen and began to dig through her cavernous bag. "Where is it? Come on, I hate how I pack sometimes...aha!"

Stella pulled out a rolled-up piece of paper. It was fastened with a rubber band.

"What's that?" Helen asked, tilting her head.

Stella unrolled the paper to reveal it was the Fruitsaders poster she had procured from her room. "Helen, we really should start this show tonight! There are a ton of episodes and the finale for season 8 is coming next week!"

Helen fiddles with her hair. "I don't know, I'm a little old for cartoons."

"Hey! I'm five years older than you!" Stella walked over and poked Helen on the nose. "You are never too old for children's cartoons. Watching them actually keeps you youthful. Besides this child's cartoon is more informative and meaningful than like every adult show combined."

There was a tentativeness for Helen to believe her friends words, but because it was Stella, her mind decided to open up to her suggestion. "Okay, I'll give a go. So, what's it about? Fruity girls fighting aliens or something?"

Stella began to gush for the next fifteen minutes, her eyes sparkling like cider, speaking about the Mighty Fruitsaders. She told her friend about how Plaqueson a mad scientist with a sweet tooth made giant size desserts that were destroying everything in sight from children's teeth to the skyscrapers in his hometown of Cavicity. His daughter, Molina was desperate to grow up healthy and strong so she fired a bottle rocket into the sky with a message calling out for help. The bottle rocket got so far out it reached an extraterrestrial planet. Just when the girl was about to give in and indulge her chocolate fantasies, three women came down from the sky: The Mighty Fruitsaders. Tammy Mato, Passionfruit Patel and Orange Ornacia, with their juices combined, beat the pulp out of the monster chocolate bar and saved the day. The girl begged the three alien women to stay and bring their messages of healthy sugar and female empowerment to the plaque plagued Cavicity. They decided to stay as long as Molina promised to eat 3 fruits of her choice every day. She agreed and the Fruitsaders all became her newly adopted mothers, raising her to fight for fruit and love. This all took place in just one heartwarming three-parter.

Stella started panting, out of breath from what she had just told Helen. Despite this, she smiled, "Well what do you think?"

"That sounds...great," Helen said, nodding her head. She really didn't know what to make of it, since it was a bit of a sensory overload, but she knew the right answer to get into Stella's good graces.

"Now you know! And knowing is half the battle."

"Yeah, it sounds very fun and cute."

51

"Aw man, I knew you'd love it." Stella grinned as she rummaged through her DVD box sets. "It sounds like it's for kids but they tackle so many meaningful themes that people all around the world have been inspired by it."

"I can only imagine," Helen said, looking at the Tammy Mato on the poster with a light smile.

"I want to change people's lives the way the show does. I want to be that positive influence for people of all races," Stella exclaimed, as she was interrupted by a mannered knock was heard from their door.

"Who is it?" Stella asked.

"Dan."

Helen sighs. "Does that include the Dorkphin race?"

Stella makes sure her shirt isn't showing off too much and then opens the door. "Oh, you're totally welcome here, Dan, come in."

Dan Dorphin in his pajamas stepped in. They were white with vertical blue stripes. His shorts rode all the way up to his smooth thighs.

Stella didn't know many men who shaved their thighs when she went to high school, but Dan told her it made him more aerodynamic. More important to Stella was how his shirt was half unbuttoned, showing the top two abdominal muscles in his stomach. She gazed at them until she was interrupted by the sharp sneer from Helen's voice.

"Oh look, Dorkphin is wearing his girly jammies."

Dan ignored her. "Stella, can I talk to you in my bedroom?"

"Sure! Oh, can Helen come?" asked Stella, grabbing her friend's hand.

Dan's eyes narrowed in hostility and he came close to spitting as he spoke, "No. I don't want negative energy polluting my new sanctuary."

Helen stuck her tongue out. "I wouldn't want to come and hear a narcissistic peacock talk anyway."

"Okay, let's talk about the importance of nice words later. See ya later, Mighty Fruitsader." Stella gives her buddy a salute.

"Do be careful, okay," said Helen meekly.

Stella nodded and then walked through the light-filled doorway with Dan.

"Follow me." Dan led her from the leisure inviting hallways with purple nightshade plants inside colorful pots to a cold empty stairwell.

She figured Dan wasn't in a mood for chit-chat so she didn't open her mouth either. They finally reached the top and were greeted with a single door.

Dan opened it and let it shut, closing it on Stella who had to push it open herself. With a huff, she found herself inside another carefully decorated hotel hallway, but this time there were only two doors, one at the far end of the hallway and the elevator door.

Stella and Dan walked on further.

Stella was a bit weirded out by the lack of rooms aside from the one at the far end. "Gee, it sure is lonely up here," Stella said, observing the passageway.

"I don't mind it," Dan responded. "Reminds me of home."

Stella's eyes softened as they finally reached the door. This time Dan held the door for her. Stella hesitated.

"Well," Dan said with a welcoming tone, "come in."

Stella walked in, stretching her arms. "Don't mind if I do."

She came to a short stairway inside a dark room. As she walked up it, the lights suddenly flashed on, and she found herself in the middle of the winner's penthouse, a total wonderland.

The first thing that caught Stella's eyes was the jacuzzi that was behind the staircase. It was almost the size of Stella and Helen's kitchen, and it made her really kick herself for not coming in first. There were several mechanical arms sticking out of the wall near it; she assumed those were there for massages and automatic bathing. On the opposite side there was an enormous floating king-sized bed, which could swallow up a sumo wrestler much less a hundred-thirty-pound, five-foot nine young man. The walls of the penthouse were all composed of large segmented windows that were specially tinted for privacy. There was also a dance floor and even a large chrome stereo built into the wall, which Dan would probably never use. Stella knew she would have blasted it to heavens, which technically Dan resided in right now.

"Whoa," Stella said, with her mouth wide, "I wish my room had a jacuzzi."

"It's a droll pond compared to the one we have at the mansion back home, but I guess it will have to do," Dan said without much consideration for the people who didn't have one at all.

Stella, without much warning, stripped herself of her shorts, long sleeved shirt and t-shirt. She was only in her neon pink glowing underwear, leaving Dan completely aghast as she plunged into the hot tub.

She went under the water causing it to bubble, and when she raised her head, her now straightened brown hair was soaking wet and dripping all over.

Dan was now standing over her with his arms crossed. "I wanted to be the first one to use it."

"Hehehe, sorry, I've never been in one," Stella said, kicking back in the hot tub.

Dan shrugged his shoulders. "I guess it's the least I can do, as annoying as you are, you did save my life. You do realize you're in your underwear in my apartment, right?"

"Yeah, but it doubles as swimwear, so no biggie." Stella leaned forward and rested her arms on the top of the tub. "Are you going to tell me why you suddenly started being so nice to me in the doctor's office?"

"Well," Dan said, sitting down and letting his feet dangle in the hot tub, "I just wanted to be."

Stella's face rested into a 'can-you-believe-this-guy' face with narrowed eyes and a disapproving frown. "Yeah, that's totally it, Mr. I'm-too-cool-to-make-friends-with-anyone."

Dan's face grew angered. "You know I can kick you out, it is my hot tub." He slid in like a proud serpent.

"I'll just leave before you can, so nyah." Stella stuck her tongue out like a grade-schooler.

Dan let out a sigh. "You don't know what it's like being raised in the public eye. People always want something out of you."

Stella was silent, but her widened eyes told Dan that she was listening to what he was saying.

"People will claim to be your friend just to get to a higher status. And sometimes they hate you for what you've been blessed with. Then there are those who are just waiting with bated breath for you to make a mistake that they can feed off of."

"Like that doctor," Stella muttered with her revelation.

"Yeah, him and the wondrous free press of the City Electric…" Dan swung his head forward, unpoised and angry. "They're scum, all of 'em!"

Stella could feel Dan's raw emotion, and his tirade opened up a whole new interpretation of his personality in her mind. "I can understand why you'd want to close yourself off; they really are horrible."

Dan rose out of the hot tub and walked over to the mechanical arms. He sat down in a stool and picked up a remote. The arms started massaging his back.

"Oh cool. I didn't know it did that." Dan smiled for a split second, his naivety towards technology lead to some amusement before he looked up at her tenderly. "That's been my life's burden. Stella, I can't just change who I am on a whim."

"Wow, I'm really, really, really super sorry. I really didn't know."

Dan raised his finger. "Now you know, and more importantly, you know not to ask."

Dan closed his eyes and let the mechanical hands pound him until his spine clicked. "You showed me kindness even though all I gave you were cold words. You barely knew me…" he looks at her deeply "why are you so kind?"

Stella gave a warm smile. "Of course I helped you! I saw someone in trouble and I had to do something. Plus, if I could get the stoic prince himself to smile, well that would be a personal trophy to add to my shelf."

Dan rolled his head from side to side. He was no stranger to a massage and wishing to gain more flexibility in all of his joints. "Well Stella, I didn't think you would risk your life for someone like me."

"You're awesome!" Stella gave her signature wink. "Plus, if you died, I wouldn't be able to beat your perfectly sculpted booty fair and square."

"I suppose that's true," Dan said, as he lifted up his arm to reveal the patch that had been there. "If this thing on my arm keeps up with what it's been doing, you might not get that rematch."

"Oh," Stella said aghast, realizing his pain was still there. "It's still bothering you?"

"Like I told you, not only does it tire me out but when I hit the camera out of that reporter's arm, it wasn't me who did that. It felt like someone else. A being of rage."

"It wasn't you?" Stella's eyes grew in curiosity.

Dan rocked his head with a suavity, causing his hair to bob from one side to another. "I pride myself in being a gentleman, even to those who don't deserve it."

Stella started laughing so hard she splashed her feet in the tub. "Hahaha yeah, of course you are Dan."

"What?" Dan shook his head in disbelief. "What do you mean?"

"I don't think I've ever seen you being nice to Helen, or any woman for that matter. You were pretty rude to me for most of that train ride too."

Dan was flustered and his choked-up words indicated that Stella had made him think. "Well I...look, Helen is a special case." He looks at Stella with pain in his eyes. "You really don't believe me. I wouldn't assault a woman no matter what."

"Yeah, you wouldn't want to harm those pretty fingers." Stella winked at him again. "I'm joking. Smile, 'kay. I know you wouldn't do that. But maybe you lost it. Anger can be pretty scary. Trust me, my mom can be a real grizzly when I just leave without any notice."

Dan turned away. "Just what was that creature that attacked me anyway? I even asked the officer who was with me and he said he had no idea."

"He didn't?" Stella grew further interested by the conversation.

"No one knew, but the doctor said that the bites are reoccurring and people tend to go missing a few weeks after they are bitten." Dan shivered with disgust. "Are these creatures really vampires?"

"I dunno," Stella responded. "They sure look like them."

"I really don't want to become like that guy." Dan held onto his head and looked around with paranoia that he'd transform at any given second.

Stella tried to remain on the bright side and gave a great big smile. "Hey at least he wasn't bald like the vampires in our movies. He wasn't that bad looking. If you were a vampire, you would be the most elegant of the whole creed."

"Is that so?" Dan chuckles a bit.

Stella knew Wintersons believed vampires were sexy romantic figures that flooded their novel centric culture. She much preferred her Summerein culture's interpretation where they looked bald and goofy with long pointed ears. Those vampires existed only on cheesy telescreen flicks and were either completely harmless or easily defeated."

"At least I don't have to worry about becoming bald...I think." Dan said, sweeping his mane.

"Well," Stella giggled, "does male pattern baldness run in your family?"

"Umm my dad...uh, well he's not even related to me," Dan said, looking away.

"But I've seen your dad, he has luscious hair."

Dan just stood in silence and refused to look Stella in the eyes.

A smile returned to her face.

"Ah, your dad he had toupee for some new hair, didn't he? If he didn't, he might just wig out!"

"Stella. I think it's time for you to leave."

Dan grabbed a towel that hung on the wall railing by the mechanical arms and started gathering Stella's clothes. As he stood over her, her laughter left, though the mirth remained in her eyes.

"I'm going to need to rest. Tomorrow, Charlotte has invited us to her winner's celebration at CharLuv."

Stella yawned and pretended like there wasn't an irate Dorphin standing by the poolside. "Ooh, I didn't know that."

Dan swept his hair to the side as he shook his head in disbelief. "Really? She told us."

"Oh yeah, I guess she did," Stella cringed. "Here comes my least favorite part."

Stella rose out of the pool, water dripping off her brown skin and falling like diamonds back into the water. She began to shiver. "I swear every time I get out of a bath, I'm like a wrinkly plum with hair."

"That's a wonderful mental image," Dan said as he handed Stella her towel.

"I'm full of them," Stella responded with a flick of her hand.

She began to rub her skin until it was removed of the droplets that coated it.

Stella looked in Dan's direction. The massage had helped, but he still had a look of total exasperation. That rainbow burn was burning him out.

"Dan, I think you might want to drink something. You know what always makes me peppy? One of those smart drinks. A Philoso Pepper." Stella wiggles her eyebrows.

"I don't think I've ever seen you not peppy."

"Hehe, yeah I guess not."

"I'll try one." He pressed the remote he had. "There, I called room service, but you better go so I can relax."

Stella lowered her head like a sad puppy. "Okay."

57

She slipped on her pants and t-shirt, then began to walk from the hot tub to the staircase.

Dan followed her to send her off. "Two things, Dan...."

Dan raised his eyebrow. "Yes?"

"I once heard something from a wise cartoon. It was something about who you are. It said," Stella took Dan's hand and continued "without the ups and downs, a roller coaster would be a duller coaster."

Dan just shrugged his shoulders. "Um, what does that even mean?"

Stella released Dan's hand and positioned her hand towards the stars. "You gotta take all the good and bad things and accept them as one big mélange of life!"

Dan felt small in comparison to Stella's metaphor. He hung his head. "I wish it was that easy. What was the other thing?"

Stella had an antsy look on her face like a child desiring a new toy. "Can I go out on the penthouse deck sometime in the near future?"

"Uh...sure...I..."

"Yay!" Stella fist pumped. "That's all I wanted to say. And don't worry Dan, I'm sure you'll be okay! After all you got me. And you know, a positive attitude is the best medicine! Well, second best."

She winked at him and ran down the stairs, slamming the door.

Dan stared at the door for a while. "That is the most hopped-up girl I've ever met," he said to himself, "But it's nice to have her around...sometimes." He turns curtly.

When Stella led herself from the hallway without doors to her floor, Helen was standing outside their room and came running when she saw Stella.

"Stella, Stella I got a problem. Please don't kill me."

"What is it?" Stella asked.

"I opened the window to get some air in the bedroom and when I was relaxing, a jeeg came in through the window."

"Wow a jeeg? That's awesome" Stella looked at Helen's terrified face. "I'd do the opposite of kill you, I'd uhhh...bring you back to life."

Stella knew all about jeegs. They were some of the most cuddly, sweetest animals on the face of the planet. They had four legs, two perky long ears and two of the roundest largest eyes that could even make a the most macho man or butch babe 'aww' at their cuteness. She desperately wanted one, but her mother was deathly allergic, so she had to settle for her friend's jeegs. When her friends all moved out of her life, she was left without one, so Stella was terribly excited at the prospect of having one infiltrate her room.

Helen maintained a look of seriousness on her face. "Stella, I hope you understand what I'm talking about."

She grabbed Stella's hand and pulled her into their room. It was dark except for the illuminated color telescreen.

Stella could feel the cool breeze from the open window on her skin. She looked around, squinting her eyes in the darkness there was a big pile of black bile on the floor staining the carpet. She looked up and saw creature on the ceiling, or at least there was one for a second. Its eyes, small and beady glowed in the dark and when they made contact with Stella's, it skittered away underneath Stella's floating bed.

Helen switched on the lights. "Hopefully this will shoo them out... umm Stella?"

In the brightness, Helen had finally gotten a good look at Stella and her eyes were drawn to one specific detail. "Stella, how come your shirt is backwards?"

Stella looked down at her shirt, grasping it. "Oh, that. I took it off in Dan's room."

Helen's eyes grew so much it looked like they were ready to fall from their sockets. "You WHAT?"

"Helen, why are you redder than a sun that just ate a pepper? I was in his jacuzzi."

Helen tried her hardest to simmer down. "Stella, Stella. I'm gonna have to give you the Dorphinology 101."

Stella's eyebrows raised as she listened to Helen continue. "It's about everything you never wanted to know about Dan Dorphin, but my mom and now I are burdened with knowing."

Stella put her hands together. "Ooh, like if he's single?" She wiggled her eyebrows.

Helen slapped her hand on her face. "No, it's like the fact that he's... a heart-breaker."

"Why do you keep saying that?"

From under Stella's bed came a sick sounding growl. Helen quickly diverted the subject. "When we find time, I'll let you know, but first, I think we have a jeeg problem to take care of."

Stella put her hands to her chest. "Aww yes, the fearsome jeeg. Or more accurately, the adorably worbly wittle jeeg." She ran to the bed, crouching to peer underneath it. "Hey Helen, do you have any kind of food?"

"There's a dead fish in the fridge."

"Eww. Fish. That's disgusting Helen. I much prefer sushi."

Helen rolled her eyes, but quickly produced the fish that she had received. "I know a lot about jeegs and if anything, they can't resist fish."

Helen handed the fish to Stella. "I'll let you handle it because well, you'll see."

Stella put her hands on her hips. "Stop treating our guest like he's a smelly hobo. From now on, it's his room too. Oh, this isn't a dead fish, it's a finely prepared meal. You're so silly."

She placed the dish on the floor. She started to hear the growling become more intense, and with little warning, a dark pile of fuzz jumped out from under the bed, smashing into the fish with such hostility that Stella jumped back with a shriek. She rubbed at her eyes to help herself believe the creature that she was seeing.

It was boney and black with limbs that stuck out at all the wrong angles. Its midsection was so malnourished that it was literally nothing but layer of bone with skin stretched over it. Its tiny eyes, the color of light piss, moved around its head almost uncontrollably as it bit into the fish with equally yellow fangs. The noises it produced were snarling and slobbering over the high-grade food that the Raveopolis hotel offered. Stella had seldom blinked upon seeing this sight. "Uh Helen, are you sure this is a jeeg?"

"Yep. It is," Helen said while nodding. "A sewer variety."

"Umm I didn't know jeegs could live in the sewer."

"Stella, you're lucky that I'm very knowledgeable about MEPs."

"MEPs?"

"Morality Exploratory Pets."

Helen, who inexplicably had what seemed to be a masters in MEPs, told Stella all about them.

MEPs were creatures engineered in laboratories in the City Electric with the intentions of becoming domesticated. The laboratories were founded by Dr. Walter Shita, a maven in creating artificial life. He had spent a large portion of his life developing biohazardous creatures for wartime in the mainland. Way past his war days, he had settled down with the intention of creating creatures that were meant to love instead of kill. He didn't believe, however, that natives of Aleatore could properly handle a creature that was only able to share affection, having seen the horrors that he and others were capable of during the war. That is why he developed Morality Exploratory Pets; creatures designed to test the morality of its master.

Basing the MEPs on the long extinct, Meeg, he created the jeeg, a four-legged creature that fulfilled the level of cuteness that most consumers expected from a pet. It was not only cute, but it was loving, affectionate, and only demanded to be fed, groomed, and treated properly. It was safe to say that as soon as it was introduced to the market, a good third of the City Electric's population was smitten with the little fella. Shita's artificial pet seemed to be an outstanding success. But, when they were finally produced in bulk, people ended up purchasing too many jeegs and not being able to properly take care of them. Many were malnourished, released or even abused. This caused those friendly furballs to change.

Helen pointed at the jeeg that had just finished gobbling down its meal and was now looking for its next prey. "This is what happens to a malnourished, abused jeeg?"

Stella put her hand through her hair and sighed, looking at the creature. She then scooped it up and exclaimed "I still think he's adorable."

The jeeg squirmed in her arms, desperately wanting to escape the grasp of a girl who had been denied one all her life. All of the squirming made her hug the little cutie tighter. "Helen, I think I'm in love. This little guy is so fuzzy and fun and…"

The creature looked up at her face and let out a giant "blllllllleeeeeeeeeegggggg" coating her face in a dark bile.

Stella squeaked and let go of the jeeg, who scrambled back under the bed.

"I forgot to mention, having to live on garbage, the jeeg's probably not used to eating fancy foods." Helen spoke, while trying to avert her eyes from the mess that stained her friend's face.

Stella shook all the bile off her face, causing specks to land on the bed, wall and everything else. "You know, if that's what a jeeg turns into when their mistreated; what if you re-treat him nicely?"

"I don't know."

61

"Well, I believe this cutie is capable of redemption. If Molderon could freshen up his attitude, anyone can change!" Stella squeezed the jeeg again. "I'm gonna keep him and raise him like my own precious son."

"Stella…the owners will have a conniption if he sees this creature and his puke in here."

The peppy pet freak waved her hand skyward like she had done with Dan. "Come on, just think: two ultra-tight roomies raising their cute little pet together. Doesn't that just sound like the perfect slice-of-life cartoon?"

Helen let out a sigh and smiled. "Yes. It sounds dreamy."

"I'm glad ya get me." Stella winked. "Now Stellen has a mascot."

Stella walked over to the jeeg which had just urinated in the kitchen. "I dub thee: Mr. Kitty." The creature growled and hissed in response.

"So, Stella. Umm, you wanna watch that show together?" asked Helen timidly, tapping her fingers together.

Stella walked to her bed in a daze and within seconds was snoring.

Helen sighed and put the blanket over her friend. "Rest well, sleepyhead."

Step 7: Getting Super Fly

"Mom....uhm. Mom....Mom...I miss you." Stella muttered as she lay in her bed. She rolled around in her sheets, tangling them up around her body like a fork twirls spaghetti. She reached up in the air, stretched her body upward and fell back down moaning and mumbling.

"Stella. Stella." A soft voice called to her. "Stella, it's time to get up."

"Mom is that you? I love you."

"No Stella, I'm not your momma bear. It's me, Helen. I made breakfast for you."

"Mwuaaah." Stella yawned and blinked her eyes open. She held the covers up to her face, hiding behind them like a little girl. "Did you say breakfast?"

"Yeah. I heard you calling out for your mom all morning so I decided to make you breakfast like she probably does."

Stella reached onto her night stand that accompanied both her and Helen's bed. On it was her phone and her bottle of Yellow Plus. Putting the smiling pill under her tongue, she let it dissolve before swallowing. She looked to her side and also caught notice of a steaming pile of heated up toaster tarts with bright green icing freshly drizzled on top.

The dazed diva took in a whiff of their flakey pastry crust and salivated over them. "Wow, thanks. I don't know if I told you that these are my absolute favorite flavor."

Helen's dimples grew as the smile on her face became wide and her eyes bright but unblinking. "I just know what you like."

Stella began to lick the icing off the tart with an equally big smile on her face. She began to mess with her comphone and noticed that someone had opened a text she had sent to her mom a while ago, reminding her to pick up more of her favorite toaster tarts. "Hey, I think someone was messing with my phone."

Helen's smile quickly vanished and she coughed like she was swallowed the air wrong. "Yeah, I saw Mr. Kitty, he was playing with it. I took it from him before he did any damage to it." Helen out of breath paused and continued. "While on my way to pick up those toaster tarts, I picked up some garbage for Mr. Kitty to eat on the balcony."

"Wow, you're a super good friend."

"Thanks, Stella! I also noticed he has a strange tattoo on his fur. I think whoever had him before was a big fan of the techno hippies. Oh, did you see the text Charlotte sent? She told us to get pick out some outfits for the rave party tonight."

"Did you say rave party? Oh man, I'll be there all decked out and ready to shine." With great excitement, she kicked the covers off her. "Come on, we gotta go shopping. I'll go ask if Dan wants to go."

Hellen frowned.

Stella shuffled into her shoes, ran a brush through her messy hair and was out the door before Helen could even answer.

Helen let out a breath of air. "Phew, that was a close one. I'm so glad she not as focused as she is pretty."

Helen waited in the lobby of the Raveopolis Suites. She sat in a sleek round chair by the window, feeling the sun beam down on her. She prayed to Ravenous that Dan would refuse Stella's offer to come shopping with them. It was embarrassing enough having to shop with Stella when she was hooked up to Charlotte's tab on those card keys. Helen on the other hand was nothing but a minimum wage employee of the Charlotte Company. Whenever she was on the clock, Charlotte yelled and screamed to bring her soy beans and gluten free products until she punched out. Whenever anyone called her out on this, she said it was in her manner to be blunt. Helen thought she was more like 'blunt' with a capital C. And the pay was awful. That was the reason why having Sir "Spend-a-lot" Dorphin with them would be equally painful. Helen hoped it wasn't just money that Stella saw in a person.

She thought about the whole reason she ended up in this predicament to start with. As much as she loved her mother Madame Mimi, she was starting to exhibit traits of an aging spinster. This involved purchasing every jeeg in existence and keeping them at their house. They came in every color, and every time a new one was developed, the Madame was the first to purchase it. It was difficult enough for Helen to become a master jam skater, when she also had to be a master pet sitter and provide for all of them as well. And if she didn't provide for the jeegs, they would go bad and be reduced to the same fate as Mr. Kitty. Naturally the funds Mimi had accumulated over the years from dancing had lowered and it was now time for Helen to be the breadwinner. With third place not being good enough, Mimi begged Charlotte to let her daughter do anything for her and eventually it was decided that soy girl was the route to go.

Stella's high-pitched voice could be heard across the lobby. "Hey Helen. Guess what, Dan decided to come shopping with us after all."

Helen grimaced, and put her cheek into her hand with a pout. She glared over at the two.

Stella was in her gym shorts and her long-sleeved shirt, looking as bright as ever.

Dan had a sullen look on his face, his collared shirt was stained with black bile. It took Helen two seconds to realize what had happened.

"I wouldn't have come if that living roadkill hadn't puked all over me. I just wanted to pet him a little."

"Dan met Mr. Kitty. Dan likes Mr. Kitty, but I don't think it's mutual."

"Well, that makes two of us," Helen said.

"And there are about half a million of my adoring fans who hate you," Dan retorted.

"Well, let's go before this gets even more awkward," Stella said, grabbing both Dan and Helen's hands. "Let's try to have a nice day. After all, it's the first day of the rest of our lives."

"Hoo-ray," Dan muttered.

"Now it's time for us to go shopping in the fashion district."

The trio could feel the late summer breeze wisp through the streets. There were many parked at the neighboring apartment buildings of Raveopolis, but the amount of people dwindled to a few street workers and some more suspicious types.

"What's wrong with this place?" Stella asked. "It's abandoned as hell."

"Well, I don't think it's as abandoned as Hell," Dan said "at least considering all the evil in the world."

"Such a great outlook," Stella frowned in disproval "but seriously what gives?"

"This place is a city that thrives on parties," Helen told Stella. "And most parties happen at nighttime."

"Aha!" Stella exclaimed, with a carefree smile. "Well, the nighttime is the right time if I do say so myself."

The three headed for the fashion district, which was uptown according to Helen. Along the way, they passed piles of garbage, ginormous elastic bags stacked along the sidewalk in front of rusty garage doors. They walked until they were accosted by a stocky, unshaven man in his mid-forties. He wore a large overcoat that looked like it held large amounts of stocks and wares. Dan and Helen looked at the man warily, but Stella didn't seem to mind his presence at all.

"Hey, that's a pretty cool shirt," he said, gesturing at Stella's Fruitsaders shirt.

"Wow, thanks." Stella grinned.

"That's my favorite show." The man responded and spread open his coat revealing several pockets stuffed with Fruitsaders plushies. "And I got all the juicy fruity goods."

Stella's eyes sparkled like a night sky and her voice grew light and airy. "Oh my goddess. You have every single one."

"The rarest of the rare! Do you like Apple Apaulita?"

"Do I ever!? She brings some much-needed aptitude to the team."

"Do you like Orange Ornacia?"

"Of course, she's wild and tangy and will beat the pulp out of ya."

"Do you like Passionfruit Patel?"

"Oh boy I do. She brings passion into fashion."

"Do you like Tooty Paste?"

"Hell yeah. He's the paste with the minty taste."

"Dan," Helen demanded "get Stella to stop talking to this con-artist."

"Why? She looks like she's having so much fun," Dan replied with a sardonic look on his face.

Helen's glare prompted Dan to grab Stella and pull her away as the man continued asking her questions.

"Aw come on." Stella cried "I finally found someone to share my interests with."

Dan dragged her along. "Go to a convention or something. It's less shifty, but probably just as homemade."

"Yeah Stella, come on. Don't you want to get your clothes for the party?" Helen added, skating backwards and facing her friend.

"Fine."

The three continued to walk on a slight incline for forty-five minutes until they started seeing shops advertising tie dye rompers fitted on mannequins with black tape crossed over their breasts. There were disembodied mannequin legs, flashing knee high psychedelic-colored stockings and black lacey boots, quite like Stella's herself.

Stella gawked at some of them. "Whoa I'm guessing that this is the fashion district?"

"I'm not sure I'd call it the fashion district," Dan responded with a smirk. "Seeing some of these styles."

Stella shook her head and smiled. "Dan you're being rude. Fashion is in the eye of the consumer!" She went back to pressing her face against the shop windows, pulling her card key out without looking.

Stella had never been allowed to spend this much money in her life, but she soon realized that these were the perks of winning a nationwide competition. "Hehe, thanks Charlotte, now I'm gonna go on a spending spree."

Dan sighed. "Stella, make sure to choose a place that we can all afford."

Helen suddenly got red in the face. She didn't want to be the person who dragged Stella down and more importantly, she wondered how her arch enemy knew that about her living conditions.

"Okay." Stella said, looking at both Dan and Helen. "You know, I've heard good things about the Flashing Tights warehouse."

They walked further up the street. They passed many clothing stores until they got to the warehouse at a dead end. It dwarfed the posh but tiny boutiques that had come before. True to its name, a large metallic pair of flashing rainbow underpants were perched atop it. The name was embroidered on the elastic waist band.

"Oh boy…I feel so warm! I've got fashion fever!" Stella yelled before dashing inside the sliding doors, leaving Dan and Helen to stare at each other before following suit.

Stella found herself at a row of check out aisles, numbered one to twenty. Every single one with the exception of number #13 was powered down. At the thirtieth checkout counter, there was a pimply teenage girl with her hair tied back. She sat at the counter by the cash register and upon closer examination, she was sleeping.

Stella, wanting to wake the girl without seeming rude, gave a loud cough.

The girl sprang to attention with an equally loud snort caused by her sleep apnea.

"Hi, I'm Stella and I'm ready to shop until I drop."

The girl gave a grumpy groan and stood up, revealing that she had flashy tights pulled over her work pants. "I just had to be a day shift worker, didn't I?"

"Back at home, everyone loved the day shift."

The girl looked unamused "Not in this town. Well, please take one of carts at the start of aisle one."

"Okay," Stella said with a smile.

"And remember" the girl said with a forced smile "At Flashing Tights, We tight…with security. Don't shoplift or you might find yourself face to face with one of our dayshift guard robots."

"Alright sounds good to me. Now let's go!" exclaimed Stella.

At least three hours passed and three entirely different people emerged from the sliding doors.

The first was a young man with a close shave on one side of his head, and a whole mess of dark hair on the other side. He wore a red robe like shirt with long sleeves that were embroidered with ancient spiral patterns. His pants were also long and baggy, continuing the same color and patterns. The shoes he wore were seven-inch black heels, resembling spikes at the toes and heel. He had a midriff that revealed bar-like abs. The man's clothes paid a tribute to his race, the Wintersons who wore very ceremonial like clothes, a heritage he was proud of. But it was his choice to leave his abdominals exposed.

"Dan, you've got to be kidding me," said the female voice that followed.

A full-figured young woman stepped out. Her round face was made up with prominent eyeliner and rosy pink cheeks to accentuate her dimples. Her brown hair was conditioned and tied in a bun on the side of her head. She wore a black dress that draped over her body, a neon green and purple zig-zag outlined the draping clothes. She wore a pixelated flower in her hair. "Only the biggest skanky hos would have their midriff exposed like that." She puffed up her cheeks. "You're only doing that so unfortunate girls will gawk at you."

"Helen, excuse me for a second, I was staring at Dan's rock-hard abs. Did you say that midriffs were skanky?"

The third person had clothes that paid a tribute to contemporary fashion in the City Electric. She had bright pink hair reminiscent of bubble gum that contrasted with her reddish-tan skin. The pink hair was tied into pig tails that swirled and twisted with the help of two floral hair-ties. She wore a flashy zippered top that showed off a midriff and a newly pierced belly button. There were stars on her knee-high leggings. Black spiked go-go boots and a brand-new plus sign tattoo on her cheek gave away the identity of this woman: Stella Grace. Her eyes were so bright and starry that a person could probably pick out a few constellations in them if they tried.

"Uh, no Stella. I meant its only skanky when a guy does it." Helen looked like she was hyper ventilating. "When a woman does it, its awe inspiring and powerful. She's not afraid to show off her body but men, when they do it, they just want a harem of drooling lady slaves or is it boy slaves? I mean this is Dan we're talking about."

"You better keep sucking up to Stella," Dan said, glaring at his heckler. "She was nice enough to buy you that dress, after all."

Dan's words were enough to shut Helen up and make her stare at her newly purchased platform shoes.

"Aw Dan, you really don't need to put it that way," Stella said. "I've been so poor all my life, that being hooked up to foxy momma's spending account has made me want to share the wealth."

Dan walks ahead. "Whatever Stella, I'm too tired to argue with her anyway."

Stella looked at Dan; his arms sagged forward despite his best ability to stand up right in enormous heels. Upon closer observation, Dan's hair was a lot longer than when she encountered him on the train and it only seemed to grow from one side of his head.

"Has your hair always been this long?"

"Stella, I it's a little-known fact, but hair grows."

"Yeah, but that fast?"

"I've been through a lot, maybe I've just been pulling strands further out of my head."

"I guess." Stella, didn't want to bother him.

"Look Stella, I know it's still early—like quarter of 5—but the party starts at 8 and Dorphins are always punctual. Let's go."

"Okay sure." Stella nodded and both her and Dan left, leaving Helen to ponder Stella's outfit choice. It was exactly the one from the Dance of the Gods, but Stella didn't seem to notice.

The three started back downtown. CharLuv was in that direction past the Raveopolis Suites; technically it was in the exact opposite direction of the Fashion District. As they walked, Dan continued to shuffle in his heels. Upon being asked if he would rather take them off, he scoffed and said that he would much rather walk with pointed spikes for his heels than set a foot down and get a foot fungus from these filthy streets.

Stella had never met someone who suffered so much for fashion before.

After another forty-five-minute walk, they were back at the Raveopolis Suite. On the red carpet stretched out in front, there stood a few men and women in bullet proof vests and guard masks. Mr. Raveopolis was with them, in his tux, contrasting with the sweaty summer weather.

"Why are the police here?" asked Stella with a look of disbelief on her face.

Mr. Raveopolis gestured to the three dancers and the police walked over. "Stella Grace and Dan Dorphin, we would like you to come down to our headquarters for questioning."

Stella's could feel heart thump and she felt as if she could turn as pale as Dorphin if her skin was lighter. She pointed at herself and no words came out her mouth.

"Don't worry." The masked officer said, surveying the two "We just want to know about the incident that happened on one of our train lines."

"Oh phew," Stella said, her tense shoulders sinking.

"Stella, did you really think they were going to arrest you?" Dan retorted. "I'm pretty sure being annoying isn't a crime, even though it should be." He smiles at Helen.

Stella stuck her tongue out at Dan and then quickly turned her attention to the officers. "Sure, though we are due for a party at eight."

"Oh no problem," the female officer said with a reassuring smile. "It won't take long at all."

Stella found herself in a small room with shiny wooden floors and a simple plastic table. The room was bright and for a room where suspects had to answer questions that put their freedom on the line, it wasn't very imposing. A man in his mid-twenties, sat at an easel that was faced away from Stella. He wore small circular shades to prevent his eyes from being seen and also had a long pipe hanging out his mouth. She was informed this guy was a professional criminal profiler and that he was using her memory to illustrate the man that had attacked the train.

"So, you were saying," the man said, as he puffed into his pipe, "the thing that attacked you, left a bite mark on your friend."

"Yes." Stella nodded her head. She remembered the monster, but she hadn't faintest idea about what happened during the incident.

"And this bite mark, takes a lot of energy out of someone?"

"Oh definitely. Dan had trouble waking up in the morning."

"Hmm, a bite mark…that takes energy." The man rubbed his chin. He took his pen and began dabbing the pencil on his paper.

"Oh, and this creature only showed up in bright flashing lights."

"Aha. Eureka!" The man exclaimed. He began scribbling with an intensity, leaving Stella to believe he had captured her minds concept of the monster perfectly.

"I can describe his appearance if you want."

"I don't think that's necessary."

Stella sat with her hands folded, playing with her new belt and her star shaped earrings that hung down to her neck. It was about a half hour before the man spoke to her again. She would have fallen asleep, but her meds kept her energized and perky.

"That's all you're needed for. Thank you."

"Okay? Okay. No problem." Stella bobbed her head and stood up.

"Thanks, dudette," he said, as she walked out.

A masked officer came in and led Stella out into the bright waiting room where Dan sat. He looked miserable. She could tell by the look on his face he was more occupied by his own symptoms and with covering them up. He had to keep his image ultra clean for the sake of all of his fans.

"You're good to go." said the officer. "And thanks. With your help we will definitely be able to keep the City Electric well-informed and safe."

Stella and Dan walked down a flight of stairs and onto the street in front of a two-story building that read "TCEPD."

"Hey Dan," Stella greeted him. "That was really fast and easy. I didn't mind that at all."

"Yeah, I was only in there for ten minutes being questioned. I thought investigations like that went on longer." Dan scratched his head in confusion. "How did yours go longer than mine when I was a victim of an actual bite?"

"I don't mind, we still got an hour to go before Charlotte's party starts. We can meet up with Helen."

"Do we have to?" Dan whined.

"Uh yeah, Helen's my friend and I'm sure one day, you guys will become good friends too." Stella smiled with a reassuring look on her face.

"Hah, I'd never let my taste in friends sink that low. I only mingle with high-class people," Dan said, brushing his growing hair out of his face in a composed but prissy fashion. "But yeah, let's get her and go see Charlotte so I can sit down."

Stella and Dan walked a few blocks until they came to the front steps of Raveopolis where Helen sat.

"You got done that fast?" Helen asked as she stretched her limbs. "I've been asked questions as a witness before and it went for a few hours."

"I dunno," Stella said and started kicking her boots up in the air. "But it was convenient because now, it's party time!"

Helen paused before talking. "I dunno that seems so shifty."

Stella reached down and struggling a bit, pulled Helen up. "Come on, pudgy pal. We don't need to worry. This night is going to be the night of awesome."

The three made their way downtown to where Charlotte's club and bar was situated, but as they did, an announcement rang over the city. The telescreens all flashed, and Daddy D's face beamed over the whole city, watching over it like a funky father.

"Rise and shine everyone, it's party time. Time for the night to slip on that cute little black dress and glosticks to illuminate the sky. It's your King Mayor and I'm ready to declare anarchy on this town yet again. Everyone in town now has a license to chill; certified by the monarch of music himself. It's time to dance dance and dance and oh..." D's face looked shocked for a second when he's was handed a clip board by someone off screen.

"Hmm, well I think it's time I bring you the latest update about what's going down around town. So, it seems people are getting bitten and they don't know why, but they've been getting all these rainbow shaped marks on their skin. Well, thanks to some superb eyewitness accounts and sleuthing from our keen detective force, we now know why. It's something called a…"

Stella put her arms on hips. "Oh, he's gonna warn everyone..."

Daddy D. put on a calming smile as he turned the clipboard around. There was a drawing on it, presumably the one that the artist sketched on. The drawing was of a fly; complete with bug compound eyes in a hip hop outfit, and a stinger coming out the rear. "It's called a superfly."

Stella was so shocked by his announcement that she nearly fell over. "What?"

"Yes, a Superfly," Daddy D. said, as if responding to Stella. "This fly is a pretty fly guy, but better watch out if he bites you. You'll get yourself a rainbow burn. They're known to make you tired and drain you of your energy, so you can't party and you don't want that. So, this is warning to all my peeps, keep covered and party on. Now that you've got the know-how, you know how to avoid an itchy situation."

Dan threw his arms in the air. "What he's saying is a bunch of nonsense. We know what we saw."

Helen sneered at Dan. "I take it from your oh-so-sophisticated reaction, that the stuff he's talking about isn't true?"

Stella put her hand to her mouth. "Uh… why would he say it was a superfly, when we all know it was these vampire guys?"

"Vampire guys?" Helen asked with a pale face. "Is there something you guys aren't telling me?"

"Helen…on the train there was…mmm."

Dan quickly put his hand over Stella's mouth as she continued to speak muffled words.

"Stella, you can't just tell anyone." Dan's eyes narrowed as he continued to hold Stella's mouth. "Especially this blabbermouth blimp."

"Blabbermouth?" Helen put her hands on her doughy hips and walked up to Dan. "I'll have you know that my lips would never sink any ships unless they were registered to the SS Dorkphin."

"Yeah Dan," Stella added, "Helen's pretty trustworthy. I've told her countless secrets, like how I like it when guys tell me to go away."

73

Stella quickly covered her mouth.

Dan laughed "So it's you who we have to keep our secrets safe from."

Stella's face turned bright red in response, but she remained on task. "Well, you know what, I think we should tell our foxy momma."

Dan raises an eyebrow.

"She's talking about mistress Charlotte."

"Mistress?" asked Dan with a smirk.

"Yeah, she's a mega influential person in this city." Stella's eyes opened wide. "If the police force is covering this whole incident up, she'd do something about it."

Helen looks at her worriedly. "You don't think Daddy D. is part of this conspiracy, right?"

"He's being lied to just like the public."

Dan nods. "I think Charlotte would listen...especially since she hates his guts. Maybe we can even learn more about these creatures and how to cure these bites from her too. You're wiser than you act, Stella."

"Exactly. And thank my tabloid knowledge too," Stella replied.

Helen lets out a peep. "Umm...I agree too. About telling Charlotte about whatever it is."

Stella grabs all their hands. "Then it's decided! The Electric Fruitsaders will uncover the truth about what happened and share it with the masses!"

Step 8: Plan D

They had reached the street where CharLuv's was after about an hour of walking and triumphantly stood in the long line waiting for their admittance.

CharLuv was built like a cathedral. It had four separate towers that were stationed at the four corners of the building. Stella knew from her tabloids that there was also a courtyard at the center of the building. When the city was first constructed, it was a building erected in honor of the goddess Ravenous. As time went on, support for the demi-Goddess had waned and the building was devalued. Using her swift business knowledge Charlotte had swept it up and turned the former place of worship into a sanctum of partying. The building's towers and courtyard added a feeling of conservatism that contrasted heavily with the front: a giant neon sign that stated the name of the bar in a vibrant, electronic fashion with light green and yellow letters. Sitting on them was the bars mascot shone in all of its flashing glory: an electric yellow thunderbolt lady with two sensual curving legs sprouting from the bottom. With dark heels that elicited sensual play, it invoked the feeling of decadence that embodied its owner.

"Well, I have to say…" Dan muttered, rampant in his reserved taste, "this place looks even more like a strip club in person."

"I think it looks awesome," Stella responded. "I can't wait until we get inside."

"It's gonna be a long time before we get in," Helen said. "We're the last people here and this line is pretty hefty!"

The line of people trailed so far that the velvet railings and carpet ended where the street began.

"Yeah…" Stella sighed. "But imagine how fun it will be when we get inside. Did you see the celeb list?"

Dan scoffed. "No. I was busy getting ready."

"Well, the king mayor himself is gonna be there."

"Great," Dan remarked with his arms crossed. "That sleazy man and his throne of lies."

"Hey." Helen pointed at Dan. "Aside from that uncool fly thing, he's one of the coolest people in town. Plus, innocent until proven guilty."

Dan rolls his eyes. "Have you heard all the outdated words he uses in his monologues?"

"Who cares? I mean, he's in one of the coolest bands in existence: The Techno Hippies. Even Mister Kitty is a fan."

"Are bands even a thing anymore?"

"Yeah," Stella nudged Dan playfully. "I keep them in my hair."

Helen rolled her eyes "Ugh, you guys are missing out. These guys have made some of the most life changing music in all of Aleatore."

"Is that so? According to who exactly?"

Helen threw up her arms in frustration. "Dorkphin this is proof you have no soul."

Stella in an attempt to break up their argument continued with the list "Well Barvarius Bop is there. And ooh, Molly Primus."

"Molly...Primus?" Dan's mouth gaped. "She's there?"

Helen perks up. "Oh, you mean Meltdown Molly."

"Shut up, you tasteless cur. Molly's craziness is a calculated stunt."

"Wow, Dan," Stella said. "I had no idea you liked Molly Primus."

"Well... I don't like her," Dan crossed his arms "but I did dance to one of her songs in my Wintermonk rite of passage. You can say I have a fondness for that memory. That's all it is. Sentimentality."

An evil smile revealed itself on Helen's face. "So, you wouldn't mind if I told her that?"

Dan who had been leaning against the wall of CharLuv sprang forward and grabbed Helen. He pulled her away from Stella.

Helen froze up from the sudden movement.

Dan pulls her in close. "Listen to me, you tell her that and I'll tell Stella about your little crush."

Helen stammers and blushes a deep crimson. "H-h-how do you know that?"

"Stella may be thick to it, but it's clearer than crystal. The way you look at her so lovingly and follow her around like a needy puppy dog."

Helen went dead silent, nodded her head and walked away from Dan.

Stella looked at Dan "What were you guys whispering about? Helen looks like she's seen a ghost."

Dan walks ahead. "Nothing to concern yourself over, right Helen?"

The meek girl nods, looking away from Stella.

Stella smiled to herself. She ignored the drama around her and began to daydream. She was so excited about going to Charlotte's party.

It was called The Penultimate Party in Charlotte's digital message. This mega bash would allow her groovy dancing to be recognized by so many influential people. She felt her heart pumping faster and her legs began to shake. She knew it wasn't just the Yellow Plus that was making her ecstatic, it was the fact that she was so close to being a star.

"I'm a VIP at this party," Stella told her without turning around. "There's no way I should be waiting in lines. You guys should join me. We got business with the Madame."

Angry grumbling came from the crowd as Stella began to sprint towards the club entrance.

"Ugh Stella, you know I dislike running in heels!" Dan yelled.

"I'm a shooting star, and they go far." Stella started singing and prancing as she sang.

Stella's triumphant move was cut off completely when she ran into the seven-foot-tall bouncer. This butch guard looked like she had lived entirely off of testosterone hormones grabbed Stella. Her hair was short and her face was long, she had two beady black eyes and an enormous snout, of which a giant ring with a ball was punctured through it. Two giant tattooed arms grabbed Stella's shoulders like tiny balls in her hands.

"Where do you think you're going?" she asked in a shrill voice.

"Oh, my goddess. Umm. Uh I didn't see you there."

"Helen" Dan said "can you please speak to that woman and tell her to let go of Stella."

"Why me, Dorkphin?"

"She is one of your kind, after all."

"Dan, that's so offensive," Helen responded with spit flying from her mouth. "I don't look anything like that. I'm tomboy not butch. That's like lady boy and fop being the same."

Dan rolls his eyes. "Just do it."

"Who are you? Why do you think you can just cut the line?"

"Set her down," said a commanding voice from the crowd.

Stella fell to the floor. She shook her head, a bit dazed from falling from such a height. She saw those signature lightning heels step in front of her and she knew it could only be one person. She looked up at the powerful business woman who held her in such high esteem.

"Helen," Charlotte snapped, "help Stella up."

Helen sprinted over to Stella, wobbling in her heels as she did it. She was nowhere as good a heel walker as Dan. She quickly yanked Stella to her feet.

"Hey foxy mom." Stella smiled, raising her hand in a wave.

Charlotte panicked and grabbed Stella, pulling her close to her. "Hush hush," she whispered. "Don't say that out here."

"Got it, other mom." Charlotte sighs. "Just stop."

"Boy are we glad to see you, Daddy D. has been mmph…"

Dan with great skill, covered Stella's mouth before she spoke.

"Stella, how many times do we have to tell you not to say classified things out loud?"

Charlotte's botoxed face managed to perk up even more than it already was. "Did you say something about Daddy D? What did that nasty man do?"

"That's what we've come to talk about," Helen said, glaring at Dan to let go of Stella.

"Well not just that, I'm here to party," Stella added.

"And I just want to sit down," Dan mentioned with an exasperated look on his face.

"Okay, come with me to my office and we can do all of those things," Charlotte said. "Gallant, please be a hun and step aside."

"Yes, Ms. Charlotte." The large female bouncer moved to the left, revealing the door that her girthy nature had previously blocked. The bouncer's cheeks turned red when Charlotte passed her. "Anything for you, Madame."

Charlotte gestured at the door and Helen heaved it open, letting the others walk in. Stella followed, sticking her tongue out at the bouncer.

The two girls walked in together and were lead through a small antechamber to Charlotte's office.

Stella looked around the room. "Wow, this place is…ugh."

The first thing about Charlotte's place of business, and perhaps the most striking or eye gouging, depending on your opinion, was the wallpaper: bright yellow and neon green zigzags over a white backdrop. The colors were so bright and intrusive that Stella couldn't focus on anything else. Her eyes constantly fluttered from the overload. She walked over to one of the many ravenwood chairs that were dark and ashy.

Stella planted herself upon one of the gaudy yellow pillows on the chair. She squinted her eyes to see Dan and Helen joining her in similar seats.

Charlotte's desk lay in front of them. From what Stella could see, all of the paperwork was neatly sorted, every neon pencil was fully juiced and lay in a dark plaster cup along with some laser quill pens. The one thing that stood out to Stella was that there were no photos of any kind. Her father sent her a picture of his desk at work. It was rife with photos of her, her mom and her two brothers. He did abandon her, but this meant he cared about them deep down inside, right? Charlotte had not one family photo to warm the room with some much need sentimentality.

Charlotte walked in beaming. "Before we do anything else, I would like to acquaint my fake children plus Helena with my real children."

Charlotte pulled out her electronic manipulator and a curtain hanging on the left wall of the office parted, revealing a spectrum of awards hung on the wall. There were plaques and headlines of acclaim that CharLuv had received over the years. Some newspapers were titled "CharLuv's Had the Wildest Party of 2992" and "If you're in the mood to groove, CharLuv is the place for you." They also saw she was a recipient for the "The Passed-Out Lampshade Award" and "Party Mistress of the Year."

Charlotte grinned "And unlike you, Stella and Dan, these babies are only a few years old."

"Look Charlotte, I know you're great and full of it," Dan said curtly. "But can we please cut to the chase. There are lives at stake, including my own."

Helen looks over at Stella worried, and Stella smiles back to reassure her everything is okay.

Charlotte put her hand to her lip and blew a small raspberry to impersonate the sound of an electric crackle. "Bzzt…Dan aren't you quite the live wire today. Tell me what troubles that poor head of yours."

"This all relates to Daddy D. so I'm sure you'd want to hear."

Dan told Charlotte about the incident on the train. He made sure to profile Crane from his long silver hair and pointed nose to his nauseating green and purple checkered suit. He then added something that Stella hadn't heard previously though. "I talked to the officers on the train who had interviewed people on the train. They said that nobody saw what this creature looked like."

"That is peculiar. Any theories on that?" asked Charlotte.

"I don't know," Dan said with utter confusion "I think only Stella and I could see it, but I can't imagine why."

"Hmm," Charlotte put her fingernail to her mouth again. "You know, you aren't the first people to come to me about these creatures."

"Really?" Dan said, raising his voice. "That's a great relief. I'm not alone." He looks to his arm.

"No, my associate says she's seen them too."

"Your associate?"

"Yes, a longtime friend of mine, Jayden. She's told me she's had a run in with one and has been hunting it ever since."

"Does she know more about them?"

"You could ask her; she's at this party." Charlotte held her hand at chin length. "Just look for an intense Neuronian woman with short dark jagged hair." She put her finger across her brow. "And don't tell her this, but she has a unibrow. Poor baby is so obsessed with her little vamp hunt, she doesn't have time to wax or thread."

Stella raised her hand and opened her mouth. She could have sworn she saw a person like that before, but for some reason her memory was blurry.

Charlotte reclined in her chair. "Now care to spill the tea on our mutual friend, the Big D."

Helen, speaking up for the first time "Well he…"

"Someone else please." Charlotte cut her off. "Girls like Helena should bring me soy and not noise. I'm thirsty. Make yourself useful."

Helen frowned and muttered, looking down at the ground as she stormed off.

Stella chimed in. "Well, we don't know if he's guilty yet. And please don't be so mean to my roomie. She's sensitive."

"We know enough." Dan spoke up in her place.

80

"You know how Daddy D. does the whole Shoot the Breeze thing every night?"

"Yes, unfortunately. Like I'd listen that schlock."

As Dan told her about how Daddy D. deliberately misinformed the public using knowledge he had, Charlotte's focus grew greater and greater until she found herself resting her hands on her table. She looked almost entranced to hear of the machinations of her business rival.

Helen, after handing Charlotte her soy smoothie, looked concerned and put her hand on Stella's shoulder. "Stella, don't you think that Charlotte's enjoying this a little too much?"

"Nah, when it comes to dishing dirt on your exes there is no ex-cess."

Helen smiled. "Yeah, I suppose you're right."

When Dan had finished, Charlotte started filling out a clipboard. "I have devised a plan of actions for you three to undertake."

"Wow, the inner macro manager of Charlotte is coming out and eeeee, I'm so excited" Stella said, bouncing up and down.

Charlotte pats her new pet. "That you should be, Stella." She then addresses the group. "Our glorious leader, Daddy D. is going to be here. He's usually surrounded by his entourage of mindless sycophants and hanger-ons." She put her finger on Dan. "Your popularity rivals that of some of the greatest idols in our city! I want you to distract Daddy's groupies."

Dan nodded his head. He looked like he didn't want to be bothered, which was something new for the normally grandstanding Dorphin.

"Stella, with your affable and bubbly personality, I want you to get as much information out of Daddy D. as possible." Charlotte held her hands over her head and smiled "With those cute pigtails and that perky demeanor, I'm sure he won't be able to resist spilling his reasons for covering things up."

Stella smiled and winked at Dan. "See I told you it pays to be cute. Though there might not be any dirt on the Daddy. I think he's just been lied to like everyone else."

Charlotte turned her attention to Helen. "Helena Wheels, I have the most important task for you."

Helen perked up in her seat at the mention of her full name. "It's so important I saved it for last because I didn't want you forgetting it while I told the other two their assignments. I want you to…bring me more soy."

Helen's face looked twice as tired as Dan and twice as angry, but she knew better than to talk back.

"The bar has some fermented soy milk, La Chateau Electric and I would love to get a hold of it for this very special occasion."

A loud pounding was heard from the office door. "Ms. Charlotte, where the hell are you? We need you to be the master of ceremonies, all of the aristocrats from Gris are arriving.

"Don't you pressure me, underling!!" Charlotte yelled at the door "Alright, my children, it's time for you to commence Plan D."

Charlotte leaned over the desk and whispered to three "By the way, you don't have to worry about attracting attention; the opportunity for that has just landed in my hands."

Everyone got up and headed for the door, Helen and Dan were not delighted by their assignments at all, but Stella practically skipped out…until she hit a sign hanging from one of the doorways.

Helen giggled and grabs Stella. "Let's get out before you accidentally break something expensive."

Step 9: Stella the Lyfisher

As soon as they were out of the office and walking behind a booth set up to separate Charlotte's office from the main bar, Helen tapped Stella on the shoulder. "Hey slow down Stella, I need to ask you something."

"Yeah, roomie?"

"Have you seen the way Charlotte treats me?"

"Yeah, I don't know why she does that but it's not cool. I tried to speak up for you, but I didn't do a very good job. Sorry, babe."

Helen blushes. "No! You did fine! She's been nicer to Dan. She hates his perfect guts!"

"Maybe she's grown to like him."

"Yeah, nope. I got it! Since Dan is now under her wing, she is no longer envious of the Dorphins. She's got the gold prize in her grip, so she's kissing and polishing it."

"Or she just realized that he's not as cold as she thought. Dan can be pretty warm."

"Eww, gross. Focus Stella."

"I am focused. Hey, look Helen, Dan is going through some difficult stuff right now."

"Yeah, and I'm out of the loop on it."

Stella grabs Helen's hand. "Please try to be nice to him. For me? Please please pleaaaaase!"

"Okay, okay, I'll try. It's just not easy when it's so ingrained in your mind. But back to the Mistress of Mean, why do you think she is so mean to me?"

Stella raised her eyebrows and spoke with an innocent ignorance. "Maybe it's because you like girls?"

Helen blushed and nearly tumbled over backwards when she stepped back. "Umm…uh. No, I don't think that's it. She has that bouncer, Gallant, who is clearly into her and she doesn't mind that at all."

Stella smiled. "Yeah, she seems quite head over heels for that head lady in heels."

"I'm gonna find out by the end of this night why she hates me so much. I promise you that."

83

"I'll help in any way I can. I know a ton about her, but no clues as to why she's so mean to you."

"Aww, thanks Stella. That means a lot."

"No problem, you're the best friend I've ever had. Wait Helen, why are you walking so fast all of a sudden?"

Stella dashed after Helen who had turned her back on her to mask her dejected expression. They walked past the booth and into the open revealing the central room of CharLuv itself.

Stella remembered images of the architecture of this building before it became a bar. The lengthy pews that were placed in the center had been removed and modified into a glowing checkered green and yellow dance floor, covering a majority of the room. The alter that once commanded a view over the pews had become a stage where ceremonies of a different kind were performed. The arch shaped ceiling was the only thing remaining that hinted of the room's religious past, but outside a few more representations of its past remained. A giant plate glass window that overlooked the whole room and the stage lay a courtyard with a giant statue of the demi goddess were a few notable remnants. Dusk had settled in and moonbeams shone down, illuminating the statue and the club itself and providing little need for further light sources. Plus like all good night clubs, Charlotte loved keeping everything dim and sensual and the moon provided just enough light to achieve that goal.

The room was large and was able to fit an army of Ravenous worshipers. The religious worshipers were now replaced with dancers and thrill seekers whose religion was partying. Stella noticed that a majority of them shared Dan's grey white skin.

"Hey Dan, your family's here," Stella said.

"Graceful with your words as usual," Dan replied.

"You know, if you don't like her, you should just go away," Helen said with a pouty face.

"Oh, I can handle her, you on the other hand."

"Hmmph…" Helen crossed her arms and teared up a bit.

"But yes, Stella, there are a lot of Wintersons here. I wonder why?"

Stella's eyes widened. "It will be soooo hype to make some Winterson friends! In Boringtown, it's all Summereins. All fire, no ice is just no fun!"

Without warning, synthetic sirens blared and an electronic encoded voice echoed around the room. "WITHOUT FURTHER ADO, MS. ELECTRA, OVERSEER OF THE PENULTIMATE PARTY."

The three dancers and everyone else as well turned their attention to the stage. The stage was lined with nodes that shot off small blue explosions of electricity that crackled loudly. Loud and dominant clops of high heels followed and soon Charlotte appeared in front of everyone with a microphone in hand.

"Hello and welcome to CharLuv, I am the proud host of this Penultimate Party. I'm so glad to see so many faces from Gris this year on the dance floor. After all, it was the glorious efforts of your chosen boy, Daniel Dorphin in the Dance of The Gods that has placed your nation on top. I applaud you."

Charlotte clapped and the sound echoed around the room.

"To celebrate, we have a special guest performance from the City Electric's very own starlet, Molly Primus. She's sure to drive the house as stark raving mad as her wardrobe and life choices."

Dan smiled and put his hands to his cheeks, but quickly pulled them away when Stella looked at him.

"Not only that, her opening act is the Techno Hippies, the outlet for our ruler Daddy D's creative indulgences. Going strong for 15 years and they're totally not washed up or out of style."

Helen gritted her teeth and raised her fist. "Charlotte, first you mess with me and now you're ranking on my favorite band! That's two out of three taboos!"

Dan pulls Helen back before Electra notices her outburst.

"That wraps up my introduction, but before I go, I would like to alert the crowd that the two finalists of the Dance of The Gods are in the house! Give a warm welcome to miss Stella Grace and sir Dan Dorphin. All you young bachelors and bachelorettes don't tear them apart now, you hear?"

Stella hopped on the stage. "And so is the third-place starlet, Hellen Wheels! Boys stay away, this cutie pie likes melons more than bananas!"

Helen blushes profusely, hiding her face before running off into a corner.

Dan rested his face in his hands as they began to hear screams from the cavernous crowd. "Ugh, I can't believe that this is what she was thinking for a distraction."

Stella's permanent chipper attitude made her energetically strike a pose. "Dan, you better get used to it. People gaze up at you when you're a star!"

Stella stepped out onto the dance floor. Dan was on the left with a crowd of Winterson people. It was as if an invisible wall separated them. Stella wanted to tear down that barrier so that all races could love and adore the first-time celebrities together.

"H-H-Hey," Stella said with a bit of a nervous stutter. "I'm Stella, Stella Grace, dancer for the Gods and starlet of tomorrow."

The Wintersons, both men and women, as pale faced as Dan, gave her no response. They sized her up, taking in her characteristics either like awestruck fans or hungry predators. The star-eyed starlet didn't possess the instincts to know the difference.

"And guess what," Stella continued "free autographs for everyone. I'm not jaded enough to charge money but better take my offer now. Who knows how pricy I'll be in a few years?"

She laughed and then coughed to cover up the lack of response.

A girl, bespectacled and clutching a drawing pad, suddenly shrieked from the crowd. "AIIEEEEEE DAN DORPHIN!"

The crowd began to ramble as Dan's name was heard throughout the room.

"He's over there!"

The crowd charged forward, with the bespectacled girl leading the ranks. They began pushing and shoving Stella's body like she was a barricade obstructing their path. Stella screamed loudly, but her voice was lost in the crowd. She felt herself being buffeted by arms, legs and chests. One misplaced hand hit her square in the jaw and she fell backwards.

On the floor she felt a rain of boots and heels hit her body. She put her arms over her head to shield her face from further damage. She felt her eyes water up and her chest feel heavy. Eventually the shoes and heels stopped, but the pandemonium didn't for Stella until she looked up and saw a friendly hand.

"Stella, are you okay?" Helen asked, reaching for her. "Should I take you to the hospital?"

"No, I'm fine…just shaken up. Why did that happen?" Stella sniffled as she was helped to her feet.

"Stella, they're Wintersons, we're Summereins what did you expect?"

"To not get trampled like a doormat."

Helen put her arm around the downtrodden Stella. Her clothes were all dirty and Helen dusted them off with her other hand. "Any chance I can get that autograph?"

Stella chuckles. "Aww, thanks for cheering me up. I kinda lost my pen in the stampede though. I can't believe the way they ignored me."

"Stella…look at it this way. If we were at a party entirely of Summereins, Dan would be the one getting crushed."

"And we'd be adored?"

"Stella, *you'd* be adored. A lot of Summereins are calling foul on your silver medal, myself included."

She looked Helen in the eyes who looked a little dejected herself, even by her own kind.

"No," Stella said "I'd make sure it was the both of us or none of us. We both hail from South Aleatore and we're both finalists. We're a team, buttercup. Like peanut butter and jelly. Wait, but then who's the bread?"

Helen looked away from Stella to hide her smile and rosy cheeks.

"Why are you looking over there, Helen?"

"Uh, because Daddy D's over there at the bar and he's all alone except for his bandmates and Molly Primus."

Stella dusts herself off. "I think I should clean myself up a little first."

Helen hands her a napkin. "That you should."

The two headed past the crowd of Wintersons.

"Boy, that Dan is lucky he has so many adoring fans...and suitors," Stella said.

"I wouldn't say those are suitors per se," Helen responded.

Stella recognized the bespectacled girl who led the mob. She was Lilia Floren, the famed Virgin of Gris, or at least that's what her father touted her as. She held her notepad and shoved it in an annoyed Dan's face.

"My poor single Danny bear. You don't have that perfect man in your life, but with all of my knowledge, I have created the perfect man for you."

Lilia opened her notebook to show a man in a flannel suit with large eyes and neatly combed hair.

"His name is Prettyboy Flanoshi and he is everything your gorgeous body desires. Please accept that the fates of you and him are forever intertwined…in my flanfic of course. He's not real. Nobody real could ever be your match, mister perfect!"

"Oh my," Stella said. "Did not think that's what she was after."

Stella quickly turned away from Helen. She reached into her side pocket and produced her Yellow Plus Pill container. She was feeling better from Helen's attempts to calm her down but still, she harbored some resentment. She believed she was just as good a dancer as Dan and should be recognized for it. Her mind constantly weighed that with the disregard she got from the people at the party. She just wanted to forget and those magical pills would soothe the agitated neurons that riddled her brain and prevent their memory allocation. That's what Dr. Proto said, at least.

"Second one, today." Stella quickly gulped it and turned to Helen. "Okay let's get over to D."

"But shouldn't we have a plan first?" Helen looks over at the band and taps her fingers. "I'm so nervous."

"I already have a plan, cream puff," Stella remarked as she strutted. "I know exactly how I'm going to coax that information out of Daddy D."

"Okay…if you say so."

"I know exactly how celeb seduction works in this day and age. It's called LyFishing. I read about it in the tabloids. Follow me."

They strolled over to the bar with Helen trailing after Stella who walked with a newly found placebo confidence. The pills hadn't taken effect yet, but Stella didn't care, she knew they would soon.

The bar was at the corner far off from the dance floor. It was even more dimly lit than CharLuv's dance floor with only the large swirling tubes full of glowing smart drinks behind the bar counter, illuminating the area. There were high stools that had been arranged specifically for the bar's guests.

The two that sat in these seats liked to assume themselves as high up as the position they sat in. They were Stormy Cecile and Grant Olson, two members of Daddy D's group The Techno Hippies. Stella mostly got all her facts on them from Helen's long praising sessions of Daddy D's outfit, but she knew some details herself from news reports and history class.

Stormy Cecile was a Winterson as dour as his name would suggest. The tall pale duke was in a dark robe with grey-black closely cropped hair on the sides of his head and a swooped slightly receding pompadour on top. His nationalism and cynicism drew him heavily into politics. It was often him who said things that would incite the groups of Summereins who opposed him. It was almost by pure chance that a man like him would have the ability to drum, and to do it with as much precision as he did. He could match any techno beat and it was for that reason that Daddy D. elected to have him join his organic compound of a band, despite the controversies.

The man next to him had the opposite skin tone, it was dark just like Stella's face, but he was twice her age. A night cap covered his bald head and he had two sunken eyes. Grant Olson was his name, but his musical abilities lead him to be known as the Sandman. He was a keyboardist knowledgeable of coaxing many sounds out of his instrument but the tones he preferred the most were hypnotic, mellow and repetitive. They added a laid-back feel to the Techno Hippies output that, when combined with Stormy's drums, could put most people into a pleasing trance that aided dancing abilities. It was often said, that said bags under his eyes were due to him staying up late every night trying to find new ways to lull people to into trances.

These two were both pivotal to Daddy D's plan of union between the Summereins and Wintersons. Fifteen years ago, Daddy D. asked Olson and Stormy to join his band and with some hesitation, they both agreed. What they didn't know is how the world would perceive one of the first multi-ethnic bands. Stormy C was related to family lineage that ruled over Gris and Grant was a high council member in the Summerein government. This move Daddy D. made was risky, but what he believed to be a noble undertaking. In the end it was an astounding success.

Long pleather seats accompanied these stools and in them lounged a laid-out silver haired Daddy D. and a female companion, a woman who made Stella's eyes dart in many different directions to keep up with her deranged getup. She had short spikey bright orange hair, held back by a rainbow hairband, a set of tie-dye butterfly wings that sprouted from her back, a skirt with suspenders made entirely out of plush jeegs, a bikini top made of swirling colors, fuzzy brightly- colored leg warmers and unicorn boots. Stella knew that instantly who this was and what relationship she had to D.

"Hey pretty ladies…and Molly," Stella said, smiling at her joke.

"Hah," Stormy C said with wide eyes. "Care to tell us who you are, young lady?"

"And why you go hating on my main squeeze?" Daddy D. interjected with a half glare.

"Before I tell you that." Stella smiled. "I want you all to check your LYFI profiles. And see if anyone visited you on Level 6."

LYFI stood for Living Your Fiercest Incarnation and it was a program built into comphones that allowed someone to plug their mentality into an avatar and live in a digital hub world known as The Power Tower. The P.T. was a massive virtual building with 41 floors, each specially designed for a different use. One floor was a digital library of information, another was a theater where the avatar could watch an endless supply of videos, and then there was Level 6 where the avatars could socialize.

Molly, Olson and D. pulled out their comphones. Stormy C, being a staunch Winterson, refused to partake in this, having sworn off technology.

"Yo, piggy wiggy tails…it's just a random person named PassionFruitGirl62 sending a winky face," Molly said.

"Yeah, but check out her avatar."

"It's uh… you," Olson spoke with a little annoyance.

"Yeah, and look at me."

"Your avatar is sitting on a couch eating toaster tarts in Mighty Fruitsaders pajamas."

"Ooh, I like that show" Molly interjected "Vitamin She, woot!"

Stella had to keep herself from puking, she quickly followed it up with a grin and a wink. "Yeah exactly. *That's* what I do at night."

"And…"

"And I sent a winky face so obviously that means I'm into you. So put two and two together."

Daddy D. raised his eyebrow. "Hoho, woman, are you trying to LyFish us? I get 3,000 of those a day and plus, that's not even how you do it."

D explained that you had to create a seductive digital consciousness that didn't resemble yourself in order to make the victim believe that LYFI avatar was actually you in real life. Stella didn't even get the basics of Lyfishing it turned out.

Stormy C, frowned. "This is all irrelevant. How about you tell us who you are, and why someone would invite an insatiable waste like you to a prestigious event such as this."

Someone in a normal state of mind would have flinched upon being called out, but Stella was a force of chaos powered by the special plus. Stormy C's rudeness, especially didn't bother Stella, because he reminded her of Dan before he had his tea in the morning. It was why verbal lashings from him were a lot easier to shrug off.

She does a fashionable but proud curtsey. "Stella Grace. Nice to meet ya."

"You should rename yourself. You are bereft of grace," Stormy C said.

"Why thank you." She curtsied with a grin, trying to prove him wrong.

"Stella Grace," Daddy D. said with a smile. "I know you, you're the runner up in the Gods tournament."

"Correct, although arguably I should have won for my spontaneity."

"And I know exactly why you were trying to LyFish us. You want to be a back-up dancer for our group."

"Umm…well I…"

"Well, why don't I quiz the boys on how they feel about adding your body to make motions over our music. Boys?"

"Absolutely not," Stormy C said. "We don't need a bubble brained, Summerein girl. She'd be much too busy checking her Level 6 updates to actually learn any dance moves."

"Now now," Olson chimed in. "Just because she's Summerein, doesn't mean she's completely absorbed in electronics."

"Yeah, but look at her wardrobe choice, it's way too busy and flashy, not like the pious and reverent designs of our culture."

"Yeah," Stella said. "Because Molly Primus is soooooo pious. Especially since the only thing covering her crotch is jeeg corpses."

Daddy D. rose from his pleather seat and glared at Stella. "That is enough. I've had enough of you, talking about my fine little girl that way. There's no way I'd want you working with us."

Stella wanted to scream. It was all Stormy C's fault. She turned around and bumped into Dan who had just escaped his fans.

"Stella, what's wrong, why do you look so angry?"

"Hey is that pretty boy, Dan Dorphin?" Molly Primus questioned. "He sure is cute."

"Molly Primus…did you just talk to…me?" Dan's eyes widened.

"Shut up, both of you!" Stella screamed and ran off, leaving Helen at the mercy of Daddy D. and his entourage.

"Um…I'm so sorry about Stella." Helen said. "I should go after her." She quickly turned. "I'm a huuuuuge fan!" She then squeaked and ran off.

"Wait hold up, what for?" Daddy D. responded "She left me in the presence of you: the true bombshell."

Helen looked around and Daddy D. raised his voice. "I'm talking about you. Helen Wheels. You're the girl who I've been focusing on since I saw you at the God's tournament."

Daddy D. held up his phone. "Did you not get the message I sent you, congratulating you with my number?"

"Um…I had no clue it was you. Thought I was being Lyfished."

"Well, it was me. You're a girl with flavor and flash. I know talent and you girl, are drenched in it."

"Oh wow," Helen started gushing. "You know I've always been a fan! I love all your music! Like I said you're my favorite band! Nobody even comes close to the style and lyrics of the Hippies."

Helen began to expound at lengths about her love for their musical outfit. Bragging about how she owned all the albums, from the critical hits: "In A Priestess Operated Chairlift" "Magnesium Flavored Sky" and "Tamika Fights the Green Ex Managers" to their most recent release "BLH BTY."

The bubbly skater was bouncing up and down. "I even have your Year Long Song hidden inside a life-size gummy Charlotte skull."

"Wow, beauty and taste go hand in hand. Helen Wheels, I humbly welcome you to our freaky family." Daddy D. offers her his hand.

"And I humbly accept it," Helen said, taking a deep breath before grabbing her hero's hands.

Step 10: Investigation & Initiation

Unable to leave the side of the legendary Techno Hippies, Helen knew she'd have to make amends with Stella later—even friendship had to take a back seat to her mission. Was D covering up the rainbow burns?

Daddy D. flashed a finger gun. "How about we get you ladies ding-dong dolled up before we burn this house down."

Helen rested a hand on her round cheek. "This is perfect," she thought, "a little snooping behind the scenes before I get to be on stage with my favorite band"—Helen gazed forlorn at the stained-glass windows. "I really do hope Stella is okay. Poor girl."

The backstage hallways contrasted heavily with the glammy sheen of CharLuv—they were narrow, dark and cavernous. They looked more like they belonged to a seedy office or medical ward than a glamorous party house.

As Daddy D. lead his entourage through the hallway, Helen kept her eyes peeled, observing her surroundings carefully. Ever since she was at the Dance of the Gods, she was no stranger to shadiness behind the scenes.

The metal floors clanked loudly as Daddy D. led Helen to a vacant dressing room. "Only the best—of Charlotte's—for you, my dear."

Helen smiled broadly. "Thanks Daddy D, I appreciate it…"

The mayor pope put his arms around Molly and Stormy C, the latter looking extremely annoyed. "You make yourself fresh, Hella Helen, and soon, you will debut with the freshest band on this side of fresh."

Helen's eyes sparkled in the dim lighting. "Thanks again, Daddy D. But uh, one quick question?"

"What is it, Chubby Cheeks?"

"Where exactly did the Superfly come from? And shouldn't someone be dealing with the crisis?"

Daddy D. bit his tongue. It was clear to Helen that she touched a nerve. She could see the gears turning in his head.

"Uh," D began. "That pesky, but super-cool, pest emigrated from the eastern islands." Daddy D. looked to Grant and Stormy C.; a confident smirk stretched across all of their faces. "We have ways of dealing with it. Now I will leave you to your lady things."

As soon as Helen closed the door behind her, she let out a sigh of relief. So far, she didn't blow her cover with D and his gang. And she found a vital piece of information.

Helen walked over to ta rotating seat by a large dressing room mirror. She squeezed herself into it. Reaching towards the cosmetics, the skater powdered her face. She coughed as the powder went everywhere.

"Bleh," Helen choked. "No idea how Charlotte inhales all this stuff, but it must go right to her brain."

Helen crossed her thick thigs in the seat. "Now that I'm done with that girly stuff. How about I get down to business."

Her eyes fixed on a mini fridge. "Hmm, I wonder..." she walked over and much to her surprise, there was a hydroponic produce generator inside. In the waterlocked metropolis of City Electric, it was hard to get any vegetables and fruits to keep fit and limber, so the Scientific Committee of Electric invented the HPG to grow delicious fruits and vegetables in small spaces.

Helen pulled out several freshy grown sticks of celery, placed them in a plastic bag. She smiled. "Nice to have some brain food for the mission."

She crunched happily for five minutes, chewing up the times as well. Then she headed out.

Helen crept through the corridors, and when the staff of CharLuv passed her, she gave a timid smile.

She arrived at a door with a Darius nametag emblazoned on it. She quickly slid up against the wall. The door was open a small crack and she peered directly through it. Fortunately, there was no one inside the gaudy dressing room, but a pyramid of suspicious bottles stacked at the center of it.

Helen tip-toed in to get a closer look at the bottles.

Closing the door behind her, she crept over to the bottles and read them in horror. In a chintzy font, which looked like a cross between a detergent and geriatric cream were the words: Ravelotion D.

In a small bubble below it, there was a picture of a Winterson rubbing the cream on a rainbow burn. In the next bubble, the Winterson smiled as the rainbow burn was magically gone. Above it read, "Super Effective on the Superfly burn."

Helen reached out to grab one, but loud footsteps outside the room startled her. With a loud crash, she knocked the bottles over. "Oh no," Helen whispered. "I gotta think of something fast or the Jeeg is out of the bag."

94

Outside the room, Daddy D. chuckled to himself. "The Superfly, what a gas man. I'm gonna make a real killin' with my lotion line. If something doesn't sell once, rebrand it, baby."

But his face changed as he heard a loud crash from inside his room. He ran inside expecting a huge mess, but instead, the Ravelotion was carefully piled in a different order, one that was much larger and accommodating.

"Why…" Daddy D. remarked, scratching his chin. "I thought there was a big mess in here, but nope, it's nothing but my glorious line of lotion."

"Hehehe," he snickered with a glint in his eyes. "Never let a good crisis go to waste."

Suddenly, there was a loud belch in the room, seemingly coming from the lotion.

"Wait a minute," Daddy D. said. "Hold on a second."

The pile of lotion was silent. "Ah," Daddy D. said, putting a hand forward. "It's probably that Jeeg belching again. I was wondering where that critter went off to."

He slammed the door and Helen cautiously emerged from the pile.

"Whoo," she said, with a relaxed smile. "Too many celery sticks."

The plus sized girl smiled and balled up her fists. Now she had something to tell Stella—a tale of celery, lotion and belching jeegs.

Helen returned to her dressing room, preparing herself for her first live performance. But unable to resist, she ate a few more celery sticks first.

As she chowed down, a wave of disgust came over her. She was livid from D's machinations. This was the first true artist she had a passion for. Other girls—even Stella, admittedly—fell for pop music. Helen loved rock.

When she was only twelve, she loved the feeling of rebellion. While electro-op promoted strict conformity and following fashion trends, rock bucked the system. And no one did that better than the Techno Hippies.

One night, she snuck out to see a local concert after her curfew. Holographic vinyl wasn't enough for her; she needed the full experience. What she witnessed was D and his bandmates jamming for three full hours. They allowed everyone inside with free admittance, and told the audience that the only true system is universal kinship. She had found herself a new "Freaky Family," as D called it. She finally had a place to fit in, a people that embraced their differences rather than their similarities. The Techno Hippies after all, were a unity between two Wintersons and a Summerein. These were the ideals that every one of their songs embodied.

Or once did…It was clear now that D had not only sold out to the system, he became the system. And now he was peddling cheap and sleazy lotion to take advantage of the greatest crisis in Helen's lifetime.

There was knock at the door and Helen jumped.

"Come in," she said.

Soon, Daddy D, Stormy C, Grant, and Molly Primus all came pouring into the room chanting, "Freaky Family, Freaky Family, one of us, one of us."

They banged GLOs on their knees and continued chanting in unison, with Grant shutting off the lights.

"What's going on," Helen asked, started with her cheeks bright red.

"Shh," Daddy D. said. "We're initiating you."

"Ooga chugga, ooga chugga," Daddy shouted as he twisted a glo into a crown and placed it on Helen's head. "We are now welcoming you, Helena Wheels, into our Freaky Family."

"You know," D said, as the ritual chanting stopped. "I knew Helen Wheel was something special on the day I laid eyes on her. I saw a young lady who wasn't a dimwitted airhead of a girl, or a vain, self-interested young man, she clearly had a head on her shoulders and talent in her heels."

Helen blushed red like a tomato. She almost forgot for a second that her favorite artist was a snake oil salesman.

"And did I forget to mention how beautiful she is? Absolutely dazzling, darling! You're gonna be an icon for girls big and small." He smiles and leans in. "Anything you'd like to tell us?"

All the other Techno Hippies gazed at her with admiration.

"Yes…" Helen said. Now was the time she could finally let loose on D for his swindling the masses.

"Stormy C?"

"Yes," Stormy C asked in his nasally voice, seemingly smiling at her.

"You are the greatest drummer in the history of Tech-Rock. I remember playing air cymbals to your parts when I was still wearing braces."

"Grant?"

Grant quietly yawned, and his baggy eyes focused on Helen.

"You have pioneered hypnotic keyboard loops in ways that electro-pop could ever imagine."

"I try," Grant responded, "The best ones come to me while I sleep."

"Molly you…joined the greatest band in history!"

"Yeah. Totally the best decision of my life," said Molly with pride.

Helen had to hold back a grown. Molly joining the Hippies was the biggest tragedy in the history of rock.

"And Daddy D?" Helen said, ready to direct all of her ire at her favorite artist.

"You are the…"

Daddy D. walked to Helen and gently put his arm around her shoulder in a respectful manner.

Helen immediately felt guilty about her tirade and instead peeped, "the greatest artist I've ever heard and you…really have helped a lot of nations as a mediator."

She felt maybe she shouldn't be so quick to judge him perhaps. Nobody was all good, after all.

Daddy D. grinned hard and gave his bandmates two thumbs up. "See, I still got it with the kids. The Techno Hippies are still the IN thing. Alright Helen, giddy up. We're about the ride this concert all the way to the bank."

All the Techno Hippies left the room, including Molly, leaving Helen alone, pushing her fingers together. "That's not the only thing you're going to be riding to the bank."

She put on her skates and tapped them to make them light up. As she came out from backstage, the whole crowd of Winterson's applauded her.

Her face lit up, but her eyes were searching the crowd for Stella.

Daddy D. smiled at her. "Eyes up, Skater Star. You're gonna give the people some razzle dazzle and blast their woes to next week!"

Helen's face lit up like a star.

He was right. This was her moment. Stella would be okay. And she'd explain everything she learned afterward. But right now, she had to soothe the electric burned with a true remedy. One that came from her heart but was powered by wheels of flame.

97

Step 11: The Bebop Tango

Stella fled in tears. She wanted to get as far away from the dance room as possible. She chose the door closest to the bar, one that was to the left of the stage. Inside, she found herself in a hallway. This room had two stained glass windows that reflected light in from the courtyard. They were painted to resemble the two heroes, Kouyate, the silver skinned, dark haired woman from legend and the red skinned soldier, Harry Fairson who had rescued her from a barbaric sacrifice. During the first war, the pair traveled through an underground temple to dance before Ravenous and gain powers to protect their nation during wartime. Through their love and chemistry, they impressed the goddess and gained magical powers for both of their people. The Dance of the Gods commemorated that moment and was held every five years to find dancers of the same chemistry as Kouyate and Fairson.

These stained-glass windows were one of the few areas of CharLuv that retained its former appearance, looking more like a castle egress than a dance club.

Stella's sobbing and tears reverberated through the room. She had to get some fresh air, her throat was dry and throbbing. She pushed open a door between the two stained glass windows and entered the moonlit courtyard. There a garden opposed the giant statue of Ravenous.

Stella took a seat on the stone wall that stood between her and the garden.

"Oh Ravenous, what am I doing here?"

This was the first time she found herself asking this question, because after all, it was her dream to bask in the glory of becoming a superstar. She knew very well of the freak-outs and breakdowns the heroes of her tabloids went through, but now she was all alone with nothing and not even her friends cared to see where she was.

"Why do I have to make such an ass out of myself?"

She gazed at the moon light adorned statue. Its face glowed with it. Seeing it allowed Stella to take a deep congested breath.

"I just need to forget all about this. Yeah, that's what I need to do."

She pulled out her case of Yellow Plus and gazed at them.

"Memories are important. Not something you should frivolously throw away." A voice started Stella and she dropped her pill container. Apparently, she wasn't the only one in the courtyard.

"How are you going to learn to prevent your future screw-ups if you can't remember your past ones?"

She scrambled to the ground looking for pills that had scattered when the container hit the ground. Her hands picked at them like a starved chicken going at its feed. After filling it up, she clutched the container hard.

Looking up, she saw a handsome man with a fiery afro. Afros were definitely not her ideal hairstyle on a man, but his chiseled face and dark facial hair compensated greatly. His outfit was a dark red pinstriped suit with an orange trim that imitated flames. Even his afro was dyed two different colors to imitate the colors of fire.

"Barvarius ...Bop?" Stella asked. "Last year's finalist? Oh geez, I'm a huge fan! It's really really wonderful to meet you."

"B for short," said the suave voice. "And I am a fan of you too, Pink Tails."

"You were the guest judge on the final episode and the only one who gave me a good score...even though I messed up."

"You had promise. As a master in the tango, I know when I see it."

"Thanks," Stella said with flushed cheeks. "But honestly, I don't feel like I have that much at all. That's why it's better if I just forget it all."

"And how do you do that?" B. Bop asked.

"These." Stella held her pills up to him.

"Ah...the Yellow Plus Pill. They sure ain't all they're cracked up to be that's for sure."

"What do you mean by that?" Stella shot back at him.

"What are you taking them for?"

"Umm...I...I uh...trauma. Yes, trauma."

"Wow. Smart girl. You don't even remember."

"Um...yeah you're not supposed to remember. That's the point of them." This guy was really starting to irritate Stella. She kicked her foot forward into the stone wall.

B. Bop smirked at her.

"Like I said, in the long run, it's better to learn from your mistakes than give yourself a chemical lobotomy." Bop narrowed his eyes and looked at her. "What even happened?"

99

"Why should I tell you?" Stella asked.

"Have you ever heard about talking about your problems?"

Stella looked around and jutted her lip out in a pouting fashion. "Well, it's not like I have anyone else to talk to this about."

"Yeah, so spill your guts, Pink Tails."

Stella was torn by his moniker for her. At first, it reminded her of how Dan would call her Grace, which was annoying, but on the other hand, it was wordplay which she liked. After all, she never liked her hair being referred to as a pig to start with. Still, she didn't want to come off as soft to him so she glared at him. "You are so rude."

"I'm also all ears."

Stella told the man how she was humiliated twice at the party. It was all because of Wintersons who discriminated against who she was. The first time, though it was fading from her head, still stuck out to her in that her celebrity and talent wasn't recognized because of her identity. The second time, which was permanently on repeat in her head, was because a Winterson nationalist caused her to slip over her words in front of someone important. And it was all just because he thought she was a fashion crazed, electronic addicted airhead, because that was the textbook definition of Summerein girls. Even if it was a little true of herself, she admitted, she also believed she had so much personality beyond those stereotypical traits.

As Stella spoke, she noticed how blended B. Bop's skin was and when she spoke, her words seemed to resonate with him.

"By the number of times they've flashed it on telescreen, I'm sure you know of my upbringing."

"Ah yes, you're Reinson right?"

"Well, someone pays attention to my television bio after all."

Stella heard about the kind of person B was. A Reinson was a person of mixed race, half Summerein, half Winterson. A relationship of this kind was a taboo to both races and often those who took part in it, did so privately, not letting their friends or neighbors know that they had feelings for the opposite race. Generally, the children of these relationships hid their history and did whatever they could to resemble whichever race their skin appeared. B. Bop was different, he was very open about it even on TV. Stella respected his grit.

"People tend to forget that the legendary hero Kouyate was a Winterson and her lover, a Summerein."

"Oh, everyone knows that," Stella said. "I'm pretty sure they were together before everyone got their powers and Wintersons became so much stronger than Summereins; that's when the true division happened."

"Well Pink Tails, there's no division in my blood. Tons of people of both races come up to me and say I'm an inspiration."

"They do?"

"Hell yeah they do, girl! it's because I dazzle them with my unbridled passion. I don't pay no attention to who's on the dance floor and who's watching," B. Bop gazed at her directly and smacked his fist into his opposing hand. "I just do it."

Stella gazed at him for a second before B. Bop spoke again. "Stella, I would like to invite you to a tango on the dance floor, I want to demonstrate how one should really go down."

"Well…I…uh."

B. Bop stuck out his hand in offering.

Stella thought about how her skill was unappreciated. She had earned her silver prize and she was gonna go for gold!

"Let's smoke them." She said, grabbing his hand.

The two partners in dance re-entered CharLuv's main hall. All of the Wintersons were moving on the floor and their pale silver skin glinted in the moon and rave lights. They noticed the Techno Hippies had mounted the stage with Molly Primus and Helen as backup singers and dancers.

"Jokes on them because Helen can't carry a note." Stella muttered, remembering their soda pop induced singalong of "We are Courage!", the opening of her favorite show.

She was sore to see Helen on stage and looking like she was enjoying herself.

Stella wasn't normally a jealous type, but she felt livid that her friend would be on stage with the man who tore her down instead of at her side, lifting her up. She was aware that Daddy D. was her pillow pal's idol, but it still left no excuse. Helen would have to watch a lot of cartoons to get on her good side again.

The band pumped out an electronic groove, with chilling minor keys set to a hypnotic drum beat that sounded pre-programed. Daddy D. crooned out some lyrics in a high pitched warbly voice that sounded like a cross between a castrated disco singer and a homoerotic space android. "I don't drink moonshine, I drink purple sunshine with a side of lime" went the chorus, repeated in a mantra like fashion with the two unlikely choir girls echoing the "side of lime" part. The crowd swayed in a techno trance to the music.

Stella made for the dance floor with great haste, but B. Bop grabbed her pig tails. "Owww, come on B, don't you want to dance everyone to dust?"

"Let's wait for the song to end first. You do want an ideal soundtrack don't you, pinky?"

Stella sighed. "You're right. And everyone's a bit too hypnotized right now to notice anyway."

B. Bop snapped his fingers. "We need the right tune and I have just the one in mind."

The two hid in the corner, out of the blinding spotlight of the dancefloor. The band eventually came to a stop. Daddy D, despite his pale skin, had a glowing facial expression. The man felt no more alive and eternally young than when he was fronting his band. "That was 'Purple Heliocentrism—My Religion' an ode I wrote to our purple sun. Now as I told you ladies and gents, we were open to requests, whether they be slow dancing or electro-funky bangers. So, call them out to me."

B. Bop quickly scrawled on a tiny tear of paper he removed from his dress shirt's pocket. He reached into his giant afro and pulled out a large fluff of hair.

Stella was surprised he didn't cringe when he did so. She watched him whip out some tape and stuck the piece to his hair. He then walked to the center of the dance floor and released it into a wind, generated by fans that were designed to keep everyone on the dance floor cool. The fluff flew on the breeze and landed perfectly in Daddy D's hands. "I see you down there, B. Bop with your unorthodox methods of communication. I'm sure there are quite a few ladies and dudes who'd want this lock of hair more than me."

He removed the piece of paper from the hair. "Hmm." Daddy's face moved into his signature toothy grin. "You are no stranger to danger, my friend."

Stella gazed over at him, her head swimming with questions.

Daddy D. continued. "Well, this is the first and probably the last time we'll get a request like this, so let's cherish it. Alright boys, let us play…The Bebop Tango."

Stella gasped.

The Bebop Tango? Out of the five most dangerous tangos, that one was ranked #2. The one she had to perform with Dan was the Foxtrot Tango, only #4 on the list and she still screwed it up. Stella knew of a contestant in the Dance of the Gods named Jumpin' Jack who had to be hospitalized from the amount of rave energy the accursed tango had consumed from him. It was concern for the health of the contestants that lead the judges in Dance of The God's to choose a much less dangerous tango for her and Dan.

Still, Stella knew exactly where B. Bop was going with his titular tango. Everyone would be fixated on them. That was exactly what Stella wanted. The amount she had been shunned made her crave sweet stardom even more. She wanted both races of people to want her and if she had to set the world ablaze with her feet, then the burn it shall.

"1…2…3…4…a gozar!" Stormy C's drums kicked into an oddly timed rhythm that sounded like a shuffle on hard crack. The keyboards played stabs of somewhat off-key notes, sounding like they belonged to a tango melody that was too sped up for its own good.

Most of the people on the dance floor just stood there in utter shock, not knowing what to do or how to react to this bizarre cacophony.

Stella and B walked onto the dance floor. B put his arm around Stella's collar bone. She spun and faced him; a look of fear repressed by an unrevealing expression. Everyone gasped and they began muttering between themselves "Those Summereins, are they really going to do it?" "That's last competition's winner and this year's runner up?"

"That's right," Stella answered "and I'm here to stay. I'm going to be the sunshine in this blizzard."

With sudden momentum, the two stepped across the dance floor vigorously. Each foot tapping the ground and moving to the perverted melody. When the two stopped for a musical pause, B. Bop pulled his face close and whispered to her.

"There's a single thing needed in a tango and a relationship: passion."

Stella looked up at him, eyes widened. He nodded his head in an affirmative motion. As they darted back and forth, Stella spun with great force into his arms. Her legs lifted and wrapped around his, all the while he continued to whisper on the edge of his breath.

"Extinguish the passion in both and they will die."

She raised her hand and he slowly moved his hand up and gripped hers. They began to mirror each other's movements on the dance floor. Stella made sure to make every step precise so she would not folly like she did with Dan.

As they moved, she could feel beads of sweat on the back of her neck. It was hard to be precise. She feared her mind was moving as fast as her legs.

103

B. Bop calms her with a look. "You're wondering why you lost, little girl, you had a partner who didn't care about you or the tango. He just wanted to win."

Stella's leg wobbled a bit, but she kept her composure. "He just used you and your passion to precipitate your own demise and leave you for dead."

"That's not Dan. Is it? He's changed. Mmph."

B. Bop took his carnation and put it in Stella's mouth; a move quite familiar in the world of tango, but oddly convenient as a silencer too.

B remained steady and unwavering. "Here's your moment to be passionate and it won't be denied."

Stella's body circled around B. Bop's. He carefully followed her, his arms around her waist. With the extra force, he thrust her up unto the air where she split her feet apart.

Everything felt like it was in slow motion, she saw the crowd make audible gasps as she flew. Her body revolved in the air at high speed, defying gravity and causing her pig tails to swing in a hypnotic motion.

B. Bop ran under her catching her with great ease. A bunch of Wintersons clapped upon impact. She broke the normally stern and sexy glare a person doing the tango did, spreading her face into a cheerful smile.

Recognition. It was finally hers.

On the stage, Helen stood behind the tangled wires and musicians who concentrated on playing their own sick version of the tango. Helen was in awe of the technical prowess of the Techno Hippies.

They played the way good friends made conversation; interacting in playful ways and never being afraid of improvisation. This was the famed interplay Helen heard on the record and now she got to see their inner clockwork front and center stage.

The other backup singer, infamous starlet, Molly Primus couldn't be less entertained. She yawned, jittered around a lot and played games on her comphone.

Aside from the irreverence, Helen had mixed emotions with this girl. Before her much publicized image change, Molly just made run of the mill pop music that saturated the airwaves and caused Helen to switch the switch the radio station. Helen only cared about Molly because without warning she latched onto her favorite band and became a part of them. She didn't read tabloids like Stella so she didn't know why the girl got scouted. All in all, she didn't know whether she should have new found respect for Primus or new distaste for the Hippies for associating with her.

104

Helen beams at Daddy D. who she swore gave a friendly wink.

She was grateful that Daddy D. singled her out though. She spent her life always being the third choice and sometimes not even that, so having D personally seek her out was mind blowing. Unlike Stella however, she refused to be so easily starstruck. She felt she was too old for that and after all, celebs were just people thrust into a flickering spotlight. They were no one to leave your friends for. She felt bad about Stella and would explain to her that she was only doing Stella's job so Charlotte wouldn't get mad at Stella; something Charlotte sure did with her a lot.

Daddy D. already let it slip he had a new product he was marketing in order to combat the rainbow burns from the supposed superfly. When they were in the changing room, Helen saw piles of a product called Ravelotion D that was going to be sold at this event.

"Whoa, check it out, cream puff. I'm so high on pot." Molly rambled.

"Uh Molly, I think you should get down from that," Helen said in reference to the tall flower pot that Molly had dragged on stage to wobble on.

"It's just I'm so bored. This song has no vocals and the crowds not even paying attention to us."

Helen looked past the stage to notice the crowd on the dance floor was swarmed around two dancers rather than their stage. Squinting, she could make out pink hair and a giant afro the color of a smoldering fire on the two dancers.

"Is that Stella and B. Bop?" Helen asked with a crack in her voice. "Why are they dancing…together?" She frowned. "If I try to stop them, she could get hurt."

"Grrrr…it's making me mad. I didn't just get cheek implants for nothing!" Molly screamed.

"I really do hope you mean the ones for your face," Helen responded, her eyes fixed on the graceful moves of her roommate.

"They were for tonight so the world could see how much I changed."

Molly hopped off her pot and raised her fist in the air. "Well, they'll see. I'll show everyone the new me, the one who can't be domesticated."

She rushed off stage, running down the steps and off into the shadows of the backroom.

Helen tried to decide what to do next. Should she go to Stella and tell her what she knew or follow Molly? Unable to determine how much of a hazard Molly was, Helen went to Stella instead.

Stella panted like she was a dog suffering a heat stroke. A big grin was on her face, but she felt like she was burning up. B. seemed unwavering and unaffected, but the tango was named after his family so he was no doubt a master of it. From every direction, there were people of pale face cheering, they clearly loved them.

"You ready to give them the grand spectacle?" B. Bop whispered to her.

"What's that?"

"The Fiery Vortex."

"...I've never tried that. I don't think I can do that."

"You have abilities way beyond your own comprehension."

"But..."

"Just let go and enjoy how naturally airborne you can be."

B. Bop placed two fireglos in her hand. They were Gel Luminescent Optics, sticks containing a gel that created fire-like energy when utilized correctly.

Stella clutched them hard as B. Bop hoisted her up over his head with very little effort. The room began to whirl as B. Bop quickly shifted his hands underneath her, rotating her fast. Stella felt a bit sick and closed her eyes as B. Bop went faster and faster.

With all his energy, he threw her body up into the air. Stella was surprised how much air she got, even compared to last time, as she soared towards a giant chandelier on the ceiling.

She thought she would hit it, but fell short of it. It was then that everything clicked. She knew what to do.

She concentrated her adrenaline into her hands, cracking the two fireglos. "Come on, come on. I've used these before."

They refused to light.

Stella's eyes squinted and she caught a glimpse of a woman in the crowd. It was her mom. "Mom? She always told me that I had abilities too. I know I do."

The caps of the fireglos flew off and Stella's body was accompanied by two long whips of energy.

Stella spun her body and the lines of fire encircled her body, creating the vortex. Everyone yelled and screamed in awe as Stella began slowly floating down with the energy twirling around her. The shining star landed next to B and fell to the ground.

The tango master helped her up as people began to clap and cheer.

"I told you, Pink Tails, it takes two to Bebop tango."

Stella, a bit dazed, rolled her head backwards and grinned. "Ah, so that's why I see two of you."

"Come on, lets grace 'em with a finale."

"B I don't feel well and I want to see my mom." Stella whined and shook her head.

"Nonsense, you can handle this. Just believe and let go!"

The room had continued spinning for Stella even though she had long stopped twirling. She couldn't even feel her legs moving anymore.

"Stella!" She heard a voice among the loudness.

It took her a moment to reorient herself and realize the voice belonged to Helen.

Helen grabs her hand. "Stella, Daddy D. has been covering things up and I know why now."

Stella closed her eyes and ignored her treacherous friend as she kept on moving.

Helen followed after her. "Stella! Can you hear me?"

"People started shouting and looking away from B. Bop and Stella. They were pointing above them. Up in the rafters, a woman in a colorful and over-the-top outfit hung. "Sup all you homeboys and home girls, it's me Molly Primus. I'm so high…up right now."

She jumped from them onto the giant, multi layered chandelier. It swung back and forth with loud creaks from the old wooden ceiling above.

Molly dangled from above. "I got a song dedicated to all of you who are as wild as me."

Down on the floor people were panicking and running.

Charlotte walked in with an air of coolness too.

Helen shouted as she ran to her boss. "I am so glad to see you."

Charlotte grimaced. "The feeling isn't mutual. Can someone get that monkey down from there?"

The monkey in question began to sing very off-key. It was obvious that when she was out of the studio she was out of her element. The chandelier moved like a pendulum, but bits of glass that hung from it fell off. "I SWUNG IN ON A CHANDELIER!"

"Hey, Molly took that song from Mia!" yelled a fan of electropop music in horror as she ran off.

The ceiling cracked further. The bolts that held the top of the chandelier fell out and flew towards the floor. And then, in a split second, the chandelier fell.

It plummeted straight towards B. Bop and Stella.

B took a dive away from the chandelier, leaving Stella as fair game to be splattered and broken. But, in another split second, someone ran at such speeds they could barely be seen and scooped Stella up in their arms.

Stella, opened her eyes and saw Dan holding her. He let out a heavy breath. "Dan, you didn't leave me for dead like he said."

"Of course not, and uh who said that?"

Stella rubbed her face up against Dan's cheek and planted a kiss.

Dan turned away. "Why'd you do that?"

Stella blushed and nuzzled him. "You're my lucky star, Dan. Heehee."

The two looked over, expecting to see a chandelier shatter into a million pieces but instead, they saw a dark-haired woman. She was dressed entirely in black and had a severe expression.

The warrior woman had somehow caught the whole chandelier right before it hit the ground and cradled it with a flashing staff.

"Wow…she's…such a cool lady," Stella said with wide eyes. "I wonder who she is."

"Good job, Jayden," Charlotte said. "You just saved an antique from the wrath of Daddy D.'s coked out chimp."

A crashing sound echoed over everyone. When everyone looked up, they saw that the giant window behind the stage had a humanoid-shaped hole in it.

Stella and Dan both spotted a winged man with shiny silver skin and a green-purple checkered suit. It was Crane. He flew in towards Molly who was still on top of the chandelier and snatched her. He began to fly with her towards the window.

"Wheeeeeee....ouch!" Molly shouted as they crashed through it.

Jayden with control, let the chandelier down. "Well Jayden looks like you should probably handle that before my club gets a lawsuit."

With all this chaos encircling her, Stella let out a snore and she passed out in Dan's arms. Her consciousness finally had given out from all that dangerous dancing, but a greater danger remained for those who were still awake.

Act 2: Knights in Training

Step 12: The Neon Knight Conference

Stella opened her eyes and found herself lying in an oddly shaped bed. She was tucked in so tight that she could barely move and was surrounded by plush jeegs. They were like the ones Molly Primus had bundled together as a dress. She surveyed her surroundings. The sides of the bed were reinforced with gate-like bars. She looked through them and around the room.

On the walls of the room were designs of the Fruitsaders. Stella observed the wallpaper closer. All three main Fruits were there: a tall curvaceous woman with orange skin and an equally enriched-in-Vitamin C afro, a squat chubby red woman with a short green tuft of hair on her head and a midsize thin yellow lady who posed like a ballerina. They were accompanied by a young girl with a giant grin that was full of dental issues, but she was clearly proud of her teeth anyway thanks to the empowering words of her Fruitsader friends.

The original logo was there; before it had been changed for the more iconic season 2 one. With this knowledge, Stella could tell this wallpaper was vintage. She wondered where she was and if she was still in CharLuv. She was almost of the impression that Charlotte had set this room up for her. She really was her other mom, wasn't she? The door across from the bed opened and Helen walked through to greet her.

"Oh Stella, thank the goddess you're awake. Dan said you passed out so we found this room for you to rest."

"Oh...hey...Daddy's best friend." Stella shot an ice-cold glance.

"Don't be like that. I'm sorry I couldn't help you. I had an important mission and..."

"Blah, blah, blah. I don't wanna hear it, Miss Abandonment." She crossed her arms and pouted.

Helen puffed her cheeks in rage. "Abandonment? What are you talking about?"

"Best friend lesson 101: When your bestie runs off crying, you don't proceed to brown nose the guy who made her cry."

"Stella...we had a mission. I didn't know you were so petty."

"I'm not the one who left her best friend's side to go sing on stage with a band of senior citizens and the latest celebrity burnout."

Helen gritted her teeth. "At least I didn't spend the night with man-whore extraordinaire B. Bop!" A growl escaped her lips.

"Oh no, you didn't just go there." Stella shot back, picking up a jeeg plush, ready to throw.

"You should know that Greasy Teen Stuff magazine voted him the person most likely to make you hate the player AND the game."

"And someone like him was there when I most needed it. Unlike my supposed bestie."

"You know what, Stella, this isn't going anywhere. Charlotte wants to see both of us in her office! Even Daddy D. is there. We've got a mission. Dan needs us. You like him, right? Then move on and grow up!"

Stella threw the plush jeeg at Helen, which didn't do quite as much damage as she had hoped.

She groaned and then emerged from her cocoon of covers. The pissed-off pep-girl slipped on her Go-go boots and ruffled her hair. Without a mirror, or a friend, it was hard to fix her hair. and she could only hope for the best. Without a word, she accompanied the tubby traitor.

They left the bedroom and went down a stairwell that led to the main dance hall. It was in shambles. The giant chandelier that had fallen was placed in the center, along with the shards of broken glass and the crystal that hung from it. The floor was rife with glo-sticks, streamers, novelty beads, stripped off clothing and spilled cocktails of smart drinks.

In the light of day, the amount of ruin and chaos was all the more apparent. As they walked through the wreck, both girls were dead silent.

Stella wasn't use to being so quiet around Helen. Judging by the quick way she skated ahead, the starlet could tell she didn't want to be around her either. As annoyed as she was, Stella didn't like the uncomfortable tension. She began thinking that maybe she didn't sort things out with Helen the way she should of.

"Helen, listen I…"

"Stella, I don't want to talk to you right now. I don't want to say something that will hurt us."

"But I…"

Helen turned around; her cheeks puffed up like an angry hamster. She lifted her finger and pointed it right in Stella's face. "I don't want to hear anything you have to say right now!"

Stella shuddered.

Helen was scary when she was angry. Stella wasn't too surprised. She was permanently heated around Dan, after all. Still, she never thought that aggression would be directed her way.

The two walked in the direction of Charlotte's office and when they got to the door, they found themselves in the middle of a conference.

The madame sat at her desk as the head honcho woman of her organization, but there were numerous others in the room as well. On the right side of the room were Daddy D, Stormy C and Grant Olson. On the left side of the room sat Dan, B. Bop and the dark haired, pale-faced woman who Charlotte referred to as Jayden.

Stormy C and Daddy D. both were standing and pointing, arguing with Charlotte. Fellow band member Olson just slept, somehow able to ignore them.

Dan looked really tired and had an I-can't-believe-they-dragged-me-into-this face, while B. Bop sat reclined and relaxed, sipping a smart drink.

Jayden sat there without batting an eye or twitching. Her face looked like a doll, one that was serious looking and rough around the edges. She had both hands on her electronic staff which she positioned towards the ground. The yammering didn't help anyone's mood and Stella could feel herself being brought down as she walked in.

"Oh sup, fine Stella," B. Bop said. "And five girl."

"Hey whoa, hey Bop." Daddy D. cut in. "The only way our newest member of the family is a five is if she's multiplied by two."

"Aw thanks," Helen said. "Daddy D. you are by far my favorite person in this room. On a scale of ten, you're a groovy twenty!"

"Come, my brash brunette bombshell and merge with your freaky family." He offers her a hand.

Helen's face lit up. "Don't mind if I do."

"I think I'm gonna puke," Charlotte muttered to herself.

"Soy?" asked Stella, handing Charlotte a cup.

"Yes, go figure you remember, but my soy girl's mind is too occupied with the big D."

Helen ignored her and walked over to Daddy D's side of the room and sat down.

"Here Stella, I saved you a seat between two flawless gems." B. Bop gestured to Stella, pointing at the empty seat between him and Dan.

As Stella sat, she waved at Dan, who gave the tiniest smile. "I'm glad you're awake."

"As am I," said Charlotte. "Quite a lot has transpired without you. Considering that party was for you and Dan, it's important for you to be here."

"It was for me?"

"Yes. I hosted this party—the Penultimate Party—in honor of the victors of Dance of The Gods. After the rather mediocre entertainment, we were going to have an inauguration for you and Danny."

Daddy D. raises a glass. "And to our skating starlet."

"For what?" asked Stella with a blank look.

Stormy C slapped his hand on his face. "This is another stunning example of Summerein intelligence. This girl doesn't even know that she was going to be sworn in as a Neon Knight of the City Electric, probably because she cares more if her hair is the color of bubble gum."

"Cecillian." Charlotte stood up and puffed out her chest further than it already was. "I won't have you talk about one of my stars that way, especially when we share the same race. Humanity is on a constant quest to feel superior to itself and you're one of those fools leading that dreadful parade."

"Lady Charlotte, I just don't want the newest recruits of the Neon Knights to be lax. I could offer you tons more talented Winterson men and women in her place."

B. Bop stood up along with them. "I'll have you know that Stella performed nearly the whole Bebop tango at your party. She's got the skills that kill."

"I fully believe that," Charlotte added. "She's got a drive and I've seen her work her way up from the bottom, getting up after every fall."

"Thanks guys, seriously." Stella blushed. "But uh, what's a Neon Knight?"

Dan, looking more confused than annoyed spoke. "Stella, you should really know that. I mean you were in the Dance of the Gods to BE one."

"I guess it just slipped my mind. Heh-heh, care for a little refresher?"

Charlotte was quick to jump in before anyone else. "Well, on Aleatore, some are just content with being dancers but the more ambitious aim to become the true legends! The Neon Knights are the rhythmic protectors of the nation. We hold the Dance of the Gods so young men and young women, like myself, can compete to become them."

B. Bop spoke next. "They're people like me and Jayden with exceptionally high Electromotion counts. You don't need to place to join the Neon Knight pantheon, just gotta dazzle the pants off the scouters! A high number isn't enough for a passing grade. You need the skill and drive to channel that motion into a typhoon of style and power!"

"That sounds amazing!" exclaimed Stella. "Hey, but why have placements at all? Wasn't the DOTG founded to, you know, unify the people?"

Daddy D. smirks. "Well, bubble gum, an event that big takes a lot of moolah to move, if you get my groove? A competition is the best way to make it rain green. Plus, a little competition can be a glue that binds minds and mends the tension between ladies and gents."

Helen perks up. "So, you're using money from your product lines to ummm foster unity and acceptance."

"That is on the dime, puffy cheeks!"

Stella nods. "And competition makes both sides give it their all. But why make Summereins and Wintersons compete against their own before the finale?"

"For peace, baby! There's enough sunny versus snowy going on in the streets as is. The stratification in the competition is just part of keeping things chill, ya dig?"

Stella gins. "I totally dig! So how long has this Neon Knight thing been going on?"

B put his arms behind his head and relaxed in his chair. "I've been under Charlotte's division since last year. The pay is awesome and you don't have to take care of much, well…until these vampire guys showed their ugly faces…"

"That's right, Mr. Bop," Charlotte said. "But you failed to mention when the Edwardian planet aligned with us. Nine-hundred and fifty-five years ago, it was all out war. Violence ravaged this planet. Without Kouyate harnessing the goddesses' powers for everyone, life would lose its motion."

Stella knew about these Edwardians. They were a menace that plagued their society for the last century. They were humanoid-insectoid creatures that were male like in appearance but with the power of special costumes, they could move at light-speed. That wasn't everything either, they were capable of shapeshifting into females. Their powers were said to increase tenfold when they took on the appearance of a woman. These aliens were said to be a hostile warlike race that had set their sights on Aleatore because their planet's resources were depleting.

115

"If they come back, dear." Daddy cut in and sat up. "I've been receiving reports that they might have wiped themselves out in a civil war. Maybe they should have held their own DOTG, ya get me?"

"That report is completely unfounded," Charlotte responded. "Someone of your leadership should not be sticking their head in the sand. Though you already done that with the Ravepires...and just look what happened."

Daddy looked at her sternly. "This never would have happened if you hadn't thrown a party out in the open like that and invited so many Wintersons."

"From what your intelligence says," Stormy C said "they tend to go after our kind. We are after all the richest in Electromotion, of course. There is no finer meal."

Charlotte ignored Stormy and continued to focus on tearing into Daddy D. "The winner of the Dance of the Gods was a Winterson and I believe he would have much rather been in the company of his people; though, I can hardly understand why. Your superiority complexes are absolute agony."

"What are Ravepires exactly?" asked Dan. "Is there a cure?"

"Ravenous gave the Wintersons twice the amount of power because we are the more deserving race." Stormy C added. "And it was because our Kouyate had twice the zeal and determination that dreg-of-the-planet Hairy Fairson could ever hope to muster. I'm surprised he was even allowed in her presence."

Charlotte shot a gaze across the room at Stormy C like she's was going to fry him. "If we were going to turn this into a race debate, I wouldn't have asked you to come. You always do this, Cecille."

"Is there a cure to the Ravepire bite?" asked Dan, more desperate than before.

"Let's focus on the matter at hand!" Daddy D. yelled. "You should have hired better people to protect them, instead of your incompetent bodyguards. Look at this girl," Daddy D. pointed at Jayden who still leaned on her staff. "She can barely talk, let alone protect anyone."

Charlotte's eyes flared up. "How dare you speak ill about her condition. Your cruelty knows no bounds, Darius."

"Don't call me that, Charlie. I ought to have you exiled from this city for putting my daughter in harm's way."

"His daughter? Molly Primus is his daughter?" Stella whispered to Dan. "I thought she was his main squeeze."

"That's all news to me," Dan responded with a confused look.

116

Charlotte smiled. "So, you're dating your own daughter?"

"That was a ploy to keep her from being manhandled!" Daddy D. raised his voice to the pitch he often sung at in an outburst of emotion. "I had just come to terms with her, her illegitimacy, the way stardom has affected her brain and despite that I truly loved her. Now she will die young because of your incompetence, you vile disgusting hag."

Charlotte's face twitched and the electronics in the room began to go haywire. Lights, comphones, telescreens and computers began to crackle and flicker. She held her hand out like a gun and began to soak up all of her electricity into her index finger.

"I...AM...NOT...A...HAG." Charlotte put emphases on each of her words. "My blood is like virgin oil; I am eternally young! Come at me, replacement hip Harry!"

Daddy D. flinched at Charlotte's ugly grimace, but quickly assumed his battle position. He wagged his pointer finger and began dancing in place.

Stella observed that this was not only a disco move, it was Daddy D's signature attack, the cold snap.

Blue energy drew from his fingertips, causing Stormy C to kick over his chair and dart behind a snoozing Grant Olson.

"This is more than I bargained for," B. Bop said. "Came here for a little drama, but I didn't expect a duel of this caliber. Such a shame I'm all out of fizz."

Charlotte pointed her hand right at D. "I'm gonna fry the remaining hair you have left. Greased Lightning!"

Right before they let loose their attacks, Jayden jumped in.

Her staff blocked a hail of icy disco balls and then absorbed the incoming lightning bolt.

Charlotte and Daddy D. were stunned, their eyes became blurry and their bodies were surrounded by colorful circles of energy that banded them.

Jayden, started breathing hard, as if out of breath.

Stella looked at this woman. She was gaunt, with dark circles under her eyes and her face was in a permanent scowl with her light unibrow hanging heavy over her eyes.

Jayden spoke up. "No fighting."

Her voice was very soft, pleading and childlike. It was at a complete dissonance with her intense face. Stella almost thought it belonged to a young girl.

Jayden's voice deepened and grew monotonous. "I will release you, but first...promise no fighting."

Charlotte's face moved slightly. Daddy D.'s did too.

Jayden dropped them.

Stella was very shocked that she had such power to best people of their caliber.

"What did she do to them?" Stella whispered to B. Bop.

"Jayden's a Neuronian warrior, her mind can lift up objects and turn even the heaviest thing weightless," B. Bop said. "She may even be able to lift up Five Girl."

Neuronia was, as far as Stella knew, the western country on the other side of the planet. Most people there were very far removed from the country of Aleatore, tending to stick to their own affairs. They only ever approached their distant neighbors for trade and commerce in their own part of the City Electric known as Neuritown.

It was a wise move not being involved in the petty fighting of North and South Aleatore. While Aleatoreans were about the body, the Neuronians were firmly devoted to the evolution of their mind and spirit.

Stella leans into B. Bop. "But what were those circles?"

"Why don't you ask her, Pink Tails?"

"She's kinda scary," said Stella meekly.

Charlotte, had taken a deep breath and returned to her seat. "Jayden, thank you for not getting me incarcerated for scorching this sorry king's pasty grey ass. Why don't you have a seat too, Daddy D. and we can continue our discussion."

Daddy D. glared at her; he was obviously not as calm as Charlotte. Stella could see that finding Molly was very very important to him. He took his seat begrudgingly but then spoke.

"So, what are we going to do about these...Ravepires?"

Dan smiled. "Finally," he said softly.

"Well, first, you need to admit to the whole city you lied to them. Otherwise, that Super Fly might bite you in the butt," Charlotte said with a bony finger.

D's eyes widened. "How did you?" He sighs. "I was only trying to cover it up so we could continue to party every night. I was only doing what a good leader would do: maintain order. If only the Wintersons are being fed upon, then they will likely blame the Summereins for their woes. That's why I even had some false Summerein reports of Super Fly bites."

"That's very considerate of you, but I'm not sure that's best," said Helen softly.

"Yes. You sure kept this party in check, Daddy. Everyone ran into the night screaming their heads off. A place where they would obviously be open to more Ravepire attacks." Charlotte narrowed her eyes as her gaze connected with D's. "As of now, thirteen more people have gone missing, all Wintersons. That includes your precious monkey girl."

"Jayden seems capable. Can't she handle it? Or will she fail again?" asked Stormy C, who had emerged from behind Grant's chair with grace and poise.

"I was getting to that," Charlotte said. "We do not have a lot of Neon Knights stationed in this town and we'll need to make more."

Stella looked at Charlotte and gestured at herself. "You mean me?"

"Yes, dear. You and Danny will be trained by Jayden and B. Bop. I'll even let Helena tag along, she can serve as water boy, or should I say soy girl."

Daddy D. shakes his head. "You really underestimate the skill of this wheeled woman."

"I'm not a warrior, but thanks," said Helen shyly.

Stella raised her hand. "I'm not so sure I'm ready to fight those monsters either."

Dan gives her a smile. "You are already did once."

B. Bop suddenly puts his hands on Stella's shoulders. "I will help awaken your true abilities, Pinky. Just as long as you refer to me as Master B."

Helen groans. "Masturbater? That's not a title you should flaunt."

Stella lightly punched him in the arm. "I'm not calling you master anything. This star has no strings!" She turned back to Charlotte "But seriously, uh I'm not sure about that commitment, I've seen some things I really didn't want to see."

"Stella, let me level with you." Charlotte smiled. "B told me all about your problem last night. You wanted to feel accepted by everyone, but the people at the party shunned you."

"It was one of the most embarrassing nights of my life, so much I had to chemically forget it."

"You didn't forget about our tango, did you?"

Stella looks at him confused.

Helen laughs. "He's lying! Why would you dance with the city's top womanizer? You're better than that."

"Am I though?" asked Stella with a grin.

Charlotte puffed out her chest again. "Dancers, even the most famous, like Dan's hack of a father are only beloved by their own people. A Neon knight is a protector of the whole nation, both North and South Aleatore, Wintersons and Summereins."

Stella's mouth pursed and her eyes opened wide. Charlotte continued speaking as her words had struck a chord.

Charlotte finished off her soy cup. "You were happy to oblige when I spoke to you at Dance of The Gods, but Stella it's really your choice if you want to be a Knight or not…"

"Why don't I remember that? You know what, it doesn't really matter. Acceptance is something I've struggled with all my life. At work, at school and I think this is my surefire shot at finally overcoming it."

"That's absolutely beautiful, Stella." Helen approaches Charlotte with a cup of soymilk. "Added a little something extra to spice things up."

"How considerate," said Charlotte, taking the cup. "I suppose you can be useful."

Stella reflected back to the people and even friends who told her that she wasn't smart and that dancing was a hopeless career unless you were absolutely flawless. They told her that she lived her life in frivolous kid's cartoons, sharing their sentimental morality. Even if that was true, Stella wanted to prove that she could succeed despite that. It was her drive to succeed and her mother's belief in her that lead her to accept Charlotte's offer. Even so, it was only coming back in fragments.

"Excellent. Daddy D. you hear that? You'll be getting your sad wannabe of a daughter back in no time." Charlotte's eyes turned to Stella and Dan. "But first I want you to do a new 'Shoot the Breeze' that covers both the Ravepire's existence and our newest additions of the Neon Knights. I want you to wake up the whole city so they can hear it. It's an emergency broadcast."

"Yes, your highness. Anything else?"

"Yes, stop trying to use this epidemic as an excuse to sell your tacky geriatric lotion."

"What? How'd you know about that?" Daddy D's face flushed and he grimaced.

"Why sweet little Helena told me, you know the girl I've been having spy on you. She overheard you bragging about your super fly ploy too. You sure you want a kiss ass and snoop in your family of freaks?"

Helen turned bright red as Daddy D. looked at her with a shocked expression on his face. The redness in her face at first seemed like embarrassment but quickly changed to anger. "It's all clear to me now why you hate me: it's all because I happen to have the attention of the one man who rejected you. You knew he was a fan of me!"

Charlotte's face, though hard to gage due to Botox, seemed to curl into a sneer. "My my, that is a bold accusation from you, my dear sweet Helena."

"You know it's true, you nasty witch!"

"Well Helena, let me dismantle your little pointed words by saying, I don't hate you."

"You don't?"

Charlotte tossed her soy cup aside. "No, I'd have to care about you to hate you. You're just D's flavor of the month and a bland one at that. Oh, pick up that up will you, dear?"

Helen stood up. She made a fist and started walking towards her.

Daddy D, grabbed her arm. "Now now, Miss Wheels, don't let her get to you. She just loves to play her pointless little hag games, why do you think I avoid her as much as possible? You're still a part of our freaky family, that is if you'll promise no more snoopin' on your fam."

Helen nods with a face full of tears.

Charlotte taps her finger against the desk. "She'll be too busy training to be a Neon Knight to be your dance floozy."

Stella began to feel sorry for Helen. She was a confused teenager who had to deal with older people who were less mature than her. As much as Stella liked Charlotte, she knew how famously petty she was with people who crossed her. It was for that reason she was happy she was on Charlotte's good side.

This had to end and Stella was going to be the one to do it. She clapped her hands.

"Okay guys, sounds like we have a lot of work to do. Helen will be too busy training to be a soy slave, so I'll take her place." Stella picks up the cup. "Oh wait! I'm training too! I can't wait for my training session! I'm gonna make you all so proud."

After staring at Charlotte with a quivering lip, Helen finally spoke. "Get your own milk, hag!" She stuck out her tongue while holding on to Daddy's arm.

"Your insults are as meaningless as you are, bronze," said Charlotte, taking a sip and smacking her lips.

Helen grins. "That drink I got you, it has etra almonds. Which you're allergic too, if I recall. Mmmm, yummy retribution!" She pats her tummy.

Electra gags and drops the cup.

Dan cracks up.

Stella takes a sip. "Oooh, I love almonds! This is fantastic, Helen."

Helen smiles warmly.

Electra, after composing herself, takes loud steps toward the girl who poisoned her. Her throat is puffed out and her skin is going into hives.

Jayden steps in before another fight breaks out. "Time to go."

"As much as I like a good cat fight, I mean soap opera," B. Bop said "I've been out of my smart water for fifteen minutes now."

Dan lowers his head. "There is no cure, is there?"

Daddy puts a hand on the boy's arm. "Not yet, but we got the slickest scientists working all around the clock to save my Molly and your life."

"Grant!" Stormy C yelled at his sleeping companion.

"Wha?" The man rubbed his eyes. "That was a nice stroll through dreamland, why'd you end it?"

"We're leaving."

Grant picks up his sheep pillow. "Oh okay. That was one of my best unconscious expeditions. I got a new idea for our next cover." He sighs. "Man, that party yesterday drained me like a Super Fly."

"Stella and Dan," Charlotte said "keep your comphones on. I'll be sure to send you your schedules for next week."

"Oh boy! Oh boy!" Stella yelled. "Dan, this is our Schedule for Awesome, we're not only going to be dancers, but super heroes!"

"Yeah. I knew that already as so should you. Stella you might need to spend more energy remembering things instead of running into them."

Stella batted her eyes and gave an innocent smile. "Ah hehe, I guess I forgot to remember."

Step 13: Boppin' with Bop

Back at the Raveopolis suite, Stella lay in her bed. She was glad to have gotten a full night sleep in her own bed, but this morning she was too lazy to swallow her waker-uppers. She tried hard to get to sleep again, but her mind continued to operate. The wind-up chimp in her head wandered to Dan and Helen. After the meeting, Dan retreated to the confines of his penthouse and stayed there for the rest of the day. It worried her that he ignored her friendly bumps via messaging.

Helen was another story. Stella peered from behind her covers to look at Helen who was over in the kitchen. She was in her pajama bottoms and a tank top. Her hair was all scraggly and her eyes squinted. She crouched over, her stomach hanging out as she fed Mr. Kitty. The pampered jeeg wasn't snarling like before, in fact, he made peace with his food and politely chewed it, before nuzzling up to his feeder. Stella had to admit it, even though the jeeg was her pet, Helen was the caretaker and she was awfully good at re-taming him.

Stella thought about the toaster tarts which Helen had stocked up especially for her and a sense of melancholy came over her. Here was this girl who did a lot for Stella but appreciate her enough. Stella was still annoyed at her, but she considered Helen's age: 18. Stella was gaga over famous people, pop stars, and the lot when she was that age and still was, knowing full well that Brenda Splenda would have to hire a small army to keep Stella at bay. Maybe it was just a moment of weakness on her roommate's part?

Helen caught Stella peering at her, and then glared.

Stella quickly hid her face.

"I'm not gonna make breakfast for you if that's what you think Stella."

"Um, no that's ok. After all, you just put the tart in the toaster, hence the clever name toaster tart."

"I don't think it's clever at all. In fact, I think it's stupid and plain."

Stella was silent, hoping to avoid Helen's warpath.

The starlet was puzzled why her pal was holding on to her sour mood. As bad as what Helen did was, Stella knew it was best not to let negativity flood her brain, so she tried to let it go. The pills were going to be a big help with that.

Unscrewing the child proof lid, she took one Plus Pill in her hand and rolled it between two fingers. B. Bop was a big pretender, but Stella couldn't help but consider his point of view on the pills. It wasn't the smartest idea to always throw away memories-that-could-be-lessons, but the idea of those bad memories coming back, well that scared Stella more. She popped it into her mouth without another thought.

Someone was saying "knock knock" outside and her attention shifted.

Stella stood up. She was in her bed clothes so she hoped it wasn't Dan.

Helen answered the door, unafraid of what the outsider thought of her disheveled appearance.

The door opened and it was B. Bop.

"I hope you know it's ten in the morning, but to me, it feels more like five." Helen muttered.

"Well, you know what they say early to bed, early to…rise."

"Go away, man ho."

"Hey now, I didn't come to see you…I wanted to ask Stella something."

Helen slammed the door in his face.

Stella ran over after slipping her shoes on. "Come on, that's not nice."

Helen walked away and went back to the jeeg and started petting him. "Look if you want to hang out with some street animal that's slimier than a sewer jeeg, that's fine by me."

"Maybe I will!"

Stella opened the door again, walked out and slammed it.

When Stella was gone, Helen spoke to the jeeg and sighed. "With the way I am, maybe I'll just become a crazy jeeg lady like my mom."

Stella greeted B. Bop with a bit of a tentative hello. "Hey, so why do you want to see me?"

"Well since you asked, I wanted to know if you'd like to watch our appearance on Shoot the Breeze with me."

"Where?"

"Back in my pad."

"Oh…well okay. I guess it's better than being in my room right now."

"Why is that?"

"Helen's mad at me and I'm still a bit mad at her."

B. Bop scoffed and put his hand forward. "Don't pay it no pretty little mind. Ugly people just like to act as ugly as they are on the outside."

Stella crossed her arms and gave B. Bop a big frown of disproval. "She's not ugly. In fact, I think she's beautiful. You know, more to hug or grab in your case."

B. Bop put up his hands to surrender. "Hey now, I was just playing."

"You better be. She's my friend."

"I was. Just trying to lighten the tension, so your frowns don't create wrinkles on that sweet face of yours."

"Well, I do want to see my first appearance on the telescreen. Let's go!"

Stella face quickly reverted back to its natural smile. She was so dampened by the incident in her room, she almost forgot the fact that Daddy D. had invited Dan, Stella, B. Bop, Jayden and Helen, much to Charlotte's dismay, to introduce themselves as the newest squad of Neon Knights.

Stella was both excited and nervous. Excited because she was seen by millions, but nervous because she was, well seen by millions. Her dyed hot pink weave was already fading, showing its roots, and in addition, B. Bop had tugged it so hard some of the tracking was damaged, making her hair look a little lopsided. Since there wasn't time to get touched up that much, she had to settle with a messy look. She hoped she played it off well in the recording.

As they began to walk to his room, B made conversation with Stella.

"So that was the wildest party I've been to since my own inauguration as a knight."

"Oh, I know," Stella responded. "You danced with Charlotte and she kissed you on stage, but not before ripping off her own leggings and giving the crowd some wobble thighs."

"Don't remind me." B. Bop laughed. "I could have taken some of your Yellow Plus medication to forget that."

"I dunno, I thought Charlotte was bold doing that. I hope I'm as awesome when I get to that age."

B. Bop's face grew stern, an unusual feeling for him, Stella thought. "Speaking of that Yellow Plus medication, well, I don't blame you if you took it after the party."

"But you said that I shouldn't take it?"

"Well, you almost died. I'm sure that's plenty traumatic."

"It really wasn't that bad. I didn't know what was going on."

"Yeah…but still, sort of pink tails, mortality is a scary thing."

126

Stella's bit her lips trying to get a read on B. Bop's motives. "That night you were anti-plus and now you're pro-plus? What gives?"

B. Bop paused to develop an answer in his head. "I thought of all the benefits of it. Medication isn't good or evil, it is a true neutrality in this world."

"Well, I kind of agree with that," Stella said. "I think I'll just use this medicine when I want to."

"Good. I like a woman who's the master of her own destiny. I was just giving friendly suggestions anyway."

The two got to B. Bop's room.

The suave man reached for his card. "So happy Charlotte broad's been paying for my stay. I love soaking up the perks of being a rich…"

"Deadbeat!" B. Bop walked in and narrowly avoided a lampshade thrown at his head.

There was a woman in his room. She was pale, but her heavy makeup gave her the appearance of a harlequin. Her hair was dyed several colors and her clothes were exposing but not as much as her diatribe against B. Bop was.

"How dare you think you could get away without paying? Do you really think you're above the rules?"

B remained cool and composed. "I did pay. That mark on your neck is a surefire sign that you will be allowed into higher orders."

The woman let out an agitated howl and scuffed her heels on the floor.

"Ease up, Serenade. I was just playin'."

Stella smirked. Her mom warned her about guys like B. Bop, saying, "Men who are only playing games are bound to lose them one day."

"Look girl." Serenade positioned her finger right at Stella. "Be sure to demand he pay you up front."

Stella turned red. "Uh…the only thing he owes me is a new weave." She lifted it part way off the side of her head, showing how it was partially torn.

"Oh, my bad. That I can cover. As can I with your costs, Serenade." B. Bop bowed. "My minds just been somewhere else."

"Yeah, in your pants."

"Sassing me won't make me produce the coins faster, Serenade."

127

B. Bop reached into his suit. It seemed to be a variant of the pinstripe suit he wore at the Penultimate Party, but this time it was tinted blue. He flipped the card at Serenade who snatched it up. "You've changed after the Dance of the Gods. That self-centered demeanor of yours, I can't stand it." The irate woman said. "Don't think you'll be hearing from me again."

"You'll miss me." B. Bop smiled.

"As if."

With the loud clops of fast walking heels, she was gone.

"So how about we take a nice dive into my pad and watch ourselves be famous." B. Bop suggested with a swing of his hands.

"Okay."

"Beautiful ladies first." He held out his hand and let Stella walk inside so she could observe his "so-called" pad.

First thing that caught her eye was a circular king-sized bed with custom designed sheets. The sheets flowed out across the bed in orange and red wavy patterns that perfectly matched up with its owner's afro.

Next to it, lay a bench and barbell set which was very obvious to Stella, the key to the banging bod B. Bop frequently showed off during the Dance of the Gods. He often said his alternative to a pinstripe jacket was no shirt at all. If you looked like B. Bop or Dan, then it's a-okay to show some skin.

There were some black and white glamour shots on the wall of skinny androgynous women with shaved heads and no cleavage.

The dresser across from the bed and weights was piled high with beauty products. He might have had more than Stella and Helen combined. There was a teeth-whitening kit; a huge mess of colognes, many with the labels torn off, a curling iron, a bunch of conditioners and some lotions.

"Take it all in, my pink princess. You've just witnessed what a real man's bachelor pad is like."

"It kind of smells in here.," Stella said, holding her nose.

"Ah the raw smell of man juice. It manhandles your senses until you'll ready to submit to it."

"I think my stomach might submit in a few seconds."

"You'll get used to it. Here, take a seat on my bed and I'll boot up the telescreen. Our moment is upon us."

Stella sat on the bed, it was very fluffy and comfy and she bounced on it. She was so nervous that her hands jittered, which may have been a side-effect from the medicine too.

The screen came on and Daddy D. stood beaming with pride.

"Greetings, all you ravers and ravettes. I'm broadcasting early this morning with a special warning. So I gotta apologize to you on the down low, the information I received on the Superfly was a sour lie. Okay, serious talk. It was fraudulent news and your Daddy knows his kids are able to handle the truth. The real thing causing the rainbow burn is much scarier."

B. Bop laughed. "I like how he isn't even admitting that he's the one who lied. That's politics for you."

A digital graphic of a body appeared next to Daddy D. It was a snarling Crane with fangs flashing rainbow. "These harbingers of the night have been given the name Ravepires. They are a parasitic humanoid creature that feeds on that groovy Electromotion inside you. They are known for their undyed silver hair, neon-colored fangs and tacky fashion sense," he said while pointing at the green suit covered in purple diamonds.

Stella taps her chin. "Does losing rave energy harm your fashion sense? I should warn Dan."

Daddy D. darkens the set. "They only appear in rave lights. Worst of all they can only be seen by those with high EM counts in their blood. Though don't freak out, because those are the ones that these tacky monsters prey upon. So don't go walking alone at night, if you know what's good in the hood. Consider this royal decree, the will of D."

B. Bop rubbed his chin and elbowed Stella. "All of Daddy D's outdated phrases never cease to amuse me."

"He could write a Daddy dictionary if he really wanted to."

"Now for some good news," Daddy D. added an effect where there were several figures, but they were blurred out behind him.

"This town's got some new heroes who are ready to protect the town from the Ravepire's evil lameness. They're the newest additions to the Neon Knights and this new squad I call the Army of Four." A hip-hop drum beat started playing and Daddy D. started moving his hands up and down. He began to rap out some lyrics that sounded made up on the spot. "The first guy, you know quite well. His electromagnetic dance moves will make your heart swell."

Dan Dorphin's silhouette came forward. "Yo, I'm Dan and I'm the man, when you mess with me... shit will hit the fan." Dan's voice stumbled when he read the second part of the line. "Shit will hit the fan? I can't believe I just said tha...." Dan's voice was cut off.

Daddy D. smiled. "The next lady has hair of pink locks. With her boundless energy, she'll rock your socks."

Stella came forward. Her faded pink weave hung over her jean jacket. She winked and opened her mouth in happy grin. "They call me Stella, if you're evil doing, I'll send you to hell-a."

B. Bop started laughing and holding himself. "You got the best lyrics."

"Well, I didn't write them, but boy I look grungy."

"You look, hella fine."

"At least you used the word properly."

Daddy continued to talk. "This next man's got flames of passion. Ladies his love is never out of fashion." He snaps his finger.

"B. Bop's the name, with fro of raging fire, Ravepires who cross me will end up in a funeral pyre."

B. Bop's mouth hung open.

Stella entered a fit of giggling.

B. Bop took a chug of beer. "Hey, come on. It sounded a lot better when I was in the studio."

The drum beat got quicker and quicker until it entered techno patterns. "The last lady got an electro staff, with it she'll have the last laugh."

Jayden came forward, her face was somber and her eyes gazed at the camera like she was in a trance. She just sat there until Daddy D's off-screen voice cut in "Er… Jayden you're on."

"My name is Jayden and I'm mad raving. You're sour, you cower, in fear of my unibrow of steel. There's two kinds of Ravepires in this world, dead and gonna be. I'll rip you apart, do you hear me, I'll slaughter every last one of you. Your souls are damned…I'll…"

After that bizarre and unconventional attempt at a speed rap, the recording cut off and went back to Daddy D. who now stood with the four Neon Knights, plus Helen who stuck her round face up behind them. "So now you've witnessed the dawn of the new heroes and not only are they mean, they can bust a rhyme. They were just featured on the latest Techno Hippie groove, Ravepires Demise which you can now buy if you place an order to my site with your comphones. And about Daddy D.'s Superfly lotion. It is known to give you smooth silky skin and cover bites from all insect kin, just not Ravepires, ya dig?"

"You know Stella, I make music too." B. Bop grinned at her.

"Do you? Like the kind of rock and techno Daddy D. makes?"

"Nah, I'm a pop sorta guy."

"Oh, so you're in a boy band."

"Ha! No. I'm in a man band. A one-man band. Just me and my guitar."

"Now you have nothing to fear, the Neon Knights are here." They all lined up and Daddy D. had forced them all to smile, which made Dan and Jayden especially noticeably uncomfortable.

Stella leaned closer to the screen, looking at Dan.

One of his back teeth was rainbow and fanglike. Stella put her hands to her chest. It all came to her at once, she knew why Dan was being so reclusive: he really was becoming a Ravepire.

Stella looked around and then something caught her eye. It was the box of Megaflash Teeth Whitener, "For the best chompers in the game." She knew she could take it to Dan and help him with his little fang problem.

"Hey B. Bop, I gotta go but can I ask you, something?"

"What's up, buttercup?"

Stella held up the box. "Can I borrow this?"

B. Bop paused, closed his eyes and then with a bright smile, he nodded.

"Oh course, when people ask you where you got those diamond white teeth that flash like the stars in the night sky you can say, B. Bop sent you."

Stella smiled. "Thanks B, you really aren't a bad guy or a man ho, despite what Helen said."

"That girl speaks nonsense. Like fire and ice, I'm cool and hot simultaneously."

"That you are." Stella stood up to go.

B. Bop shot Stella an intimidating look. "By the way, you don't think Dorphin looked a bit odd, did you? He's very pale even for a boy of his breed."

Stella shook her head as she backed away. "No. He seemed fine to me."

Stella kept backing up until she bumped into the dresser, causing everything to fall off it onto her lap. Bottles of cologne spilled open.

Stella let out a scream and the door to B. Bop's apartment flew open.

Helen ran in. "Stella. What are you doing? Did he lay a hand on you?"

"What?" B. Bop shouted, "I didn't do any such thing, you're crazy." He started groaning oddly, causing Stella to stare up at him.

Helen looked at the bottles on the floor and let out a scream before grabbing Stella and running out.

Stella looked around disoriented.

"Do you realize what could would have happened?"

"Wha...what?" Stella's eye started blinking and she shook her head, slowly returning to the clear headedness of reality.

"The sleaze had Mone-Cologne."

Stella's eyes widened. "What is that?"

"It's this highly illegal cologne you can only get from obscure mail orders. It heightens hormones of anyone who sprays it."

"Helen, he didn't use any of it...but still, thank you for saving me."

Helen rolled her eyes before looking away from Stella and crossing her arms. "Do me a favor and never hang out with him again. Something bad could have happened. I'd never want that. Please, promise me."

"Promise." Stella looked at the box in her hands. "Oh, I gotta see Dan."

Helen's face of concern shifted into panic. "Not while you're oozing man hormones. You know Dan loves playing ball with his team."

"It's really important Helen, his life depends on it."

Helen covered her face. "And it's not something you can explain? I'm always out the loop."

"Well, I'll explain another time."

Helen sighs. "Just go."

"Thank you." Stella raced off to the nearest stairwell. "You are doing me a world of favors."

Stella was shaken up by the whole Be Bop fiasco. She had to hurry and find Dan before somebody discovered his rainbow-colored secret.

Step 14: Zero-Gridlocked

As Stella began to sprint up the stairwell, she became lost in thought. Helen really cared for her and she hoped this rift between them would mend immediately. The peppy girl let out a smile. She came to rescue Stella despite the current tension between them. Stella wondered how she was going to properly thank her.

Her mind then wandered over to B. Bop. Did he know about Dan's state of transformation? She knew he was very shrewd and perceptive and probably could have discerned Dan's fang from the Telescreen. Why did he have Mone Cologne? She knew he hadn't used any, but even having that bottle is very suspicious. That smooth talking tango pro was definitely up to something underhanded.

Stella reached the top of the stair-case. Her breath drew fast, but she had no time to catch it.

She had to see Dan!

The speedy teen made a mad scramble across the doorless hallway to Dan's door. She started pounding and thumping it with her balled up fists.

"Dan! Let me in, please. I want to help you. It's important!"

No response. Stella frantically slammed against the door hoping to break it open.

"Dan. You're very important to me and I can make it so no one will find out."

The door opened and Dan grabbed Stella by the collar of her shirt, pulling her in with tremendous force.

"Whoa, who knew you were that strong."

"Keep your mouth shut. This could not only be the end of my career, but the end of me."

Dan led her down the hallway toward his penthouse. He looked back and forth before looking her dead in the eyes with his own bloodshot ones. "How did you know? How the hell did you know?!" He shook Stella by the shoulders.

"Dan…Dan, stop shaking me. I just had a whole incident with B. Bop, so I'm already on edge."

"What did he do? If he laid a hand on you, I'd thread his whole afro through a needle."

"Whoa, where's this coming from? I've never heard you talk so…abrasive before." Stella blushes and turns away.

Dan looked down at the ground. "It's not me, look around."

Stella took his whole room in. There were empty bottles of the electrolyte-loaded smart drink Fizz-XL was all over the place. They were stacked on the bed and on the floor. There were even a bunch that lined the Jacuzzi, probably enough to bathe in."

"I need energy, Stella. If I don't get it, I get scary."

"I can see that. This place looks like it belongs to a soda-pop-head."

"There's no time for joking. You take those pills, so I didn't think you'd judge me. I need to do something…I—"

Stella ran and fetched him another large tube of the beverage he craved. With a snarl, he grabbed it and held the bottle top down above his head, guzzling the whole thing in a matter of seconds.

When he stopped gulping, the bottle of several liters was drained and Dan had a placid look on his face. "I guess we're both junkies now. Maybe we should go to addicts anonymous together!"

"Ah, that feels better…for now."

"You know, you could have just grabbed that yourself. I don't want to be an enabler."

"Stella, you don't understand. I can't think straight when I don't have my juices."

"Well, let's keep one handy just in case you freak out again. Now listen up, I need to talk to you."

Dan looked at the gaudy box Stella was waving around in her hand. "What's that?"

"Something that will help you, but I want to talk out on the balcony."

"What? Why not here?"

"Hey you said we could before, remember?" Stella smiled at Dan. "I want to admire the penthouse view."

"You just have to make this difficult, don't you?" Dan sighed and led Stella to the window next to the bed that doubled as a door to the outside of the penthouse. Stella referred to it as the gateway to the sky.

She could feel the chill of the higher elevation and a sudden need to catch her breath. Once she did, she smiled wide like she was overcome by a sugar rush.

"Wow. This is soooo amazing! Do you ever come out here?" Stella took in the air with a deep breath and let the wind flow through her hair.

"No."

Stella ignored his response and continued to look at the buildings. They all were tall towers, but the one she was in towered over them all! The altitude was taking her breath away. She could hear the internal beat that rose from the streets and tapped her foot alone. When she looked up, she saw the floating skyway levitating over the city.

The long metal tube-like spaceship was powered by electromagnetism. This massive ship was where the Zero-G riders flew their modified sky-cruisers at high speeds. Due to the highly reactive nature of the vehicles going not only 200mph, but being in ultra-tight proximity, the people of the City Electric turned to this as their sport of choice next to dancing.

Stella didn't care at all about stupid aerodynamic cars. She'd much rather stay with her feet planted on the ground where they wouldn't explode.

"I see the great cans of fire are racing today. Boring. I'd much rather rave." Stella snorted. "Right, Dan? Dan?"

Dan stood silent and still, staring up at the sky.

"You ever feel like you're doing the wrong thing in your life?"

"What do you mean?"

"Like you're born for one thing, gifted even, but something else catches your eye and you want to do it, even if you're less good at it."

"Oh, I know exactly what you're talking about. I used to want to be a celebrity, but now I just wanna be a star!"

Dan's hand collided so fast into his face that Stella cringed. "Stella be serious for once, is there anything that you haven't done that you wanted to do?"

Stella's eyes looked at Dan earnestly as she recounted an available memory from her past. "You know, I really wanted to be a scientist because this world's biology fascinates me, but I just couldn't understand anything involved with it."

"See, you know. Now think about me, I'm a relatively good dancer, aren't I?"

"Relatively? You're the winner of a nationwide competition."

"In the span of this world, I am very little and in the span of this universe, I'm microscopic. Who can compete with the real giants?" He looks up at the planetoids in the night sky.

"Still, I think you're pretty darn great! You barely beat me though." Stella muttered under her breath.

"What I'm saying though is that I'm damned to be a dancer." Dan pointed at the sky "But sometimes I'd rather be up there."

"If you want to be a Zero G Rider and claim those air trophies, then go ahead. You're rich. You can probably afford one of those fancy cruisers and just go zoom!"

"It's not that easy, especially with my father."

He didn't have to say anymore. Stella understood.

To Dorian Dorphin, dancing was every facet of a man's life. He wanted his son to continue his legacy with the highest levels of electromotion in his blood stream.

"When my Dad adopted me, I had just left the caverns high in the mountains behind Gris."

"The caves? You mean where the Wintermonks live?"

"Yes, that was my tribe."

I move in a little closer and send warm energy his way. "I'd like to know about them. The tabloids aren't interested in frugal living, but I really admire those who only have one pair of shoes."

Dan smiles and looks out at the city. "It's like you said, the Wintermonks were the most frugal of all Wintersons. While Wintersons that inhabited cities like Gris lived in buildings and wore robes, the Wintermonks lived in caverns and wore scant clothes. They believed their body is an offering to the great goddess of dance herself."

"I certainly like to show off my bod." Stella winks.

Dan chuckles. "Yes, I remember the jacuzzi." His face becomes lax. "Their lineage was always straight and kept close within their ranks. When they were…caught in that volcanic eruption…I couldn't see a future for myself." He looks at me with watery eyes. "Stella…I was the only survivor."

"Yeah, but then you got adopted, moving from cramped caverns to large rooms in the city!" Stella turns him around to show him his awesome pad. "You were adopted by Dorian and given a new lease on life."

"I suppose that's one way of looking at it. After Madame Mimi destroyed his ability to continue his bloodline, he had to get the next best thing." Dan frowned. "That is why I have to be a dancer and also, why whenever the Zero-Grid flies over the city, I remain inside."

Stella took a moment and pondered about Dan's predicament and the second a thought entered her head, her face lit up.

"Why are you smiling like that?" Dan asked.

"Oh, you'll see." Stella responded, taking his hand and leading him back inside.

"All I know is when you smile like that it can't be good."

In the penthouse's living room, Stella sat Dan down on the hovering couch in front of his enormous telescreen. She grabbed a remote on the couch and waved it in front of Dan. "Do you have a second one of these?"

Dan reached inside the cabinet and pulled out an identical remote.

Stella brought up a menu on the screen and flicked through it. She highlighted an option that said Virtual Game Zone and it brought up a selection of video games both past and present. She shuffled through them.

There was Super Guidio Funtime 128, a platform game Stella had played inside and out as a kid. There was also M.E.P. Monsters, a simulator and RPG that allowed the player to own and battle with a numerous amount of Morality Exploratory Pets. Stella had used it frequently in place of having a real jeeg. There was Collector Man, a man obsessed with collecting every knick knack in the kingdom of Aristillus. Stella flicked past these and other classic games of her youth. "Oh wow, they finally have Down2Earth. Only took them fifteen years to rerelease it."

"Come on, Stella. I have no time for games." Dan flicked his fingers across the elbow of the couch.

"This one you do."

She scrolled onto a retro game with blocky looking graphics. There were two floating 3D rectangles with numbers on them. Upon closer inspection, they were something Dan loved greatly.

"Are those cruisers?" Dan exclaimed; eyes widened.

"Yep, just look at the title."

"Gridlock Racers 128, originally for the Funtime System."

Dan was silent, but an open-mouthed look of awe said to Stella what words couldn't.

"I just need to put in Charlotte's card number and then we can play this baby."

Dan still silent, but with his knees trembling in anticipation, watched as Stella put the digits in. Once they were entered, heroic 128-bit music filled the room on Dan's surround sound and the intro began.

The blocky racers from the pictures zoomed by on the sky grid. The cockpits of the racers showed two distinct characters. An action-figure like space man with a chiseled smiling jaw, large muscles and a helmet that covered half his face mugged for the camera.

The racer that he battled with for the lead, in contrast was a thin insectoid like woman with pincers sprouting from the sides of her face, piercing red eyes and a swelling cranium. A black crown was placed upon her head. The character was rendered as menacing as a character in 128-bit fashion could be with gashing teeth and dilated eyes that betrayed some psychosis.

"Who are they?" Dan asked.

"Well, that's Commander Funtime. A Summerein hero who races not for money but to protect the world from the Edwardian menace."

Stella waited until his challenger appeared on the screen before she continued talking.

"And that's Dictator Divabolical, the leader of the Edwardians. She's entered the grid to win the prize money. It will allow her to purchase weapons to destroy Aleatore."

"Could these characters be any more stereotypical?" Dan asked, with an eye roll.

"Hey, it was back in the day. Like eight-hundred years ago. Things were a lot simpler back then."

Stella quickly selected a two-player mode to take Dan's mind off of the flat characterization. "Turn your remote sideways. They also function as controllers."

Dan complied.

On the screen they found themselves on the gridlock, Dan as the evil Edwardian Dictator and Stella as the legendary Commander. There were several rectangular racers ahead of them ready to ignite their engines before the starting line.

"Wait, why are we in the back?" Dan asked.

"That's how all racing games start."

"Sorry, I haven't played any."

Stella remembered, being a Winterson, even a rich one, often meant that your home was absent of all electronics. They used books for all of their entertainment needs.

There was a tower next to the race track with a light attached to it. It flickered from red to green and the race was on. Stella and the other racers sped off, but Dan remained in the same position.

"Why can't I move?"

"Are you pushing 1?"

"No, I'm not." Dan jammed his fingers down as fast as he could on the 1 button.

Dan began to accelerate and drive straight. "Hah, wow! I'm doing it! Look Stella, I'm making it move!"

His car continued to move straight…even when it entered a turn. The car went sailing off the half pipe that was designed to block the edge. With a glorious somersault, it plummeted out of the sky to its demise.

Dan's screen turned black and blood-red lettering appeared with a stamping sound. The word read "Retire."

"What the…?"

"Oops Dan, looks like you're dead."

"What, I don't get to retry?" Dan looked disappointed and upset.

"Nah, it's one of those hardcore retro games where you only get one shot."

"That's stupid as hell."

"Hey. at least you saved the planet by killing Divabolical. You're a hero."

"I guess I am." Dan laughed. His face had brightened into a smile that radiated with genuine joy. Stella couldn't remember him ever smiling like this.

139

Dan looked at her with soft eyes and showed his teeth in a grin. His canines were slightly rainbow-colored on both sides.

"Oh," Stella said. "I forgot."

"I got this whitening kit for your teeth. So they're less rainbow-y, you know."

"Damn, I never expected you to be so practical, yet here we are."

"You sure do love your complinsults don't you, buddy?"

Dan's face, though pale, reddened a bit. "Oh, um my bad. I need to work on that."

He pulled out a tiny hand mirror to gaze at his teeth. "They're getting really bad, aren't they?" He looked at the Mega Flash box and then at Stella.

"Yeah, but once you use that, nobody will suspect a thing. You'll look super...fly." Stella giggled. "And about the game, I'll be your mentor. By the weeks end, you'll be making those squares eat your pixelated dust!"

Without warning Dan took a lunge and hugged Stella. She was completely taken aback by this, but she didn't feel uncomfortable or scared. Dan was her friend.

"Thank you," Dan said, his voice a bit wavy and almost sobbing. "I never was a normal person and now I might lose myself entirely. I'm...scared."

Stella put her arms around his body and embraced him. "I've always seen you as my fellow dancer and rival. After all, we competed on the same dance floor, didn't we? You can absolutely consider me a friend! I'll protect from creepers fanged and fro'd."

"I never saw us becoming so close. You were just a clueless girl in my eyes. A stepping-stone to help me rise to the top."

"Well, I'm not gonna just lie down! Next competition, you better bring you're A-game!"

"Will I...last that long?"

"Um, duh, of course you will. You have your mom's lucky pendant right?"

"I told you I don't believe in luck."

"Well, I do." I grab his pendant. "Whoa, you won't believe the powerful luck energy emitting from this ancient relic!"

"Lately I've been feeling cursed." Dan turns away. "I need to tell you something. I was scared to say it out loud…but just listen, okay?"

Stella holds his hands and nods.

"Ever since I was bitten, I've been hearing quiet voices. They speak in some other language and torment me while I sleep." Dan paused and then whispered. "But whenever I'm with you, they go away. What do you think that means?"

"I really don't know anything about being a Ravepire. I don't think anyone knows. Unless you count Victor Crane."

Dan shivered and moved a little closer to Stella. "It scares me so much how uncertain my future has become."

"It's uncertain for everyone. The only thing that's certain is the ups and downs on the rollercoaster we all ride."

"Not that silly show again," Dan said.

"Hey, the simple morals in cartoons are often better than those from a haughty philosopher."

Dan let out a sigh but then smiled. "Don't ever change, Stella." He gave his dear friend a light kiss on the lips before pulling away from her and returning to where he sat on the couch.

Stella sat there stunned. Her head was spinning from what just happened.

Her phone started going off, but she was caught up in thoughts about Dan.

"Uh, your phone is. Oh wait, mine is too." Dan said.

He checked it. He was keen enough to learn how to use his comphone in the time he moved to the city. "Hmm, our first training session is today. We're supposed to meet on the Bi-Rise. Wherever that is."

Dan snatched the box of Megaflash. "Well, I just gotta put this on and I'll be ready to go."

He stared at Stella, still on the couch, and yelled at her. "You know you can stop sitting there smiling! We have to go. Oh, and maybe you should take a shower too, you reek of cologne."

Stella couldn't hear him. All she heard were bells and the crackle of her heart.

141

Step 15: The Warrior of the Sound Mind

Stella, after a warm shower and snapping out of her "The #1 dancer in all of Aleatore just kissed me and he has washboard abs" pseudo-coma, discovered where and what the bi-rise was. She didn't even feel the need to forget about the Bebop incident. Dan's kiss had washed away the slime entirely.

Charlotte had them come to the bi-rise for training. The bi-rise was an above ground railway line, situated on high rising platforms. Where once a dual monorail—a monorail that could split and go in two separate directions— traveled, was now a boardwalk. Plants grew in the hollowed-out train tracks as young hipsters mellowed out on the benches, drinking their neon-green mocha swirl lattes and smoking. Vegan moms jogged by, training for their fundraising triathlon. They were the early risers, people who would wake up early in the evening just to have the place to themselves before the tourists arrived.

It was an unusual place for the Neon Knight training to be held.

Stella expected a top-secret underground facility that only Charlotte, Jayden and Daddy D. knew about, but Stella enjoyed this even more.

Being up so high was a calming experience for her.

Stella enjoyed the view it gave her of the purpling skyline and metal buildings. The Bi-rise was a place she could see her and Helen or even Dan hanging out at…if they didn't have a battle to prepare for.

After walking from the suites to the uptown area, charging up a flight of steps leading to the Bi-rise itself and taking it all in, Dan and Stella saw Jayden, Charlotte and Helen waiting for them at the top.

Jayden stood with her staff, unwavering to anyone or anything around her, but her sickly white face and large eye bags made her look positively undead to Stella.

Charlotte mentioned to the pink-haired girl that Jayden frequently gave up sleep in favor of her duty.

Stella was devoted to her craft too, but she also made a personal effort to not let it interfere with her cuteness.

Charlotte, was Jayden's opposite. She reclined in an extended chair, allowing her body—exposed except for a tight, very tight two-piece bikini to lavish in the purple sunshine. She was out to capitalize on this bright shiny day and keep her skin the shade of platinum it was.

Accompanying her was her disloyal soy girl. To make up for what will only be mentioned as the 'almond incident', Helen was told to lather sun cream all over the body of her ruthless employer. The girl normally appreciated the female form, but had to refrain from gagging as Charlotte's demeaning nature disgusted her.

The foxy woman didn't give a damn; she savored mocking and belittling the girl who was up to her head in jeeg debt.

Charlotte smiled as her deep voice filled the air. "Ah Daniel and Stella, my most promising protégés. It's time for your first lesson. Helen, you'll never lose weight if you don't work those arms more. Really rub me good!"

Helen sighs and continues.

Stella heads to confront Charlotte but is stopped by the scary tall lady.

"Being on time." Jayden said.

"What, what do you mean?" Stella asked.

"It is 5:01. A minute of training is lost forever."

"Jayden, Jayden love. They're still young. Let them have their youthful adventures and romantic follies."

"Understood, Charlotte."

Stella let out a strained sigh. Jayden was ultra-intimidating; the shaky monotone and her furrowed unibrow being the things that made her most uneasy. She was just glad that for whatever reason, Jayden submitted to her other mom.

"I'm ready." Dan said, standing firm. "My father has been training me for the day I can become a Neon Knight like him."

"Just like the cute guy on my left, I'm ready too," Stella said, her eyes shifting in that direction.

Dan looked at Stella and narrowed his eyes. "Uh, what?"

"Sorry, I shouldn't objectify you like that, hehe." Stella giggled.

A suave voice came from behind. "Break it up, lovebirds."

B. Bop strode up the stairs of the Bi-rise. This time, he was only wearing a grey tank-top. It revealed his muscular arms and refined pecs that caused his shirt to bulge. His right arm was tattooed up and down with a twisting and turning red dragon that for some odd reason sported a similar flaming afro and sunglasses. If it weren't for the odd incident earlier, Stella would have admitted that, aside from the dragon's questionable choice of attire, the combination of muscles and the tattoos that adorned his physique made him look smoking hot.

"Today, Jayden and I will teach you how to turn your dance moves into fighting moves."

"The essence of Neon Knight battle tactics," Jayden said with a nod.

Stella decided to be snide with him. "Hey Jayden, B. Bop's late. Aren't you gonna scold him?"

"No."

B. Bop glared at Stella, his bushy eyebrows making him look extra annoyed.

"Uh okay. Let's uh get to that lesson then," Stella put her fist in the air. "Oh, and Charlotte, ease up on Hellen please. Almonds are healthy for you anyway."

Charlotte gagged and growled at Helen.

"Stella please, stop helping," said the sad girl, rubbing the lotion on Charlotte's feet.

"Okay, sorry. I'll make it up to you, 'kay? How about we bathe together. I can soap you down 'till you're sparkling like a star!"

Helen blushes deeply and focuses on the job at hand while her mouth trembles.

Jayden closed her eyes. "Every dancer has Electromotion in their blood. You're either born with it." She positioned to Dan. "Or you accumulate it," she pointed at Stella. "When you have large amounts of it, you are a conduit of great energy, some say it can even make one enlightened."

"How it interacts with a Winterson's blood and a Summerein's blood is different." B. Bop said, eyeing Dan. "For instance, yo stud, I want you to strike a Frost Dance."

B. Bop tossed Dan a pale blue glowstick, known better as an iceglo.

Dan caught it and slid his feet together. He closed his eyes and brought his hands up over his head, shaking them back in forth in a zig-zagging motion as he lowered them. He then slid his feet apart and moved his clenched hands around each other. His iceglo began to emit a cold grey aura.

Stella could feel the chill from where she stood, despite how hot he looked.

"Good job, my prince," B. Bop said. "Seems like you're like you've done this before, Mr. Winner."

144

Dan nodded his head. "I am well-versed. I already know the abilities of it, how I can freeze the seconds and minutes around me so I can move at high speeds."

Stella felt she had seen this miraculous ability in action when Dan saved her from certain death by chandelier. She was out of it, but she felt him whisk her away at an ultra-fast speed. Now she knew why.

Stella shivered with a familiar chill, but was also awed. The dancing-before-doing-a-magic-spell reminded her of one of her favorite aspects of the Fruitsaders. When the heroes would combine their powers and become one, they were known as fruit smoothies. Different juicy warriors could combine to form different flavored smoothies and each had a new flavor and a new power.

"As you know," B. Bop told his protégés. "You can only do basic magic with GLOs but the better you get, the further you can get your personal magic to meld with your dance moves, creating dance magic combinations."

B. Bop imitated Daddy D's disco movement with his fingers. "Daddy D. is the master of the cold snap."

He fluffed his hair so his fro glowed in the sun. "I'm the premier talent in using the Greatest Balls of Fire."

"And," B. Bop smirked, "Jayden's is the robot."

"Oh, like the dance move?" Stella said.

"No. She acts like one."

Strangely enough, Jayden did not retaliate or glare. She gazed at B. Bop for one second, before speaking to Stella. "Your turn. You are Summerein. Your electromotion must be utilized with passion."

B. Bop smirked. "It's time to teach the newbie her powers."

Stella rolled her eyes.

B. Bop moved in close, getting a glare from Helen. "Being part Summerein, I know all about the fire burning bright within your heart and your eyes. That burning passion you have will be converted into power. That is why I want you to concentrate and do a passionate dance."

He stuck his hand out, causing Stella to flinch in repulsion. "Might I suggest the...tango."

"No! Never again!" Stella yelled, causing everyone to take notice.

B. Bop even recoiled from the way she screamed at him.

Dan looks at B. Bop suspiciously.

145

B. Bop strolled behind Stella and whispered softly so the others wouldn't hear. "Hey. I'm aware why you needed that teeth whitener. It wasn't for your pearly whites. Dan is going through a little transformation."

Stella gasped, but quickly regained her composure. "You better not tell anyone."

"Don't worry little girl, I won't. Just as long as you promise not to tell Charlotte about what happened in my room. It's a fair trade."

Stella knew she had to keep cool. She dealt with a boyfriend like him before and knew the only way to win was to remain calm and look for a way to escape his game. She didn't even know why he was playing a game because nothing happened in at his pad.

"My lips and legs are sealed." Stella glares at him.

She grabbed his hand and pulled him in front of her, digging her nails into his skin.

"Hey, ow!"

"What, I thought you said I had to tango?" She sneered in his face.

"Okay, sheesh. Just keep those claws away from me, jeegy."

"I'm not doing the Bebop tango this time though, that's for sure."

"Are you sure about that? That's what awakened your powers last time." B. Bop said.

Stella took a step back. "What? It did?"

"You were flying high, almost touching the ceiling of CharLuv. You flew in the Dance of the Gods too."

Stella paused for a second to remember. She remembered almost hitting that chandelier, but not reaching absurd heights in the Dance of the Gods.

"If you want, we'll do a simpler tango. I just want to show everyone what you're capable of." B. Bop and Stella began a simple step and twirl routine while holding hands.

"I want you to focus as we do this, baby girl."

Stella closed her eyes and visualized the motions in her head.

B. Bop's hand was cold and clammy, but she just concentrated on the deepest recesses of her soul. She remembered her mother and suddenly her hand lit up with an orange aura.

146

B. Bop pulled his hands away immediately. "Whoa, this is awesome."

He pulled some fireglos out of his jean back pocket and tossed them to Stella.

"Hey I remember these." Stella jumped and found herself gaining altitude at an alarming rate. The fireglos sizzled. They felt different from the ones she had at the dance, they were burning and stung her hands. The long ropelike fires emerged from them and she began to swing them around into the air, brandishing them like whips. They left trails of fire wherever they went and made crimson flames rain out of the sky.

They seemed like great weapons to use as long as she concentrated on not getting singed by them. She landed on her feet and looked around. There were mini fires everywhere on the Bi-rise. Some plants had caught ablaze, as did B. Bop's hair. Some of the onlookers were shrieking at the sight of these sudden brushfires.

"Hey not the hair! My perfectly permed fro."

Helen drops a jug of soy milk over B. Bop's hair. "Don't try anything with my Stella, bub. You better not have been threatening her when you whispering," she said with dagger-like eyes.

B. Bop's fro fire ended with his giant perm soaked so hard it looked like someone took a piece of road kill left out in the rain and dropped it on his head. He spit some plant milk out that had landed in his mouth and gave an annoyed pout through the dripping hair hanging over his face.

Jayden handed Dan some more iceglos and gave him a simple nod.

Dan dropped his mega sized bottle of FizzXL and took his stance. He closed his eyes and the caps popped off his iceglos. They emitted laser like projections of ice and he began firing them at the small fires. Every time they hit a fire, the ice would melt, liquefying and dousing the target. Dan's aim was virtually perfect and nailed every single one.

Stella smiled. Dan was so talented he got all the fires…but one. She turned around and noticed her rear end was ablaze.

"Oh damn, oh damn!" She yelled as she ran around the Bi-rise. "This girl is on fire! Dan, help me out."

"Stella, hold still! I can't cast when you're running so fast."

Stella tried to stop, but it was too late. She ran into him full force, knocking both of them over.

Dan casted the ice beam above Stella's rear and it melted, causing both Dan and Stella to get drenched.

147

"Whoa, you just saved my ass again…literally this time?"

"You need to work on controlling your powers."

"You're my hero." Stella leaned in and started kissing him on the cheek. "And my booty's hero too!"

"Ugh…can you stop with the kisses?" Dan demanded.

"Don't be like that, Danny." She gives him a playful peck on the lips.

Everyone around him stopped what they were doing and took notice.

Dan seemed physically uncomfortable; his face changed to a shade of green. "Look Stella. It took me a long time and a heartbreak to know this, but…"

Stella put her fingers over his lips. "Please don't say it…I'm too annoying…is that it?" Her eyes watered up.

He pulls her hand aside. "I'm not and I never will be…into girls."

"Wha? You kissed me!" Stella punched his perfect chest.

Helen let out an audible squeak.

Charlotte tapped her on the knee. "Helena, get me a triple soylent blue shake, this is getting spicy."

Helen dashed off to the nearest kiosk along the bi-rise.

Jayden watched with a look of annoyance.

"See Jayden, this is why we let them have their romantic follies. You get more drama than the theatrical presentation of Divita I starred in." Charlotte's face stretched into a smile.

"Correct as always. Still, they need training."

Dan looked both horrified and astounded at Stella's answer. "Wait, I kissed you when?"

Stella with an antagonized glare, shoved Dan off of her. "Do you take me for a fool? In your room, you kissed me."

"Why don't I remember that?"

"Dan, are you serious?"

"Hmm, all I remember is the wonderful time I had with you playing that game. I went to hug you and things got all hazy."

148

"Do you remember anything else?" B. Bop asked, a smirk creeping upon his face.

"Yeah, Stella smelled funny, like she was wearing some cheap pick-up artists cologne."

"Maybe she was," B. Bop's grin got even wider. "And maybe that cologne has something to do with what happened."

B. Bop walked over to Dan and hung his arm over Dan's shoulder, unprovoked.

Dan was too bothered to even notice. "For my main man, Dorphin, Detective Bop is on the case."

Stella felt a sharp pain of anger twist inside her stomach. She knew exactly what B. Bop was doing. If she tried to stop it, Dan would be more than uncomfortable, his life would be in jeopardy.

"I don't get it. What does cologne have to do with altering your..."

"Dan, Mr. Stud. You need to be made aware of the wonders and horrors developed in the pharmaceutical world of the City Electric."

Dan was still and quiet, his hesitation caused by the ignorance of his Winterson roots.

"It's called Mone-Cologne, playa. It allows the wearer to attract anyone who comes in close, regardless of gender or sexuality."

Dan began to choke on his words every time his sentences came out. "You're saying that...? Stella did...? I can't believe this."

"You're being absurd! Ugh, you're always a drama queen. Maybe she just smelled like it because she was in his pad," said Helen, glaring at B. Bop.

"Keep spitting poison, you viper. I don't need that nasty cream to get the ladies to come," said B Bop with a confident grin.

"Well, what do you have to say for yourself Stella?" B. Bop's sickly grin turned towards Stella.

Stella knew she had to be passionate to fight and now she had the ultimate reason. B. Bop had set her up and she had no idea why. At this moment she felt like her whole body would envelop itself in flames; from her fists to her eye sockets, everything would emit large fireballs to consume the fro wearing freak and burn his perm to a crisp. But she had to keep it inside. She could feel the fire turning and twisting, tickling and pounding inside her, but she took her hand and slammed her stomach. She coughed and bits of ash and smoke came

149

out her mouth and her nose. She dusted it off and spoke to Dan in short quick murmurs.

"I'm…sorry…Dan. I didn't know what it did."

Helen sighs. "Next time listen to my warning please."

"I can't believe like everyone else, you had to deceive me. My friendship wasn't enough for you." Dan finally stood up. "Charlotte, Jayden, I'm sorry but I don't know if I can continue training today."

Helen blocked his path. "You got to kiss Stella and now you're running away! You know her. She wouldn't do that." Her eyes went wide. "Creep Bop was blackmailing her! That's what's going on!"

B. Bop turned away. "I ain't standing for this shit. Your jealousy is truly hideous. Now that this case is closed I gotta re-frizz my fro. Later skaters." He shuffled down the steps of the bi-rise, out of harm's way of Stella. Her glare suggesting his death may be imminent.

Dan started to walk away too, snatching his FizzXL can. Tiny tears formed in the corner of his eyes and he turned away to conceal them from the prying eyes of the world. Before he did though, Jayden began to mutter in a sour tone that cut through the dry air of midday and gestured in the direction of Dan and Stella.

"You. You devote your lives to meaningless drama. Don't you realize what's at stake?"

Jayden's voice though quiet was becoming progressively loud and trembling. Her staff began to emit lights flashing violently enough to plague anyone who looked directly at it with a seizure.

"You know nothing of the Neon Knights. Do you even know the founder?"

"Harry Fairson." Dan interjected.

Jayden nods. "Fairson was the legendary Summerein soldier in all the history books, the savior of Kouyate. What principle were they founded upon?"

"Uh…"

Jayden's face moved closer and closer to Dan, not realizing how violated he already felt. "Prioritizing protecting those in a grave situation."

The warrior woman gritted her teeth and flashed her bright orange eyes, her lip wavered and she displayed emotion for only the second time Stella had been around her.

"Fairson did so for Kouyate. I do so for the people. These citizens are facing matters of life and death. If you don't prioritize them, I'll do so alone."

With that Jayden sprinted and jumped off the bi-rise.

"Geez…" Stella said, flustered by the incident with Dan and from seeing Jayden leap off a bridge as high as five stories "won't that hurt her?"

"My sweet Jayden. Her bodies survived worse wear and tear. Plus, she's in control of how she falls." Charlotte removed her heart shaped sunglasses that either a teenage girl or someone trying to look young would wear and gazed at Stella and Dan with her large hazel eyes. "But seriously, as great as that display of drama was, next time, you two need to leave your troubles at the door. You really upset my baby."

"I'm sorry," Stella said "I didn't mean to upset anyone."

Dan responded softly. "I don't like having my emotions played with." He walked off.

Helen tried to sneak out, but Charlotte's gaze froze her like a gorgon's.

Stella knew she had to tell Dan the truth as soon as she got back to Raveopolis. He would listen, right? Stella knew Dan hated conflict because it tired him out. Right now, Stella realized it wasn't best to dwell on this subject; she couldn't just expose Dan's issue in front of Charlotte.

"Jayden…" Stella spoke "she's not just loyal. That was…she took it personally, didn't she?"

"Well with good reason" Charlotte responded. "I know she looks like she could gracefully remove your head without a hint of remorse for either you or the furniture she'd be staining, but inside she's a scared little girl."

Curiosity reflected in Stella's eyes. She had no idea who this Jayden character was, but hearing more would distract her from thinking about other more negative things. "Charlotte, I am one of the biggest tabloid readers, but even I don't know Jayden. How long have you known her?"

"You won't find her in any of those horrid magazines and that's the way it should be."

"Then who is she?"

"She goes under many names, the one most people know her as the Legendary Masked Rave Stepper."

Stella's eyes lit up upon command. "The one who mastered the Rave step machine when it was in its heyday?"

151

"Yep, the one and only."

"I used to watch those competitions on the telescreen when I was little."

"You were a fan of LMR? Did you know you're looking at her manager?" Charlotte said as she raised a sharp finger nail to her lips.

Stella dramatically put her hand above her head. "I'm in the presence of a real legend, I feel faint."

"Now now Stella, settle down. We don't need any more accidents to happen today."

"Can you please tell us about Jayden?"

"You're lucky that I'm releasing a memoir as of late, one that is going to delve into every beautiful and gory detail of my life. Of course, it will still be left open ended enough for readers to feel an aura of mystery."

"Ooh, yay." Stella clapped and danced in place. "What's it called?"

"Lightning Never Strikes Twice but I Do: A memoir of the most electrifying business maven in Aleatore."

Charlotte pulled up her comphone and flicked through it until she found what she was looking for. Upon seeing it, she began to beam in the sunshine. "Listen 'round kiddies, I'm going to tell you an abridged selection from my wonderful, fabulous, soon-to-be-novella life. Helen, bring back Dan. Tie him up if you have to. Where is that worthless girl?"

Dan comes out from behind a pillar.

"I wanted to hear about Jayden," Dan said, looking up at the sky.

"She's one of many colorful characters I've encountered in my lifetime."

Helen returned, holding a large neon blue shake with a plastic dome lid and a bendy straw sticking through the middle. "I brought you your shake, Ms. Charlotte."

"No need for that. This backstory is really going to shake things up enough for everyone."

Stella takes the shake, but it gets swiped by Charlotte.

"Now, where was I?" Charlotte takes a seat and beckons the others to do the same.

Step 16: An Abridged Excerpt from Charlotte's Autobiography

Rags to riches. My story is nothing new when summarized in a few words, but it's all in the details where originality thrives. Granted, the locale I grew up in wasn't wholly original either. It was a place known as Lethal Town, a district in the City Electric that no longer exists because my wealth restored it to its finest state. But back when I was impoverished, so was my hometown. It was the only place in TCE that wasn't brightened with rave lights that flickered in the night. Those who maintained the buildings couldn't afford to flash them, so aside from a few dim street lights, the place was often just people and their shadows.

I was a dirty dancer, and before you get any naughty ideas, that was what they called the backup dancers in Thin Brady's entourage. Yes, back then Thin Brady lived on the streets of Lethal Town with me and several other dancers and rappers. We weren't always so well received because he was a Winterson who completely shirked his roots, and embraced Summerein electronics and music. His flagrant display of defiance toward his culture and his multi-ethnic backup dancers often lead to hecklings from the audience. We didn't take them seriously because they were mostly criminals and drug addicts. Eventually, when they saw what kind of show we could put on, they shut their yaps and lost themselves in Brady's lyricism and our big hips.

I was walking home one night from a particularly fiery gig. You know all that ass-shaking over lusty cheers had really worked me up. I know I'm a luscious vixen now but back then, I didn't have to dress all conservative. My hair was loose, unrestrained and flowing, spilling out unto my bare shoulders, I wore a low-cut, crop top, decorated with costume diamonds and tight, elastic pants that hugged my thighs and bum quite tightly. I had my breadwinners right on display too, loud, proud and right below my collar bone. As I strutted the streets, lamplight and all, I came upon a boy who was rather cute.

He sat alone on the steps to an abandoned building, his brunette hair scruffy and in his face. His eyes were wide and dark and his clothes were robe like. He had a look of worry on his face so I thought I would cheer him up.

"Hey," I said, my voice deep and sultry. "Are you new to this town?"

I slowly put my right heels forward and put them on the steps, two below where he was sitting. "Mind if this lady steps into your life?"

The boy recoiled in shock; his eyes widened as they skimmed over me. "Just take me in and…"

I stopped because I found a sharp object positioned right at my throat. If I had moved just an inch, well then the world would have lost a true treasure.

My eyes shifted towards my attacker. It was a woman with harsh unblinking orange eyes, she was wearing imperial-type armor. She would later be known as Jayden but right now, she possessed her foreign name.

"Away from this woman, Amyg, she may not be intelligent, but she might be dangerous."

"Dangerous? Me?"

"You might be in possession of a thousand diseases."

I wasn't the type to normally feel embarrassment, but this woman knew where to hit where it hurt. It was almost like she had no verbal tact.

"Well, that's a pretty bold accusation. Though, I can say it's false…" I sneered and moved my head a little and felt the pointy stick move too.

I also wasn't above putting a little emotion into a tight situation. There's nothing a cornered jeeg likes to do more than bring out those big jeegy eyes.

"Please, I don't want to die," I said, laying it on nice and thick for this woman, swooning and swaying and drawing out my words. "I have such a long and promising life ahead of me."

"The only thing promising about your life is what your organs will do for the black market after you're punished for seducing a teenage boy."

I closed my eyes in resignation. I didn't know how I was going to get out of this one. I was doomed until the voice of angel spoke in defense of me.

"Come on, Cere, stop it. She didn't do anything to me. We don't need to cause a scene here."

Cere, the woman, looked at Amyg, who I surmised was the boy's name, and softened her brow just a tiny bit to indicate that there was a change in her emotion. The pointed staff, as fast as it was at my throat was retracted. Her detached emotional responses and machine-gun reflexes, told me she wasn't raised in Aleatore. Their appearances further roused my suspicions because they were from the opposite side of the globe, the scattered islands of Neuronia.

I showed my gratitude with a sweet tone of voice, one that I was capable of in my youth. "Thank you, my sweet boy. Amyg, right?"

He nodded, refusing to make eye contact with me. It was the way the inexperienced did in front of attractive members of the opposite sex. "Yes."

"I can understand why she'd want to protect you. But I assure you, I'm as harmless as a jeeg, but twice as playful."

"Okay." Was Cere's response.

154

"You don't like to talk much do you, but I get it, brevity is the wit of soul or whatever."

"We must be going now, Amyg."

"Well, it was nice meeting you…foxy lady," Amyg said, sneaking a mischievous smirk.

"Ha-ha you scamp, you just called me foxy; I'm so flattered." With a wave of my hand, I saw them off. "Bye, sexy boy!"

Three men had emerged from the subway steps. They were concealed, or should I say encased, in armor with only a slit for their eyes. Their masks possessed a large cannon-like appendage that rose from their head. I was surprised they could walk without their head being pulled forward and smacking on the ground. The one in the middle pointed at Amyg.

"Prince Amygdala, by order of the Knights of the Poisoned Mind, we place you under arrest."

"How'd they find us so fast?" asked Amyg.

"We were out in the open." Cere assumed a battle stance in front of Amyg. Her staff was drawn forward to protect him.

"Don't think a single guardian will protect you. You should give yourself up right now."

Cere didn't even respond. She just lunged forward, her staff swinging on its own with the command from her mind. The staff extended, nailing the soldier to the left with a sickening clang.

"Ready men? Fire." The cannons on their heads began to shoot a bright pink plasma.

I had heard all about the weaponry of Neuronians. These guys were capable of some incredible feats with their minds. Their thinkers could harvest energy and transmute it into a deadly weapon. The mind cannons would most likely deal severe brain damage if they hit her.

Fortunately, Cere's stepping was impeccable. She moved with a dancer's precision. Every blast of pink matter never came within a hair of her.

Sensing I was in danger, along with the boy, I grabbed Amyg and ran toward some trash cans that had yet to be collected by the street management. As we made our escape, several blasts nearly hit us and if I wasn't so light on my feet, well we might have both been left drooling tomatoes from their blasts.

As I observed from the metallic sheen of the adjacent cans, I began to notice something with twinkle toes. Cere could predict where every blast was

155

headed and with grace, she subverted it. She would make a damn fine dancer and even though I might not live much longer, I was seeing K signs so hard that Amyg had to shake me back to reality. It was a good thing too, because a soldier stood right over use.

"I'm going to have to wipe the prince's mind along with this broad."

Cere looked over and I could sense weakness from her. It was in that moment she was blasted square in the chest with pink matter.

"Noooooo!" Amyg screamed.

Cere stumbled over, her head looking at the ground and her hair drooped over her face. Then, as if broken, her head snapped forward in utter hostility.

"You can't break what is already fragmented." She snarled with a stare that condemned her foes to death.

Cere's gaze seemed to have a power of its own because the two soldiers who stood over her suddenly held their heads, and their mind cannons exploded. The soldiers fell forward onto the ground, both of them muttering in disturbed incomprehensible gibberish.

The third who stood over us aimed his cannon in an attempt to still have leverage, despite his fallen comrades. He didn't know he was messing with a girl who grew up in a district where self-defense classes were a necessity.

"Prince, are you going to come with me or not? Just surrender or I'll…"

"White Lightning."

"Ahhhhhhh."

I had raised my hand in a flamboyant twirling manner and electricity had generated from the telepole and struck him. His armor consumed the electricity. The energy crackled around the armor until it burst. When it did, his heavy cannon head fell to the ground along with his charred body.

"That's what you get for cosplaying as a lightning rod." I smiled at my handiwork. Last time I did it, it was a drunk man who wanted me to comply with some twisted fantasy he had. But doing it for someone else felt even better.

Cere appeared over us. She was so fast, it was like she was warping.

"Amyg, did they damage your body in anyway?"

"No. She protected me." Amyg pointed right at me.

Cere looked at me the same way she did at those guards and I assumed everyone else too. But once again there was a little twitch of her face that indicated she was relieved. "Thank you."

156

"Can you tell me who were those guys we just had a huge brawl with?"

"No."

"I'm sorry that happened," Amyg said, "but we really have to go."

"Where are you guys going?"

"I don't know. We usually have to drift around town to avoid them." The boy responded.

My natural sympathy got the best of me. I did want to help the boy. Plus, I will admit, Amyg would turn into a fine specimen of man in the next few years to come and I had a good feeling of that even back then.

"The name's Electricia. I know a place you can stay that they'll never think to look."

"Whoa, really? You hear that Cere?" Amyg jumped up and down.

Cere narrowed her eyes. "Where is it?"

"The Holy Halfway House."

Hard to believe in this modern day and age but yes, this was what CharLuv once was. Back in the day, it was a derelict church that Thin Brady's crew once squatted at. We had our share of flying rats and sewer jeegs. The paint chipped off the statue of Ravenous, the stained glass was shattered in several places and I lived next to a dancer and rapper who used to test out their bed springs every night. But to a girl who lived a hard life, it was a suitable home and made my eventual rise to glory all the sweeter.

Cere didn't respond, but Amyg was enthusiastic enough that I took them to my home.

Walking in through the antechamber, I could tell from the lack of chaos that most of the crew was still out. While I liked to get out of gigs fast, most of my coworkers enjoyed throwing themselves a little after party in the bars, whether the barkeeps liked it or not. The joint was usually pretty dark, so I led the way with my two Neuronian neighbors keeping up with my brisk pace.

"Don't worry, in my room we have a couch with one of those pull-out beds. Only problem is it pulls out slower than some of my boyfriends."

Cere glared at me and pulled Amyg aside. "Please, don't stand so close to her Amyg."

"Hey, I was only joking. Oof."

I bumped into one of my many partners in crime walking through these halls. It was a woman much taller than me, and I already was quite tall for a lady.

"I told you already, Thin Brady said no more tenants."

The high pithed voice belonged to Gallant, a woman who was the bouncer for Thin Brady and later for me. This was the defining moment the allegiance shifted.

"Thin Brady says a lot of things, but he doesn't mean them. That's called playing."

"How do I know you're not playing?" Like Cere, Gallant didn't talk much, but you could tell there was a war going on behind those brown eyes.

I stood on the tips of my toes to reach a head above my body and planted a big kiss right on Gallants face.

"Even if it is a lie, that kiss wasn't," I said with a foxy purr.

It took a moment for her to shift her whole attitude. Her cheeks shone red against her light Winterson exterior like blood in a snowfall. "Electricia, I didn't know this about you."

"There's a lot you don't know about me. By the way, dinner, you and I, 10 P.M. tomorrow, Greasy Tiger, dress nice."

You may be asking was I lying to her about myself? Well, as a true business maven, I'm willing to try everything at least once. Gotta explore your options if you want to climb that slippery social ladder.

I took Cere and Amyg to my room where they could take refuge.

You could tell a couple things about me from my room. Though I lived on a budget, I still worked my hardest at making this a nice living space. My best efforts went into making those light piss-tinted walls as white as possible. My clothes were all jammed tightly into my wardrobe so they weren't thrown all over the place. I had hung some pictures I picked up at the flea market a few blocks down to cover up the scuffs and skids that coated the walls. They were all of blackness speckled with shiny white dots, and water-colored bodies of gas; outer space. When guys described me and said I was an "out of this world" kind of woman, they meant that in multiple ways. One, I was fantastic and two, there's nothing I'd want more than to travel beyond the sky. One planetoid wasn't enough for me, I wanted more in my life.

My humble abode was a sanctuary. Amyg jumped on my old couch like a child. The hovering mechanism was busted so the couch was slanted.

"How do I get it to turn into a bed?" He asked with giddy curiosity.

"You press the button on the arm."

Amyg did just that and a groaning sound came from the couch. It slowly began to stretch out, almost at the couch's own expense. The arms folded into the couch. All the while this happened, young Amyg crossed his arms behind his head and relaxed. His body let out a deep breath and I could tell he felt safe.

I looked over at Cere. A tiny smile, and by which I mean, her lip twitched upwards, came across her face. Her arms were all stiff and rigid, but I could tell her mind was at ease.

"Well, somebody likes his new home."

"Where do I sleep?" Cere asked.

"That's a one-person bed. Looks like you'll have to sleep with me."

For those keeping score at home, this is probably the first time I ever got emotion out of her.

"I am NOT sleeping with you. I don't, nor do I ever sleep with women."

I could tell as I had some intuition in this field, that for a woman as uptight as her, this wasn't because she hated the Gallants of the world. She was raised to be a prude and had fear of her own feelings. It was nice to know she had some…fear, that is.

"Aww Cere, I don't bite. I save that for the men."

Cere planted herself on the floor, among the dirt marks and scraggy brown carpet on the floor. She lounged a bit, spreading herself out. "This will be my bed."

"Suit yourself."

"Hey, wow," Amyg said. "Electricia, you didn't tell me you had a telescreen."

"Oh, that thing? It's so tiny and insignificant."

"In Neuronia, we don't have telescreens. We have to use our imagination for our entertainment."

"That sounds painfully dull."

Amyg sighed. "It is."

He tapped at the screen across the bed which was a bit scratched up. It switched on and a man appeared on it. He had hair that used to be fuller and a demeanor that was once cool. He wore dark shades that covered the most remarkable eyes I'd ever seen.

"Yeah, me and the boys, we caught our manager embezzling us. I was like, hey man, that's not cool. And we threw his ass out of there. I know music's a pretty raw deal, but sometimes you gotta bite that nasty bullet and deal anyway. We're currently in the process of looking for a new manager. I sure hope Mr/Miss whoever is more of a charmer than the last guy."

This was interrupted by Amyg, whose timing was not so hot.

"Electricia, why are you so red?"

I ignored him. This man was Darius, someone who today everyone knows better as Daddy D. and there was once a time…admittedly, where my heart would thump over him rather than my bowels. I could get hot guys aplenty, but he was different, he had power. He was one of the most influential celebrities in all of the City Electric. He was surely destined to become King Mayor. That was the dominance I craved in a man. Let's just be honest, I'm a power-hungry bitch and the only man I could truly respect would be one who could rule the world and take me to the stars. But I had dreams of reaching his level on my own terms and merits, and when he said he was looking for a manager, an idea began to sprout in my head. I started working on it in my head rather than getting lost in his eyes.

While Amyg was all curled up tight in his floating bed and Cere somehow managed to ignore the itchiness of the carpet long enough to sleep, I wracked my brain. How could someone of street urchin status ever be considered good enough to manage a successful band? I really wanted to stop dancing and become a manager myself, but I couldn't just go there now. The wish-granting fairy takes on odd shapes sometimes, and in this case, it was a young boy.

Amyg, whispered softly, "Electricia, come outside with me."

I followed him. Cere, must have been exhausted from fighting. She barely budged as we snuck through my room.

Outside, Amyg spoke with the honesty I had known from him since our first meeting.

"I just wanted to fill you in. I know you don't know much about my sister and I so listen."

"All ears, baby cakes."

"I'm a royal from the Kingdom of the Sound Mind."

"Ah, so that's why they called you prince."

"Yes, and Cere, she's my guardian."

"Is she actually related to you?"

"No, she was a knight trained in the ways of the Mind's Eye warrior and selected to be my guard." Amyg's eyes softened like a dream. "But she's been with me so long; she's my sister."

Now like I said, I was naturally curious so I asked him something I probably shouldn't. "Is there…something the matter with her?"

Amyg looked a bit hurt, but I feel like he realized I had a valid question. "She was raised to be an elite at a very young age. The elite go through difficult mental training."

"Oh. I see. What kind? I hope they aren't too rough on the poor thing."

"Training that's meant to suppress the part of your brain that holds all your feelings. Everything she feels within her, she was taught to hold it back no matter what happens…even if it caused her pain."

Amyg looked down at the ground. "I sometimes blame myself because she was raised to be my guardian."

"It's not your fault, Amyg." I patted him on the shoulder.

I never liked being motherly, but the time was appropriate.

"It's not your fault she's like that. People decided that for you, didn't they?"

"It's just, I owe her so much. She saves me almost every day."

"From what? Those men?"

"Cere likes to keep it a secret, but there's a bounty on us since my uncle took over our kingdom."

"Let me guess, your uncle is an evil guy who wanted the throne for his own gain?" I smiled, knowing my literary clichés quite well.

"Well, sort of. You're acting like this happens all the time."

"Uncles are the most nefarious of relatives. Especially when they're royalty."

"I guess, but Uncle Pons sort of had a reason."

"Ah, so he's a more complex character than I thought."

"My uncle was a commander in the Mind Games."

"The Mind Games?"

"A horrible civil war where people who wanted to free their minds battled against those who wanted to restrain them."

"And your uncle was the one who…?"

"He was someone who was under my father, who wanted to keep everyone's minds from going places they shouldn't."

"That's stupid. All minds and bodies should be free!" I smiled at the kid and nudged him. "Free to get as dirty as they desire!"

"I don't think your mind is dirty. You just have ways of being friendly that scare people."

"Aw, thanks hun."

"But my uncle, he and his men were tortured by free thinkers and forced to see things that couldn't be unseen in their minds. After the war, it made them go crazy."

"So, he just snapped and staged a coup?"

"Yes, he blamed my father for what happened to him. He formed the Knights of the Poisoned Mind, attacked our capital and locked our family up. Only Cere and I escaped."

I had to lean back against the dirty wall of the hallway we stood in. "Kid, that's crazy. If it wasn't for that attack, I'd think you were just trying to take me in with a sob story you came up with while high on shrooms."

Amyg gasped and with a drowned look on his face spoke. "But you believe me, don't you?"

"Hun, I may look young, but I've seen enough of this world to know when someone's telling the truth. I know those aren't just debt collectors after you and Cere."

"Oh, thank you, Electricia." Amyg hugged me tight.

I ruffled his hair and whispered to him. "Hey, let go of me before your sister sees."

He did just that and I told him the solution that had been percolating in my head. This is where the future business maven came forth and shined. I knew a way they and I could both have what we truly wanted.

"I know exactly how to fix things."

"How?"

"You take on a new identity, now that you're here in this new world."

"That's what I've been saying to Cere, but she won't listen."

"Look kid, you can't run forever. Cere, she's gifted and in fights, she knows exactly where to step and I have an idea of how she can make a living."

I told Amyg my plan in full detail.

There was a recent innovation in the entertainment industry. It was said to have revolutionized competitive dancing. People today just know it as a fad and a sign of the times, but back then it was hot. It was called the Rave Stepper and for those who aren't so knowledgeable on antiques it was a machine with two platforms, one red, one blue, and several dark panels in between. Two competitors would stand on both of these platforms and take turns stepping in patterns. They would enter basic dancing steps and the person opposing them would have to repeat it faster and add one more move each time. This tapestry of dance moves would create a game of volley and continued until the first slip up.

These matches could get pretty heated and intense and while they started as small competitions, they quickly began filling up small rings, and soon to be stadiums. The fast-paced sports nature of Rave Stepping drew crowds almost as wide as the Dance of the Gods.

One thing I knew was as many skilled dancers as there were, no one could match the mathematic precision in a game of memory and reflexes as a Mind's Eye Elite warrior. And I just had one imported, lucky me. If Cere agreed, I would not only be the manager I always dreamed of being, but the amount of K that would be mine—ours would be enormous.

Cere needed me because she wasn't much of a talker. Contrary to the common belief, I was just as important. I just hoped and prayed to Ravenous that she'd say yes. I'm just glad I had a little mediator for me in this situation.

Amyg, fresh faced and captivated by our dancing culture grew more and more excited when I gave him promises that his sister would see stardom. He was quite a lively sort too and wanted to dance just as much. He started dancing in the hallway, a really cheesy dance. He started shaking his hips and crossing his legs in steps. He must have seen this dance from a rare tourist in his country and I admired his enthusiasm.

"Whoa, chill out there, Electric Slide Clyde."

"Sorry, I got so happy by the thought that we'd be dancers."

"Oh, I have just one question."

"What is it?"

"If Cere gets famous, the knights might find her. Won't they?"

"I know. That's why as a competitor she'll wear a mask. She'll be the first masked rave stepper. People eat up that masked gimmick because it adds an aura of mystery."

"Whoa, that's so cool."

"Yep." I patted him on the head. "Now let's sleep on it and we'll break it to her in the morning."

"Thanks, Charlie, you're the best."

Despite all the raised endorphins from the thought of a promising future, both Amyg and I got to sleep. When morning and our opportunity dawned, we were met with predictable skepticism, but luckily, I had my cute mediator.

"Please Cere, you know what we can do when we get the money."

"Yes, and that's the only reason I'd even consider it."

"Oh, so you are interested?" I asked with a sultry look.

Cere answered me, frank as always. "We will do it as long as we get enough money to make our expedition to the mountain caverns of Gris."

"Why…why would you want to go there?"

"The Wintermonks welcome those who are skilled dancers. We will be in a place where Pons can't find us."

Being the master of negotiation that I was, I agreed. "Cere, I swear that will be my first priority."

Cere, still disbelieving, glared at me. "And with some of the other money, we'll need to purchase new weapons to protect us."

"Okay sure, but don't worry. I'm sure your enemies will never think to look in the world of Aleatorean sports."

"I hope so."

And with those words of uncertainty, Rave Master Jayden and Electric Slide Clyde were born. And not only that, I began a slow rise from the low heels of poverty to the seven-inch stilettos of luxury.

Step 17: Gifts from the Gods

Charlotte switched off her comphone and with a broad smile, questioned the dancers.

"Well, how did you like them melons…?"

"Melons?" Stella said as wide eyed as ever. "I thought they were apples?"

"Do you like melons, Stella? I…do," said Helen shyly.

Charlotte snaps her fingers. "Apples are too small and honey; there's nothing small about my story."

"Yeah, melons are yummy." Stella grins.

Dan stood upright, his hands on his hips and a look of annoyance on his face. "I can't believe you made me sit through your self-indulgent story while I was having an existential crisis."

"Oh, get off your high horse Dorphin." Charlotte waved him away like a stray dog. "Some of us have been forced to hold in burdens that make yours seem like a stubbed toe. I mean is it really so bad you kissed a girl while intoxicated. I kissed many men and women while riding high and it didn't so much as stir a beat in my heart."

Dan shriveled away when he heard this, he knew not to argue with this big boisterous woman. Stella sensing this, tried to defuse the tension with an attention shift.

"I thought we were going to hear about you managing the masked rave stepper and Daddy D's band as well as your ensuing romance and breakup with Daddy D. and…"

Charlotte wagged her finger and interrupted Stella "Easy there, child. If you want to know all my secrets, just buy my book when it's released. This was just the appetizer. Gotta pay up if you want me to fill you up."

"Fine." Stella pouted.

"Hey, all is not fair in the game of capitalism. It's jeeg eat jeeg."

"Can you at least tell me one thing, Charlotte? Can you tell me what happened to Electric Slide Clyde?"

Charlotte paused to contemplate. When she opened her mouth to speak, she was interrupted.

"Charlotte, I would like to answer her question." Jayden appeared out of nowhere, her orange eyes blazing.

Stella flinched. "Whoa, where did you come from?"

"By the edge of the bi-rise. Train well and you will be able to mask your presence."

"Figures," Dan said "she probably wanted to hear our reactions."

"I desire to hear the story. Charlotte hasn't permitted me to read the draft."

"Charlotte turned to Jayden so she could see her face nice and clear. "Here I thought you didn't care; you were there after all. You lived quite a bit of my story."

"Yes," Jayden said, her tone calm and self-assured. "But I did not experience from your perspective."

Charlotte's face stretched itself into a smile. "So curious. This is why I like you, dear. But you know I'd never say anything cutting about my favorite associate."

"I know," Jayden said, her voice soft and sighing like that of a young girl.

Helen who had been silent up until then, launched into a tirade. "Oh yeah, Charlotte. What if Pons finds your autobiography and knows what Jayden and Clyde have been doing this whole time?"

"History lesson time: Sweet Helena." Charlotte said, extending her claw like nails as if to ensnare Helen within her grip. "Pons is history. When Daddy D. was under my control, I had him throw a diplomatic party that not only made Pons an ally of this country, but he also stopped searching for them."

Helen's face shaded like a burnt strawberry. "I didn't know that."

"The angry don't know anything because they don't think. Sorry Helena, I'll need to dock your pay for failing my history class and for serving me sass when I didn't ask for sassafras."

"Please Charlotte, don't be too hard on her," Stella said. "Can we just hear about Clyde?"

"I'd much rather watch what's going on now. Wonder what Helen will do next." Dan muttered while Helen pleaded.

Charlotte smirked from her recliner. "I'm quite inclined to agree with young Danny here."

Jayden shakes her head. "No, Charlotte. They needed to hear this. Clyde was kidnapped."

Charlotte's currents of malice towards Helen seemed to subsides. She folded her arms, hiding her neatly manicured claws.

"He was?" Stella asked. "By who?"

"The Ravepires."

"Way back then?"

"During my time as a rave stepper. My fame brought me unwanted attention. A jealous rival wasn't fond of my unknown origins."

Charlotte's eyes narrowed. "A young man, her self-proclaimed rival, loathed Jayden. The whole mystery of her drove him to less than legal methods."

"He could not penetrate the defense of my identity. He recruited an augmented Neuronian to probe me."

"Is that bad?" asked Stella.

Jayden harrowed her voice. "They are Mind Readers. They are gifted Neuronians who've been modified with tech that enhances their powers. They can see through objects as well as people."

"That sounds impossible," said Hellen with a nervous look.

"It isn't. They read neurons in the brain to predict their opponent's attacks."

"And pry into their thoughts. You really don't want to be two timing with these fellows," Charlotte added.

"With the Augmented's help, my rival uncovered who I was. Soldiers of Pons came to kill me and take away Clyde."

"So, what happened?" Stella asked.

"I was cornered. I killed all the attackers."

"I managed to cover up the incident by labeling the whole thing as a terrorist attack," said Charlotte.

Jayden's face was stark, but gave way to a bit more emotion. "After our enemies were slain…Clyde ran off in fear of me. I never heard from him again."

"That's not fair! Didn't he realize you were just protecting him?"

"My fame put us in danger. I was foolish. I won't ever see him again. It's for the best."

"Just because he ran off doesn't mean you won't see him again," said Stella.

Charlotte stood up and put her arm around Jayden.

Stella knew what happened was a glimpse of something rare: the cold, calculating Charlotte almost never seemed to be a very motherly person except around Jayden and strangely enough, her.

"I tracked him on a train heading out of the City Electric."

Jayden's lip quivers. "That train was attacked by Ravepires. Not a single soul was saved."

Dan's face goes pale. "Then Stella and I were…"

"Quite lucky indeed," said Chalotte.

"Do you see now?" Charlotte said, patting her assistant's head. "She feels it's all her fault."

Jayden grasped her hand in a fist. "These Ravepires have singled him out but why? All those I've conquered know nothing. They're mindless wretches."

"Mindless?" asked Dan with a pale face.

"Well, maybe they're just shy," said Stella with an awkward smile.

Jayden gives her a dark look.

"Hey, relax!" Stella. with a sudden burst of energy, bounced back "Don't you worry about a thing. You can count on me. I'm going to help you find out where Clyde is!"

This was the second time Stella felt invested in taking down Ravepires. Jayden was the most devoted sibling she'd ever encountered. Her family bond touched Stella. They weren't even true blood relatives, but her endless searching and fighting showed something Stella had never seen from her own siblings. Now despite her uncertainties, she wanted to discover a way to help Dan and to also rescue Clyde.

Jayden's eyes shimmered a little. "Rescue. An often-neglected duty of the Neon Knights. I have vowed to return all those who were taken. Your assistance is appreciated."

Charlotte laughed and rubbed Stella's head. "So, you finally understand your duty as a knight. You're a bit of a late riser, but I'll cut you some slack, Stella."

"I'm sorry if I've been lazy. I've got a lot on my plate." Stella looked to Dan and Helen, both who she had been experiencing some turbulence with lately.

Dan avoided her eye sight, but Helen returned her gaze and even managed a shy smile that made the inside of Stella's chest feel soft.

Stella pumped the air. "But now I really feel I can devote myself to it."

"Good, because I have no need for employees who slack, even if it's someone with promise," Charlotte responded with a chuckle.

"Help! Someone help catch my Princess Fluffy Pants."

Everyone turned their attention to the scene behind Stella. Stella quickly spun to witness a chubby yuppie woman in her forties, jog by as she followed a swiftly scurrying jeeg that indeed had puffy pink pants crammed over her blue body.

Stella could see that the jeeg was heading straight for the edge of the platform where she would fall to her death.

Stella sprinted into action, shoving her way past others who jogged alongside the walkway. She dove for the jeeg, sliding and tumbling across the wood, squeaking in pain as she brushed up against the girl's body.

The jeeg was startled and made a mad dash under the railing, blocking the edge, but Stella grabbed her just in time.

Unfortunately for Stella, her body continued to move and slipped headfirst under the railing, allowing her a terrifying view of the cruisers and asphalt that she'd soon kiss. But as she fell, she could feel a bit of a delay in the drop. She looked around, her body hung and she could taste the air, it was dry and stale.

Why wasn't she moving? Could it be that time was frozen? Immediately her mind jumped to Dan. "I can't believe Dan's saving me again."

Then she saw it was a womanly figure that had grabbed onto her.

"Helen!" Stella exclaimed.

The bubble popped and the three plummeted, hitting the sidewalk but only getting a little scraped up.

Stella was held tightly with Helen's arms wrapped around her back. "Helen, what did you do? I had no idea you had time powers."

"There's a lot you don't know about me," Helen said with a small smile.

Stella realized that her arms were around Helen's waist. "Squishy." She giggles and then releases her savior.

Helen's cheeks turned pink, contrasting greatly with the harsh red they were when Charlotte confronted her earlier. "You can squeeze me anytime, Stella. I mean…if you wanna."

"Helen…" Stella opened her mouth into a wide smile.

It was good to have her friend back. She embraced Helen really hard, nuzzling her with tons of affection. "I'm so happy you like me again."

"You're lucky you're so hard to stay mad at." Helen pokes Stella's tummy. "And you're squishy too."

They went back to the top of the Bi-rise.

Dan rolls his eyes. "I think there's something wrong with your princess."

Something wasn't right with the jeeg. It was making the kind of buzzing sounds that happens when you hold two baby monitors together.

"Uh, lady," Stella said, putting her hand behind her. "I think your jeeg is broken."

The yuppie woman with her fluffy overcoat and grey brown hair stood with Jayden and Charlotte.

Jayden was hiding her face, containing something that almost looked like laughter while Charlotte looked a bit more severe and uncomfortable.

"Congratulations," Jayden said. "You passed the test."

"Test? There was a test?" The two girls asked in unison.

Jayden nods. "That is not a jeeg. It is an artificially test dummy. The intent was to jumpstart your potential. More specifically, it was Charlotte's idea to awaken Helen."

"We'd never put a real cuddly wuddly jeeg in danger, just our dancers. The former would attract annoying protesters." Charlotte added.

"Gee, thanks," Helen said. "I didn't know the queen cougar paid any attention to me."

"Oooh, I love the sound of that. And of course I pay attention. It's important to know the weaknesses of those close to you," said Charlotte with a chuckle.

"Still...it did work. I...really passed," said Helen shyly.

Jayden without warning or prompting let out a loud shriek and stomped her legs. This display of emotion shocked everyone around them. Even Charlotte who had known the weathered and stolid woman for the longest time. "EEEEEEEEE! Helen, you did soooo good! I'm soooo proud of you!"

The flustered dancer looked around her, almost believing there was some alternate Helen this rabid Neuronian was screaming at.

Jayden instantly calms herself and stands tall. "Helen should accompany B. Bop and me."

"What are you saying?" Helen asked with wide eyes, taking a step back.

Jayden bows her head. "Helen, I beseech you to fight alongside me. Become a Neon Knight."

"Well..." Helen fidgeted, she closed her eyes and tried to shut out the world around her. Would being a knight solve her problems in debt? Yes, most likely. Her mother would be proud. She thought about her social standing; she wouldn't be known as a runner-up anymore.

Helen's eyes opened and she observed the faces around her.

Jayden was beaming, her smile wide and she was wincing as if it pained her to hold her face in that position. Stella gave Helen a thumbs up and winked at her.

Her eyes then moved to her critics.

Dan had his arms crossed and refused to even look at her. "Screw him," she thought. But then her eyes locked with the paralyzing gaze of Charlotte.

Her tyrannical employer had a disproving stare that could sever her neck and poison the air that she breathed. But it was her deep, guttural voice that really made Helen feel pain and anxiety.

"Jayden, I forbid it. Helen isn't capable of such responsibility."

"Why not?!" Stella demanded. "It was your idea. Don't you at least trust yourself?"

Charlotte raised her eyes, though her face was static due to being botoxed. "It was Daddy D.'s idea. I just lied to Jayden to steal his credit. Plus, it would be fun seeing her plummet."

Stella covered her mouth and shrank away, leaving Jayden to finish up where she started. "Charlotte, did you not see her powers? She manipulated the flow of time and if you saw the competition, she has blazing wheels! Only one possible reason to have those conflicting powers. My pen pal is a Reinson."

"No way." Helen scoffed and blushed. "You think too much of me. That was a gravity bubble I made. And I...don't even know how I did it."

"Tell me about your father," said Jayden sternly.

"Well...I don't really know his nationality or anything. Mom doesn't like to talk about him after he woke up gay one day and got with his coworker."

"What drivel," said Charlotte, rolling her eyes.

Stella grabs onto Helen's shoulders. "Wow! I just realized something! Now I know a Reinson who isn't an asshole. I'm looking at you B. Bop."

"I already said I'm not a Reinson. We're Summer Sisters, right?" asked Helen with a blush.

Jayden shakes her head. "You cannot deny your heritage. Doing so will only cause ruin."

Charlotte continued on the offensive. "Exactly, she's too immature. I don't know if Helena is *fit* for the job, she might *weigh* you down in those long hard battles. Just dealing with her is a *ton* of stress."

Stella holds her friend close. "Well, I think she's a *ton* of fun!"

Helen spat on the ground right by Charlotte's foot. The saliva fizzled in the sun, as did the woman who congealed it. Her eyes watered a little "Charlotte, you are the most immature, childish, vindictive person I've had the displeasure of knowing. You're a...child in a grown woman's body. And your ugly Botox face is a total eyesore!"

Jayden nods and then looks away.

Charlotte's eyes lit aflame. "Well, tubby...I got a little surprise for you, you're fired."

Helen gritted her teeth. "Bitch, I quit!" She flicks off Charlotte.

Jayden stands between them. "Charlotte, you are a business woman. You mustn't allow feelings to impede rational thought. This is a purely beneficial decision for the city at large."

172

"Feelings?" Charlotte responded with a guffaw. "I don't have feelings about this. It's all merely hot air masquerading as feelings."

"Then why did you fire my pudgy pal?" Stella asked with teary eyes.

"I grew bored of Helena's little tantrums. Day in day out, there's only so much one can take...even for a child in a grown woman's body."

Stella smiles. "Acknowledgment is the first step to recovery."

"Charlotte," Jayden pleaded in an almost wining pout, "think of what Helen can do for this city?"

"Well, she does bring me tons of soy products. I suppose she's good at being an obedient pet, but she's no warrior."

"I strongly disagree."

Charlotte's eyes bulged.

"What?"

Jayden puts a hand on Helen's shoulder. "She showed great courage when she confronted you about your abuse."

"And got fired for it," said Charlotte with a sneer.

"Her position as your assistant is irrelevant. I personally induct her as a Knight. Any finalist in the Dance of the Gods is worthy to apply." She looks to Helen and gives off some warmth. "A bronze is still a noble metal."

Charlotte holds her hands to her cheeks. "Oh, how nice of you Jayden, charity for the weak."

"If refined, the power she'd yield would be an unstoppable force."

"Do you really think that?" Helen's eyes glistened.

"With all my spirit. I've seen your skill as a skater. More than that, I witnessed your empathy for your competitors. You have something I cannot access."

"You seem pretty empathetic to me," said Helen with a small blush.

"If there's anyone who can end this plague, it's you. And I shall hone your body and mind into the sharpest of blades."

Charlotte pokes Jayden with her fingernail. "This is really heartwarming, but even with your decision to recruit her, well honey, I'm in charge of the Neon Knights. Without my approval, there's nothing you can do."

Jayden lowers her head. "That is…true."

Charlotte beams and looks at Helen from the side of her eye. "Maybe I'll consider it if she begs like a good puppy."

Jayden lowers her head. "Charlotte, I have done everything for you. Please, accept her for me. I ask this as your friend. Please consider."

Charlotte recognized the power play Jayden made and understood it well. "I'll let her train with you, but if she messes up, well, its curtains for our little starlet's noble career."

Stella's face and Jayden's face brightened at the same time, but Jayden tried to mask it with her hands.

"Congratulations on your knighthood, milady. Ha-ha! We're gonna be the coolest knights ever! I'll bring the sizzle and you bring the style," Stella said patting her friend on the back.

"Wow, thanks."

"But don't think I'm gonna give up on being the best just because you're a Reinson. I'm gonna be the gold Neon Knight! My name shall echo through the ages!"

Jayden sighs. "It's not a competition."

"Not until now!" exclaimed Stella proudly.

Dan put his arms behind his head. "Can I finally go home now? I think I need to sit in my room and brood over a FizzXL. My life is Helen's hands," he mutters to himself softly.

"I'll join you for that, hun. We can toast to decisions we'll soon regret," Charlotte said.

"Sorry, I think I'd rather be alone…for a long time," Dan responded.

Stella grabs Helen's arm and nuzzles her. "Well, we're gonna train together! Dan, we're a trio! A trio of legendary knights!"

Step 18: Pen Pals' Playdate

Helen walked dejectedly along the streets of The City Electric with Stella. After the first training session, her mind had reached great highs from saving Stella and becoming a Neon Knight. Regrettably, the lows had brought that joy below the surface. Charlotte had fired her from an occupation that supported her mother and all those poor innocent jeegs. It was truly a time of great elation and dejection for Helen. Would she be able to keep up with the most elite soldiers of The City Electric? Or would she flounder like all of her foes expected her to.

Stella hopped in front of Helen's path. Her bright blue eyes were shining and she bore a cheerful smile on her dimpled face. "You look like there's a lot on your mind," she said, leaning closer to her friend.

"Oh girl, is there ever," Helen responded.

"That's why," Stella said, and pulled out her comphone "I dialed up Later-Skaters. That's the Rave-n-skate rink that's only open in the evening time. But I'm sure you know that, the star skater you are! I reserved us brave knights in training two pairs of roller ravers. That'll take your mind off all this hooplah."

Helen blushed and shook her head. "You don't need to do that for me. Just the thought is enough."

"Nonsense," Stella responded with a wink. "If I learned one thing about you as your perky pen pal, it's that you skate to leave your worries behind in the dust."

Helen put her hand to her mouth and squeaked. Perhaps Stella paid more attention to her than she realized. That was indeed her one true ticket to freedom from her burdens: lace up her skates and zoom away.

Before Helen could even answer, Stella grabbed her by the hand, pulling her into the crowd.

"Let's go before they give our skates away"—she turned to Helen and winked—"and after that I've got something special planned."

Though Helen was captivated by the something special, she was concerned as Stella laced on her skates. The skates Stella had chosen had orange and red rocket boosters on the sides.

"Stella," she said nervously "those are Fireball XL-9 skates."

Stella tilted her head in confusion. "You know me, Hels, I love to go fast."

"B-but," Helen stuttered "not even I've used those skates and I'm a semi-pro skater."

Stella grabbed Helen's hand. "Remember the Fruitsader's creed, Helen. Without the ups and downs…"

Stella waited for Helen to finish it.

Helen did it with a nervous smile. "A roller coaster would be a duller coaster." She sighed and smiled. "Alright."

She was so flustered that she couldn't disagree with Stella. Perhaps she could let go of her motherly side for this one night.

Later Skater's rink was famous for its funnel shape, allowing people to truly skate, "on the edge."

Helen had plenty of practice here, but she wasn't sure how Stella would fare. At least there would be plenty of opportunities to hold her bestie's hand.

As they watched people roll around the rink like K coins, Stella and Helen stood at the gate.

Helen cautiously slid the gate open as Stella tapped her shoes. "Now, how do you ignite these dragons?"

"Wait!" Helen screamed and grabbed Stella's hand. "Don't do that."

A loud clank sounded, followed by a sonic boom as the jets on Stella's shoes ignited.

"Oh noooooo!" Stella screamed as she zoomed forward with Helen onto the rink

Like a rocket, Stella blasted forward and began knocking over hapless skaters, wiping them out as they tumbled down the funnel to the bottom.

As they zoomed around and around, Helen's cheeks sucked inwards. "Stella, take them offfff!"

"I'm trying!" Stella screamed, but her hands struggled to reach down. Many of the skaters had already rolled into an enormous groaning pile, but Stella kept blasting around in circles.

Helen ducked and swirled around the fallen skaters with graceful pirouettes before grabbing onto Stella's hand.

"Nice going," Stella smiled at her friend. "You truly are a rave skater supreme."

176

Wait," Stella exclaimed, looking at the fallen people.

"I'll wipe myself out. That will stop us from moving."

She threw all her equilibrium backwards, but instead of falling, she blasted straight into the stratosphere with Helen in tow.

"Whooooo, we're blasting off!" Stella screamed with wide eyes as Helen held onto her for dear life.

As her feet pulled her into the sky, Stella reached towards her shoes, trying desperately to undo her laces. Her fingers untangled the laces of one shoe. It shot off from her foot, spiraling around the sky until it vanished into the stars.

Stella quickly undid the other one.

Stella and Helen had finally stopped blasting through the sky. What came next was a sudden plummet.

"No worries! I'm a gravity girl!" Stella danced as they fell towards their doom. She focused her rave energy into her feet, creating a gravity well.

The gravity only served to slow them down. A collision at their current speed would still leave them severely injured.

"We have to do this together." Helen recalled her power and how she saved Stella before. She clutched Stella's warm hand and spun with her in the air, focused deeply on protecting her. Their descent gradually lessened. It wasn't long before their feet made gentle contact with the floor of the rink.

"Whoa Helen," Stella said with a warm smile. "You saved us again."

"It was a group effort, cutie," she nudges Stella playfully.

"Cutie?" asked Stella with a light blush.

Helen goes red.

Unfortunately, the people at the bottom of the rink were furious. They were all complaining and cursing out the girl with the XL-9s.

The owner of Later-Skater stood before them. Her arms were crossed and there was a scowl on her face.

Both Helen and Stella gasped in terror.

Stella and Helen walked back to the Raveopolis building, and as they did, Stella praised her time defying dance partner.

177

"Way to go," Stella said, pumping her fist in the air. "Who knew I could put the cost for the whole day, the damages and potential lawsuits on Charlotte's tab."

"Well," Helen said, a satisfied smirk on her face, "you are her employee. It's only fair for the employer to be responsible for all the damages their chaotic workers cause."

"That's right," Stella said, clapping her hands. "Helen, you're a genius. A problem-solving sorceress!"

Helen arrogantly puffed out her cheeks as her eyes glinted. "I am pretty clever, aren't I?"

And Charlotte will know better than to mess with me, she thought to herself.

"Come on," Stella said, pulling her friend's hand. "Now we can have that surprise sleepover I planned."

"A s-s-s-s-sleepover," Helen stammered and wobbled.

"Yes-s-s-s-s-s." Stella giggled and rushed ahead to get a cab.

The sky over City Electric was dark making the neon glint all over the town. Stella admired the view from the Raveopolis Suite's wide window.

"What's this for?" Helen looked at a pile of Ravelotion stacked near the door.

Stella picks up the note by the bottles and does her best Daddy D. impersonation.

"Dear Hella Helen,

I only do this with my closest compadres, but here's some Ravelotion D to apologize for misleading you and a lot of others. Even if it's not particularly effective on rainbow-burns, it will still allure any man or woman that comes within your vicinity.

Catch you next time I shoot the breeze,

Daddy D."

"Ugh, that's gnarly, and not the good kind," Stella said, sniffing it as she walked over. "This stuff could only allure the living dead. I can't believe this guy. He's trying to bribe you to keep hush hush about his faulty product by giving you said faulty product. That's not just sleazy, it's really dumb. I mean is he really that thick-headed that he doesn't see the irony in this."

178

Helen softly said, "At least I figured out his sales scheme. I still don't think he's all bad though. He has helped unify people all over the world, after all."

Stella flickered her fingers at Helen, causing Helen to blush. "Good job on your awesome spywork. Is that why you were chilling with D? To expose him?"

"I was, Stella but that's not the entire reason. I really was excited to meet my favorite band. I'm sorry I wasn't there for you when you needed me. I won't let it happen again."

"Awww, come here." Stella spins her friend into a hug. "I'm sorry I was too bubble-headed to realize things," Stella responded. "And to think I was trying to LyFish them instead. Oh, speaking of which…"

Stella excitedly grabbed Helen's hand and lead her over to the bed. As they reclined on Stella's bed, the pink haired raver girl showed the plus-sized skater her phone. "Wanna Lyfy together?"

"Oh uh, I don't have that. I made an account, but I never got into it."

"Well now I'm here to peer pressure you in person." Stella grins. "I'm going to show you how to make a Lyfy avatar and then you can metamorphose into a beautiful social butterfly." She spreads her arms out like wings and then turns to Helen with a smile. "Like me."

"Beautiful," said Helen gently. "You're not gonna let me say no, are you?"

"You really don't want to?" asked Stella softly.

"Actually, it sounds fun. Like pen pals in a brand-new world, right? Thanks for helping me out. I'm not social media savvy."

"What are roomies for?" Stella winked.

Stella traced her fingers on the padscreen to Room 5 in the Lyfy building. "Now if you remember the old console known as the Why, you could create mini-avatars of yourself known as the Mys. It's a lot like that but they actually look super fly! Umm, cool, yeah, cool."

Stella started with a faceless body and a torso on the padscreen. She moved into features. "First, you design the face. I'll give your avy some nice big eyes, some round dimples when she smiles and that cute short hairstyle you're always rockin'."

Helen blushed. "You really think my hair style is cute?"

179

"Totes adorbs," Stella responded, folding her hair in attempt to make it short. "You know me. I don't tell people things if they're not true. I can be a bit forgetful, but I'm also beautifully honest." She turns her attention back to the screen. "Now how about the body. Unlike the Why, this app has a boob slider so we can either be ourselves or adjust a bit." She looks at Helen. "No real need to adjust in this particular instance. Hmmmm…round and full and…"

Helen looks away with deep blush.

Stella pops up when her comphone jingles. "Ooh, I got a ping from of my new Winterson friends. They were sceptics who became believers after watching me tango with…someone. Oh, wow I got a ton of new pal requests."

Stella's short attention span led her to start checking her messages. Minutes passed and Helen sat there awkward, she was turning redder than B. Bop's fro and her cheeks puffed out in jealous and irritation.

"Er…Stella how about we get washed up." Helen asked to break the silence. "We wouldn't want to stink up the place like a poor sewer jeeg."

Stella smelled her armpit. "You're right, my bodacious buddy." She winked. "And I know the perfect place." She turned to her phone. "Brb, heart, smiley face, plus sign."

Helen sighs and chuckles to herself.

Helen and Stella stood in their undergarments in Dorphin's dark room.

"Where is Dorkphin?" Helen asked. "Won't he flip his lid when he sees us in here?"

Stella replied quietly. "Shhh. He's asleep at this time. Chillax, his lid won't flip if he doesn't know we're here. Hey, so you wanna tell me why you have it in for the guy? Don't be upset with him on my behalf, okay? Despite our current turbulence, I want us all to get along. I want us *all* to be friends."

"He's a heartbreaker."

"Wait, you dated him? So he's not gay? That's fantastic news!" Her eyes shimmer.

"No, he is super gay, but he uhhh…pretended not to be. He learned my weaknesses to exploit them at the DOTG." Helen looks away with watery eyes. "He's a liar and a bad friend."

"Well, I think he's changed a lot since then. Give him another chance, for me. Please, bath buddy."

180

Helen blushed again. "I only hope my hairy legs don't shed in his jacuzzi."

Stella turned on the faucet and filled the pool. She quickly shed her clothes, her underwear flying in Helen's face. She leaped into the bath. "Come on in, Hels, the water's hella fine." Stella smiled as she eased in.

Helen's whole body was redder than Tammy Mato.

"But Stella, I've never been in a tub nude with another girl…"

"Come on, my peachy pal. Don't you believe that there's a first time for everything?"

"But Stella you know I like…umm…."

"Hey now," Stella responded, beckoning her friend into the tub. "There's a lot of people I like and maybe more that I don't even know I like. I wouldn't bathe with someone I don't like. Well, there's mixed bathing, but that's a totally different animal."

"But Stella, I uh…" Helen held out Stella's panties. "Perhaps you should…undies on. For now at least."

"Well, you know me," Stella responded, beckoning her friend into the tub. "Undies or commando. I go both ways with everything. Even in jacuzzies. Come on in, my new Lyfi sista. Don't be afraid of the unknown." She holds her hand out.

Helen exhaled her worries and whisked them away with her hands. "I'm being silly. Nude is fine. For you. Not me. I hope that's okay."

"It's fine and dandy. Whatever you need to do to chill, do it sista. If it makes you uncomfortable," Stella claps her hands and bubbles come out from the jets of the wide jacuzzi "just add bubbles."

"Thanks." Helen slipped out of her clothes, but kept her underwear on. "You can do this," she said to herself. She gave a gentle smile and stepped into the tub.

Stella was so accepting, and she was ready to bathe with her crush for the very first time.

As Helen settled into the warm water, Stella sped behind her. She then started rubbing shampoo into Helen's hair. "Don't worry Helen. I know your secret and why you're so shy."

Helen immediately covered her chest and turned bright red again. "Wait what?"

181

Stella started washing Helen's back with a soapy washcloth. "You like to play for the same team," Stella said with a wink. "So tell me, do you got your eyes on any lovely flowers? I could scope 'em out if you want." She rubs Helen's legs with the cloth. "So thick and...hey, these aren't hairy. Girl you are too self-conscious. Your legs are beautiful and plump. Just like all of you."

Helen pulls her legs in. "You really think that. You don't think I'm..." She lowers into the tub and looks down "fat?"

"Fat is what people call someone when they can't find a real insult. You are pleasingly plump and don't let nobop tell you otherwise."

"I won't," said Helen with a small smile.

"Great! Now what were we talking about?"

"Oh, I totally forgot too. It probably wasn't important. So, let's just forget it!"

"Oh, I remember! It was about secret crushes. Let me think, were any cute girls checking you out?" Her eyes widened. "Oh, do you like Jayden? I noticed her noticing you. Want to live out some steamy teacher student romance? Wink wink." She grins. "Going commando or bathing suit isn't the only thing I go both ways on." She hands Helen the towel. "I'm just joshing ya. Hey, you wanna get your front, right?"

Helen slid so deep in the tub that she blew bubbles beneath the water before rising again. "Uh nobody at this time. Jayden is too distant for a relationship with anyone honestly," she said as she washes her front.

"Oh, so I can't be your wing-gal?" asked Stella with a pout, she leans against Helen and wiggles her hair to signal her friend it's her turn.

Helen squeezes out too much lotion when she squeezes the bottle. "Just uhh, let me know if there's any you come across who catches your eye. You have good taste."

"You know I like Dan, right? Hey wait, what if they're Wintersons?"

"Yeah, that's fine too. Actually, let's put this idea on hold. We should focus on training, not romance."

Stella nodded and gave her a thumbs up. "Will do, my best friend. I'm sure Jayden would appreciate that." She leans back and wiggles her eyebrows.

"Hold still, silly," said Helen, before grabbing the washcloth.

Stella's ears perk up. "Do you hear that tapping sound?"

Helen covers her chest. "It's just my nerves. Sorry."

"Oh crap. It's Dan. He's training at like three A.M."

Helen put the bottle of shampoo back where she remembered it being before. "What do we do?"

Stella stands up. "Time for the Neon Knights to courageously sneak past him."

Helen reflexively looks away. "Yeah, good thinking. But before that...I have to tell you something about Dan. He didn't break my heart. I just...made that up."

Stella tickles Hellen. "You shouldn't lie to your bestie. Now promise me you will be nice to Dan and I'll stop tickling you. Nod if you agree. You don't want him hearing you giggling. We'll both get caught."

Helen covers her mouth and nods. "Stella, I won't lie to you ever again. I promise."

"Don't worry. Our friendship won't ever be broken. That's my promise." She puts on her underwear and grabs a soap bottle, holding it out like a sword. "A Knights promise is their vow. Now let's vow to get out of here while Dan is training on the balcony."

Helen and Stella snuck back to their room, wrapped in towels they had pilfered from Dorphin's room. They dressed themselves in their pajamas that were freshly laid out for them by the concierge. Stella's were pink with blue stars and Helen's were beige with pixelated lilacs.

As they snuggled into their comfort clothes, Stella asked her friend, "Are you feeling better?"

"Yeah," Helen responded, and snatched a pillow from her bed. "But I'm still pissed at Charlotte, I could..."

Without warning, Helen whacked Stella in the face with a pillow. "Oh my," Helen said, with her hands to her face "I don't know what came over me."

"No fair," Stella pouted. "At least warn me before"—Stella snatched a pillow from the bed and whacked Helen in the face "bam!".

With some loud giggles and fluff flying everywhere, they had begun smacking each other with pillows. Mr. Kitty hops onto the bed and takes turns hissing at whoever whacked his friend.

"We should probably stop before Mr. Kitty gets all bitey. Oh, won't Mr. Raveopolis whine about the mess?" Stella asked as she laughed.

Helen ducked Stella's pillow and smiled. "Stella, you still aren't used to the 'tabs' thing. That's what Charlotte is for."

As Helen pillow whacked Stella in the stomach, she put her hands on Helen's shoulders. "Listen, are you still hurt by what Charlotte did to you?"

"A bit," Helen said, bashfully hiding behind a pillow. "I'm feeling a bit better, but it's still kinda rough. Revenge is like a warm cushion; it softens the blow." She hugs her pillow with a relaxed look.

Stella's eyes glistened and warmed her friend. "I'm going to give you all my paychecks so your mom and jeegs can be supported even if you can't."

Helen's mouth trembled in response and she let out a sob. "Stella, please. You don't have to be so generous."

"Think on it, okay?" Stella asked, as she embraced Helen tightly. Even if Helen didn't like handouts, it was still nice to cozy up in a Stella hug.

"Wait, I'm a Freak now."

"Huh?" asked Stella.

"Daddy D. hired me to be a dancer. That has to pay well, right?"

"Yeah, just be careful he doesn't lotion you. I'm just giving you the same sage advice you gave me."

"Thanks. I appreciate it. If any guy tries something with me or you, they'll get a face full of flaming wheels."

"Yeah! You go girl!" Stella was about to high-five her pal.

The starlet's short attention span had diverted her. A familiar theme blared over the Telescreen. It was the legendary credo of the Fruitsaders.

"Oh boy," Stella exclaimed, her eyes transfixed "Fruitsaders. Come on Helen, pull up a seat. I'm going to show you the greatest cartoon ever."

A simplified two-dimensional cartoon depicted the main Fruitsaders as the theme song played loudly. A catchy ukulele song serenades them as they swooped in front of the screen:

"And the world will turn to Tammy Mato, Passionfruit Patel and Orange Ornacia to save the day for all that is good and juicy."

"I thought you wanted to wait for Dan," said Helen softly.

"Dan's a sourpuss. One day we'll binge the entire series as a team, but we can't miss this opportunity! It's destiny calling us! We have to answer."

"Sounds fun," said Helen, giving Stella a warm hug from behind.

The pals pulled up a pair of fluffy seats next to each other.

"Aww shoot." Stella pouted. "It's the filler episode where they help out the townspeople. At least rerun a real episode."

"Aw come on, Stella," Helen responded with a dimpled smile. "There's nothing wrong with having a filler episode if they're handled right."

Stella looked deeply into Helen's eyes. "Whoa. You're so wise!" She put her arm around her pudgy pal.

Helen nuzzled into Stella's shoulder, and they got cozy with each other. The day was finally ending for Helen, her worries had been whisked away by a wild, fun and heartwarming night with her sweet gal pal.

Step 19: Hard Motion

"Come on Stella, today's the second day of practice," Helen said, shaking her friend awake.

"Uh please, fifteen more minutes, mom." Stella mumbled, tossing and turning.

"Mom? Stella, I am not your mother. Just get up, please." Helen put her hands on her hips.

"Stella blinked her eyes and squinted. "I'm tired from training and…did we finish the Fruitsaders episode?"

Helen smiles. "Actually, you fell asleep in my lap. I can't believe how late we were up."

"Not late enough! Sleepovers should be all-nighters!" Stella rose from the bed and grabbed her Plus Pill container from her dresser and swallowed one. She smiled as a placebo effect took hold before the actual medication and her eyes shot open. "Well, I was having the best dream. I was at a rave and it was embarrassing, I found that I was in my underwear."

"That doesn't sound good." Helen answered with a chuckle.

"But then," Stella exclaimed "I realized it was a day glow underwear themed party! And we just raved all night, everyone was too glowy and happy to judge each other's appearance." She changed her clothes and pouted. "I want to start doing stuff like that."

"Well, Stella…" Helen answered, slipping into a comfortable gym outfit with a black t-shirt with a green stripe and matching gym shorts. "Being famous isn't just raves and parties; you have to keep doing what made you famous to stay there. You chose to be a Neon Knight, after all. You gotta keep at it!"

Stella sighed and smiled, untangling curls from her pink weave. "More sage advice from my bestie. I'm lucky to have such a wise friend."

"I'm lucky too." Helen smiled back at her. "But let's get down to the Bi-rise. We don't want to be late for your training."

"Our training." Stella added. "You're a knight too."

"Potentially…" Helen corrected her. "Jayden is intent on it, but Charlotte has other plans."

"Well, Jayden won't give up, so you're doomed to be knight like the rest of us." Stella winked.

"I'll try it out I guess," Helen said, cheeks flushed. "Hurry up, or we'll be late again."

The two arrived at the Bi-rise, on the cloudy and humid summer day, and were met with Jayden's unblinking gaze of steel emotion. "You're late."

Stella let out an exasperated yell. "For Rave's sake, we got here on the dot."

"Forty-nine seconds off. Every second is crucial in the field. If this was a rescue, there would be dire consequences."

"But it's not a rescue. It's training," said Stella.

"We need to train you as fast as possible."

Stella groaned and Helen turned to her and took her by the shoulder and whispered "Don't take it personally. Neuronian warriors are notoriously precise, though it can cause them to waste a bit of precious time…ironically."

Jayden's eyes narrowed. "You must have punishment for your tardiness. And for disrespect as well. Show me your best combat dance, now."

She pressed her finger to Stella's forehead.

Stella screamed. "Craaane!"

Jayden tapped her staff on the bridge with authority. The holographic Crane stopped in place. "He is a mental projection. Now, when I grab my staff energy is transferred into it this projection. If you attack when it glows you will be shocked. Attack it when it's dim."

"This is just the second day."

"Excuses! Dance or die. These are the options for a Knight."

"I don't know any combat dance."

The Ravepire thrusted forward and she felt wild electromotion surge through her, causing her to jump backwards and fall to the wooden floor.

"Come on, Stella!" Helen shouted. "Don't you remember Summoeira the Summerein martial arts dance?"

Stella dazed, shook her head. "I don't. I don't know why?"

"Are you kidding me? You knew it at the Dance," she said, running circles around her projection. "Eat fire ball, creep!" She threw a tiny orb of flame that quickly fizzled out. "Ugh! I suck at this. Come on, back me up."

"I don't remember the dance. I'm sorry."

Jayden's unibrow curved heavily, signifying that she was not feeling merciful. "Pitiful. If this was real, you'd be dead." She turned to Helen. "Do not doubt yourself. You must unleash your power with great confidence."

"Yeah, I feel like there is some serious bias here," said Stella, backing up against the wall.

"Do something!" Helen screamed as the Ravepire loomed over Stella. "Just rave or something." She kicked the Ravepire with her flaming wheels but got zapped.

Stella's eyes illuminated. She pushed off the ground with her hands into a twirling breakdance. Her legs extended into a kick, knocking the energy projection Ravepire back.

Stella began to shuffle when she got to her feet. She kicked her legs on the floor, cutting shapes, her favorite rave move.

The energy Ravepire tore back at her, glowing with hostility. The Ravepire threw another punch, but this time Stella gave a spin and a duck while remaining light on her feet. She allowed the punch to miss her and then with returned momentum from the spin, she punched the Ravepire hard in the chest.

Stella did a straight jump and slammed her arms down on it while sliding her feet in the air, creating a stream of gravity to ride upon. When the Ravepire hit the ground, she spun counterclockwise, creating beads of heavy gravity energy on her legs. Her feet hit the jaw, causing the projection to explode.

Stella put her arms in the air, clapped and grinned. "I call that Ravoeira."

Jayden looking none too amused, slammed her staff, causing the Ravepire to disperse. "Ravepires won't die that easily. I suppose that's satisfactory for an improvisation though."

Stella turns to Helen. "Did you hear that? The mean lady complemented me. Can you believe it?"

Helen blushes. "Sorry I wasn't much help."

Jayden points her staff at Helen. "You are holding yourself back. Perhaps you need a different projection." She creates a hologram of Helen. "Take down your insecurities first hand."

Helen squeaked and rode off on skates as she was pursued by her double. She turned her head to look far in the distance of the of the long bi-rise bridge. She saw a figure with a giant afro and a white tank top, accompanied by a pale figure with dark flowing hair. "Isn't that Dorkphin and man dog?" she asked, making a sharp turn that her double followed like a shadow.

"B. Bop and Dan?" Stella spun around. She danced in place. "Oh man they're really going to get it. Look how late they are?"

"Wow, you're being spiteful today," Helen said, tricking her double to drive off the edge of the building. "Even I don't care that much."

"Oh, I just want to see what kind of punishment Jayden will dish out, considering what she gave us."

When B. Bop and Dan arrived, Jayden stood tall, her lanky form allowing her to intimidate easier. "You're considerably late, B."

B. Bop grinned, he had dark angular sunglasses that shined with his smile. He believed he was so cool that he'd look fly, wearing shades on a cloudy day. "Hey just got the stud and me some good eats at the Petite Three's mall."

"No excuse, lives are at stake."

B. Bop left Dan's side to move closer to the angry woman. "Come on Jay, lighten up. Have some fun; it's summertime…" he pointed right at Jayden's purple highlighted armor "and you're wearing that sweat suit. "Come on, this is the season to show some skin, Jay."

He moved his arms to flex, causing the twisting and turning dragon tattoo to writhe like a snake from his shiny bicep to his forearm. "I worked all winter for these, and these." He then made his abs ripples against his white fabric tank top.

Jayden's face was unflinching, but her words came out in a stutter. "I…I can't have fun. Fun is only accessible when in a good mood."

"Not true," B. Bop responded. "Fun is what you have when you want to forget your bad mood."

"Well…I…I'm not in a bad mood. I'm in no mood. I'm focused on the mission."

B. Bop shrugged "Well you must be in some mood; you are a woman, after all. At least I think you are. Maybe if you showed more skin, I could confirm it."

Stella couldn't help but grin, she knew B. Bop was finally going to get his dues for mouthing off to Jayden.

Instead, Jayden turned red and shied away from B. Bop with a hurt expression on her face.

Helen figured out the unspoken truth. "Come on B. Bop, stop harassing her. We have important training to do." She turned to Jayden with a warm smile. "And for the record, you have the bod of a warrior goddess. I bet those thighs could crack Bop's hollow skull."

Jayden raised her hand and seemed to regain her composure as the color seemed to drain from her face. "Right. Well, before we delve deeper into training, I believe it would be beneficial to discuss the origins of your powers. Connecting to your roots is necessary for growth. Doing so should allow you to harness them efficiently."

"I think my gravity belt was pretty efficient," said Stella.

Jayden turned to B. Bop but tried to avoid his direct glance. "B, I am an outsider when it comes to knowledge on Summereins, Wintersons and Reinsons. Perhaps you can shed some light for the trainees."

"Of course, Jay. Finally, a subject that interests me. Gather round boys and girls."

Once Dan, Stella and Helen all stood around in a circle with Dan trying his hardest to avoid the gazes of the other two trainees, B. Bop spoke. "So, who knows the story of Kouyate and Harry Fairson?"

"I do," Stella gushed. "It's sooo romantic."

"Gee, is that all you get out of it?" B. Bop muttered. "It's the birth of your powers."

"Really?" Stella chirped.

B. Bop nodded in response. "They may not be your ancestors exactly, but they are where your powers originate from. When Kouyate and Fairson danced before Ravenous in petition and prayer to turn the war against the Edwardians, the goddess was moved and took note of their dance styles."

B. Bop raised his hand in a refined pose and pointed at Dan. "The Winterson Kouyate was elegant and graceful. Every step was perfect. Ravenous granted her and her race blue electromotion in their veins."

B. Bop's feet moved energetically and with a forward sing of his hands he said "The Summerein Fairson lacked that grace, but he made up with sheer energy and devotion. He was granted red electromotion for him and his people."

B. Bop whipped out two glos from his pocket, a red and a blue one. He held them in both hands. "The blue and the red motion, both had different attributes, the blue could create ice and manipulate time with perfect dance

190

moves and the red could channel fire and control gravity through passionate dance moves."

B. Bop rose his hands and put his feet apart and the iceglo ignited. He shuffled quickly swinging his arms again and the fire glos whipped extended. "Glos were created to make the transmission of fire and ice so much easier with a quick dance, but trust me, both polarized elements sleep in your body, begging to be awakened!"

"What about Reinsons?" Helen asked, a little proud of herself.

"I didn't forget us. We're a blend of both races but…we have a hidden power. If an enlightened Winterson and enlightened Summerein mate, the electromotion they create is purple and that kind is nearly limitless. Reinsons are capable of wielding advanced powers that mold to their own personality."

Helen took a step back "Whoa…I didn't know that."

"Soak it up." B. Bop smiled, raising his hand. "Bask in the knowledge of why we are feared and mistreated. Now you know why your momma was so hush hash about your daddy. With me as your teacher, you can be woke."

"Well well." A very snide and theatrical voice quaked through the warm air. "That is quite the history lesson."

Everyone turned to see Charlotte. Her brown tanned skin shining on a cloudy day when it wasn't covered by a neon yellow and green two-piece bikini. "Don't mind me, I'm just going to be a casual observer and tanner in the crack of afternoon."

"Let's get things going," B. Bop said.

"Jay set up some targets appropriate for each of their powers." He tossed Stella and Dan some glos.

Jayden tapped their foreheads and then tapped her staff again, creating three Ravepire projections. One who leapt several feet off the ground, another who move at blinding speeds and a third that just stood there.

"Wow, so we can all see them?" asked Stella with stars in her eyes.

"Indeed. It is a shared mental projection," said Jayden.

"I'll handle these two, Jay. I'll let you take care of the man hater," B. Bop said.

"Wow, you couldn't just keep it professional. So childish," said Helen, crossing her arms.

191

In a rare expression of emotion, Jayden put her hands together and quickly grinned before her face became neutral again when she walked over to Helen.

Jayden took her protégé to where Charlotte had set up her floating expandable tanning chair.

"I'm not going to fight one?" asked Helen.

"Not yet," replies Jayden.

B. Bop dug his fingers slightly into his jeans as he eyed Stella as she watched the jumping Ravepire. "Well, do your dance of passion, soar to the skies with your fireglo and nail that sucker."

Stella smiled with confidence. "This will be easy."

"Even easier if you know there is a heat seeking function on your fireglo. Cast your mind to your target and the fireglo will zoom towards its prey."

"Got it." Stella nodded. She did a little cha cha and the fireglos cap popped off, leading the fire to extend in a snake-like whip. "Oooooh, this is awesome!"

Stella squatted and then leapt in the air. Her face pushed back against the gravity until she didn't feel any resistance. The starlet grinned from ear to ear as she realized she was in sync with the Ravepire who had leapt too.

She concentrated on the Ravepire and the whip shot out, but with a crack, it turned around and smacked her hand.

The girl squeaked loudly causing B. Bop to shout. "Stop focusing on other things. Those negative thoughts lead back to yourself."

B. Bop was right…this time. She had to forget about her stardom and Dan too. She had to get this mission done and save all of those who had been kidnapped.

It might have been the plus pills helping her, but Stella quickly emptied her mind and she slung her whip right at the Ravepire before touching down. With a direct hit, the energy faded. The rave-stepper was delighted to see that B. Bop's idea worked.

"Bravo." Jayden shouted across the Bi-rise. "Now do it again."

Another Ravepire appeared with the stamp of her staff, causing Stella to groan.

Meanwhile, Dan did a frost dance and began to watch as the Ravepire that had been shuffling back and forth at extreme speeds had slowed. He fired his iceglo like a pistol, but every shot missed. "Agh, I can't believe this. I was the winner of the Dance and I can't even hit this one target."

"Well stud, I think you're over thinking it just like your ex-friend," B. Bop said. "Your jaw is clenched and your hands are gripping the glo too tightly. Maybe you should loosen up."

"I am not uptight. I performed the most perfected Frost Dance at 31.7 seconds. Though I have done one in under 30 before. Why am I slipping?"

B. Bop gave him a just-listen-to-yourself smirk and said, "Gee, you're worse than the Neuronian chick."

Dan sighed. "How do I…"

"Well, I ain't much of a chiropractor but try this…" B. Bop strolled over to Dan and grabbed the lower part of Dan's back.

"Hey I don't like to be touched…" He pulled back.

"Don't worry, we're bros, bros do those things for each other." B. Bop said with a smooth dulcet tone.

Dan sighed again as B. Bop began to massage his back. "Actually, that feels good."

B. Bop put his arms alongside Dan's arms. "Now loosen up on the iceglo."

Dan did just that. "Let go of all those tense emotions stud. Focus on my sultry voice. I'll make those worries leave town."

Dan breathed and did a Frost Dance at a much more leisurely pace. He hit the Ravepire on his next try.

"Told ya," B. Bop said. "All you need is a man who's got your back literally."

"Thanks," Dan gave a soft and shy smile. "I think you're right."

Jayden and Helen stood apart from the other two.

Stella gave Jayden a curious look.

"I've kept you separate because you can do so much more."

"What do you mean?" Helen asked.

193

"Unlike those two, electromotion flows in vast amounts to your brain. It's the same with us Neuronians."

Jayden's eyes went from dull to bright. "We were founded by Medulla the warrior, a powerful Neuronian matriarch who traveled to the same place as Kouyate and Fairson to gain powers for her people. The goddess was amazed by Medulla's wisdom and she filled her brain with powerful electromotion to allow her and her people to perform psychic feats."

"Whoa, so I'm similar to a Neuronian?" Helen asked, her eyes aglow. "Are all Reinsons like that?"

"No, they are not. It is why you have no glos. Your mind is your glow. Now, you're going to annihilate that target with only your focused mind."

Charlotte cut in. "I don't know why you bother, Jayden. Helena is quite mindless. Her head isn't full of hot air."

Helen's face grew bright red but she knew better not to lash out. The best way to shut up Charlotte was to excel as a Neon Knight.

"Now try, Helen. Attack that Ravepire with your mind. Imagine they are someone you want destroyed."

"Oh, I got this!" Helen concentrated on the Ravepire. She could feel her mind rumble but she was cut short by Charlotte's sneer.

"Aim for the stars honey, you'll never be one." Charlotte laughed in an unpleasant and deep tone.

Helen cried and covered her face. "I can't do this." She looked at her teacher through her hands.

Jayden's face was still and sad, it looked as helpless as her protégé felt.

"Come on, Helen. I know you can do it!" Stella shouted. "Be that girl who kicked so much booty at the Dance. Ignore the bad vibes of the haters."

"You only say that because you don't remember a thing that happened at the dance, dear," said Charlotte before her smoothie was frozen.

Dan glared at her. "I'm trying to concentrate. Why are you even here?"

"For a tan," said Charlotte, taking a sip from her silver straw. "And to torment Helen, of course."

Stella grabs Helen's hand. "You totally got this. Show her who's the boss!"

A hope welled up in Helen's stomach and she could feel motivation spring from her core.

194

Helen turned to Charlotte who continued her husky laugh. She began to feel her consciousness tug at Charlotte's chair. Her floating holochair began to rumble and Charlotte ceased laughing. Without warning the chair flipped Charlotte flat on her back and sped towards the Ravepire. The energy in the chair and Ravepire fused until there was a small explosion.

"Whoa!" Stella exclaimed running, to Helen to hug her. "You're really powerful. And a lil bit scary." She giggles.

Jayden covered her mouth to mask her face of awe. "I can't believe you can do that, Helen. To stand up to Charlotte."

"What did I do exactly?" Helen asked shyly.

"In time you will learn the extent of your power," Jayden said with a gentle happiness.

Even B. Bop acknowledged Helen and began to clap, leaving only Dan and Charlotte silent until the latter spoke up.

"Ouch." Charlotte said, dazed. "I just got plastic surgery on that." She dusted off her prized ass and rose up with a proud pose. "She couldn't have done it without me here."

Jayden smiles. "You truly bring out strong emotions from her."

Stella looked at Charlotte curiously. "Wait, how can you feel that if you just got plastic surgery on your butt? Isn't it still numb?"

"Oh no." Charlotte put her hands to her face and her eyes bugged in horror. "I've been botched...again!"

Everyone gave a hearty laugh before Charlotte growled about Helen's salary being docked to buy her a new chair.

"Bitch, you fired me." Helen flicked her off.

Even Dan let out a chuckle.

Helen turned to look to Stella. She grabbed her hand with confidence. They both were determined to break past their limits and become Neon Knights side by side.

Step 20: Bonding over Bubbly Tea

As weeks of training flew by; Stella took notice of two things. The first was that some days Helen's powers didn't work. They mostly coincided with Charlotte's presence at the training site. When she wasn't working to get CharLuv refurbished, Charlotte would show up for sunbathing and heckling. To her sunbathing was leisure time and heckling Helen was both a sport and a pastime. Every time Charolotte would try to bring her friend down, Stella would cheer for Helen. This encouraged her from the sidelines, improving her accuracy and focus tenfold!

The second thing of note was that Dan made very little contact with Stella after the first day of training. He was always there, but said very little either to her or anyone. Occasionally, B. Bop would tease him, but he would just brush it off. Usually, Dan would have had something snarky to say about B. Bop's brand of provocative nonsense, but recently, he just took it in stride. The way B. Bop would refer to him as a "stud" and "handsome" made it clear that B. Bop was hoping for more than just friendship with the Winterson. Stella wanted to tell him that B. Bop was a liar, but he never responded to any of her messages. The alienation her friend imposed on himself, made her feel all the more guilty about making him feel uncomfortable with that kiss.

After a few more days of this alienation, Stella was at her wits end. She wanted to bury the feelings deep inside her brain. Drugs weren't the answer for something so small, so she found a better way. After a day of rigorous training near the end of summer, Stella asked Helen and Jayden a question in the evening.

"Hey guys, want to come shopping with this pretty thing?"

"What." Jayden stated rather than questioned, her piercing orange eyes looking like fires that would burn Stella to a crisp.

"You know, shopping? It's not the most progressive of hobbies for a girl but hey, we all have our guilty pleasures."

"Actually, I have a question about that. When do Stella and I, get paid?" asked Helen, shyly tapping her fingers together. "I remember hearing that the pay for being a Knight is awesome."

Jayden shakes her head. "You are still in training. When a true Knight, you will be paid a respectful sum."

"Then I don't think I can afford going shopping, Stella. Until we get a gig, I don't get paid for dancing. D has been too busy for parties recently. I've tried to get a side-job, but I'm overqualified," Helen said with a look of shame.

"Nonsense, you know I…Charlotte's got you covered."

Helen looked around and seeing no Charlotte in her presence, a devious smirk creeping onto her normally plain face. "Well, if it's on Charlotte's K, then I'm all in. Who knew she could be so generous?"

Jayden's incinerating eyes shifted to Helen. Normally, if she heard some plan to take advantage of Charlotte, she would have taken her staff and impaled the person's foot into the ground. In this instance Jayden simply muttered. "If Helen's going, count me in."

Stella winked at Hellen. "You hear that?"

Jayden readies her staff. "What did you hear?"

Stella chuckled. "Nothing. You won't regret a thing, trust me! Oh, we should invite Dan! Or not. He's still upset with me."

Helen perks up. "Leave that to me! I actually bought him something sweet to make amends for me being so bratty to him. We'll meet you there, buddy!"

"Nah, we can wait for you here, right Jayden."

Jayden nods.

Stella hoped that this experience would allow Jayden to learn more about Helen and for herself to possibly even become friends with her fierce teacher. More than anything though she hoped she could finally bridge the gap that formed between her and Dan.

Helen came back about fifteen minutes later. "Dan was uhh…busy. Maybe another time."

Stella grabs her hand. "You look shaken up. Is everything okay?"

"Yeah, just some crazy drivers on the streets. I'm fine though. Let's enjoy the night together."

"Can I still come?" asked Jayden meekly.

"Yeah, silly. I'm gonna teach you how to chillax," said Stella with a big smile.

The newly formed trio walked along the wooden boardwalk of the Bi-Rise until they came to the second-floor entrance of a triple decker mall. The mall titled "Petit 3's" welcomed them in with reflective glass paneling that ushered in the purple sunlight. They stepped through the sliding doors and into a utopia for those with fashion sense and an upper middle-class budget. The three floors were all visible as there was a railing protected gap through the center of the mall. Lively stores sprang from every direction. Each of the levels were distinctly coded with black floors and neon pink, green and orange patterned on the floor, walls and guard rails.

"Wow, it's so surreal reading about places like this and suddenly you're there," Stella chimed in.

"This place…" Jayden whispered with a harshness, clenching her fist and shaking it.

"Jayden, have you been here before?" Stella asked, keeping her distance in case Jayden went berserk.

"Yeah, you're looking like you fought in a war here." Helen added with a nervous chuckle. "Did you fight a war here?"

"Only a war of clothes."

"Well, that's cryptic enough." Stella smiled. "I think we should get down to business."

The first shop they decided to hit up was the Boutique of 3. Racked in orderly rows were colorful accessories, eye-catching dresses and pants with fancy designs. Everything was very in league with the color scheme of the City Electric, but this was for casual clothes as opposed to garments to set the scene at raves. In the corner of the shop, next to the dressing rooms, was a station to get your eyebrows waxed and threaded. Jayden shuddered like she was confronting her biggest fear.

"What's wrong Jayden?" Helen asked.

"Charlotte takes me shopping here frequently."

"Aww, that's nice," said Stella.

Jayden looks down. "I perform my duty as her glorified coat rack."

Helen put her arm around Jayden. "Don't worry, we're not Charlotte, but she's here in spirit if you miss her." She flashed the credit card.

Stella grabbed Jayden by the hand. "Come on, let's crush those bad memories with some good ones!"

Stella decided her new mission was to make Jayden a little easier on the eyes. It wasn't that she was ugly, but the way she dressed, in a black rave-suit armor made her look more like a warrior and less like the hot babe she was. The peppy girl wanted to soften her new friend's image because she noticed a few people flinch when they walked by. They were probably thinking Jayden would decimate them if they coughed in her direction. She must have been lonely because of her fierce demeanor. She observed Jayden's stonelike face and knew the first place to start her makeover.

"Okay Jayden, close your eyes and I'll lead you," she said, leading her through the store. She sat her down at the station in the back of the store. "Okay, now you can open them."

A perky woman with darker skin and an apron to keep hair off her clothes, smiled at Jayden. "Hi there, unibrow, I can see you want me to do something about that caterpillar on your face."

Jayden's eyes bugged out. "Caterpillar? Where is it?"

She launched from her seat and pulled her glow staff out. She twirled it toppling a clothing rack before pointing it right at her face.

"Jayden, she's talking about your unibrow," Helen said.

"My what?"

"Your eyebrows, they're connected."

"Y-yeah," the salon woman stuttered to Jayden while cowering in place. "It's not exactly a beauty standard."

Jayden pointed her glow staff right at the woman. "Stella, you can't remove this. Or my clothes for that matter."

"Are you sure? I wanted you to be happy."

"Making me look like Charlotte won't bring happiness. Finding my brother is my mission. I will neither shed this armor or my unibrow until he has been reclaimed."

"I'm sorry Jayden. I didn't know they meant so much to you."

"I'm sorry too," the salon woman cried. "I just remove unibrows, not symbols of familial devotion. Please, don't kill me."

Jayden lowered her weapon as the woman continued to hyperventilate and sob. "Your life has been spared."

Stella brushed her forehead to remove some sweat. Shopping with an intense Neuronian warrior was two handfuls and two footfuls of stressful.

Helen nudged Stella. "Did you really think the old makeover trick would work on her?"

Stella whispered back to her. "She seems like the type it would help."

199

"I think…what she really needs is a makeover…in her heart," Helen said, her cheeks rosy.

"Aww, Helen. Yeah, we'll do just that. Come on guys, let's go before someone calls the fuzz."

Navigating the clothing racks that were still standing upright, Stella heard the sound of quiet vacuuming. She turned and saw someone in the beauty products aisle with a giant bag slumped over their back. Attached to it was a nozzle that seemed to be sucking up the products. The face was wrapped in purple bandages, save for some neatly mascaraed eyes which caught a glimpse of Stella and her crew. "A thief. Oh boy, it's hero time!"

In a split second, the figure made a break for it, toppling racks in order to create obstacles for potential pursuers.

Stella grinned "This looks like a job for a mighty—err, Neon Knight" and she ran off without Helen or Jayden.

Bounding over clothing racks, Jayden's speed dash training had made her light on her feet. Stella knew this was the best way to prove her abilities. She reached the bright lights of the outer portion of the mall and saw the thief's figure in the distance, pushing people in their attempt to make a break. Stella closed her eyes and with sensuous arm movements in the air and a wiggle of her hips, she did a small cha cha. She pulled a fireglo out from her jean pocket and leaped into the air. The girl flew over many piles ups of people.

"In the name of the Neon Knights I order you to stop," she said, one hand on her hip and the other gripping a fully activated sparking fireglo.

In response, the thief held the vacuum nozzle up and shot her in the head with Illusionary Face crème. "Owwwwww," Stella said, rubbing her head and taking a few steps back. "That's not fair."

The thief shot her again, this time in the gut. Stella could feel her stomach churn as she looked down in agony. Skin Reviving lotion fell at her feet. She looked up and growled at the thief. After twirling down the hallway she ran up the side of the wall and lifted her glostick. "This time you're going down. Fire wall!"

The wall of flames appeared as Stella planned, but it appeared on the thief causing their body to burst into flames. High-pitched screams were heard along with the crackling of the inferno. The burning body rolled and Stella saw the bandages on the person's face had caught fire.

Helen, using her roller shoes to catch up, appeared on the opposite side of the firewall. "Stella, we aren't supposed to kill people!" She held up an iceglo and after performing the frost dance, a coolness emitted from her being. Ice coated everything, crystalizing the railing and freezing some nearby people. The ice formed over the fire, washing everything clean.

The thief, was frozen to the floor.

"Whoops," Helen said. "I think I got a little carried away," she leaned against the wall, about to fall over.

Stella laughed and supported her friend. "You gotta be careful Helen. You are more powerful than me, so you gotta be frugal with your powers. Don't spend them all in one place."

Helen blushed. "Yeah, good advice. Sorry."

"Hey, cheer up buttercup. Now we got an ice rink."

TCE Police rushed the scene, some too fast and slipping on the ice. Two grabbed mecha-truncheons and smashed them into the ice, freeing the thief.

"Oh Goddess it hurts," the person said sobbing. The bandages were burnt and the face of the person was revealed.

The face was corpselike and long, with tiny eyes and large eye sockets. The hair was scraggly and charred, it draped over the raised skull-like cheekbones. The nose was large and pointy in a witchlike way. The face and its voice contrasted greatly as it was feminine, shrill and crying.

The masked police looked at Stella and Helen and gave them a thumbs up. "Good job girls, you caught yourself an Ug-Thief."

Stella heard about Ug-Thiefs on the news. Illusionary Beauty products were the latest fashion trend in the City Electric and they were a slippery slope. People who were dissatisfied with their face, whether due to aging or perceived ugliness, could use corrective skin creams to symmetrize their face, enlarge or shrink parts of the face including eyes, nose and lips. All of this happened overnight. As miraculous as that sounded, the products were costly and had the ultimate downside. If you didn't use them, your face would not only revert, but your genetics would be permanently scarred, resulting in deformed faces that looked halfway between the original look and the new look.

When Stella was younger, she was tempted to use one because she perceived her nose too prominent, but her mother stopped her. She was very thankful because soon after, news stories of backfiring products started becoming prominent in the media. The change was gradual but once it took ahold it, the damage was hard to reverse without more of the product. That's the excuse the company who made it used and they raised their prices to match the afflicted's demand. That is how Ug-Thiefs were created. They were lepars who wasted all their money on these products and couldn't afford to buy more.

Charlotte was rumored to use them by the press, but there was no clear evidence of this besides her obsession with youth.

The woman cried "I just wanted to look like myself...I wanted to look beautiful again. Oww, my body is burning all over." She pointed at Stella. This woman, she's no hero, she's a monster."

Stella felt like she had been hit with the wall of flames. Even though the woman didn't pay for the products, she didn't deserve to be disfigured and injured the way Stella did with her uncontrollable powers.

"I'm sorry...I hurt you."

"My life is over." The woman put her face on the ground and began wailing even louder. A stretcher was produced and the woman's charred body was taken away.

"Good job, Neon Knight," the officer said. "We'll be sure to put your noble effort in the paper."

When everyone left and the only people left were janitors trying to remove the ice and water, Stella started crying.

Helen came to her side and put her arm on her shoulder. "Stella, you were just doing what you felt was right. But you're inexperienced, you and me both."

Stella turns to Jayden in tears. "Why didn't you help us?"

"It is not our job to capture thieves. We are not police. Nor are we superheroes. We are Knights. Besides, it was good training for you both."

Stella looks away. "I don't know if I can be a Neon Knight if it involves bringing pain to people."

"It was an accident. I screwed up too. Guess being a Reinson isn't all good? Too much power is...scary," said Helen, looking at the ice being cleared out.

Stella forced a smile. "I don't think you're scary at all. I think it's wonderful you're a Reinson."

Helen smiled warmly. "I was...worried when I found out I was a Reinson."

"Cuz you didn't want anything in common with Bop?"

Helen chuckled. "No, well maybe a bit. But really, I was worried we wouldn't be Summer Sisters anymore. You used to call me that, remember? Back when we were Pen Pals."

"Oh yeah, you're right." Stella looked out at the scorched mall. "That seems like a lifetime ago."

"Yeah, it kind of does. Stella, you're so great. You never got jealous of me. Instead you always supported me."

"I'm not an angel, pal. I mean I was jealous. You can use fire and ice and gravity and time."

"And perhaps a personal power," added Jayden.

"Yeah! But like I want to help you. I'd like die of jealousy if you had all that power and were no good with it. As long as you shine, I'll shine too. We're still summer sisters! Remember, my fluffy cloud, even if it's raining the sun is still shining. That's uh, you know like you're a Reinson, I'm a Summerein. It's like a pun. Oh, but it's not a joke. It's uhh...complicated."

Helen puts her hand on Stella's. "It's the sweetest thing, Stella. Thanks."

"Hey, you'll be fine without me, right?"

"What are you saying? Don't talk like you're gonna run off! Please, that's what my dad did. Don't...do that to me," said Helen, holding onto Stella tightly.

"Oh don't worry. We'll still be chillin' in Stellen each night." Stella looks up at Jayden with a serious face. "I can't be a Neon Knight. Hurting people...like I did back there...it hurts too much."

"Cast your worries into the furnace," Jayden said, unmoved by this whole incident. "The Ravepires aren't people like her. They are monsters. Do not be fooled by their similarities in appearance."

"Jayden," Helen said. "Not now." She turned to Stella, "That woman, she's going to get the help she needs now. I'm sure the prisons have some kind of rehab."

"Doesn't change that I hurt her."

"Stella...please don't leave. I can't do this without you."

"Okay, I'll just cope with it...for my best bud." Stella produced a plus pill and downed it.

"Stella, what is that medicine? I see you taking it all the time. I convinced myself it wasn't my business...but I can't keep quiet about it anymore."

"A yellow plus pill, don't worry this day isn't ruined. I'm just gonna forget this all happened and then we can have a ball."

"Is that why you were falling asleep the moment we got back to the hotel those times? And during training too?"

"Helen, please, just…today has been too much already. These help me. Have faith in the yellow plus, kay?"

"I don't know, Stella." Helen looked away.

For fifteen minutes the trio sat in silence as hundreds of other people sat at other tables. They were in the mall's wide dining hall where numerous chain restaurants were lined up next to each other.

Stella, abruptly got up and smiled. "Guys, I'm gonna buy you something and it's on me."

"Okay sure," Helen said, a bit startled by the sudden mood change. "Thank you."

Jayden sat with Helen and observed her quietly. "Good job, my student."

"Oh thanks. For what? The ice barrier? I overdid it though. Those people are gonna have frostbite because of me."

"I meant for the tough love you gave your friend. Without you, she'd be lost."

Helen blushes. "Well, I don't know if I am helping. She has these new market pills she's been taking. I think they've been helping her? I dunno much about this stuff. I'm just worried about the side-effects, but looking at her now…I think I'll leave it be."

"You're a really kind friend, Helen," Jayden said with a tiny smile. "You remind me of Charlotte."

Helen's eyes bugged out and if she was drinking anything, liquid would have been spewed out all over the table. "What?"

"Charlotte came to my aid at the darkest moment of my existence. When Clyde left, she was always there to take me out and keep my mind busy. Even if I didn't like being a clothing rack or how she dressed me up against my will, or

204

the uncomfortable flirting…and touching…" Jayden swatted away the thought. "I was still happy to be with her. That's what I meant by a 'war of clothing.' It was a battle within myself."

"Ah I see…" Helen muttered. "I guess. But if there's any other nice people in your life, please compare me to them…not her."

"I don't know many people," Jayden said in deep thought. "Ah, I could compare you to you."

Helen smiled and rolled her eyes. She really couldn't believe that someone like Jayden was real. Jayden was a stunted person. Her body had aged into a young woman in her late twenties, but parts of her mind hadn't developed along with it. Helen heard all this from the queen of mean's sob story. Still, Helen thought it was cute and sweet how much her teacher obsessed over her powers.

Stella returned, holding two cups with her hands and a third with her elbow. She carefully laid them on the table. "Drink up."

"What is this?" Jayden asked.

"Bubbly Tea."

Jayden paused. "It is unwise to drink this."

"I just thought it'd help lighten the mood. Please. It will just make you feel good, promise."

"Okay…" Jayden put the straw in the side of her mouth and drank some.

Stella took a long slurp.

Jayden's face grew from the stolid seriousness to a strange smile with eyes full of mirth rather than anger. She gave an uncharacteristic giggle and drank some more.

"Wowee zowie, that's some great stuff, hehe." Jayden said, her voice with more inflection.

"I told you," Stella responded with a wink. "Now let's get fizzy."

Helen rolled her eyes again. She knew all about the tea in her hand.

Bubbly Tea was kind of like alcohol. It gave you a bubbly buzz, and silly personality. It didn't impair your senses. It just made you more annoying. Helen knew that this was Stella's attempt at lightening the mood and she pretended to sip some.

"Wow…everything looks so pretty. You're pretty, Stella," she said with a little blush.

"Aww, you're super pretty too, hee-hee," said Stella, putting an arm around Helen.

"Well now tee hee, I want to ask you cuties something," Jayden said.

"Yeah, pretty lady?" Helen responded, batting her eyelashes.

"Out of all the sexy sexy people in the world, who do you like the most?" Jayden rested her head in her palms.

"That's an easy one." Stella said with wide-eyes. "I like Helen. She's beautiful."

The skater pro was happy she wasn't actually drinking the Bubbly Tea or it would be all over her lap. She turned away for fear that Stella and Jayden might see a big ripe tomato in place of her head.

"And my mom…and Dan…and Charlotte…and you, Jayden and this really cool salesman I met who knew about The Fruitsaders. I like everyone, but B. Bop."

"Aw really?" Jayden asked. "That's good. That froed flirt is all mine!"

Stella spat Bubbly Tea out, but she made sure it wasn't in the faces of her friends. "What the? You like B. Bop, Jayden?"

"Yeeeeeeah." Jayden responded drawing out her voice "He's so handsome and manly. He's the coolest guy in Aleatore."

"Hah. He's a real tool," Stella responded.

"I knoooow," Jayden said, she rested her hands on her cheeks like a yearning schoolgirl. "But I like that about him. Oh this one time, he smacked me on the ass and said that he liked Neuroi chicks that were out of their mind. I wanted to maim him so bad, but I didn't."

Stella did a double take. This was a new side to Jayden. She didn't know if it was Bubbly Tea or if this was really her feelings. "Jayden, you're crazy."

"I knoooow."

"Now I know why you like Reinsons so much." Stella laughed and pointed at Helen.

"You do not."

"Yeah, you think they're sexy. I see the way you look at Helen, like a bear thirsty for snuggling."

"Umm...do not." Jayden looked back and forth with a bashful expression, before hiding her face. "I don't think Helen is sexy. I liiiike guuuuuuyyyss."

Helen finally got the courage to talk but avoided the issue. "You know Stella, I can't tell the difference between you on Bubbly Tea and off it."

"That's cuz I'm naturally bubbly. They could take concentrated blood from me and serve it as a drink and it'd probably produce the same effect."

"True that." Jayden's eyes widen. "If the Ravepires bite ya, they'll become peaceful..." She rests her head in her palms "and easy to destroy," Jayden responded in a very perky, but soft voice. "I wasn't happy today. It's the anniversary of Clyde's disappearance so I was prepared for a day of misery. But just getting to chill with you gals and drink this awesome tea has really flipped my day. I love you suckers like sisters."

Stella grinned too, having forgotten the gruesome images she saw before. "I don't know how this day can get any better."

Helen looked at her comphone "Well, looks like it can." She held up her phone showing off a message from Charlotte.

"Charlotte says she wants us down at the TCEPD station, they've found the location of the Ravepire's lair."

Jayden lifted her arms to flex her arms. "Look out Ravepires Jayden baby's gonna pay a visit to your house."

"Well, she's excited," Stella said. "Let's go Helen. It's time for us to truly be Neon Knights. Let's head to Stellen and get ready?"

"Stellen?" asked Jayden.

"Stella plus Hellen is Stellen. It's our room name."

"Ha! Do you have a kid too?" asked Jayden all loopy.

"We sure do! Mr. Kitty! I bet he's hungry!"

"That is just soooo sweet," said Jayden in a daze.

"Yep!" Stella poked her buddy's boob. "Let's go, buddy."

Helen covered her chest. "Don't poke me there!"

"Aww, but it was soft."

Helen blushed deeply and then grabbed Stella's shoulders.

She just sat there for a moment, staring at her friend.

Was it really ok that her life was a series of being traumatized and then forgetting it? The consequences were unknown, but she prayed that there wasn't a gradual descent the way there was for Illusionary Beauty products.

She checked up the history on her comphone. Both the products should have been outlawed, but there was such a great demand for them that Daddy D. just vetoed the ban with his signature veto slide.

Helen reached into Stella's pocket.

"Are you groping my booty? Is it squishy like your lady melons?"

"Yeah, it's...really great," said Helen with forced chipper. She looked at the back of the bottle, reading the side-effects.

"Oh, you wanted a happy pill?" Stella snuggled up to her. "Consider me your pep pill, cutie."

Helen nearly fell over and begrudgingly pulled herself free of her crush's grip. She handed her the pill bottle back.

There were things in Stella's past that she didn't seem to care about and Helen began to realize that maybe she just didn't remember them. From now on, Helen would be Stella's backup memory; remembering things she didn't want to by keeping them in storage so Stella could be a complete person.

Step 21: Dan Bop in Zero G

Dan reclined in his penthouse apartment chair, resting his head on his hand.

After becoming a Ravepire, his insatiable appetite was only quelled by a can of Fizz XL. He was becoming closer to Stella, but right when he thought he could let her into his private world, she infiltrated it. She hurt him in a way that was even his most rabid fans and haters couldn't.. It was his nature to close himself off more and more, each time someone broke his trust in them. At this point, the cage around his heart was a fortress.

His intercom rang, and he pushed up against the chair to get out of it. He hoped desperately it wasn't Stella or that rotten Wheels girl. He was relieved to see it was simply a Summerein butler with a snooty upturned nose, red bow-tie and tuxedo standing before him.

The butler presented a plate wrapped in tin foil. "Present for you, Sir..." he said.

Dan raised an eyebrow. "From who?"

"Miss Helena Wheels, sir."

Dan growled. "Why would that bothersome pest send me a..."

"Unraveling the intent behind this gift is beyond my paygrade, but that rather rotund girl expressed her deepest concerns to give it to you."

Dan rolled his eyes. "I guess I'll take it."

He grabbed the tin foil plate and closed the door. Walking back up the steps, he noticed a note on it.

"Dear Dork...Dorphin... ," Dan realized the word 'dork' was crossed out.

"I know you're going through a rough time lately, so I thought I'd make an effort to share some of my light with you. I know it's hard to believe, but I baked you a cake. Hopefully this will cheer you up.

From, Helen"

For the first time in a long time, Dan was shocked. That terror on wheels was being nice to him? What kind of bizarre occasion was this?

He removed the tin foil and winced. It was a fruitcake with gooey letters that said "a tasty treat for my fruity friend."

Dan gripped the table and let out a tormented howl. "That plastic tub of lard! She dare insult me!"

He threw the fruitcake at the wall with a splatter and started rocking back and forth. His rainbow teeth gritted into a grimace.

Dan was ready to tear his whole room apart in a Ravepire induced tantrum when his comphone rang. He removed it from his pocket, and for once, breathed a sigh of relief. It was not Stella, or that bothersome Helen Wheels, but rather Barvarius Bop.

"Yo, stud," Bop said, his handsome face flashing on the padscreen. "There's an important mission. Top secret stuff, my brother. Just you and me. No girls allowed. I picked you because I need someone I can rely on. Things could get dangerous."

Dan took time to breath. He was skeptical, but three things made him feel a bit better. B. Bop's chiseled mug, his dapper fashion sense and the phrase, "no girls allowed."

Considering lustful girls were the bane of his existence for many years now, perhaps he could finally redeem his wasted years by spending his time in the company of a real man.

Dan forgot his Helen-induced woes, grabbed his coat, and headed to Bop's pad, not knowing what awaited him. Whatever it was, he knew it was better than sitting alone in his penthouse. As he left, he heard roller blades going down the hallway.

"She is right to flee from me," he thought to himself.

Dan knocked politely at the door to Bop's pad. His father always taught him to remain mannered in the presence of anyone, man or woman. When he answered the door, his mouth nearly dropped. "Oh, hey stud," Bop said, completely shirtless.

"Homina homina hey…B-B-Bop," Dan stammered.

"Oh, don't mind me, I simply finished showering, "Bop said. "Don't let that stop you, son. Come on in."

Dan put a hand to his cold face to make sure he was still conscious before walking in. He stared in awe at Bop's pad. It wasn't anything like Stella described. It wasn't gaudy at all. The flame bed was truly cool and matched the aesthetic of its owner. The telescreen was huge, and then there was the dresser and enormous mirror. Dan eyed the cologne on it, but shook his head. Bop was actually looking out for him, unlike Stella.

Even more interesting was the plate-glass window. It was entirely open, revealing a gorgeous balcony. Wind blew into the room.

"Wasn't Bop cold?" Dan wondered.

As B. Bop fastened on his signature pinstriped outfit, he grinned at Dan. "Stud, you may be wondering: why have I invited you to my trendy pad for this top secret mission?"

Dan admittedly had the shameful thought of cuddling with a shirtless Bop before he watched B click the remote and the second most wonderful sight flew in front of him.

A Zero G racer hovered before them. It was sleek and modular with neon-red flames traveling the length of the it and a reddish brown fro at the top. Aside from Bop's shirtless torso this gorgeous racecar was the second most sexist object Dan had seen all day.

"I call this…" B. Bop said, flashing a shine grin "the Flamefroer. I thought we'd take a break from the chicks and cruise the skies in style. I didn't think you'd come unless I made it sound important. You're very serious and I respect that, but we need to seriously chill. I noticed you weren't feeling well. I thought maybe you'd want to chill with me, mano y mano? So, Stud. What do you say? Fresh air, the night sky and two bros in the slickest ride around?"

"Sounds great," Dan said, and immediately looked at the ground.

"What's wrong, Stud? Are you upset about my little white lie?" Bop asked tenderly.

"You know, Helen Wheels?" Dan asked softly.

"You mean Hell on Wheels?" Bop said, laughing at his own pun.

Dan wanted to laugh, but Helen had seriously hurt him.

"She sent me a fruitcake," Dan whined. "And called me a fruit."

"Oh, stud," B. Bop walked over in his pleather boots. He placed his arms on Dan 's shoulders, causing him to look up at the handsome fro'ed playboy.

"If I captured every hater of my Reinson heritage, I could fill a whole stadium. Each one of them would desire to see me fail, but I'd turn the tables and dazzle them into applause."

"It still hurt me," Dan said soflty.

"You ain't no fruitcake to me. You're a stylish stud!" B. Bop flashed another signature grin, and it made Dan smile too. "Now how about we cruise and schmooze the suave skies."

"Boppy," Dan cooed softly. "Can I drive?"

B. Bop winked at him. "For you, stud, anything."

Much to Dan's XXXisappointment, he was not cruising the skies with the greatest of Zero G. pilots, but instead they were down in the hustle and bustle of the street cars. He did not possess a Zero G license, so he could only operate his cruiser on the ground.

As they drove through the neon-brightened City Electric, Dan smelled the air inside the car. It smelled a lot like the cologne Stella was wearing. "Uh, Boppy?"

"Yeah, stud?"

"Do you use…that cologne Stella had?"

As they weaved through traffic, Bop paused for a second, before he smiled. "Yeah, but I'd never use it to take advantage of anyone."

Dan thought for a second. "Then why do you use it?"

"I uh…" Bop paused. "Like the way it smells… on me."

Dan was silent, but somehow, he didn't buy Bop's excuse. Perhaps he was wrong to rashly condemn Stella so fast, but he'd never learn the whole truth from either of them, so he put it aside.

As they neared the intersection of Building Forty-Two, where Daddy D offered the evening Shoot the Breeze, Dan heard something in his head.

"That Masquelaro, that's where we shall feasssst…"

Dan twitched and he looked over to B. Bop. There was a similar expression on Bop's face. "Did you hear that?"

"Hear what?" B. Bop's hand struggled, looming over Dorphin's thigh as he sped through the side streets. Dorphin couldn't take his eyes off the road. He heard the voice echoing from a dark alley way. All he had to do was find it. After a sharp turn that had Bop lean into him, he felt the squeeze of a hand on his thigh.

"What gives, Boppy?" Dorphin exclaimed, but Bop seemed to be in a trance.

Immediately, Dan swerved the Flamefroer in the direction of the voice. He turned down a side street.

"What's wrong, stud?" Bop responded, coming to. He shook his head.

"You grabbed my thigh!" Dorphin shouted.

"You're driving crazy. I had to grab onto something. Slow down, man."

"I can't stop now." Dan swerved the Flamefroer in the direction of the voice. He turned down a side street.

"Whoa, stud?" Bop responded with panic in his voice. "Where are you taking my fro bro?"

"I hear it!" Dan exclaimed and he pulled the car into a dark alleyway.

"Calm down, man. You're going too fast!" His eyes widened and he was sent into silence when he noticed an extremely pale man in a trench-coat who stood at the end of the alleyway.

His skin was even paler than a Winterson's and he had a ravenous expression on his face.

"Ravepire!" Dan screamed and attempted to run the fiend over. Right when he was about to, Bop grabbed the wheel and swerved it into a pile of trash.

Temporarily stunned, Dan shook his head. "B, why'd you do that?"

"I can't let that creature damage my car, son," B snapped. "Their blood has already ruined a really fine set of loafers. That glowy shit never washes out."

"I'll keep that in mind." Dan nodded and they both leaped out of the car.

The Ravepire leered at both of them.

"I'm going to stop each and every one of you scum!" yelled Dan with a bit of feral rage.

The Ravepire leered at both of them and Dan screamed, "Where are the Wintersons? Where have you taken my people?" Dorphin demanded, fury in his eyes.

The Ravepire simply gave a sickly laugh, fangs spread from his mouth. "Food," he snickered, but Dan didn't spare another second. He drew an iceglo and channeled his ice energy into it with a twirl. He brandished it and swung it forward, whipping him.

"Tell me now!"

"Stop! Please!" yells the Ravepire in agony.

"You don't get to make demands!" He sliced into the Ravepire with claws of ice.

"The Masquerlo! It's at the underwater palace!" The Ravepire looks at B Bop with desperation. "Don't let him kill me. That's all I know!"

"You monsters ruined my life!" yells Dan, readying his claws for the killing blow.

Bop sent out a small fireball that melted the ice around Dan's hand.

"Boppy, what are you doing?" Dan demanded. "You're acting strange. First you grab my thigh, then you crash the car and now you're protecting the Ravepire?"

"You're the one screaming like a madman. Chill bro. Ravepire blood is acidic. I'm merely being practical, stud." Bop sighs. "Listen man. Killing that guy isn't going to make you happy it's only going to…"

The Ravepire shoved Dan aside and bit into Bop's sleeve, causing him to wince.

"Boppy!" Dorphin exclaimed. Electromotion soaked Bop's sleeve as he knelt on the ground. "Damnned beast. Save yourself, Stud. I was careless."

"Noooo!" Dorphin screamed.

"Your weakness won't stop the transformation. You'll join us! It's inevitable!" the Ravepire snarled.

Dorphin leaped in front of B. Bop, but the Ravepire merely chortled. "We never travel alone. The location of the base will follow you to the grave, child!"

Several figures in trench coats dropped around them. A sickly groaning filled the air as each Ravepire lowered their hood, revealing sick, gaunt men and women with rainbow-colored eyes and teeth.

Their groaning sounded like an unnerving buzz that drained Dan of his energy. "One of ussss, one of ussss," they chanted as they approached from all sides.

Dan covered his ears and twitched painfully. "I am not one of you! And I will never be! I will resist you with every ounce of my Winterson blood."

"Stud!" Bop exclaimed as Dan dropped to his knees and started rocking on the ground.

B. Bop's fro ignited as he did a jig by sliding his legs with fierce energy. His eyes became focused and heated. "Burning Ring of Fire!"

Flames billowed up from the ground, surrounding B and Dan.

The Ravepires all leaped back and groaned.

Bop, with his hands held above him, used the flames to push the Ravepire's back.

"We shall return for the boy," they hissed before fading into thin air.

Bop, out of breath, got down on his knees. "Stud," he said, scooping Dan into his arms. "Did they hurt you?"

Dorphin's sight was blurry. He saw multiple Bops before his eyes came into focus. "You saved me, Boppy."

"That I did, Stud," B said proudly.

Dan pushed Bop off him and fell into a muddy puddle. "I don't want to hurt you. Don't get so close."

Bop's face grew serious. "Why would you think you're one of those fiends?"

Tears seeped down Dan's face. "Because…I was bitten by one. Please don't hate me. I couldn't tell anyone. I wanted to tell you, but only Stella knows."

Bop massaged Dan's hair and grinned. "Think of that setback as another chance to dazzle those haters."

Dan smiled, displaying his rainbow teeth.

Bop's eyes widened, causing Dan to feel bashful. "Oh shit! You're one of them?" Bop asked, backing up in fear.

"I hope that's not a problem. If I've s-s-survived this long…you'll b-be fine. You're s-so strong," Dorphin stammered.

After his shock receded, Bop gave a firm smile. "You're clearly one in a million, stud. Especially with that rainbow grin." Bop laughed.

"Boppy," Dan said softly. "Thanks for protecting me."

"Hey," Bop said, a coy look on his face. "Anything for a man like you. Just be careful who you show off that charming smile to, stud."

"You think my smile is charming?" asked Dan all flustered.

215

Without further provocation, B. Bop leaned in and kissed Dan. If the Ravepire's weren't going to send Dan to the land beyond, Bop's long kiss was.

The two of them remained there, gazing into each other's eyes until a police siren was heard off in the distance.

"I called the fuzz," Bop said at last. "I figured they'd be able to sort out this situation."

"I hope you're okay," Dan said, looking at Bop's wound.

"It's merely a nick," Bop said, covering his sleeve. "Nothing to worry about."

"Are you sure?" Dan asked. "He bit you real bad."

"I've dealt with women who have done a whole lot worse," B. Bop said and he turned in the direction of the sirens.

Police cruisers pulled into the alleyway. Men and women in uniform stepped out.

Dan closed his eyes softly, wishing to rest after such a hectic evening.

When Dan opened his eyes again, he found himself in the front entrance way of the police station, lying on one of their couches. Bop was the first thing he could see sitting on the couch beside him.

"Rise and shine, stud," he said and fluffed Dan's hair."

"Was that all a dream?" Dan asked, praying deeply his kiss wasn't the product of a wet dream.

Bop gave a winsome grin. "Nope, but it sure felt like it."

Bop's face grew more serious and he removed his hand from Dan's hair. "But stud, tell me…what did you hear in the car. What lead you to the Ravepire? The coppers want to know."

Dan scratched his head. "Something about the Ravepire's feasting at a masquelero. They also mentioned a palace underwater."

B. Bop ruffled the hair on his chin, before his eyes ignited like flames. "Stud, you're a lifesaver."

"I am?" Dorphin asked stupefied.

B. Bop pulled Dorphin to his feet. "Time to call the calvary, boss. "You single handedly uncovered the location of the Ravepire's lair."

216

"I…did?" Dorphin asked with a stupefied expression.

B. Bop's eyes glinted. "What a good boy." He leaned in and kissed Dan on the forehead before getting up and walking to the sheriff's office.

Dan slid back in his seat. That day out with Boppy had truly awakened something within him. He felt love and passion within in him despite the coldness of being a Ravepire. All it took was a kiss to remain himself and now that he knew that Boppy loved him, he was ready to take on all the Ravepire's himself with the power of love.

But as he looked at B. Bop talking to the sheriff, he still wondered about the look on Bop's face when he first heard the Ravepire. And how he beat around the bush with the cologne. Perhaps he could afford to apologize to Stella, if she apologized too. Dan gathered his wits. He knew the battle and the mysteries were far from over.

Step 22: The Yellow Sub

Dorphin entered the sheriff's office with B. Bop. Questions were swimming in his head. What was the Masquelaro and what did it have to do with a palace?

The sheriff reclined at his desk, shuffling through his desktop telescreen. He turned his head to address B. Bop.

The sheriff himself, a grey-haired man in his early fifties was cut and fit. It made Dorphin think to himself. "My dad only wishes he was that fit."

The sheriff squinted his eyes at B. Bop. "You sure about this, Barvarius?"

"Surefire," Bop responded with a grin. He put his arm around Dorphin's shoulders, causing him to turn red. "My boy would never lie. Tell him, stud."

Dorphin looked nervously. "I uh, heard the Ravepire's talking about a Masquelaro at a palace of some sort."

"And where did you hear this?" the sheriff asked.

Dorphin looked nervously at B. Bop. Did he tell him he heard this inside his head? Was he going to tell the sheriff how he went berserk against that Ravepire to acquire the information?

Bop rubbed Dorphin's shoulders. "We both heard them talking about it when we fought off those creatures."

Dan's tension left him and he felt so fortunate to have someone like Bop to protect him.

"Well," the sheriff responded. "There is a location out in the Electric Sea and…."

"Whoa," a boyish voice cried out in astonishment. "Who is that foxy lady?"

Dorphin turned his head. A spikey-haired Summerain man in his twenties stood before them. He wore a police uniform and a gas mask.

"What a silver fox," the young man said again. "Such poise, such elegant curves, such foxy-tude."

All three occupants looked around the room, trying to find who the young Summerein man was talking about.

"You," the young man said, pointing at Dorphin.

"I'm a guy," Dorphin said, angrily placing his hands on his hips.

218

The Summerin did a double take and stepped backwards. "Whoa. My apologies dude. It's just...wow. Like, you got a more curvaceous body than my sister."

The sheriff narrowed his eyes. "Pardon my son, RJ. He is not known for his subtlety."

"I can see that," Dorphin said, glaring at the masked man as he put his hands behind his head.

"Before we were so brashly interrupted," the sheriff said. "I have a theory that the lair of the Ravepires is somewhere in the east electric sea."

The sheriff looked to Bop and Dorphin. "I will dispatch my men immediately. And Barvarius, I ask that you accompany them."

Bop raised his hands. "I'm sorry fellas. I gotta tend to this wound." Dan gazed at Bop's arm which had a bandage around it. "Tonights been a bit too exciting for me. Best I rest for now, later skaters."

Bop put his arm on Dan's shoulder before walking out of the room.

Dan was a bit disappointed that Bop couldn't come along, but he was being responsible by taking the Ravepire bite seriously. Dan on the other hand, was determined to save Primus and the others.

"I'll go. You need a neon-knight to protect your son, right?" he asked with a serious look.

The sheriff immediately stood up. "I will not stand for a knight in training to go on such a treacherous mission."

RJ winked at Dan. "Aww come on, pops. We could use someone trained to fight with dance magic! You never know what is going to happen on a mission, right? Pleeeeeaaaaaasssseeee. Pretty Pleeeeaaaaaaassee. Pretty please with a Jeeg on top?"

RJ's shrill begging seemed to do the work that his words couldn't. The sheriff cringed and at last said, "Oh alright. But only because I've only heard good things about the young man from Barvarius." He looks at Dan sternly. "You are sure about going, right? It could get very dangerous."

"I take every aspect of my life very seriously."

Dan's response put a big smile on the sheriff. "Looking forward to when you get properly initiated. Imagine a neon knight as my detective. That would be stellar."

RJ lead Dan down the dark hallways of the police station to a subterranean harbor. Several submarines were in the docking bay, all colored in neon primary colors: red, blue and yellow.

"Welcome to our substation," RJ said. "Unfortunately, it doesn't serve hoagies."

"I'm vegetarian," said Dan, rolling his eyes.

"That explains the figure," said RJ with finger guns and a grin.

Dan ignored him and marveled at the aqua subs. They were fascinating, even if they weren't Zero G racers. They were built like this shark-shooters; racers often used in aquatic races around City Electric. They were bullet-shaped with fins and powerful turbo rudders.

"Which one should we pick?" Dan asked, his excitement increasing the pitch of his voice.

"Hmmm," RJ said, putting his hand to the chin of his mask. "The yellow one."

"Why?" Dan asked, somewhat interested in RJ's color-coated choice.

RJ flashed a peace sign. "I dunno, it makes me think of peace and love."

"We're not going to find love down there."

"Ha! That's good, ba...bro! But think of it. We're bringing the peace and love."

"Whatever," Dan said. "Let's find this hidden base and save Molly Primus and my people."

RJ looked back and forth. "Molly Primus, eh?"

Dan blushed. "What's wrong with liking her?"

"Uh nothing," RJ said quickly. "Let's hop to it."

Dan and RJ sat in the cockpit of the yellow submarine. Immediately Dan marveled at the controls. They were a dashboard of beautifully colored buttons, levers and switches.

RJ pulled the front level and the motor started, causing the whole submarine to rumble. The radio at the center switched on and began to blare loud pop music, which Dan didn't recognize.

RJ blushed from behind his mask and switched it to the communication channel. "Err, this ain't my sub. Some wierdo must have been listening to the Fire Five."

"Fire up my life? That's kinda cute. Makes me think of Stella," said Dan with a chuckle.

A voice blared in from the radio. "This Red Leader reporting in," a professional voice called out from the radio. "Blue Leader and Yellow Leader, do you copy?"

"Do you copy? I don't. I never plagiarize." RJ responded, humorously repeating the words to the other submarine leaders.

"Knock it off, RJ," Red Leader reported, and Dan could hardly agree more.

"This is Blue Leader," another voice responded. "I can't believe the sheriff is putting that goofball in charge again. Pure nepotism in his decisions again."

"My dad...believes in me. I just wanted to bring some levity." RJ sighed, causing Dan to feel a bit sorry for the young man.

"Anyway," Red Leader said, "we're drawing heavy signals from the sea bed to the east of the beach. If I was to venture a guess, that's where the Ravepires are stationed. Let us head over there and RJ, take this mission seriously for once."

"I will," RJ sighed. "Hold on to your perfectly preened hair, Mr. Dan, because this is going to be a speedy ride."

"As a future Zero-G pilot," Dan said, "no speed is too fast for me."

"Nice to know, dude," RJ nodded and cheerfully pressed the engine button.

With a bubbly blast, the submarine zoomed out of the docking bay and into the ocean, followed by the red and blue submarines.

As Dan and RJ cruised the florescent seas, Dan got to marvel at a sight he had never seen before: the marine life beneath the City Electric.

The purple, spiny balls of coral flashed brilliantly like a mirror ball. They were filled with electro-motion that illuminated the whole sea, even in dark waters. Neon colored fish grooved rhythmically to the pulsating coral. Even beneath the waves, the ocean had a funky beat.

A blip appeared on RJ's radar. "That's the concentration of electromotion that we're looking for."

"It's beautiful," Dan said with starry eyes.

RJ looked at him. "Yeah, just gorgeous."

Dan turned away annoyed. "Enough sight-seeing. I want to save my musical heroine."

"Primus is great. Such super fantastismic electro pop," RJ said, causing Dan to lift an eyebrow. "Err...I mean that's what my sister told me."

Dan shrugged his shoulders. RJ seemed to be quite a flamboyant fellow for someone who flirts with a girl the moment he enters a room.

The blips on the radar moved closer.

"Is that really a palace?" Dan asked. "It seems to be moving closer."

"Hmm," RJ said, putting his hand on his mask again. "We'll see."

"Dan craned his neck to see through the glow-weed reef and the murky waters ahead of them. "This is Blue Leader," a voice came over the radio. "I'll go on ahead."

The blue submarine zoomed forward into the glow-weed, but soon there was a sickening growl, and a scream. "This is Blue Leader. Do you copy? Emergency maneuvers."

Red Leader quickly chimed over the radio. "Blue Leader, what's wrong?"

"It's an enormous AAAAAAGGGGGGHHHHH."

The feed went dead silent, and with a roar, an enormous fish burst out of the glow-weed. Its teeth were rainbow colored in its huge gaping maw. It swallowed the submarine whole. A large antenna extended out of its head, flashing like a strobe light.

"What is that?" Dan exclaimed.

"A really big Raveglar fish," Red Leader shouted back. "The concentration of electro-motion in his antenna must have set off our radars."

"You see those whiskers? That means it's a male," said RJ with pride.

Dan gives him a blank. "I don't care about their biology!"

"Yeah, me neither," said RJ flustered. "Oh, but did you know some people say that the pollution of glows causes monsters like these to be born." His eyes widen. "Don't look now!" RJ screamed. "But it's coming straight for us."

As if spurred on by RJ's words, the monstrous Raveglar fish swam after them, opening his maw wide. The faint of the blue submarine flicker in the back of his throat.

"What do I do?" RJ asked panicking, but Dan immediately grabbed the panel. "If this is anything like Shark-Shooters, then I think I can pilot it."

"Yeah, I love that game! I modeled the controls after it. Well, best I could."

"I thought this wasn't your sub." Dan grabbed the joystick lever, and swiveled the sub around.

"Yeah…I just…modeled this one…umm…yeah, okay it's my submarine. But I didn't touch the radio last."

Red Leader followed them in his red submarine. He zoomed back through the reef as the fish started chomping hard after them.

RJ held onto Dan as the ship zoomed even faster than he had driven it. Dan didn't mind too much. Despite being obnoxious, RJ was kinda cute.

As the Raveglar got closer, it chomped even harder at Red Leader's submarine, biting into the left fin. The Red Leader struggled in spite of the damages and kept driving.

"I've been hit," he called out. "But the damage doesn't seem too structurally significant."

"Keep going!" RJ called back. "Last thing you want is be a late-night snack for this big fishy"

Dan looked up ahead. There was a weird wavy plant up ahead. Electric blue crackles came off of it.

"A Sea Electronemone," RJ called out. "Dan, go for it!"

"Wait, why?" Dan asked. "I'm trying to escape this thing. We can cruise the ocean some other time, captain."

"Captain, yeah. I like the sound of that." He turns his attention to the problem at hand. "Can you pivot around that Electronemone at the last second?" RJ asked. "Are your skill with the sub that good?"

"I'll try," Dan responded back. It would really be by the skin of his teeth. "I might need to try a somersault."

223

"Mind if I hold on a bit longer then?" RJ asked.

"Fine by me," Dan responded.

As they sped closer and closer to the Electronemone, the Raveglar drew closer and closer.

A loud gulp came from behind Rj's mask. "Here we go."

Dan spun the joystick upside down, causing the ship to spin like a loop-de-loop roller coaster. They could see the skin of the fish narrowly avoid the top of their sub as they zoomed over it.

As RJ and Dan flipped around to the back of the fish's tail, they had achieved what they were aiming for. They had avoided the Electronemone and the Raveglar.

The Raveglar wasn't so lucky and it plunged into the Electronemone, causing it to roar as it got zapped with electricity and zoom off in agitated anger.

"Gonna have to call you a Rageglar now! Haha, take that, big fishy boy." RJ laughed, and gave Dan a high five.

"Thanks for believing in me, captain."

"You too, first mate," said RJ with a big smile.

Red Leader's damaged submarine pulled up next to them. "I gotta hand it to you, lads," he said, his voice coming in over the radio. "I didn't expect such fine driving. I wasn't so lucky on the other hand."

"What's your plan?" RJ asked.

"We're going to have to retreat for now," Red Leader said. "Repair our submarines and report our loss of Blue Leader to the Sheriff."

Dan thought for a second. "You do that. I want to keep searching for Primus and the others."

"Are you sure about that?" Red Leader asked.

"I uh…" Dan grabbed his head. He heard a voice, calling out from the depths of the ocean.

"Sssssoon…soon we shall feast on them."

Dan immediately hit the switch, turning the motor on. "Wait, Dan," RJ cried. "Where are you going."

Dan let the direction of the voice guide him with closed eyes. He didn't even need to see. He was interconnected with the Ravepires whether he wanted to or not. He maneuvered the controls as he sped off into the depths again.

"Are you alright?" RJ asked, but Dan kept his eyes closed.

"I'm fine. Watch me."

Dan saw in his head, several men and women, Primus included, standing solemnly in a dark temple. They weren't moving, but they weren't dead either. Their minds lingered between life and death. He felt the pulse of electromotion course through his body guiding him to them.

He wouldn't give up on them, much like his friends wouldn't give up on him. As much as he didn't want to admit it. He witnessed the currents of electromotion, invisible to the eye, but seen in the mind as it guided him.

"Whoa!" RJ exclaimed. "Dan, open your eyes."

Dan looked beyond a giant red barrier and out onto an enormous valley of ruins. They had to date back centuries, with dilapidated houses, churches and even a stadium. But even more daunting was the building that floated over them. It resembled a cross between a palace and a theater.

The electromotion reader went off the charts, and RJ smiled from beneath his mask. "Stop the presses, Dan. I do believe you found the hostages. And uh, we better head back up because we are really low on fuel. I'll just take a picture and ask the Sheriff what that red energy is."

Dan puts his hand to the glass. "I'll come back for you all."

225

Act 3: The Lair of the Puppeteer

Step 23: Sorry to Burst your Bubble

The two aspiring female knights, and their more than a little inebriated teacher, returned to the headquarters of the TCEPD to be questioned.

They were escorted immediately to a planning room where Charlotte stood poised over a sleek metallic conference table. B. Bop and Dan both sat in chairs and who Stella assumed to be the chief of police stood behind them.

Tall and fit, his dark grey hair stood spikey and his five o' clock shadow was the same shade. It made him look gritty and hardened, something Stella certainly didn't mind. She thought he looked ten times more attractive than Daddy D. for someone around the same age. The mask that units usually wore was around his neck and had been removed for formalities sake.

When Stella came in, he locked eyes with her, and they were the most peculiar eyes she thought. They shined a rainbow of colors through his irises. "What's with his eyes? They're kind of funny," Stella whispered to her friends to avoid offending him.

"You don't remember Sheriff, do you?" Helen whispered with a sad look on her face.

"Who?" Stella asked.

"He led the security force at the Dance of the Gods."

"Oh yeah, I know that. But what about his eyes?"

"He had to fight with people who used seizure inducing rave staffs. Most don't survive and those that do…"

"Oh."

Jayden popped her head into the conversation and then shouted loud. "Hey Sheriff, Stella thinks your eyes are funny. But they didn't even tell a joke!"

Stella looked up at Jayden and glared as mean as she could but Jayden just let out an unrestrained giggle and covered her mouth in response. She let out a heavy breath.

To her luck, Sheriff just rolled with what she said. "Hah, I get that a lot. It's no big deal. I get people looking into them all day long and sometimes it's someone I like looking at too."

Stella felt suddenly shy and with a lot of tentativeness, moved her way to where everyone was.

The Sheriff smiles at the shy girl. "I heard about you and Ms. Wheel's first attempt at catching an Ug-Thief. Good job."

227

"I did what now?" Stella asked, wide-eyed and dumbfounded, putting her finger to her lip.

The Sheriff looked at her like he didn't understand her response.

Helen covered her face and shook her head. She had no idea how Stella could have a professional career when she didn't even remember her track record.

Charlotte, sensing awkwardness cut in. "So, everyone, we have excellent news…"

Jayden, ignoring her friend, sat down next to B. Bop in one of the revolving chairs. "Hey what you been up to, cutie?"

B. Bop raised an eyebrow at Jayden's disposition, "Uh, I was just been hanging with my bro, Dan."

Jayden held her hands together and put them to her chest. "Aww, male bonding…that's so adorable, hehehehe."

"Everyone," Charlotte said, a bit of tension in her voice, trying to reign the conversation back in. "I have important news."

B. Bop shook his head in disbelief. "It's not male bonding; it's called hanging. This is what I hate about women, they can hang out together and it's not called girl bonding, but everyone thinks that what we do is some kind of fanfiction shit."

Dan, winced a bit at B. Bop's tirade and spoke softly in order to ease him. "B, calm down. I know we were just hanging." He looks away and blushes.

"You guys were probably spooning and making out," Jayden said, while sticking her tongue out.

"I could totally imagine that." Stella was holding her sides as she laughed.

"Why won't anyone take this seriously?" Charlotte was growing very irate.

"I take it very seriously," Helen said.

"You do. Thank you, Helen….wait, Helen?" Charlotte's eyes bugged out. "I can't believe my brain formulated that sentence. Whoo, I need to sit down." Charlotte held her hand to her head, dazed, sinking into another of the rotating chairs.

"You secretly like Helen," Jayden said giggling. "I bet you fantasize about kissing her every night."

Charlotte shook her head just like B. Bop. "Something tells me that my little baby Jayden got into some Bubbly Tea."

"Yeah, miss chubby wubby thighs."

Charlotte swallowed hard and turned to Stella. "Stella, did you give her Bubbly Tea?"

"Yeah, I did. Is that bad?"

"It's very bad. Bad for her functioning."

"I think she's kind of fun this way."

Jayden stood up from her rotating chair and bent down, sticking her face into B. Bop's fro. "This conditioner is sooo yummy. It smells so mmmmmanly."

"Ahh, what the funk is wrong with you, psycho chick?" He leaned backwards, causing him to slip out and fall on his rear.

Charlotte narrowed her eyes at Stella and pursed her lips into her famous resting bitch face as if to say, "really, you call this fun?"

Stella found herself in a giggly mood too, but not because of the Bubbly Tea. "Hee-hee. I still think she's fun this way."

Charlotte's eyes narrowed. "Stella, I want you to go into the next room and get me some seltzer—make sure its flat. This is not the time for this."

Stella quickly stood up and headed straight to the break room. She reached in the cabinet next to the fridge and found the bottle. She then ran back at a rapid pace and passed the bottle off to Charlotte.

The scene had changed from when Stella was last in the room. Jayden and B. Bop were on the floor. Jayden was on top of him, her face fully submerged in his fro.

Jayden's voice was mewling and sounding like a small animal in heat.

"Mmm, I want every inch of me covered in your sexy sexy fro fluff."

"Get off of me! Seriously, never stick your crazy in my fro."

Charlotte towered over the two and kicked her pepped up protector's boot. "Jayden, girl it's time for you to sit up."

"Why?"

"I have some seltzer for you. It's time for the bubbles to go."

Jayden turned around and flashed big jeeg-like eyes and a trembling lip. She cooed in the voice that Stella had only heard once before.

"Please Charlotte, don't pop my bubbles."

"Jayden, it's imperative. You must be mindful, if you want to save your brother."

The bubbly warrior looked down at the ground, in deep contemplation.

Stella felt really sorry for her. It was incredibly hard for Jayden to have emotion and this tea let all of her emotions run free, even if they were unbearably uncomfortable. The sense of freedom she must have been feeling was enormous. And seeing that sleaze B. Bop get his space violated was enormously satisfying too.

Jayden's face hardened ever so slightly.

Stella could also tell Jayden knew it was time for her to calm down. There was just something in her eyes, letting everyone know it was time to say goodbye to easy emotion.

Jayden drank the seltzer without a second thought and before Stella knew it, everyone was sitting around the table.

"I'm sorry, you all saw me like that," Jayden muttered.

"You're lucky I didn't knock you out for the shit you pulled, pycho chick. This fro is a cultural treasure," B. Bop said, preening his fro.

Jayden, though having returned to her near emotionless state, sank in her chair in silence. It was clear to Stella that her feelings towards B. Bop weren't just brought on by the tea.

Stella tried hard to changer her soft high voice into a menacing growl. "Stop it, B. Bop. It's my fault she was acting like that."

"Her fault...her fault...her fault." Jayden echoed.

Her eyes pierced Stella and Stella could feel her heart speed up. Jayden looked like she was ready to crumple Stella and chuck her like a wadded-up piece of paper. She didn't know if Jayden was furious because she gave her Bubbly Tea or because she accidentally served as the ultimate vaj block. She hoped an apology and maybe some pleading for her life would suffice.

Charlotte spoke with the sheriff beside her. "Before I was so rudely interrupted, more times than I can count, I have good news to share with you."

Charlotte put her arm around the sheriff, causing the man to look around nervously with his rainbow-colored eyes.

"Thanks to the perseverance of the City Electric's own police force and Danny here…"

Charlotte put her hand on Dan's long mane of hair and ruffled it.

Dan immediately worked to fix the damage with an "ugh."

"Whoa, what did Dan do?" Stella asked.

Dan remained silent like his answer was confidential information.

"I hurt…" he spoke, but was cut off by B. Bop who despite being recently violated, was still as touchy feely as Charlotte.

Hanging on Dan, B. Bop relaxed and said, "Dan and I were hanging out at the grid when he told me he *heard* someone speaking."

Dan, a shy expression on his face, spoke again. "Their base is at the underwater palace."

"I don't know how he heard it," B. Bop said. "His ears must be supersonic to hear that with all that wind in our hair. Right, Stella?"

"Quiet people always have better hearing," she said with a smile.

The Sheriff nodded. "And it's a good thing he did because we had our top detectives dive in. Sure enough, we picked up some odd readings. Dan himself accompanied my pride and joy. He's got the spirit of a detective himself."

The Sheriff clicked a small rectangular remote that was on the table and the darkened telescreen behind them lit up to reveal an image of an antiqued dancing hall, complete with amphitheaters and large pillars featuring moldings of the visage of the angelic Kouyate.

"The Electric Blue Theater." Helen's eyes narrowed. "I remember that from architectural studies."

"I slept through that," Stella responded, dead pan. "What is that place?"

"It's one of the original theaters built in honor of Kouyate that's been long submerged underwater."

"Who did that?" Stella asked.

"Stella," Charlotte intoned like a mother, "it was built on a fault line so you can say it was…nobody's fault."

Stella broke into a fit of giggling, showcasing a wide grin. "Ha-ha, I swear if the teachers used more puns, I'd pay waaaay more attention in class."

Looking around at the other serious or disgusted faces, Charlotte smirked. "At least my play daughter didn't see it as pun-ishment. But anyway, see these sunken ruins…?"

"Yeah?"

"We had cruisers patrol the foggy water and found something as far from physics as possible."

The screen changed; a giant red bubble encircled the ruins. The Sheriff paced around. "Inside a thick fog, the scanners picked up extreme levels of electromotion. Further exploration, found the ruins floating inside an enormous bubble. We've examined and it and well, our hands are tied. The only ones who can get admittance are those trained with rave energy. Neon Knights."

"So, you just heard the good news," Charlotte said with a wave of her hand. "Now for the bad news I strategically didn't mention."

The sheriff's eyes darkened as much as a rainbow could. "You're going to be going at it alone. There's no way to disperse the shield."

"Now, now, being solo doesn't mean you can't have fun alone." Charlotte winked. "Helen knows that."

Helen lit up bright red. "How the heck would you know?"

The Sheriff looks at Charlotte. "Should I be concerned?"

"Oh, I'm just teasing her. She's always going to be single, so it was just an educated guess."

"I do that kinda self-love too. Ignore her, Helen," said Stella, holding her friend's hand.

Helen nuzzled up to her friend. "You're so sweet."

Stella nuzzled back, taking a whiff of Helen's strawberry scented hair. "You're even sweeter."

"Can we focus, please?" Dan sighs and then looks at Charlotte. "You always put things so eloquently," Dan quipped. "Glad to know you're so happy we might die."

"Why thank you, Danny. And I'm sure you'll do fine. Need I remind you you're with a woman who has been plotting the Ravepires demise since the day they crossed her?"

"I have already killed several," Jayden said coldly. "I would do this mission alone. But you Neon Knights need hands on experience."

Hellen smiles at Jayden. "You'll never have to fight them alone again."

"I want to finally prove myself," Stella said. "There was a reason I became a knight; to be famous and adored by both parts of the nation. I haven't messed up so far."

Helen scratches her cheek. "Um, you kinda did. Oh, and don't forget about saving Clyde and Molly and well, everyone else too. You didn't forget about them, did you?"

"Of course I didn't forget about Clyde. But what does Molly have to have to do with this?"

"Yellow plus," Helen said with a blunt tone of voice.

"Uhm hehe, I dunno. My mind probably just auto erases anything to do with that skank."

"Well Stella, you'll certainly be famous and a hero if you are successful," Charlotte said. "Just be sure to pay attention to the infiltration briefings. If you get lost, we can't call your parents over the intercom."

"Oh, I won't get lost," Stella replied with a salute.

"Then let us commence."

Two hours passed and Stella was unable to keep her promise. She paid attention for about fifteen minutes, but things started veering into discussions about the buildings layout every possible way to move around it. The hostages were also profiled and things got ultra-specific with personal histories and medical records being detailed.

Stella had no idea why Gary Silva being allergic to soy would be vital to know on this mission to anyone except Charlotte if she planned on dating him. And it only got worse from there. By the time the discussion ended, Stella's attention had shifted to the Power Tower levels on her comphone.

Helen, who sat in front of Stella, had to jostle her awake and tell it was time to go. She walked with Stella out of the room and into a hallway where she readied a strict lecture for her friend.

"Stella, you knew this was important and you blew it off."

Stella's eyes grew in her head. "You noticed?"

"Just because the Sheriff's half blind and Charlotte's got her head so far up her ass that she can only see eternal darkness, doesn't mean I didn't see you on your phone."

"But, Candy Birds Saga released a new character, the Chocotu. He's sooooo cute."

"This is life or death for some people, you know."

"I'm sorry, I've always had attention issues since school. I had medication for it, but I had to go off of them for the Yellow Plus."

Helen pulled Stella aside so she stopped moving and gazed into her eyes. "Because I am such an incredible friend, I copied down the most important information to give to you."

Stella's eyes lit up so bright Helen could swear they sparkled. "ZapNotes for this mission. Sweetness! Come here, buddy," Stella grabbed ahold of Helen, spreading her arms around her body so she could feel the love. "I wish I had a friend like you during school. Feel the warmth of my hearth of gratitude." She gave her a sweet smooch on the cheek.

"I thought…you did fine in school," Helen stumbled over her words.

"Nah, I was much too busy learning new dance moves because I knew someday I would end up in the Dance of the Gods."

"That you did Stella, but sometimes I wonder if you truly know what happened there."

"I do; don't worry. I keep the most important stuff locked safely in my brain suite."

"I don't know about that," muttered Helen with a sad look on her face.

"What? I didn't quite catch that," Stella responded.

"It's nothing."

Jayden ran up to them. "Helen, I desire your presence."

"Oh? Is this important or do you just want to spend time with me?" asked Helen, her head tilting.

The warrior's normally unflinching attitude faltered as if Helen's words hit her. "Well, I have some last-minute training to give you."

Stella looked to Jayden with a naughty grin. "You mean training or…*training*?" She winks.

Jayden's gaze turned to Stella and her voice grew cold.

Stella began to tremble and hold onto Helen tighter.

Jayden looks at Stella darkly. "I want to be certain someone doesn't drug you."

"Oh, okay." Helen realized she was still hugging Stella and moved her arms. "We were hugging for a very long time, weren't we?"

"Is that bad? Molina always says 'Longer hugs means longer happiness.'"

"Is that from that Fruitsaders show?"

Stella closed her eyes and smiled with a tilt of her head. "We still gotta binge it sometime together. Dan, you, me…" Stella looks up at Jayden "you wanna watch too?"

Jayden gave her a blank stare.

Helen's face was both red and smiling. "We can watch it together, just the two of us… after the mission if you want. Just remember to read the notes I gave you."

"Got it, study buddy."

Helen and Jayden departed in the direction of the TCEPD's training room while Stella headed for the locker room. She walked the cold, grey office hallways until she found the gender labeled locker rooms. She found Dan outside the male locker room. He had his foot to the wall and gazed perpendicular to the opposing wall. His lips held tight like he was retaining some tension.

"Dan."

"Stella."

Stella tried to be all cool and composed around Dan, but found it hard. She found herself tripping on her words. She waved and at him and he did not even elicit a turn in her direction.

"So, now you're hanging out with B. Bop?"

"He's a really good friend. We had a fun night together. Barely touched me inappropriately. Definitely no kissing, despite what Jayden thought."

Stella pursed her lips. It was very obvious B. Bop was using Dan, but his true agenda was a mystery still. Either way, Dan actually responded to her. This meant it was time make him see the truth.

"Dan, I want you to come with me." She took him by the hand and not paying mind to his reaction, lead him into the female locker room.

The filthy and stained, blue and light-brown tiled floor and dirt covered benches with lockers that were missing numbers, showed that the janitorial staff might have been even more inept than the police force.

"Great, Stella. Do you really want me to catch some foot disease?"

"Don't take your shoes off, silly."

"So, why have you brought me into this bio hazard?"

"So B. Bop won't find us?"

"You really think a ladies only sign will prevent him from coming in here? You know nothing," Dan said with an eye roll.

"No, but the smell will. He gets upset when he doesn't smell like himself."

"Fair enough. But I don't see why you're doing this."

"It's because B. Bop tricked you and he's trying to manipulate you."

Dan clutched at his heart. "Don't speak ill of him!" He notices she looks jostled. "He's a good friend to me. Like...you used to be." He turned away from her to hide his vulnerability.

"Hey, just hear me out okay. First off, he set me up with the cologne. Well not exactly, but he blackmailed me to keep it from you."

"What?"

"He's going to use you too. He knows something about you..."

Stella expected Dan to try as hard as possible to dispute her claim but he didn't.

"I was suspicious too because I saw so many colognes on his dresser. But you know, B. Bop was a gentleman to me. And get this, he owns a Zero-G cruiser and he took me for a ride in it."

Dan's eyes glistened in a way Stella never saw before and she felt like no matter what she said it wouldn't get through to him. Still, she tried.

"That's the wrong way to think Dan. Didn't you hear me? He blackmailed me! Helen saw it too. Helen was telling the truth. I didn't back her up because...well, the whole blackmail thing."

Upon hearing the words, Dan lashed at Stella with his head jerking forward in a rage. "I can't believe you'd say that. You have no proof. Stella, don't you want me to be happy? Please, drop this."

"B. Bop...makes you happy?" Stella asked softly.

"Well, I mean...I just like that he wants to spend time with me. No, that isn't true. Yeah, he makes me happy." Dan's face gently moved into a smile.

Stella's worst fears were true. All of the suspicion B. Bop roused was alleviated for Dan because of his powers of seduction. And the only proof she had was one thing she could say.

"You need to listen, B. Bop threatened to tell Charlotte about you being a Ravepire."

"I told him about my condition and that's because I trust him. He helped me get out of a bad situation. He protected me from...me."

"Huh?"

"And he told me what it's like to be a minority. He hasn't had it easy, Stella. Please, just leave us alone."

Stella turned her eyes away from Dan. She was very saddened by this change in him.

B. Bop must have been a sorcerer because he knew how to put people under a spell. Stella had one last shot to fire and then she'd resign to the realm of the unbelieved.

"He was aware you were a Ravepire before you told him."

"I don't believe you. And I won't just stand around arguing with you all day. Look Stella, I'm not mad at you anymore, so stop testing my patience."

You're going to find out the hard way, was in Stella's thoughts. Her crush on Dan, was completely crushed. Not just because of his admission to everyone about who he was in the bedroom, but because she had no idea how someone who was so critical of everyone and everything could put his full trust in a sleaze ball.

Hopefully things would resolve themselves with B. Bop's tendency to crumble any relationship, platonic or otherwise. Stella, as much as she still considered herself Dan's friend, couldn't see him in the same light anymore. It was time to give up, for now at least.

"I'm sorry. Maybe he just hates me. I...hope he is really your friend."

Helen having returned from training had entered the scene and gasped when she saw Dan inside the women's locker room.

"Eek, what the freak is Dan doing here." Her eyes popped. "No way. He's a sister?"

Dan scoffed at her. "It's none of your business, it's just between me and Stella. Sister talk," he said with a grin.

"I was joking. But yeah, it's okay if you want to be a woman. People are more accepting of that these days…and those that aren't…just ignore them. I just don't know what that has to do with Stella. Was she giving you make-up tips, pretty boy?" Helen chuckled.

Stella gave her an angry look and she froze up.

"You're acid-tongued as always, but I've moved beyond our petty squabbles." Dan turned his head to Stella. "I wish you luck, Stella. I hope we will stop these Ravepires together."

He held out his hand for Stella to shake it. She did with only a moment's hesitation. "I wish you luck too and not just with this, with your life. I hope you can work everything out."

"Thanks, friend." He walked off without another word.

"Dan, I'm sorry for what I said. I didn't mean to," said Helen, trailing after him. "And why did my cake upset you? Was it…bad?"

He ignored her and walked off.

Stella watched his shoes disappear behind a locker. She felt she wasn't just saying goodbye to him, but to a part of her she had developed when she first came to this city. Stella opened up locker 123, a locker she was assigned at the conference and found a brand-new set of rave armor, much like the ones Jayden had. It was time for her to suit up and embrace the true reason she came to the city.

Step 24: The New Masqualero

The cruiser skimmed across the purple waters of dusk. Its black and white body was sleek and compact and its motor, silent. It was a police-issued vehicle designed for infiltration. The riders consisted of a quintet of Neon Knights and a single pilot.

There were two rows of seating with three chairs each. The two in front, Stella and Helen were still wet behind the ears, literally as they peered off the side, droplets were hitting their faces. They were clad in flexible armor made of elastic and neon.

Stella had her faded-pink hair tied back and a powder blue and hot-pink suit. She had many fireglos strapped around her waist. She still wore large, dangling star shaped earrings, similar to the ones she wore the night of the Penultimate Party. While it did not seem like the most intelligent choice of attire for combat, these were different. Each point of the intricately shaped star was sharp. The way the earring connected to her lobe made it easy to transfer rave energy from her body and create a potent throwing weapon.

Charlotte had seen what Stella was wearing the night of the party and, using her one woman think tank, devised a way how the accessory could also be used for fighting. She wore special black goggles on her head too, everyone did. They were tinted rainbow and allowed them to see their targets even when they weren't in the rave lights.

Stella had a confident pose as she peered over the water. The outfit she wore could very much be a rave outfit; it was light and could easily stretch to fit as many dancing or battle positions as possible.

Helen leaned off the boat with her, wearing a flexible green and black suit, but this one was fuller-bodied than Stella's. The pixelated flower she often wore, was still in her hair. Charlotte wasn't nice enough to turn it into a weapon for her. She possessed both fire and ice glos, both of which she could wield equally. She kept these wands on straps over her shoulders.

Helen kept a conversation going with Stella, trying to keep her focused on the objective at hand.

Those who sat behind them were a lot more reserved, leaving all the talking for the front seaters. Dan, in his ice blue armor and Jayden in her trademark black and neon pink sat still, wrapped up in their thoughts. Dan discussed about the many ways they could die and proper battle tactics, while Jayden pondered her options for eliminating her targets.

B. Bop was the most focused, seemingly in deep thought with his eyes shut and legs crossed.

The pilot, who Dan knew as RJ, seemed the liveliest of them all. He wore a large mask with several tubes jutting out in random places and a digital screen to represent his mouth.

"Any of you here vegetarians?" he asked, with a nonchalant tone in his voice.

Helen and Dan both raised their hands. "You're in luck, your blood is the most tasteless and watery, so they'll go for you last."

"Hey, that's not fair," Stella pouted.

"It's also not true," said Helen, rolling her eyes.

"Indeed," said Dan, holding his arm. "And just so you know, it's not a diet…at least not to me."

"Well, what can I say, Ravepires suck…and they bite too," the pilot responded.

Stella giggled. "They suck and they bite and they're horrible people."

"True that," said RJ, with a digital smile.

Helen fake laughs. "Good one, Stella."

"Some of those monsters are victims too," said Dan softly.

Stella's eyes suddenly widen. "Wait, Helen, you're vegetarian." She grabs her buddy's booty. "So, all this is organic?"

Steam pours out from Helen's head and she just mumbles.

"Can you chicks can it? I'm trying to mediate here. I got a big battle ahead of me," B. Bop demanded, his hand shaking a bit.

Dan places his hand on Bop's and smiles.

"Oh really?" Stella pivoted her head to glare at him, her earrings swinging. "You never stuck me as the spiritual type."

"There's a lot you don't know about me, baby doll."

A line like that inspired Stella to roll her eyes. "Yeah, you're such a mystery."

"I'm a mystery wrapped in an enigma." B. Bop made a hand gun and pretended to sling it in the direction of Stella.

"Wrapped in a douchebag," Helen added, sticking out her tongue.

The whole front seat erupted into laughter, leaving the backseat quietly steaming.

"Take this seriously," Jayden advised everyone with a hushed tone in her voice.

Stella felt a sudden change in temperature as the boat sped into a thick bank of fog. She shivered despite being fully clad.

"Are we here?" Dan asked, looking up.

"I haven't the foggiest," replied the pilot.

"I can see why Charlotte chose you," Dan said, great annoyance in his voice.

"Wait, what's that in the distance?" asked Stella.

An unnatural red-orange mist swirled in front of the cruiser, intermingling with the fog. Slowly, the red mist began to form shapes and the shapes began to form features. An enormous head appeared from the cloud with a hooked nose and eyes like ghostly fires.

Its voice boomed.

"Go back, or the missing ones will suffer."

Stella looks to Dan. "Is this the reason you guys didn't proceed?"

"No...this is new," said Dan with wide eyes.

The cruiser continued to drive forward and into the mouth of the mist. A cold chill fell upon everyone. The head began to laugh before dispersing into the fog.

Everyone was silent, confused and a bit shook up until the pilot spoke. "So guys, were you scared?"

Stella was the first to speak. "Hah, me? Nah, that was straight out of an episode of Hysterical Mysteries, one of the cheesier ones too."

Helen laughed too. "I remember that show from when I was a kid. There's probably a projector somewhere that casts it."

"Haha yeah, what do you guys in the rear think...uh?" The pilot turned around to face Jayden, Dan and B. Bop.

Stella was surprised to see a petrified shaking Dan and Jayden hanging onto B. Bop. Both of their faces even whiter than the shade of pale they were before.

241

Upon seeing Stella raise her eyebrows, Dan became defensive. "Stella, if you had your motion sucked out of you by a Ravepire, you'd do the same thing."

Jayden's face had a tiny smile on it. "This is nice."

"Get off me! Stop pretending you're afraid!" yelled B. Bop.

Both Dan and Jayden quickly removed their hands from him and placed them in their laps.

Dan looked a bit sad and started. Upon seeing this, B. Bop realized his mistake and aimed to rectify it.

"No, it's all good, stud muffin. It's fine for a guy to show feelings. So many women frown upon it, but who cares what they think."

"How's your foot taste, B. Bop?" Helen smirked.

"And who would put studs in a muffin?" Stella added. "That's a good way to get janked- up teeth."

The boat pulled to a stop and rested against a giant red bubble. Beyond the bubble they saw a building. Inside the building was a fallen wall that had given way, presenting an entrance to a dimly lit hallway to the theater.

"Well folks, we're here. Hate to interrupt you since you guys are basically your own sitcom," the pilot said laughing.

Stella looked in his direction. "Hey, I'm gonna miss you uh…what's your name?"

"RJ," The pilot said giving her the thumbs up. Stella could tell that behind the mask, RJ was a young man and quite the cute one at that.

With spikey brown hair, reddish Summerein skin, bright blue eyes that enlivened his face and an upbeat attitude to boot, Stella was ready to enter rebound city with him.

"So, what're you going to do while we're inside, RJ?" Stella asked, grinning at him and batting her eyes.

RJ rested his arms behind his head. "Waiting here for you to return with the hostages and being bored out of my skull."

"Yeah, that's really dull and what if they found you waiting out here?" Stella tilted her head in a way she perceived as cute. "Why don't you come with us? I…I mean, we, can protect you. We are noble knights, after all."

242

"Hmm, that doesn't sound so bad. I've always wanted to see a real live Ravepire. I've never seen a suit so tacky, other than at my uncle's wedding."

Stella giggled. "Daddy D. would wear one, I'm sure of it."

"Hey!" Helen shouted. "Don't we have a mission?"

"That's correct," Jayden said, "now let's see what this force field is made of."

Jayden entered a sealed hanger. She opened the window quickly and levitated her staff up to the red force field. The staff prodded the bubble for a weak spot. It stopped and then pressed into the red barrier. About half the staff was submerged inside the bubble. She moved it with a surgeon's precision or like a king's vassal tasting a glass of wine for hints of poison.

Her head twitched and her eyebrow raised, sensing the power before she just as cautiously removed her weapon. With her harsh eyes, she looked at everyone. "I think if the count of electromotion in your body is high enough, then you can enter. I'll try first."

RJ hit the motor, and brought the cruiser parallel to the barrier's weak-point, with the blast sliding exit door pressed firmly against the entrance.

Jayden put her hand up to the bubble. "This barrier was made by someone. A warrior with advanced knowledge of electromotion." She turns to Be Bop. "Do you know of a missing neon knight who could have done this? It's a Summerein power, right?"

"Could be a Reinson too. We better be on our toes if we are gonna fight a twisted knight," said Bop with a serious expression.

Helen looks worriedly. "So this means only we can enter, right? This is definitely a trap." She pulls Stella close to her.

"Oooh, this is getting spooky," said RJ, popping his head out between them.

Jayden pressed on the bubble and pushed through it. Helen, followed by Dan and B. Bop, went through after doing a cramped dance to make a barrier of energy around them.

Stella watched as they entered. She looked at RJ with beckoning eyes.

"He can't enter," Jayden said.

"What? He's a Summerein. And I bet he can dance." She nudges him playfully.

"I'm a beast at DDI."

Jayden rolls her eyes. "He's not a warrior. He doesn't know how to create a protective barrier. He's weak."

"Hey, I resent that," RJ responded.

Stella thought for a second before her eyes brightened and her mouth widened into a smile. "What if I try this?"

Stella stood halfway between the inside of the entrance and the outside, the red bubble dividing her body. She shuttered as the energy began to tear on the fabric of her being. "H-h-here, RJ, grab my h-h-h-hand."

RJ did just that and she pulled him from the cruiser. Helen joins in by pulling on Stella's other arm. Heaving a sudden amount of weight from a fully armored pilot, caused Stella to stumble backwards and RJ to fall on top of her.

"Ugh, you're so heavy. What's weighing you down so much?" Stella said, groaning and trying to ease him off her.

"Uh, regrets and painful memories?" RJ said, checking his body for injuries.

Stella looks up at him with tearful eyes.

"I was kidding. Members of the TCEPD have to wear these body buckets as I call them even when we're directing traffic."

"Really? That's stupid," Stella said.

"Dad wants it. In these increasingly insane times, he wants every officer to be as safe as his civilians."

"Your dad?"

Helen, after rolling back onto her feet went to help Stella get up. "He means the Sheriff."

Stella had to take a deep breath. "The Sheriff's your father? I can see the resemblance."

"Really?" asked RJ as he managed to lift his armor-clad body to his feet. "How so?"

"You're both cute."

RJ put his hand behind his head. "Well, if you could see underneath my high-powered gas mask, you'd think I was a tomato." The digital mouth his mask possessed was upturned in a smile with slight blush lines flashing on it to indicate he wasn't exaggerating.

"Do you want to be left behind?" asked Dan, turning around with an annoyed look.

"Agreed," said Helen with a groan, pulling Stella close to her. "Didn't that hurt?"

"It pinched a bit, yeah. But I didn't feel right leaving our new buddy out there alone."

Jayden, who had already moved on without Stella, tapped her staff. "Stella, you've jeopardized this mission. Silence." She points her staff at RJ and Stella. "You are forbidden to speak, barring emergencies. Focus is key. We must not give away our position."

"Sorry, can you speak up?" asked Stella, still in a bit of a daze.

"Seriously, Pink Tails, get your mind on something other than new boy toys," B. Bop added.

"Stella doesn't see people as toys," said Helen with a glare. She nudged Stella to make her own retort.

Stella bit into her lip. She instead surveyed her new scenery and tried her best to remember everything Helen had copied down for her.

The group travelled down a dim and frigid corridor. Everything had a hue of sunken blue from being underwater for so long. Still, this passage way had all the trappings of a theater. The moldings on the wall were crown-shaped and regal, fitting because the King Mayor who existed long before Daddy D. would frequently attend the building for shows, according to Helen's notes. It was said the king himself perished when the building tumbled into the sea.

The show he was witnessing before the crash was now the stuff of legends. The Masked Masqualero was one of the five most powerful arcane dances granted to the world by Ravenous herself. The Electric Blue Theater was the only place one could witness mysterious dancers whose bodies showcased all emotions without the use of their face and had abilities to all but vanish and let their masks dance in the air. As the art was lost with the theater, this show, and the urban legend that surrounded it, created the City Electric's fascination with masked dancers. Old water damaged posters hung from the wall with images of elaborate performers from the last show ever performed.

Their hollow white faces gave Stella a chilling feel.

"I can't believe we're the first people to set foot in here since the place got destroyed from that disaster," said Stella from the back of the group.

245

RJ, who had become Stella's partner in conversational crime responded. "Bet you don't know how it really sunk, miss knight. Most of us at the headquarters know that the Edwardians did it."

"Wha?" Stella was dumbfounded.

"Yeah, the Edwardians caused Blue-27. Us high-level officers know there's a secret pocket of them that have remained on Aleatore. They planned Blue-27 so the City Electric would fall into chaos."

"You really believe that?" Helen asked, her voice heightened in skepticism.

"Nah, I don't believe that bullshit. Urban legends to mess with people 101!" he slapped Helen on the back and laughed.

Helen's eyes almost popped out upon impact.

Jayden moved over to eclipse Helen, her tall thin form towering over her. She talked sternly to RJ. "Don't touch Helen."

Stella could tell it was Jayden's killer eyes that made RJ stop cold in his tracks. The soldier just nodded his head and continued walking.

B. Bop and Jayden led the way as the group continued down the long corridor to the lobby. When they reached the lobby, both observed their surroundings carefully.

It had a water-damaged wooden front desk, as well as some benches that had been reduced to driftwood so attendees could rest while waiting. There were two large doorways, presumably leading to the main theater to the left and right of the desk. Seeing what was behind the desk, Helen let out a shriek and quickly covered Stella's eyes before she entered the foyer.

"Helen, whoa, what's going on?" Stella asked.

"T-T-There is a skeleton sitting at the desk."

"Oh, my goddess," Stella lifted Helen's hands off of her. "Helen, I LOVE skeletons! I can't believe this is real!" She ran over and hugged her bony bud with a great big smile.

Helen was left with her mouth gaping and stuttering in place of words. "But what? Wouldn't this terrify you?"

"You kidding me. They're always dancing and making puns. They'd be my spirit animal if they were actually an animal."

Helen shrieks and steps back. "Don't touch it."

Stella observed it closer. The skeleton was covered in rags with shreds of faded neon all over it. There was an empty glostick, encircled around its hand. Like all skeletons, it sported a hearty grin, but Stella was sure that back when it was alive, it was anything but grinning.

"This girl," RJ said, "she makes no bones about… how much she likes them skeletons…" He let out a cough and an 'ahem', which at first sounded comical, but he continued to hack, resting his arms on his knees. "Ack…someone, I can't…I feel…." His feet slid on the floor, and the soldier face planted with a loud thud.

"RJ!" Stella ran to him and lifted his limp arm. "What's happening?"

"I knew this would happen," Jayden said, her voice not giving a hint of concern.

B. Bop smirked. "Somebody check his liver. He's probably drunk off his own awful comedy."

"Boppy, please stop that," Dan said. "He's a friend. I'm concerned about him too. Jayden, what's wrong with him?"

"He's weak. The force field wears on our trained bodies. I'm surprised he made it this far."

Stella immediately realized it was her fault. She had jeopardized the whole mission and RJ's life just to flirt with a fellow jokester.

A tear trickled down her face.

Jayden bent over and put her hand on RJ's wrist, sliding his metallic glove up so she could feel his pulse. "His life is fading. He needs to get out of here."

Stella knew she should be the one to carry him. "Let me do it." She tried to lift his body, putting her back into it, but she could barely get him off the ground. His body slumped back down.

"That's that. We must proceed. Clyde awaits," said Jayden, walking ahead.

"Look Pink Tails, if you're so concerned, I'll take him," B. Bop said.

"That's so nice of you." Stella sniffed and mucus ran down her face alongside tears.

"Surprisingly," Helen said with wide eyes.

"Just uh…do something about that face. It's leaking all kinds of nasty," B. Bop replied. With great strength, he hoisted RJ's body onto his back. "This guy should learn to dress to impress, not depress." He trudged away.

As relieved and amazed Stella was by B. Bop's sudden kind gesture, she still couldn't shake off that she had caused all this. She didn't want to do anymore damage, so she decided the best plan of action was to forget it all happened, a reoccurring trend in her life. But this time, it would be for a good reason; she could finish the mission without worry or fear to trip her up.

Stella turned away from Helen, Jayden and Dan and popped a pill in her mouth. She swallowed quickly so they wouldn't notice.

Helen lightly tapped Stella on the shoulder. "It's going to be okay. As much as I can't stand him, B. Bop is being nice for a change."

Dan looked at Stella tenderly. "We're here for you. I know you just wanted RJ to not be left alone." He sighs. "I'm sorry I've been distant. I've just been dealing with a lot of things. You understand." He grabs her hand. "I'm here now, Stella."

"So, what are you going through? It has to do with that bite, right?" asked Helen shyly.

"I have nothing to say to you," said Dan coldly.

Jayden turns her head. "B. Bop doesn't have to go far to get him out. He should survive. Eighty-percent."

Stella smiled at her friends and Jayden, and then felt pangs of regret. Maybe she overreacted and didn't need to take the pill, but it was too late. In a few minutes, she'd be ignorant of the whole issue. It probably was for the best. She knew thoughts of RJ would interfere with the mission.

"Thanks guys, I love you." Stella smiled and bobbed her body.

"Argh," Dan clutched his head. "I can hear voices in the next room. They're so sharp and painful."

"I don't hear anything Dorkphin, are you sure you aren't going schizoid? B. Bop said you heard Ravepires on your bro date too. Are you okay man?" Helen asked, wanting to comfort him but scarred to touch him.

"They're in there waiting for us. I can hear them…talking about devouring energy."

Stella braced herself, inside was a cabal of Ravepires waiting to feast on her. She checked to see she had all her fireglos and felt to see if her secret weapon, her earrings, were still on.

"Let's do this Neon Knights!" She said with a dramatic pose. "Let's make them see rainbows."

Everyone raised their eyebrows, or in Jayden's case, her eyebrow at Stella's call to arms, but they all proceeded through the left door just the same.

Walking up a dark-sloped hallway where the carpet had been torn and revealed concrete, the four came out on the left of the stage.

The room was dark and towered over Stella. Rows of seats continued higher and higher until they reached a second level. Even higher were five different amphitheaters designed for those who were even more aristocratic than the people who sat in the regular seats. These window-boxes all had the same crown-like moldings. The pillars attached to the walls were decorated with painted masked dancers. She could sense the posh air of the building, despite it being ransacked and submerged for at least a hundred years.

"I'm surprised this place is so intact," Helen said. "I never thought I'd be inside to see it. It is like...really expensive...and buried in the ocean."

"We must be cautious," Jayden said. "The Ravepires are here. I can't see them. But I sense them."

"Check that stage over there?" Dan suggested, mustering up courage.

Rusted spotlights made the only light in the room. They were powered by brand new glos. A spotlight shone onto the stage where the group observed the largest amount of damage in the room. Wood boards and nails were unhinged in several places and two large statues of Kouyate had been knocked over onto the apron of the stage.

At the foot of the stage, a bunch of bodies lay, victims of the fault line that had long since decayed into skeletons.

Helen shivered and Dan covered his eyes as they walked past them.

"That's so sad," Stella said. "They came here just to have a good time."

Everyone walked one by one up the creaky steps on the side of the stage until they reached the platform where the spotlight shone brightly. As soon as the limelight was cast over them, they heard a booming "WELCOME!"

Dan jumped and held his head, "That voice...it hurts."

Stella pointed up at the highest amphitheater. "It's coming from there!"

"So glad you could come this evening. Welcome friends, to the Electric Blue Theater!" exclaimed a voice that surrounded them.

"That's definitely him," Dan said with dark eyes. "Crane."

Jayden struck a combat pose, with her staff pointed towards the source of the voice. "Give me Clyde. Return those you've taken and you may survive this night."

"Friend, are you lost? This is no fighting ground." Crane gave a theatrical laugh. "I just want you to enjoy the spectacular show I've orchestrated."

"What show? Where is Clyde!?" Jayden yelled.

Crane proudly announced to his audience of knights. "A spectacle is happening soon. It will be a gala of gladness."

Helen puffed up her cheeks in anger and let out a sharp breath. "Stay behind me, Stella."

"The first Masked Masquelaro in one-hundred and three years held just for you lot."

"What…how can he?"

Doors and latches creaked and people poured out from several different entrances into the theater.

Stella squinted in the darkness; they were all masked and dressed in black. Their masks glowed and floated like possessed relics.

"Wow, I can't be the Ravepires are preserving the culture of that ancient dance," said Stella with stars in her eyes.

Helen groans. "What?! They want to kill us! There are a dozen of them. Let's give this everything we've got!" She pulls out her glows.

"Whoopsie! Did I say this was for you? This show will be for me and my guests! Better perform well, Neon Knights, their lives depend on it." The Ravepire laughed again, his echoing patter taunted them.

Jayden, Dan, Helen and Stella all assumed positions for their dangerous dance with death.

Step 25: The Power of Empathy

Stella's eyes shifted from each of the dark figures. In the shadows, only their masks could be discerned. They all possessed the same emotionless mask with a dead, black-eyed stare. Their looks reflected a hollow feeling, like staring at a mannequin. The only thing that differed for each mask was the shapes of the horns and a different luminescent color to each of them.

"Are those the dancers who died?" asked Stella.

"They look like they could be, but I don't know," Helen replied.

"They're not," Jayden muttered. "They're Ravepires."

Dan covered his face to shutter privately. "Oh, sweet Kouyate, help me."

Stella put a friendly hand on his shoulder. "Just pretend it's training,."

"Yeah…we can do this. It's just so much easier when they're digital. No voices."

"Yep, and we have luck on our side?"

"We do?"

Stella clanked her shoes together and smiled. "I may not be wearing my lucky shoes, but I'm a walking good luck charm."

Dan rubbed her head. "Maybe some off that luck will rub off on me?"

A Ravepire leapt at Dan from across the room. They flew with a precise trajectory until Stella with med-aided speed, detached her large earrings and whipped them right at the flying vamp.

The stars with surprising strength, dug into the masked figure and pinned them to the wall left of the Neon Knights.

The creature growled and roared, struggling to break free as Jayden stepped in front of it. She licked her lips. "My favorite part." Her eyes intensified. "Revenge."

"Look away Stella," Helen warned her friend. "She's gonna neutralize the Ravepire."

Stella did just that. There was only one way to kill a Ravepire and it was absolutely gruesome.

Jayden had explained it to her in a blunt, matter of fact way that made her recoil at the cold sound of the words. A person who was full of rave energy had to use their powers to give the Ravepire exactly what they wanted and transfer copious amounts into them.

Having just that, the Ravepire would be sent into a fit of ecstasy until their body would shut down and burst. Jayden said it was a fitting way for them to die, bloated from their own gluttony.

Stella was thankful that her job was just to stun and distract the Ravepires. As a Neon Knight, she had already decided she wanted to protect rather than kill.

The hum of Jayden's electro staff powering up began and Stella kept her face hidden. The Ravepire's body went into a spasm, attempting to escape and suddenly there was a loud plop, something sounded like it had fallen to the ground.

Helen gasped. "This creature...is Gary Silva."

Stella turned around and saw the unmasked grey face of a young Winterson man with a short buzz cut. He was one of the fourteen who went missing after the Penultimate Party. He grunted and groaned just before Jayden had rammed the staff into his shoulder.

"Jayden NO!" Stella screamed, but it was too late.

"More! More!" The Winterson's eyes were completely deranged and his mouth was drooling.

Stella watched as his shoulder blade swelled larger. The man continued to giggle in an unrestrained manner. With a sickening popping sound, the rainbow electromotion came through a giant hole in his body. The man's face slumped down.

"What did you just do Jayden?" Helen screamed.

Stella hid her face and began to shake. "I did not just see that."

Even the other Ravepires kept their distance, trying to process what just happened.

"The masked dancers, they're the missing fourteen?" Dan exclaimed.

Jayden didn't have a look of remorse on her face, instead she beamed with pride. "I killed a Ravepire. They're the enemy. Don't overthink it."

"That...was a person," Stella shot back at her.

"One of my people," said Dan softly with tears in his eyes.

"Not anymore," Jayden replied with all the sensitivity of a numbed appendage.

"Jayden, the Ravepires that you killed, did they look like him?"

"They were unmasked, silver haired and looked just like their leader."

"You can't just kill them!" Stella grasped her head while writhing. She grabbed her pill container and popped one. Her eye twitched as she swallowed.

"We need a new plan." Helen said to her teammates. "One that doesn't involve killing the people we came to rescue."

"This is sooooo hard!" Stella cried, sliding her feet to create a small wall of fire to protect her from an approaching enemy.

"I'll hold them off," Dan responded, grabbing an iceglo and doing the requisite frost dance. He fired an icicle at one of the Ravepire's feet. The one he was lucky to hit, froze solid to the ground while the others shuffled to avoid a similar fate.

"So, what in our goddesses name are we going to do?" Stella asked, purposefully missing when ejecting fireballs from her glow.

"You know my answer," Jayden replied, her floating staff charged and on standby.

"I'm sorry," Helen gently intoned. "We're not going to do that. But maybe we can get some answers from Crane."

"He's up high. We gotta just get past them," Stella said.

"Get to the second floor…yes, that's the plan," Helen said in return.

"But how?" Dan talked while continuing to beam ice with the help of his glo. "We're outnumbered."

"That's where Helen comes in," Jayden said, bearing a proud smile.

Helen shook her head. "Oh, I hope I get this right."

"It should be easy for you, just remember your breathing."

Helen held her hands to her temples and whipped her head around.

Stella watched with stars in her eyes as her gal pal's hair flipped around.

"Are you sure she isn't going to screw it up again?" Dan asked, still dancing and shooting.

Jayden's response was in a sing song-y voice as she rested her cheeks in her hand. "Helen won't fail."

Everyone looked at her confused.

Dan freezed a Ravepire without looking.

Jayden coughs and becomes stoic once more. "This time is different. This is battle!"

Helen focused on a statue of Kouyate that lay on the floor. With one hand to her head, she began to raise the other with a slow but steady motion.

"Very few people in this world have empathy," Jayden said, marveling at her student. "Many Neuronians have telepathy."

Helen began to grunt as the statue rose.

Jayden knocked a Ravepire away with her staff. "But only Reinsons have telempathy."

The statue dropped down, with a powerful thud. "I can't do it, Jayden. All I see is Charlotte."

"She's your inner saboteur," Jayden told her. "Find a way to block her out."

Helen looked around until she locked eyes with her best friend.

"You can do it Helen!" Stella smiled despite her frazzled nerves.

Dan blasted another Ravepire with ice that nearly struck Stella. "Be more vigilant!"

"You're right, Stella. Thanks for always believing in me." Helen turned red and the two statues of Kouyate, normally a very stern, stately woman began swoon with their hands clasped together and their legs turned inwards, cracking in the process.

"The statues," Dan said, stopping what he was doing. "They're actually moving."

"She is able to place a piece of herself into an object."

"How?" asked Dan, sliding away from a Ravepire and then having the ice trail jut up as spikes as he raises his hands.

"Using ultra-high electromotion…and empathy," said Jayden with a tender look before throwing her staff at another enemy.

Stella's eyes widen. "So your secret one on one training really was actual training?"

Helen blushes. "I told you I'm not into Jayden!"

"Focus!" exclaimed Dan, using ice blades to fend off two Ravepires at once.

Jayden nodded her head towards Dan. She raised her hand to sic the statues on the Ravepires. "Destroy them, my student."

The two statues leapt from the platform over the decayed bodies and with a thump, began plowing through chairs towards the Ravepires. The masked attackers were hardly rattled and began to fight back.

A circular ball of energy flew in the middle of the fray between the Ravepires who began to claw at the statues and swing on them. The globe of light enlarged and detonated, sending the Ravepires flying and causing one of the statues to explode with arms and legs launching into the air.

Helen held her head and gasped. "Ugh…that…hurts so deep."

Jayden ran to comfort her.

B. Bop strode in. "What no, thank you?" He asked with a casual air. "I just took care of all your problems."

"What on Aleatore did you do to 'em?" Stella wondered "I really hope you didn't kill them."

"Just something I call the Great Balls of Flame…and why not?" B. Bop said, holding a ball of fire above his hands with a smile.

"They're the people the Ravepire's kidnapped. Now they've been transformed into Ravepires too," said Stella.

"No shit. Either way. It's too late to save them," said B. Bop.

"Indeed," Jayden said, resting on hand on her hip. "Stella, the energy won't kill them. I will."

B. Bop steps in Jayden's path. "Chill those crazy tits. We should go after the boss before more show up."

"Yeah, I agree with Bop," Stella said. "I want to find a cure for them."

Bop looks at her with a blank expression. He then chuckles. "Ha! Pinky cares about the Ravepires. You really are a saint. Hey, aren't you going to ask me how RJ is?" He made a motion towards Stella.

"Who?" She asked, completely oblivious.

255

"What the hell?" B. Bop replied. "This bitch for real?"

Helen stormed up to B. Bop who was only slightly taller than her and jabbed her finger right on his nose. "Listen here, man-whore. She's taking pills which alter her memory. She's not a bitch. And she doesn't whisper threats to people either."

"Ease up." B. Bop flinched. "I forgot she was a user. I would have never expected her to forget a man she was playing conversational footsy with."

"D-d-did I really forget someone?" Stella asked, worry spreading upon her face. "I don't know who this RJ is."

Dan looks at her confused. "RJ isn't someone you can forget."

"Stella, I'm gonna need to talk to you about these pills. After we survive this," Helen told her.

"I had no idea that Stella was taking pills," Dan said, his face showing concern.

Helen ignored him and continued to press B. Bop. "And how is RJ?"

"He's alive, but let's beat this freak with fangs fast just to be safe."

"Alright, that's good. Let's head up now."

"Wait," Dan said, pointing towards the seating. "What's that statue doing?"

The remaining statue of Kouyate sat kneeling at the remains of the other one.

"I think she's mourning," Helen said. "Those two statues must've been together for so long."

"Aww," Jayden cooed, her intense orange eyes strangely big and shimmering. "The pice of Helen gave it empathy. You make everyone feel warm, my squishy Reinson."

Stella winks at Helen.

The skater's cheeks went rosy, but her eyes were still watery. "I do? Jayden you make me…actually forget it. Let's focus on the mission."

Stella, taken in by the image, walked over to the crouching statue and patted it "Hey, it's okay. It's sad seeing a woman so big and powerful like this crying."

The statue turned its granite head towards Stella slowly.

256

Helen shakes her head with tears in her eyes. "Crying doesn't make us any less strong, Stella."

"You're right." Stella put on a big smile for the statue. "She was so kickass and mighty, and she died protecting you. She was truly awesome."

B. Bop shook his head in disbelief. "Is she really comforting an art exhibit?"

"Shh Boppy," Dan whispered. "This is what I like about Stella."

"Me too," Helen said even quieter.

"So, let's stand up and fight for her." Stella grinned as the statue did just that and rose up. But not before putting an arm around Stella and squeezing her until she couldn't breathe. "Ugh, I like the affection, but I'm squishy and you're stone-y."

"Statue!" Helen yelled as the rest ran up the aisle. "Let go of her."

The statue snapped to attention and began to follow everyone as they proceeded up the aisle to the second level.

Step 26: One Final Serenade

Pounding up the steps to a higher elevation of seating, the knights arrived at a door behind the second-row seats. Hearing the groan of Ravepires from the level below made Helen pause.

Dan finished his ice dance and created a wall of slowed time. "I'll hold them off."

Helen shook her head. "That won't be enough. And we need you fighting alongside us, Dorkphin. I hate to say it, but we need the statue to stay back and guard us."

The statue's head and arms sank and Stella leapt to its aid. "Aw come on, Helen. We're barely up the stairs and already we have to say goodbye?"

"We need a lifeline so that we can take on Crane alone. Don't worry Stella, she's a warrior."

Stella waved to the statue. "You hear that, stone Kouyate? You get to be our lifeline."

The statue stood triumphant with its hands on its hips and its head raised high.

"Good job tricking stone tits over there," B. Bop said to Helen with a snide smile and held the door for Dan and the knights accompanying him.

Helen shot a hostile look at him.

Darkness devoured the whole room and quickly swallowed everyone up. "Ooh, what room are we in now?"

Stella's voice had returned to its chipper heights with the wiping of her brain.

"Here, I'll just light it up...and we'll see," Jayden's voice answered.

"Don't..." A raspy female voice cut through the darkness.

Stella could have sworn she had heard the voice before.

"Don't listen to filth," said Jayden to Stella.

Jayden's staff crackled, but as soon as it did, a high-pitched aria rung through the room. The notes being hit were dissonant and made the knights who heard them dizzy and unnerved.

"Is it pleasing?" The voice asked. "I'm delighted that someone is here for my performance."

"What's...going...on?" Stella asked her teammates. "And why is the darkness spiraling? This is soooo trippy."

"This woman."

"You know her?" asked Helen.

Jayden coughed. "Her electromotion is focused in her voice box. Cover your ears else be broken."

The voice continued to sing in its disorienting, jazz vocal stunts, but this time with lyricism tangled along with it, tapping into everyone who listened.

"When I've been cheated blind,

I can't even see the poisoned wine.

As my skin turns the lightest pale,

I hide myself beneath the darkest veil.

I'm waiting, waiting, waiting, as my lips fade to blue.

Because I'm dying, dying, dead over you."

Stella let out a scream; the lyric reeked of sadness and betrayal and gave Stella a fuller picture of this mysterious singer. She was taken in not by the actual words, but the mournful tone of voice. The weight of her burden, whoever she was, hung heavy on Stella's chest.

Stella musters her strength. "This looks like a job for...the Mighty Fruitsaders." She starts humming to herself, slowly rising to her feet.

"When the Evil Dentist Pacqson infected the world with cavity,

Who will save us from this needless depravity?" Stella muttered the opening of the song as she took a step toward Serenade.

"What are you saying?" asked Serenade, stopping her song. "It doesn't matter. I'll blast you to pieces!"

Stella spun in place and leapt out from the way of a blast of sound.

"Everyone runs..." she ducks behind a pillar "and some people hide."

She looks out at Dan and Helen who are crippled. "But these gals from another planet stand side by side!"

Serenade released three sound blasts in quick succession.

Stella leaped in tune with her

259

"That's O for Outragously Orange!" She twilred in the air.

"T, for Terrifically Tomato." She sommersualts behind a wall.

"P the Perfectly Passionate Fruit." She jumps up and spins, riding a gravity well she created.

"Together we are the Fruitsaders. We shall fight those gum invaders!" She sent out a fireball that gets blasted by a particularly shrill scream from the banshee woman.

Serenade sets her sights on Dan. "Stand down or watch your friends die!" She blasted a stalagmite growing at the top of the amphitheater.

Stella twirled and focused her energy as the stalagmite came crashing down over dan.

"Orange Ornacia, that's me." She focused her fiery energy in her glo. "I deliver a helping of Vitamin She." The fire comes out like a snake that bursts into the rock."

Dan looks up at Stella with gratitude. "Th-thanks."

Stella winked. "A sip of orange juice helps prevent scurvy." She waved her arms around and then emitted her gravity well horizontally, heading straight towards Serenade. "And sends all my enemies topsy turvy."

"O for Outragously Orange! T, for Terrifically Tomato. P the Perfectly Passionate Fruit." Stella sent out fireballs that came out from the sides of the gravity well and sent toward Serenade.

The Ravepire songstress had to let out quick "aaaahs" to protect herself from being scorched.

"Together we are the Fruitsaders. We shall fight those gum invaders."

Serenade suddenly takes flight and blasts Stella against the ground.

Helen suddenly rises to her feet. "Tammy Mato, I'm squat and red." She ignited her skates. "I love flipping criminals on their head." She sends out a fireball and iceball after skating around to dodge a barrage of small sound blasts. "People think I'm a veggie. But identity don't matter to me."

Stella beams at Hellen as she slowly gets back on her feet. "You...learned the song."

Helen flashes a warm smile and then makes a circular shape on the ground, creating a time bubble in the area in front of Stella. She gives Serenade a fierce glare as she races up to her. "I don't give a hoot." She leaps up. "Haters will get the boot." She spun several times and then slammed her skates down into Serenade's face.

Stella cheers and spins rapidly in place. "O for Outragously Orange! T, for Terrifically Tomato. P the Perfectly Passionate Fruit. Together we are the Fruitsaders. We shall fight those gum invaders." Her entire body becomes engulfed in flames. "Passionfruit Patel, it's my passion."

Serenade is pelted by Helen's ice bullets as Stella rages towards her like a tornado.

"To keep the city neat and clean in good fashion." She created a gravity well that coiled around the air.

Serenade flew around, using her soundwaves to escape the path of the flaming tornado.

"With my star shape and fancy ways. Those baddies will see the end of their evildoing days."

Stella converged on Serenade from below while Helen skated up an ice slope Dan had made for her.

Even Dan sang along with the trio. "O for Outragously Orange! T, for Terrifically Tomato. P the Perfectly Passionate Fruit. Together we are the Fruitsaders. We shall fight those gum invaders."

"You will all perish!" yelled Serenade, letting out a screech that knocked the three knights in training out of focus.

Their accumulated energy exploded and they all fell to the floor as limp bodies.

"I've…had enough of this!" B. Bop screamed and grabbed his head in tearful agony. "Great balls of flame!"

A flashing orb of light brightened the room, showing a figure dressed exactly like the Ravepires were, with a mask and a dark cloak. The orb flew towards the monster and sent them screaming into the wall where they were impaled by a sharp piece of rubble. She then fell with a slump against the ground and a large hole in her chest.

Everyone slowly found their footing and stood up.

Jayden's staff emitted a light so they could all see once again.

B. Bop was the first to his feet and walked with a slowing hesitation over to the stunned body.

"B…" Stella said. "You look a little pale. Are you still sick from the music?"

"No. I'm fine. Shut up."

"You don't need to be so tough about it."

B. Bop crouched and gently removed the mask from the woman's face. Multi colored hair fell from it, and B. Bop brushed the hair from her face. The heavy use of makeup to an almost clownish degree made Stella realize who it was and she grasped at her heart.

It was Serenade, the angry prostitute Stella encountered when she arrived at B. Bop's room.

"B," she said, her chest moving in an out as Stella noticed a wound oozing rainbow electromotion from it. "Why did you do this to me?"

"I wanted to be with you," he said.

The dying woman looked down at his shoes. "After all this time…you're a deadbeat. After the Dance…you changed, you didn't want to see me or Crimson anymore."

"I know I am, but still…I wanted to be with you."

"You didn't even pay child support for us." She raised her hand to slap him, but it lightly came down on his cheek like soft rain before sinking to the ground. A solitary tear drop followed her hand landing on it.

Stella's heart throbbed in her chest and her brain felt punctured.

That woman was not some lady of the night, but B. Bop's baby mama. Her mind rushed to reevaluate the situation.

She looked at her compatriots, who all watched the saddening scene unfold.

Jayden's face twitched as if sensitive nerves were trying to manipulate her face. Her eyes showed real emotion with shimmering orange pupils.

Next to her, Dan started sniffing and with a choked whine he said, "Boppy…its okay, she loves…."

"Shut it, you vanilla fruitcake. I don't need your sympathy."

Dan let out a loud sniff before bursting into a wail.

Hellen's eyes widened. "Oh…I think I get it now."

Stella felt so bad, she ran over to Dan and put his head on her shoulder to absorb his tears.

Helen spoke softly to Dan. "A woman that was very important to him just died by his hand. Dorphin, I think you need to let him grieve."

B. Bop let out a scream and in a piston-like movement fired several pulsating balls of energy from his hands at the wall above Serenade. Each blast dug deeper and deeper into the wall, representing B. Bop's psyche. "Crane, I will see to it personally that you feel every blow."

"She was a Ravepire," Stella said, still letting Dan cuddle her. "How come she came to her senses and could talk like normal?"

"I don't know," Jayden responded with some weight in her voice. "That's the first time I've seen that."

"She was strong. That spirit. Her music…it was ensouled." Bop weeps against his arm.

Serenade wasn't the only Ravepire Stella had seen who was normal. There was Dan. Though he was barely affected in comparison to the others.

That meant there was still hope, right?

B. Bop turned around; his fearsome face hidden. "Uh…hey."

Dan looked at him to speak, but could only muster a choked gulping sound.

Stella put her arms around him. She noticed that he let her touch him even after what had happened between them.

"I…uh…I'm sorry stud," B. Bop put his hand behind his head. "Those remarks…they escaped my mouth. I am emotional and I'm man enough to admit it."

"Who was she?" Stella asked. "I thought she was…a prostitute."

"Serenade, we were tight at one point in my life. She was a singer. Our life together was her finest song. You could say our child was one of the high notes."

"Whoa, they never covered that in the tabloids," Stella said.

"It was all on the down low, we both had our careers and they didn't coincide. She was a singer; I was a dancer. And also, I was a Reinson."

Dan trembled a bit in Stella's arms. "It's okay," she whispered into his ear.

"Please stud…I lost her. She was so special to me." He looked up in tears. "Think how I feel. I was just lashing out."

"You just…" Dan quivered "after what we did together. I didn't think you'd call me a fruitcake. I told you…that hurts."

"Hey I…" B. Bop turned red a shade that highlighted his tanned skin further. "It wasn't me saying that…it was my rage. I've been called that too, I get what ya feelin', bro."

Helen approached him. "I'm sorry. I didn't know that word or my cake would offend you."

"I don't know what to say," Dan responded, looking at B. Bop.

Bop shook his head. "Then don't say anything. I have an urge to stake Crane through the heart for what he's done."

B. Bop hustled towards the door leading to the amphitheaters, opened it and stepped inside. Jayden followed him, leaving Dan, Stella and Helen trailing behind.

Helen gazed at Serenade. "That poor poor woman. B. Bop wants us to feel sorry for him, but she's the true victim here. Even I got swept up in his misery for a moment."

"I feel so bad," Stella said. "I feel bad for both of them."

"I just don't get how he didn't know it was her," Helen said. "Hasn't he heard her voice before?"

Dan was deep in thought but spoke to confirm what he knew. "He probably wasn't thinking. It was the heat of battle." He let out a small sniffle.

"Then you forgive him?" asked Helen. "Do you forgive me?"

Dan sighs. "Grudges are just deadweight."

"Thanks…I think. We should be careful around Bop. I don't know what's going on, but I don't think a deadbeat dad is the only kind of person B. Bop is. He might do anything to get revenge. We should steer clear of him."

Dan shook his head. "I know Bop. He's good. He knew it was her…yeah. He only struck her down to protect me."

The three followed B. Bop and Jayden's lead, hoping that the stairs would lead them to a solution; the answer to the Ravepire affliction and the identity of Barvarius Bop.

264

Step 27: The Raven's Den

Tap…tap…tap.

THUMP…THUMP…THUMP….

The two elder members of the Neon Knights traveled up the dilapidated staircase. Jayden with an inherent swiftness on her feet and B. Bop as if the weight of his soul was iron tied to his shiny shoes.

Both had motives that expanded far beyond the mission. B. Bop in particular was so determined in the path he blazed; he didn't realize the rookies had barely set foot on the stairs.

Jayden, on the other hand, used this time to her advantage with making other advances.

"My condolences, she must have been very important to you."

B. Bop tilted his head upwards as he continued to trudge. "Yes, yes she was."

"The Ravepires took someone away from me too. If I lose him, I don't know what I'll do," Jayden said, a certain softness undercutting her monotone.

"I just hope you don't have to see him… the way I saw Serenade," B. Bop said.

"I will end all of them before that happens."

B. Bop stopped abruptly, causing Jayden to stop too. He sized her up, but not in his usual ogling way. "You know, you got good motivation and I respect that. I'd like to apologize for calling you a psycho."

Jayden put her hand to her mouth, she felt tingly with this sudden surge of chivalry. "I…I…uh…" She let out a high-pitched giggle before scrambling to cover her mouth.

B. Bop's gallant expression changed to one of doubt.

Jayden's mind raced to come up with a proper response. "Sorry, my body gets indigestion easily and is having trouble processing that Bubbly Tea." She began to nod over and over.

"Right. No more hesitation. Let's get to what we truly came here for," B. Bop responded as determined as ever.

The trio of junior knights trailed after them, a few flights below.

"Gee, this stairway. Did Craneykins put it here just to tire us out?" Stella asked.

Dan sneered. "I would prefer if you didn't come up with a cutesy nickname for the menace that's been terrorizing this city."

"You're one to talk about nicknames: Boppy." Helen shot back. "This staircase was most likely for maintenance and for Wintersons who couldn't use gravity to reach the amphitheater."

"Those Summerein builders have a sick sense of humor," Dan said, keeping the subject off him. "Why don't you just fly to the top, Stella?"

"And take that creep on alone? No way!"

"Wishful thinking," Dan replied. "I really don't want to see his face again."

"Don't worry, I'll be there," Stella jogged next to him. "We can fight him side by side and we also have a scary Neuronian woman hell bent on revenge with us too."

"True. It's five on one. How bad can it be?" Dan stumbled on a step. "Urgh." He swatted at his head to ward off invisible tormenters. "The voices, they're so loud."

"What voices?" Helen asked, stopping to turn around.

"Oh uh." Stella paused. "He can hear Crane talking upstairs."

"Really?" Helen asked. Her lips pursed and her eyes widened in concern. "I don't hear anyone."

"There's two people talking in a different language. They're arguing."

Stella wondered in her head who the leaders of the Ravepires were. Who was Crane talking to?

Helping Dan to his feet, the three continued on a brisk pace and caught up with Jayden and Bop. The staircase that spiraled in a square had reached its end and they were met with two horizontal wooden doors, carved with masks and roses.

"This is the moment we've been waiting for," Stella said all antsy.

"Yeah, Pink Tails. Since you want to be a hero so badly, the hand of fate just dealt you an ace," B. Bop said in his deep manly voice.

Stella looked at the faces of the people who accompanied her. Everyone looked solemn but mentally prepared for whatever faced them.

Stella twitched. She wasn't sure what waited for her on the other end, with only a moldy slab of wood dividing her and the unknown.

An idea then popped into her head. She'd use a pill to forget this feeling of malaise. Doing that would allow her to handle it just like the rest of them. She stepped forward and slipped the cap off without a sound. It was her third of the day, the most she'd ever taken, but tonight was extra important.

As she popped the pill in her mouth, she heard someone cry. "I don't know if I can face it."

She turned around. Dan had his face hidden behind the veil of his hand, trying to hide his tears to protect his pride.

Stella ran over to her friend and put her hand on his shoulder. "There there, you can face that monster."

"I saw harsh bright lights when he sucked the energy right out of me. It hurt so much."

"I wish I could have been there to help you through it."

"Stella, you were there."

"I was?"

"Good Goddess Ravenous. What's wrong with you?" Dan turned away.

Helen stepped forward and turned to Stella. "This is why that pill is so bad for you, it fries holes in your memory when you might need them. Did you take anymore tonight?"

"No. I didn't." Stella said, face turning pale and with a sharp breath she continued to speak. "Let's not talk about this now. We have people to save."

"Yes," Jayden said. "We do."

"Dorphin, you should stay behind if you're not up to it," Helen told the shivering young man.

"No." Dan wiped his face and looked at everyone. "If I'm cursed with keeping memories of that monster, I'll use them as fuel to destroy him."

"Good job, my man." B. Bop held his hand up in a high five. "We'll both destroy him for what he's done to us."

Dan walked past him and left him hanging. He reached for the door. "Are we ready?"

Everyone looked to Jayden, the unofficial group leader and she nodded.

"It's time."

Jayden signaled to Stella and Helen to push the wooden door, along with Dan, while her staff lit up with a sharp crackle. It hovered before her as Jayden arched her back like a predator ready to stalk her prey.

B. Bop's afro began to glow with pulsation. The three rookie knights grunted as they pushed towards the heavy door. They knew they'd be well covered by their superiors.

Stella turned around and found herself in the interior of the box that overlooked the whole stage. There was a raven wood table at the center. Years of wear had made it moldy with purple barnacles sprouting from it.

There were two throne-like seats, designed for viewing, carved out of the same wood. Arrow-shaped arches sprouted from the top, giving the people who sat in them a horned appearance. Crane sat rigid in one, his silvery jagged hair glinting in the dim surroundings and his rainbow fangs brightening them.

Next to him was Molly Primus dressed in the same outrageous plush jeg and bikini dress combo she wore on the night she was snatched away. Her Winterson skin also shining as she gave a sedated grin.

At their feet lay a skeleton in a regal, but torn leisure suit, similar to Daddy D's.

Helen's eyes widened. "Is that the drowned king from the stories?"

"Geek out later. Focus," replied Dan.

Jayden and B. Bop stood feet apart, ready for battle.

"Your time is up you disgusting perversion of life." B. Bop growled. "Give her up."

Dan cried out from behind them. "Molly, did he hurt you? Did he suck out your energy?"

Molly Primus scoffed and stuck out her hand, almost to deflect Dan's words. "Nah, Danny Bannany. Mr. Ravepire's been mega chill with me. He taught me a sweet new dance move."

Molly made a constipated face and began to square her hands around her face. "Vogue." She muttered. "Vogue."

"Silence." The Ravepire said, his normally jolly attitude buried in wrath. "I did not invite you to my sanctum, Neon Knights. You should be downstairs providing us with the show of a lifetime."

268

"We're not killing anyone else downstairs," Helen said with cheeks of rage. "They're not your puppets."

"We'll save them when we take you down," Stella added.

Crane, standing up, returned to his causal rainbow grin. "They'll soon to be just like me and share my sexy white mane. There is no cure for my fashionable affliction."

Dan looked to Bop. "He's lying, right?"

Bop kept his focus on the enemy and said nothing.

The Ravepire laid his hand on Molly's head who still vogued like a robot. "This girl though, she's still of your kind. If you want her back, I propose a trade." Crane's yellow eyes came to Dan. "Her for my delicious Danny boy."

Dan tried his best to hide behind Jayden and Stella.

Stella's feelings burst out of her. "Why are you so evil, man?"

Crane laughed as his face stretched into a wider and wider grin. "We were created with malicious intent, but we are not evil. We just seek to feed and expand our ranks. We are surviving! But I want us to thrive!"

"It's bad when you kidnap people we love. And if you wish to expand your ranks, upsetting me is truly foolish," Jayden said, giving one of her patented cold steel glares. "Where the hell is Clyde?"

"He's in safe hands, and that's all I'm saying."

"Why do you want Dan so badly?" Stella continued.

"Even for an Electromotion sucking creature of the night it gets lonely and I feel my Danny will make the loveliest companion. You know what they say en-Dorphins are stimulating."

Stella clenches her fist, realizing she should have been the one to make that pun.

Dan's face peered out from behind Jayden's lanky figure.

An honest curiosity rose from Crane's voice. "And I don't know why you don't obey me like everyone else I've bitten."

"He bit you?" asked Helen.

"Crane is our enemy now," said Jayden firmly.

The Ravepire Lord outstretched his hand. "I am the only one who can cure you, Danny."

269

Dan's hair visibly stood up on its ends as he shivered in repulsion but stood his ground. "I'd rather kill you."

"Oh, but what if killing me dooms you?" Crane ran his hand through his hair and giggled.

"Ugh, why don't you just give me a straight answer, you freak?"

"That's nothing straight about me, pretty boy." Crane chuckled. "But enough dawdling, if you won't give up Dan, I'll take him by force."

Jayden stepped sideways, blocking Dan from the Ravepire's twisted view. She spoke with authority. "You clearly aren't aware of this, but you're outnumbered. The only reason you aren't dead yet is because I have questions you will answer."

Crane's eyes widened in his skull. "Am I outnumbered? How many of your gang actually belong to you because I'm never alone with the mind spread."

"M-m-mind spread?" Dan stammered.

Crane took an invisible knife and began to use it to decorate imaginary toast. "Like delicious jam spread over bread, the mind spread works fast to cover an entire brain in my own special mind control jelly. Everyone who's bitten is tethered to my mind…including…B. Bop."

B. Bop walked across the room, silently, never looking back until he pivoted forward, revealing yellow eyes much like Crane.

Crane grins at Dan. "Mr. Bop's brain is covered in my special jelly."

"Wait…all this time…," Dan shook his head, "you've been controlling B. Bop?"

"Let's just say you respond more favorably to him, than you do me. That kiss! Ahh, I'll never forget it."

Dan's eyes began to water and his voice became shrill and fragile. "You didn't mean the things you said to me, Boppy?"

"Dorphin, I don't think that now's the best time. Let's kill Crane, then you can chew him out. Right now Bop's dirty mind belongs to this freak," Helen said, trying hard to be the voice of reason.

"That's right. After I made him murder his lover, whatever part of him resisted me is now gone. He's broken," said Crane, having Bop move along with the waves of his fingers like a puppet.

Dan thrust his body forward to cry out to him again, but B. Bop with even less remorse fired a ball of energy at him.

270

Stella ran and grasped her hand into a fist, using her powers to gain control and halt the ball in midair. It just hung, there levitating and flashing until Jayden swung her staff at it, sending it to blow up the wall to the left of B. Bop.

"Don't stop firing until they're just crispy crisps on the floor, my man toy," the Ravepire Lord commanded.

Showers of flame spread out in the direction of the trio.

"Get behind me!" Jayden flipped the moldy table down to work as a shield, Stella, Dan and Helen followed.

Helen took out her glows. "Let's think of a plan."

Jayden took a firm stance. "It isn't B. Bop. It has no style or potency. That puppet is a glorified machine-gun. I can deflect anything it sends at us. Stella, I want you to hold those fireballs at bay. Our best chance at taking out Crane is by a surprise attack. Dan, you're going to rescue Molly. Helen, you're going to draw the fire away from me."

"Understood." Everyone nodded.

Stella walked out in front of the table. "Hey B. Bop, do you have the balls to shoot a girl?"

B. Bop responded with a heavy barrage aimed right at Stella's face. "Eeek!" She covered her face and held out her hand. Each of the balls halted, much to her relief.

Jayden jumped over the flipped table and began to batter each ball with her staff, sending them flying in different directions.

Blasts ricocheted off walls and the arched ceiling, causing bits of debris to fall. One well-aimed ball of energy went back at B. Bop, who used his fro to absorb it. He slid back towards Crane as his fro flashed a white-hot light.

"Did you forget Mr. Bop's fro has powers of absorption, Neuronian?" The Ravepire asked. "And he can release that energy back tenfold!"

Jayden had a satisfied smile on her face. "I didn't forget. I learned everything about him."

Helen came out from cover, firing small icicle bullets that were melted by Bop's aura.

"Go now, Dan!" yelled Jayden as a massive fireball came her way.

Stella created a gravity well that sent the reflected fireball bursting into the ceiling.

The Winterson boy performed a frost dance from behind the table, and appeared between Crane and B. Bop. Dan grabbed Molly Primus out of her chair while she was still in a robotic trance and the two zoomed away just before B. Bop's fro unleashed a blast of energy.

Dan created a trail of ice and Helen grabbed onto Jayden. The Reinson girl skated and then flung Jayden at Bop.

"Foolish!" Bop released his energy, setting the area around him aflame.

Jayden blasted the flames aside with her staff before whacking it into B. Bop's head.

The Reinson man closed his eyes and fell to the ground.

Jayden's staff was suddenly pulled out from her arms. "You're mine!" Crane sent out thin strings that sliced and coiled around Jayden.

Several other strings came out and held the staff in mid-air as Jayden called to it.

Jayden looks to the knights in training, scorched and bloodied. "Finish the battle for me."

Crane does a frost dance, sending his cool energy spiraling up the strings.

Jayden's body is frozen.

Stella readies a fireball to burn the strings, but her arm suddenly twists back. She screamed out wretchedly.

Helen is hit by the flame from behind and topples over.

Crane sprouts wings of ice and fastens strings to his throne to lift himself out of range of an ice spear thrown by Dan. "Serenade was going to kill you all. I had B. Bop rescue you. I only need Dan. The rest of you will die if you oppose me." His eyes intensify. "Last chance."

"You made me hurt Helen!" yelled Stella, wrapped in a dress of flame.

"You broke Stella's arm!" yelled Helen, taking control of the other throne to slam into Crane's seat from behind.

The Ravepire slides along a thin string in the air to dodge a barrage of ice spears created by Dan's frost dance.

Jayden's eyes widen. "St-Stop…" she said weakly.

Crane dances in the air, causing the spears to join him before sending them flying at Helen.

272

Stella sends her tornado of flame toward Crane, but Helen gets pierced in the leg by one of the spears.

"Don't you see it? I am the Conductor of Calamity!" The rubble around the room spins in a hurricane, heading towards Hellen who is pinned down.

"Stella, thanks for always being my friend," said Helen with tears.

Stella burned the spear impaled in Helen's leg. "Fruitsaders don't leave people behind, especially their friends. And Neon Knights don't give up!" She sends Helen out of the room with a gravity well.

Dan looked at Stella in tears. "I'm going to surrender to him. Get everyone out of here."

Stella fiercely grabbed his hand.

He looked at her intense face and nodded.

"Oh, what do you have planned?" asked Crane, swinging on the ice spears while sending out more strings.

Dan placed his hand on Stella's hip.

"Let's tango!" they exclaimed.

As they danced, Crane sent ice spears reigning upon them.

Stella's fiery energy came up like a shield and Dan's cool aura sent out tiny blades at the ceiling as they danced across the hall.

Crane slid out of the way of incoming onslaught, unable to create enough strings to control the icy blades. "I should be the one dancing with him!"

A fireball from blasted into his wing, sending him falling off the string he was balanced on.

He shielded himself from the icy blades that tore at his body.

A monster leapt onto Crane.

"Killing Serenade broke your control!" B. Bop bites into Crane, filling him with electromotion. He then sends him flying with a burning fist. "Die from the monster you made!"

"Stop! Clyde!" yelled Jayden in tears.

Crane crashes into the ground, his body bloating. "No…I haven't lost yet." He pulled his strings toward him to shield himself, his legs trembling in terror. "Dan, you're my puppet too. I'll make you kill the girl."

273

Dan and Stella clasp their hands together, sending out a perfect spiral of fire and ice at the Ravepire menace.

The strings melt.

Jayden slams into the monster, knocking him out of the way.

Crane slides back, falling off the balcony.

"What did you do that for? Now he's going to get away, just like Captain Cavity," Stella said with a groan.

"Umm, no…he didn't," said Helen, looking away, her wound sealed up by ice.

Stella peered over the balcony to witness a gruesome sight.

Crane was impaled on the Kouyate statue's staff, his body was bloating with electromotion.

Jayden leaps off and lands on the statue. "You have to tell me where Clyde is. You…know where!" She shook him with a faceful of tears.

"It feels so good! I'm free, I'm finally free." His eyes became at peace. His body swelled up; his arms and legs becoming rounder and circular, his face grew several chins and his eyes bulged. The electromotion began to overflow in his body until it could take no more and exploded, covering the room down below in rainbow goop.

"I got it! Poseferatu! Damn, way too late," said Stella with a tearful chuckle.

Stella, Dan and B. Bop all stood at the balcony, watching the destruction of the Ravepire when B. Bop dropped to the floor gasping.

Jayden turned around and glared at him.

B. Bop backed up against a wall of rubble. "So now you know…about Dan and I."

Jayden looked at Dan and B. Bop and with a whip, put her staff to both of their necks.

Step 28: The True Enemy

Stella quickly dropped down to avoid being killed by Jayden's current quest for vengeance. "Jayden stop," she cried, grasping onto the dead king as if he could protect her from future electromotion being shed. "They're not evil. I know for sure Dan's still good."

"It is impossible to be certain." Jayden's eyes were fixed on her foes.

"I've known Dan was one the entire time. Crane said he was never controlled. And he wasn't lying. I am absolutely certain Dan's on our side."

"Stella, you've been hiding this from us? And you actually remembered it?" Helen asked with a shocked face.

"I didn't want anyone to hurt him. He's still the same we all know. He helped us rescue Molly." Stella turned to Molly who was knocked out.

"She tried to bite me," said Helen with a glare.

"Like a Ravepire bite or a molly bite?"

"What does it matter!?"

"Yeah, the point is Dan is good." She has Molly give a thumbs up.

"Your schoolgirl crush has blinded you. Hoe long before he infects you or my Helen," Jayden said with the emotion and rigidity of a lie detector.

"He'd never do that!" Stella cried "He's just been trapped in his room, terrified of what everyone would think of him."

"Stella…" Her name escaped from his lips before he was interrupted.

Helen put her arm on Jayden's shoulder. "I don't think Dan has hurt anyone. He's just a scared victim. We couldn't have beaten Crane without him. I'd be dead, Jayden. So would you. Crane would have killed us all."

"Don't mention that name," said Jayden with a dark tone.

Dan smiled, still staring at Jayden's deathly staff. "Thanks for vouching for me, Helen."

"I should thank you for protecting us," said Helen with warmth, tending to her own wounds.

"That doesn't change what Dan is," said Jayden, although her staff lowered a bit.

B. Bop grabbed Jayden's tool of death. "Dan is clean. But me…I've been an inside man the whole time."

Jayden's eyes darted between the supernatural and the earthly.

With a small hesitation adjusted her staff from two necks to one.

Dan moved away slowly.

"Stella you can get off that dead guy now." Helen told her. "Jayden's not going to kill you, only him. If you need someone to cling to…" She taps her fingers together and blushes.

Dan grabs Stella's hand. "I'd volunteer for that."

Stella's eyes bulged. "Thank Ravenous for that. This guy is so icky." She picked herself up and scurried over to where her friends and Molly Primus were, leaving B. Bop to his fate.

"I knew you were sleazy. But why throw yourself under the bus now? She will kill you. I mean I don't care, but I don't exactly want you dead either," said Helen, bandaging up Stella's wounds.

B. Bop lashed his neck as close to the staff as possible just to egg on Jayden. "It's so damn funny…"

"What is?" Jayden asked.

"To see Jay here, who's been making goo goo eyes at me for months, be attracted to the very thing she vowed to destroy. It was hard not to break character and just laugh at the irony."

Jayden's face remained composed and statuesque. Her staff was unwavering, but her face's tint changed to bright pink.

B. Bop vocalized a laugh, but it was a laugh weighed down by misery. "After all, who could love such a desperate monster?"

"Stop teasing her! She'll burst you like a bubble! You fought uhhh…Poseferatu in the end, right? That means you're free," Stella said with confidence.

"Not that simple, pink tails," said Bop, with a shake of his head.

Jayden, feeling no more love, jabbed her staff against his throat.

The Electromotion on the outside of the staff slipped through a fresh wound into his veins, causing them to pulse with a slight rainbow.

B. Bop let out a pleasurable "ssssss" through his lips, biting them and closing his eyes as he let the power course through his body. "I'm one of them. I know how good that feels," he whispered. "But I'm human enough to know how bad it is for me." He gave a stare that could rival Jayden's when it came to lacking emotion. "Are you woman enough to put that stick through me? Can you kill me, Jayden? Because if not, you're wasting our time!"

"Yes," Jayden replied, solemn.

"That's not very ladylike, psycho chick," B. Bop arched his eyebrows and smirked.

Stella could see weakness in Jayden's posture as her staff wiggled.

"And this won't bring your brother back either," B. Bop added firmly.

As if she had an off-switch, Jayden dropped her hands. Her staff retracted and her head and arms slumped.

"Come on Jayden." Stella tried her hardest to rally her. "We don't have to kill him. We can learn more about Ravepires if we interrogate him. He's Dan's Boppy. You wouldn't take away someone's Boppy, would you?"

"Please don't kill him," said Dan with pleading eyes.

"He's right about me," Jayden muttered, her face perpendicular to the ground.

"I'll deal with him." Two glos, a fire and ice, sizzled and crackled as they activated in Helen's hand. "You have nowhere to go Bop. You jump and you'll get impaled by my statue. So just surrender like a good boy."

B. Bop, with a resounding calm, spoke to Helen. There was not an ounce of anxiety in his voice. "Calm that spitfire soul. I just want to talk."

"Then why'd you talk Jayden down?" Stella asked with a glare.

"Because I like playing with her."

"Everything about you disgusts me," Helen slammed her foot on his crotch. "Speak, man-whore."

"Geez, careful with my prized jewels!" yelled Bop, shielding himself.

"Were you really under Crane's control? Or are you like still evil?" Stella asked.

B. Bop gazed beyond the people who confronted him. "I was infected with his influence since the Dance of the Gods."

Stella's ears perked up. "That long ago, huh?"

"I was at a gig and thing is he prays on handsome young men, and well…" B. Bop points to his face "can you deny the handsome?"

"No," Dan whispered.

"I can't deny the vanity," Helen muttered.

B. Bop ignored her. "He bit me in my dressing room. Came dressed in full lady drag. I thought he was a Winterson fan. He had a very convincing falsetto and a wig and everything, plus…" B. Bop flashed a grin guaranteed to irritate Helen. "B. Bop never turns away a fan, even an unfortunate one."

"More like you can't go five seconds without having some girl massage your throbbing ego."

B. Bop crossed his arms and frowned. "Seriously, do you want me to tell you what happened or not. I'd appreciate letting me speak without you blasting my style."

Stella approached. "I want to know more about the Ravepires."

"Thanks, Pink Tails, I can always count on a fellow dime to make the words pretty again." B. Bop flashed a smile at her. "So as I was saying, before I knew it, I was out performing Crane's will, biting people, turning them into people like him and me; the regular jazz when you're a Ravepire."

"So then…," Stella said, looking away. "That time we hung out…" She started. "Why do you have Mone Cologne?"

"Yeah, I have been wondering about that too," said Dan.

B. Bop looked pained and then grabbed Stella by her shoulder. "You can't let the ladies know, but I have to use that on myself. I'm completely cold and non-vital without it."

"Okay," Stella said, regretting her answer. "I'm glad that's what you use it for…I think."

"I'm gonna barf," said Helen, leaning over.

"Listen, pink tails, I had to blackmail you because someone like Charlotte would always take your word over mine. You're a cute perky Summerein girl and I'm a big scary Reinson male. If she found out about the cologne, I'd be dead. Stereotypes always create the harshest bias."

"I'm sorry you didn't trust me enough to explain," Stella said, her eyes widened by the sudden revelation. She nudged Helen. "Apologize too."

Helen murmured to herself before saying. "You're right. I'm sorry you blackmailed my best friend to hide your malfunctioning dick."

Stella grabbed her hand. "Don't you feel better now?"

B. Bop's hand blazed into a fiery fist and hot tears poured down his face. "You do not know how angry I am having lost everything important to me, my family, my vitality and my freedom. I'd never abandon my family. They were the only people I had, but that Ravepire took it all away."

Jayden spoke. "Family."

Helen readied her ice glow. "Put the fire out now, limp dick!"

B. Bop smothered the flame and wiped his tears. "I fought hard to keep my consciousness while doing his deeds. I knew all I'd have to do is ride it out until some decent Joes and Janes came to save me, which you did."

"Boppy!" Dan burst out. "All those things you said to me. Stuff like how you'd do everything just for a boy like me, was that you who said them? Or was it the Ravepire Lord?"

"That wasn't me, I'm sorry, stud. He had control of my lips. That kiss, not my move man."

"Oh," Dan said, turning his head around into the darkness. "It's okay. I understand."

"Why would you ever think he's gay?" asked Helen. "He'll jump on anything with melons."

Bop sighed. "I lead you to believe Stella used Mone Cologne on you. I, not Crane, used it to pull you closer to me. Like in a bro way. Being around someone suffering from Ravepires, it's therapeutic."

"I liked being around you too. Bop...apologize to Stella," Dan said.

"Sorry pink tails. I'm man enough to admit that was messed up."

Helen shrugged. "Wouldn't Charlotte just assume you were a creep who drugged ladies."

"Don't underestimate that woman." Bop sighed. "Well now that all of us are free. We can get proper medical treatment. That means you, stud."

"There's a cure!" Dan broke down into tears. "We can be saved."

Helen looked at Bop suspiciously. "Why didn't you lead with that? Did you...really want to die?"

"I was just getting off my boy Dan." He turns to Jayden. "And don't worry, tall and scary. We'll find your bro too. We just gotta investigate this creeps crib for deets. Oh, and get those Winterson's home." B. Bop observed

279

Jayden who still had her head hung like a depowered robot. "And sorry about before, I was just trying to disarm you. I didn't mean a nasty thing."

Jayden bobbed her head forward and looked up at him. Her features weren't as frozen as they normally were, in fact, her eyes shimmered to show there was something working behind them. "Thank you," she said "that's the first time I felt emotion—actual emotion since I saw Helen's abilities. I won't find Clyde if I just keep mindlessly cutting through those who oppose me. My search…" she dried her eyes "must continue."

B. Bop for the first time that Stella had seen him was flustered, he put his hands up as if to protect himself. "Uh…awesome. Cool. That was exactly what I was intending. Help a sista out, ya dig?"

"I dig." Jayden strained her face and let her tongue stick out for a second with a wink that looked more like a wince. "Thanks again…cutie."

"Uh right. So uh, let's hit up this place for some clues." B. Bop said, rotating away from Jayden's face on his heels.

Stella pulled on Helen's arm. "That was me. Jayden was imitating me! How cool is that?"

"Never change," said Helen with a giggle.

Stella hugged Helen. "We really did it."

Dan joined the hug. "Yeah, we're all going to survive."

Jayden hugged B. Bop.

"Hey, not so damn rough!" yelled Bop, struggling in her arms.

Stella took out her comphone and took a selfie.

No amount of Plus could ever erase this moment.

To be continued in _On the Plus Side: Soul Fire_

Books from *Sphere of Compassion*

THE MAIN CHARACTER!

Hero's Epic Journey Arc

1. *The Hero's Epic Journey Begins*:
2. *The Hero's Epic Journey Continues*:

The Main Character: Legendary Origin Stories!

-1. *Guardian Angel:*

-2. *Broad Spectrum Assassin*:

The Main Character! Manga

1. The Main Character! The Manga! Issue 1
2. The Main Character! The Manga! Issue 2
3. The Main Character! The Manga! Issue 3
4. The Main Character! The Manga! Issue 4

OF THE EXPS

Rebellion Arc

1. *Exp 8*: Rebellion of the Exps

Resurrection Arc

2. *The Hero of Sel*: Resurrection of the Exps
3. *Sellum*
4. *Destruction, Creation, Absence*

Origins of The Exps

1. *Fate's Apotheosis: Origins of the Exps*

Rise Arc

5. *Sacrificial Savior*

Manga of the Exps

1. *Awakening* (Fall 2023)
2. *The Crimson Coliseum*

About the Author

Jhonny Steppes is a chronicler of secrets and a historian of the Aleatore planetoid. Once Daddy D took charge of the City Electric, Steppes dedicated himself to providing a bias free account of all the primary figures in this tumultuous period. Operating from an underground bunker, beneath the city, Stepps lives humbly on black beans and the affection from his Jeeg roommates. He is currently preparing for when the Edwardians resurface at the end of the millennium. His hobbies are scribing ancient text into a more modern language and listening to disco music.

Please contact me with a link to where you placed a review for any Sphere of Compassion books (Of The Exps/ The Main Character/On the Plus Side/Planetoids) and I will answer any single question as one of my characters for **FREE**.

Bloggers who wish to review a book may request "Review Copies" at the links below.

authoralexandermccarty@gmail.com

facebook.com/authoralexandermccarty

Dan's Special Message

A healthy lifestyle is about more than being fit and active. It requires a healthy mind as well. To put it simply, eating properly means eating ethically. This means we must live vegan, free of animal flesh and animal biproducts. We are all animals, after all. We all share a love for life, family and freedom. One cannot truly be at peace if they participate in the exploitation of others. Now, take my hand and seize control of your life. A healthier body, mind and life are the boons that await you.

If you need resources, the ones below are the absolute best.

http://www.adaptt.org/

http://www.abolitionistapproach.com/

veganeducationgroup.com

www.ingramcontent.com/pod-product-compliance
Lightning Source LLC
Chambersburg PA
CBHW070853180626

46817CB00003B/754